STRANDED

THE SHORTEN CHRONICLES BOOK 1

ROSALIND TATE

The past is a foreign country: they do things differently there.
L. P. Hartley

CHAPTER 1

The university website had promised lawns and trees and a pretty medieval church.

Up ahead was a concrete tower block, its pitted surface painted in primary colours to resemble lurid Lego bricks. Narrow rectangular windows lay flat against the cliff face of the building in six horizontal lines, dull and dark in the late September sunshine.

Trundling her scruffy suitcase behind her, Sophie grimaced. What an idiot. Why hadn't she visited first?

The school had laid on visits to Oxford and Cambridge, but she wasn't in that league, been too focused on A level assessments to sort long road trips.

Students were pushing by, earnestly talking, and Sophie shortened Charlotte's lead. Bringing a large brown labradoodle along wasn't ideal but kennels were expensive. 'I bet our room's in that tower block,' she said, addressing Charlotte.

Charlotte ignored her, weaving happily around a heap of cigarette ends on the grubby path; she had few expectations so was rarely disappointed.

Sophie squared her shoulders. Be more like Charlotte. Go with the flow.

The squat building beyond the entrance had sharp edges and a flat roof. A mottled, plastic panel had fallen off a wall, partly blocking the pavement.

'It's no good. This really sucks. Let's go home.'

Charlotte promptly pulled on her lead towards reception.

Sophie sighed, imagining dragging her to the road, getting a taxi to the station and when they arrived back, Aunty Wendy's disappointed face… No, Charlotte was right. Pathetic to drop out before they'd even walked in.

But the lecture-sized room with municipal flooring and yellow walls was jam-packed with new undergraduates and their families, queuing to register on the first day of the Autumn term, and Sophie paused, nerves swirling. This many people usually triggered undisciplined Charlotte bouncing; her fluorescent jacket might as well have been emblazoned *I AM NOT A SERVICE DOG*.

Charlotte leaned against Sophie's knees, sensing her anxiety. Sophie knew she had to relax. Or Charlotte wouldn't. She drew a deep breath. 'Okay, let's go.'

They joined the queue for A to E surnames and Charlotte immediately caused a stir, but she posed, enjoying being petted by impressed strangers. Genuine service dogs, focused on their work, weren't supposed to be petted, but Charlotte was calm and looked the part. So far, so good.

As she waited, Sophie closed her mouth and breathed through her nose, fending off pungent teenage aftershave and celebrity-branded perfumes, the scents intensified by the unseasonal, humid weather and the stuffy room. No air con … she should have worn a thin dress, not jeans and an over-sized shirt. She hauled off her black cardigan and tied it about her waist.

A tall, dark-haired boy in a different queue was staring at

his phone. Hugo Harrington? Couldn't be him. Wouldn't be seen dead in a place like this.

Her mobile bleeped in her bag. Isha, her BFF, had sent predictable pictures of her Oxford college. Hushed, immaculate lawns and dreamy spires.

Can we visit next weekend? xxx Sophie texted.

Isha replied immediately. *Term hasn't started yet. Come weekend after. Send Charlotte pictures!! xxx.*

Will do xxx.

Isha understood about Charlotte. Six years ago, when Sophie's parents had died in a car accident, she'd grieved in private but confided in Isha, and, four years later, when Aunty Wendy had given her a puppy, Sophie had confided again, explaining the unexpected surge of maternal love and how Charlotte helped fill the parent-size void. And Charlotte was still an anchor in a lonely sea, would always trump getting a degree, socialising, *anything*—

'Name?' The woman behind the front desk glanced up from her computer screen. She had short, spiky hair and shrewd eyes.

'Sophie Arundel.'

The woman frowned, eyeing Charlotte. 'You're not on the special needs list.'

'Oh, I filled out the form.' She hadn't, hoped she could wing it.

Unforgiving, overhead strip lighting revealed lines of annoyance around the woman's pursed mouth as she scanned the screen and typed, the faint clicks from the keyboard sounding rapid and professional.

Sophie swallowed.

'I hate to ask,' said the woman, 'but would you mind sending it again?'

Sophie hid her relief, adjusting her bag strap, securely slung across her chest. 'Of course.'

'I'll put you on the waiting list for a ground-floor flat. I'm afraid you've been allocated a fourth-floor room.'

Right. The Lego Tribute. 'No worries.'

The woman handed her an envelope, her eyes still scanning her screen. 'Your room key.'

'Thank you.' Sophie stuffed it in her bag and hurried away, struggling to wheel the suitcase through the crowd. 'Don't worry,' she whispered to Charlotte. 'Before they realise the form's still missing, I'll think of something.'

The boy who looked like Hugo was in front of her, strolling towards the exit. Six foot three and gangly in his pale knee-length shorts and red T-shirt, he had a navy hoodie casually tied around his neck. He turned as the door opened, and she saw his profile. Strong jawline, broad shoulders, annoying air of easy confidence. It was definitely him.

To get his attention, she touched his arm.

He stared at her as if she'd beamed down from a spaceship, his thick black eyebrows surprised. 'Sophie?'

She pulled Charlotte close; Hugo might not appreciate joyful doggie bouncing. 'I didn't realise you were coming here.'

He examined an envelope he was holding. His room key. 'Missed the grades for Oxford.'

Puzzling. He'd always aced exams. In the last school debate, he'd argued climate change didn't exist — without notes, just to show off. They'd never been friends. But he was a familiar face in a squash of strangers and Charlotte was earnestly leaning into his legs. Odd. She didn't usually do her full-on love-lean to people she'd just met.

Hugo's T-shirt proclaimed *San Diego Surfing Co. California* in bold, black letters, interwoven through a faded, dark ring. He could have bought that anywhere but, being Hugo, he'd have visited. She pointed. 'Souvenir?'

'Yes, my sister lives there.' He pushed his unruly hair from his forehead. Cut neatly around his ears and nape, but his fringe was way too long. 'Going to the tower block?'

She nodded. 'You've no luggage?'

'In the car. I'll get it later.'

Hugo and his mates all had cars, courtesy of Mummy and Daddy. New, sporty, pricey. Why couldn't one of *her* friends have turned up, not posh boy Hugo?

Outside, students were handing out Mexican beer, promoting some new brand.

'We had to bin the sombreros,' said a tanned, cheerful girl, handing Hugo a plastic cup. 'Cultural appropriation and all that.'

Sophie reluctantly declined the beer. Both her hands were fully occupied trundling the suitcase and holding Charlotte's extendable lead.

'It's good to be sensitive,' said Hugo, as they followed a path around the reception building, 'but where does it end? Banning people from selling Scotch whisky in kilts?'

She shrugged. Today was stressful enough. She wasn't up for an earnest discussion.

They turned a corner. Boxed in by blunt, angular buildings was a stone medieval church with gothic, stained-glass windows. It was like the chapel at school, but the steeple was larger and taller.

The church on the website ... the other buildings had been airbrushed out. Unbelievable.

'That's unusual,' said Hugo.

'Sad.' The lone survivor of a concrete massacre.

'Over there.' Hugo was pointing at something above an arched window at the near side of the chapel.

Half concealed by a buttress was a carving, attached like a gargoyle, but it wasn't a devil or grotesque figure. Two young faces looked in opposite directions, the back of their heads touching. The identical faces could have been male or female.

Sophie walked closer, stood on tip toe and touched it. The lines of the carving were confident and flowing, executed with real skill. For a moment, the church shimmered, there but not there, like a mirage. Feeling dizzy, she took a slow breath and the air tasted fresher, like a rain-swept draught into a dusty room. Summer smells … grass and pollen.

'Are you okay?' Hugo was regarding her with concern.

'I'm fine, shouldn't have skipped breakfast.' Curious. At school, he'd rarely deigned to speak to her.

They walked past the church and downhill, through a maze of square, two-storey buildings, the path levelling off as they drew nearer the tower block. No one seemed suspicious about Charlotte. Sophie had googled *Invisible Illnesses*, memorised a convincing lie, but few people would be crass enough to interrogate a stranger about a disability. English reticence plus political correctness. Result.

'Must be somewhere to practise cricket,' said Hugo. 'A pitch…'

'You think?' A cricket pitch here was as likely as a magic garden. But his doomed quest didn't affect her. She'd always been baffled by the appeal of cricket, with matches lasting whole days. Could have played at school; the mixed team had been quite good, but she'd been happy with kickboxing and javelin.

She paused wheeling the suitcase to brush an annoying strand of hair from her face. 'The sports complex looked cool on the website.' Maybe she could do kickboxing? Javelin was impractical, required a field.

'They'll have cricket nets. Better than nothing.' Hugo opened a door at the base of the tower block and went in. Above the doorframe, *STUDENTS' UNION AND ACCOM-MODATION* was signed in red, bulky letters.

Sophie followed with a skittish Charlotte. Beyond a convenience shop was a huge hall that took up most of the ground floor. Despite its size, it was as crowded and stifling as reception.

Charlotte pulled back towards the exit. She loved her day trips, exploring wind-swept beaches or the quiet gardens of stately homes; this hectic space was downright scary. Sophie gave her a reassuring pat. 'Honestly, you'll like it once we've settled in.' Charlotte sat, put out her front legs and held them ramrod stiff. So began a well-rehearsed battle of wills. There could only be one winner and — after two treats — Charlotte consented to walk to heel, attracting respectful and admiring glances.

'Wow, he's a big dog.' A podgy boy with ginger hair patted Charlotte's head.

She should have bought a harness signed *I AM A GIRL*.

He handed her a leaflet. Behind him was a poster of a caged, brown and white beagle with haunted eyes.

'They're doing testing *here?*'

'Not yet, but they've been granted funding. You're welcome to join our protest. Noon tomorrow, outside the science labs.'

'I'll be there.' Sophie walked away, putting the pamphlet in her bag. 'When we get to our room,' she told Charlotte, 'we'll call Aunty Wendy.' Sophie's aunt had Parkinson's disease and checking on her was a daily routine.

A boy wearing a cap walked by and Charlotte shrank against Sophie's legs in a very un-guide-dog way. Charlotte didn't like hats, because she couldn't see the person's face. Sophie leaned against a partition wall and hugged her.

As she straightened, Sophie's head nudged a small sepia photo, sending it wonky. She adjusted the dusty gilt frame and read the caption. *Little Shorten, 1910.* Two young girls wearing white pinafore dresses and solemn expressions were sitting on a bench by a village green. The fine hairs on the back of Sophie's neck stood up and her skin prickled. Someone was curious. Watching, assessing.

She turned around. Busy, noisy — nothing weird.

The younger girl in the picture was about four, her round face gazing defiantly at the camera. 'The university's main entrance is on Shorten Road,' she told Charlotte. 'Little Shorten won't be far. You'll love all that green space.'

Without warning, Charlotte bolted, the crowd parting like a knife slash as she moved at alarming speed. Holding the lead, Sophie hurtled after her but couldn't hurtle *and* keep her footing. She lost the lead and careered into grimy, vinyl flooring.

CHAPTER 2

For a moment Sophie lay winded, but galvanised by panic, she hauled herself up and sprinted.

At the far end of the hall were two lifts. One was plain, grey metal, matching the building's brutalist architecture, the other was painted gold. Hugo was waiting nonchalantly in front of the gold lift, his eyes on his phone. Charlotte was right beside his feet, almost touching his black trainers, oddly still, as if sitting for a portrait.

Sophie reached Charlotte, took her lead and paused to catch her breath.

On the gold lift doors were maths symbols for infinity and Pi, and two she didn't recognise. And there were pictures, simple and child-like, drawn in the same dark, swirly strokes: a mansion in the countryside, a man rocking a cot, a girl gripping an enormous sword and a cottage on fire. Framing the door was a classical-looking mural, depicting graceful urns and stylised leaves, and at the top was an old-fashioned round dial, showing only three floors — decorative not functional. By the dial were leaping stags with craggy antlers and noble expressions.

Sophie put her palm against the drawing of the country house. The paint wasn't textured as she'd expected, but smooth and cold, like stone. Odd jumble of images … must have been done for some art project. She shivered and pulled on her cardigan. Finally, air-conditioning. But it was far too cold.

Hugo put on his hoodie and zipped it closed, his eyes hardly moving from his phone.

A high ching noise like a bicycle bell rang out and the gold doors shuddered open, rattling as they slid completely back. Charlotte strained to get in, making pitiful strangling noises, smelling a dropped sandwich or forbidden burger.

Sophie checked out the grey, laminate floor, efficiently illuminated by a boxy light on the ceiling. Fine. No trash.

She let Charlotte scrabble over the threshold and followed her. Hugo came in, glancing from his phone just long enough to press the button for the sixth floor. Sophie pressed for the fourth, glad they were on different levels. She'd meet like-minded people at the protest, hopefully make friends.

The doors slid shut and Sophie frowned at her reflection in a mirror. The white shirt skirting her thighs was streaked with grey dust from the students' union floor. And her face was smeared with grime. She found a tissue in her bag and hastily wiped it off.

Charlotte pricked up her ears.

The lift was moving but there was no sound that Sophie could hear, not even a vibration hum. She took out the leaflet. *Animal Testing Is Torture.* Underneath the headline were distressing photos. She was already Online Petition Girl but here she could do proper activism. She folded the paper in half to hide the pictures. Seeing them was too difficult. She found a lot of stuff too difficult. Veggie for half her life but had never managed to go vegan.

A loud clang, and the doors on the far side jerkily opened, making a grinding sound, metal on metal, like they needed oiling.

She stuffed the leaflet in her bag and half-turned, reaching for the handle of her suitcase behind her. But it wasn't there. It was in the hall, forgotten when she'd dashed to catch Charlotte. Sophie swore under her breath and stepped forward to press the button for the ground floor.

And gaped. What was beyond the lift couldn't be real. She blinked. But the scene in front of her didn't change.

Charlotte was wagging her tail, trying to leap out. Sophie pulled her closer and with her free hand grabbed a curved handrail, keen to hold onto something solid. If this was a window, it was a long way down.

'Top of the range and the stupid thing's died.' Hugo pocketed his phone and looked up. 'Impressive 3D projection. And nice birdsong.'

Right by the threshold was the sturdy trunk of an oak tree. Beyond it, under an intense, blue sky, was a sunlit country road, bordered by a tall bay hedge.

'The IT facility here is world class,' said Hugo. 'The different perspectives are flawless.'

Of course. 'Probably been done for Freshers' Week.' The coming days promised non-stop excitement: big name music acts, live comedy and awesome parties.

Sophie took her hand from the rail. Explained why they'd gold-sprayed the lift — happy party colour and wacky art. She turned to the side wall to press for the ground floor but the black metal facing on the control panel was glossy walnut, the digital floor display had gone, and there were only two buttons — for closing and opening the doors. They were also made of wood, protruding and chunky. She gasped, disorientated.

Hugo was turning slowly around. 'This makes no sense…'

A dainty chandelier was hanging from the ceiling. Droplet-shaped crystals, artfully arranged in tiers, floated amidst three silver branches that curved upward, cradling tented bulbs. These gave out an unusually bright white light, eerily illuminating the lift walls — no longer innocuously grey but a swirl of different wood grains, from ebony to light birch.

Sophie pushed down a whisper of fear. The drab, austere ceiling was now a round mirror, framed with raised gold petals, reminiscent of a flower or the rays of the sun. Her reflected upturned face was anxious and slightly rippled. Had she been knocked out when she'd fallen? She didn't remember banging her head. She traced a curved groove on the wall with her forefinger. More likely she was asleep on the train.

Hugo pressed to close the doors. Nothing. He pressed again with more force. Nothing.

The lift was bigger than before; enough room to sleep, with space to spare. Beneath the translucent flooring was a purple, ragged cobweb, as wide as the lift, rhythmically glowing, pulsing like a heart. Sophie bent and gingerly touched the floor. It was slightly springy, like a piece of eel she'd tasted years ago by mistake. The memory still made her shudder. She snatched her hand away. Her fingertip was numb, as if she'd held it under icy water.

'The fancy light's working, so it's not a power outage.' Hugo frowned. 'Did you notice an out-of-order sign?'

'No, but if the doors were painted recently, it could have dripped, jammed the doors?'

He shook his head. 'Whatever the problem, there should be a way to contact the lift people. Perhaps the help button's on a separate panel?'

They both searched. There was no other panel.

Hugo drove his hand through his hair. 'I don't understand. Basic health and safety.'

Sophie pushed the clunky button to close the doors; it felt spongy, broken. Alarm was now souring her throat. 'We should climb through the top, like they do in films.' Even as she said this, the prospect of carrying Charlotte between them seemed too dangerous. Impractical. 'You could do that, by yourself.'

Hugo was tall enough to inspect the ceiling, including a circular brass plate that secured the chandelier. 'Might be an access door underneath this glass. Have you anything sharp in your bag?'

Keeping a firm hold on Charlotte's lead with one hand, Sophie extracted her phone and put it carefully on the floor, grabbed a bottle of water, then tipped out pens, mini umbrella, a bag for Charlotte, room key envelope, pocket mirror, comb and something foul. 'Ugh.'

'What is *that?*'

Sophie peered at the mouldy gunge. 'An apple. I bought it on the train.'

'Strange.'

'Random dream stuff.' Sophie pushed the apple out with her boot, a few putrid bits wedging in the door tracks.

She opened the room key envelope, hampered by her numb finger. A thin, electronic card dropped out. 'Useless.'

Hugo took car keys from his pocket. 'I might get the glass off with these.'

'But mirror glass is mega sharp...' A fatally injured Hugo would be a seriously sick dream.

'We should phone the fire brigade.' His hand went to his pocket and he sighed. '*You* need to.'

She picked up her phone. Had she accidentally turned it off? She pressed the on button. 'It's dead, like it's run out of charge.'

Hugo swore and checked his watch. 'Eleven twenty. About ten minutes since we walked in.'

With a dead phone, she could only guess the time. She'd never worn a watch.

'Won't last long between three.' Hugo glanced at the water bottle, his face pensive.

She repacked the bag with one hand, trying to keep her nose away from the rotting apple smell. She'd wake soon.

Charlotte was still straining against the lead towards what appeared to be a gnarled tree trunk and sun-dappled leaves.

Hugo sat on the floor against the interior wall by the open doors. 'Never liked lifts … I'm dreaming.' He hugged his knees and frowned. 'Or that beer was spiked?' He didn't expect an answer. 'But if this is a drugs trip, it'll wear off.'

So, he did drugs. Russian roulette with criminal substances instead of bullets. Life was risky enough. Her parents' faces swam into her head and she focused on Charlotte restlessly turning in a circle. 'I don't know how long drug trips last, but it won't be long before Charlotte needs to, you know…' Sophie pressed the clunky button again. It felt solid but empty, like a façade or stage prop. 'Maybe it wants us to go out?'

'Who's *it*?' Hugo squinted at the sun or what looked like the sun.

'The lift, if it's magic.' She didn't really think that. No such thing as magic, only mysteries science hadn't solved yet. 'If we walk along the road and come back, the doors might close, and it'll go to the tower block.'

'Or when we get out, we'll be stuck, wherever.'

'Or that.' Sophie sucked her numb finger. This felt real but had to be a dream. Or nightmare. Stuck in a lift with Hugo Harrington. Dreams could be so … random.

Charlotte turned and fixed Sophie with a preoccupied

stare. She squatted and peed, ensuring her paws were clear before perkily straightening up. The amber pool steamed and expanded, and Hugo scrambled to his feet.

Survival shows about drinking urine... 'If we had another bottle,' said Sophie, 'we could have scooped it.'

'What?'

'Aren't you supposed to drink urine, once you run out of water?'

'Yes.' Hugo wrinkled his nose.

Sophie stepped sideways to avoid warm pee and Hugo cautiously put his left arm out of the lift.

CHAPTER 3

*H*ugo waved his hand like a swimming fish beyond the doorway. 'I can feel a breeze. That might be part of an IT installation on the top floor, but it might not be.' He peered over the edge and stepped back.

Sophie sneezed. On the breeze were traces of birch pollen, like by the chapel.

'Let's see if it's solid.' Hugo took his phone from his pocket and hurled it out of the lift. It landed with a clatter on what looked like tarmac.

They could still be on the ground floor. The lift hadn't lurched or juddered; there'd been no sense of gliding ascent.

With his left foot, Hugo slowly prodded what appeared to be grass, and gradually shifted his weight, levering himself out, holding on to the side of the lift like a human stick insect.

Finally, he was completely out. 'Feels like a regular place. A bright summer day. Fantastic virtual reality.'

She touched her head. 'How can it be? We're not wearing headsets.'

'Good point.'

What an interesting dream. Real Hugo would never have admitted she was right.

Charlotte strained harder towards the lane, wheezing as the lead pulled her collar tight.

'If there's a dangerous person or animal lurking,' said Sophie, 'Charlotte would sense it.'

Hugo bit his lip, dubious.

'Right, we're coming too.' Keeping a firm grip on the lead's sturdy handle, Sophie stepped gingerly onto what felt and smelled like tree-shaded grass. She fished out Charlotte's plastic bag and tied it to a knobbly branch. 'This can mark the spot in case the lift doesn't stay or only comes here sometimes.'

'You know what you're saying is bonkers?' Hugo picked up his phone and put it in his pocket.

In a few steps, Sophie reached the tarmac strip. 'No road markings.' She looked one way, then the other. Bordering the lane were unbroken high hedges, fronted in places by oak and silver birch trees. 'We could wait here and if the doors start to shut, run in?'

'The doors have been open for a while. Might be stuck.'

The slid back doors weren't there — they should have been visible outside the structure. A self-contained box, with no shaft or haulage mechanism … not a real lift at all. And the angular outer walls were barely discernible, had taken on the complex green and brown shades and textures of the surrounding vegetation.

'This is tricky,' said Sophie, 'right or left?'

'No idea.'

Shame Hallucination Hugo wasn't a dream guide.

Charlotte was hauling on the lead again, wanting to go right.

'She must smell food,' said Sophie, giving in and walking. There was nothing unusual here, but that in itself made her uneasy. Why would she dream about a deserted lane?

The air tasted freshly washed, pure and sweet, suggesting countryside beyond the road, but the hedges were too tall to see over, looming like brooding sentinels; the sunlight that felt warm on her shoulders didn't penetrate them. She took off her cardigan and secured it on her waist. Hugo pulled off his hoodie and tied the sleeves around his shoulders.

Charlotte was also too hot and panting, so Sophie removed the fluorescent coat, folded it and stuffed it in her capacious, smelly bag. Good thing this was only a dream.

Charlotte bounced blissfully along, breathing in imaginary scents, but before the road twisted left, Sophie stopped and looked back at the lift. Even in the sunshine, the lit interior was bright. From a distance, the inside appeared to be the same size as a regular lift, as was the square external shape; a mismatch of perceived dimensions and reality, like *Dr Who*'s Tardis. If the doors closed now, she wouldn't get in if she sprinted.

She turned reluctantly and walked on, past another bend. More tarmac and high hedges.

Hugo gestured at bright yellow flowers on the verge. 'These primroses are pretty.' He took sunglasses from his pocket, put them on and looked at the sky. 'No vapour trails.'

No vapour trails meant no planes meant … she couldn't resist winding him up. 'Perhaps we're on another planet, where we haven't trashed the climate?'

He shrugged, seemed puzzled.

Okay, the Hugo she'd imagined was as laid-back as the real one.

A shadow swooped over the lane and Sophie pulled Charlotte close in a heart-stopping panic. 'Go away.' Her voice sounded harsh in the rural quiet.

'A hawk,' said Hugo.

Sophie took a long, relieved breath. Charlotte was too hefty to tempt an eagle, so a hawk was no threat. She examined her finger and flexed it. Fine now.

Further along, breaking the hedge line on both sides, were rough wooden gates. Sophie leaned on one, resting her elbows on the top plank; the wood felt slightly damp from recent rain. A patchwork of green fields stretched for miles, dissected by a broad river, azure and sparkling in the sunshine. Near the river, sheep were grazing, and in a different field, cows were huddled under an elm tree. Sophie reached through the gate and touched tall, golden grass rustling in the gentle breeze. 'Beautiful.'

'Barley.' Hugo smiled. 'This is a nice dream. My grandparents' farmhouse must be nearby.'

Charlotte barked and raised her head.

Someone was whistling.

Hugo turned towards the road. 'That's not my grandfather.' He gulped, his Adam's apple wobbling.

A man carrying a walking stick was striding towards them. He had a squished brown hat and wore black trousers, a dark green waistcoat and a sandy shirt, rolled up to the elbows. He drew nearer, still whistling, neither quickening nor slowing his pace.

The unfamiliar shrill melody repeated, giving Sophie's forearms goosebumps.

Charlotte was watching the man, unconcerned. But in dreams she often acted oddly. Once she'd started talking. That had been *really* weird.

The man drew near and stopped whistling. He was short and stout with lined, ruddy cheeks. 'That's a strange dog. All that wavy fur.'

His accent was a thick country-type, so thick, Sophie had to listen carefully. 'She needs a groom.'

He stared at Sophie's jeans, so Sophie stared back.

Hugo took off his shades. 'What's this place called?'

'This is all Lacey land.'

Sophie chewed her lip. None the wiser.

The man's gaze shifted to Hugo then returned to her. 'You need to go to the Manor.' He gestured vaguely up the lane. 'They'll see you right. It's not far, 'bout twenty miles.'

Twenty miles … on foot? She went running every day at school, had even run a marathon, but this man made it sound like a casual hike.

'What's the other way?' asked Hugo.

'Stansbrook. Just a hamlet. You'd be better off at the big house. They look after … strange visitors.'

Unease curled around Sophie's spine. What did he mean?

The man gave a sort of salute, walked past them and resumed whistling.

Sophie had been holding her breath. Did you have to consciously breathe in dreams? She'd once dreamed she was suffocating. That had felt real.

'A regular guy, maybe a farmer?' Hugo was reassuring himself. He cleaned his shades with the bottom of his T-shirt. 'It's not these sunglasses.' He returned them to his pocket. 'The green of the verge, blue of the sky, the flowers … all slightly off. Like a sunken dream.'

'Seem fine to me.' Crisp, strong shades, deep and vivid.

'No idea why I'm still dreaming about you.' He frowned. 'But you're behaving differently in this one.'

Hallucination Hugo dreamed about her? That made no sense.

'Let's make it nicer.' He took her right hand and theatrically kissed it. She was so surprised, she didn't react.

He slowly drew her closer and, intrigued by her mad subconscious, she let him. His eyes were on her mouth.

This was one wacky dream—

He kissed her, such a soft dreamy kiss she went with it.

She breathed in the faint scent of his aftershave, freshly cut grass wrapped in sunshine, and when the kiss turned intense, she responded, relishing a delicious energy right down to her toes. His fingers were on her shirt, caressing her breast.

Sex with Hugo Harrington? *Too* wacky.

Charlotte was jumping against Sophie's back, trying to join in the snuggle, and Sophie stepped away, resisting a tantalising tingle. Her imagination was splintering into crazy tangents. The dream must be winding up.

Hugo shot her a reckless smile. 'Let's go into the field, find a secluded spot…'

'We can't.'

'Sorry?'

'That man was a guide. To complete the quest, we have to reach the Manor.'

'Like a computer game?'

'I guess.' But this was a product of *her* brain. 'I've just finished my pre-course reading. A knight on a quest story. So, there'll be King Arthur but no elves or orcs.' English medieval literature was a cool degree course, if not obviously useful for finding a job.

'I'm searching for the Holy Grail?' Hugo seemed baffled.

'The best quests are tricky. The nature of the quest will only reveal itself at the end.' She let out Charlotte's lead.

Hugo put on his shades and watched Charlotte darting to and fro. 'To win the game, we'll have to trade something for shelter or weapons when we get there.'

'Obviously not Charlotte.'

'Of course not.' Hugo sounded affronted.

He was all right. Well, in this dream.

Her bag seemed heavier and on one of her cheap, looka-like Doc Marten boots, the sole had come loose. And her right foot was sore — a blister. Stupid shoes to wear on a quest.

~

Hugo checked his watch. 'Four-thirty, so we've been walking for five hours.'

It felt like ten. But time in dreams was deceptive. The road frequently wound left and right, but the lane and high hedges hadn't changed since the field gates. Perhaps only minutes had passed?

'This was my great, great grandfather's,' said Hugo. 'Survived the Great War better than he did.' The watch had a thick leather strap and a round face with plain, clear numbers.

Really not interested. He was like those magazine adverts for watches so expensive you inherited them. She willed him to disappear, but he didn't even fade.

They walked past wooden gates; interrupting both hedge lines, the gates faced each other. Identical to the previous ones. So were the fields. She'd been going around in a circle.

Charlotte was determinedly panting, had long ago stopped bouncing, and the water bottle was taunting Sophie. *DRINK ME*. She'd resisted; this might be a quest test: temptation, delayed gratification or endurance. But she was beyond caring. She only drank a third — a small, reluctant part of her worried this wasn't a dream. She tipped another third into Charlotte's throat and offered Hugo the rest.

He drained it, handed her the bottle and she returned it to her bag.

After a sharp bend, they continued along a lengthy straight stretch before the lane twisted right.

Sophie sat on the verge and thought about lying down. 'Knights rest on quests.'

'Chimneys.' Hugo pointed. 'Must be the Manor.'

Ignoring her protesting feet, Sophie stood, shielding her eyes from the sun.

Beyond yet another bend, an array of chimney stacks was just visible in a faint haze of woodsmoke.

Charlotte gave a half-hearted bark.

Coming towards them were two young men pushing empty wheelbarrows, chatting among themselves. Their trousers and shirts were muddy brown; they had no waistcoats but sported leather braces and cloth caps.

Hats *and* wheelbarrows were a canine call to arms but Dream Charlotte stayed sitting on the verge, quiet and watchful, as knackered as her mistress.

Hugo took off his sunglasses and cleared his throat. 'Good morning, lovely day.'

Both men were staring at Sophie's jeans. After a moment, they tipped their caps and hurried by.

Sophie glanced down. Was something wrong with her legs?

Up ahead was a broad stagnant pond, covering one verge and half the road. It smelled rank. But like the chimneys, it was new; she hadn't been walking in an endless loop.

'We shouldn't drink from that,' said Hugo.

'Agreed.' Sophie shortened the lead as they walked by. Real Charlotte loved dirty water.

They came around the bend and there was the house.

Sophie shaded her eyes again. 'All those chimneys belong to this building.'

'Elizabethan gables,' said Hugo. 'Georgian extensions and Victorian.'

Hallucination Hugo had morphed into a tour guide.

It was a mansion, not a house. Countless stone-framed mullioned windows, huge and ornate, others tiny, and beyond the glass ... movement?

One of the crenellated gables was entirely covered in dark green ivy, like a rustling green shroud.

They look after strange visitors.

Sophie took a long, shuddery breath. She didn't have to go in there, could doze in a meadow. Opposite the house, across the lane, were more neat fields.

But if this was real, a place with cows would also have agitated bulls...

Open ironwork gates marked the start of an unnecessarily long gravel driveway. It wasn't just her feet; her whole body ached. Keeping Charlotte's lead short, Sophie followed Hugo up the drive.

CHAPTER 4

The Manor was fronted by a steep, dried-out moat. Serving as a path to a more modern front door was a thick, iron gate — the original drawbridge. Hugo tugged on a large bellpull and a jangling ring echoed inside.

The door was opened by a skinny woman in a black maxi dress with a high frilly collar. Her coarse salt-and-pepper hair was drawn sternly back from her face into a tight bun. 'You've come from the lane.' Her lips tightened, pulling at her wrinkled face.

'Yes,' said Sophie and Hugo together.

'You'd better come in.'

'Bad feeling,' hissed Sophie. 'It's like we're expected.'

Hugo pocketed his shades and walked in.

Was this the end of the quest? She'd wake now—

Charlotte was pulling on her lead after Hugo. Sophie mostly trusted Charlotte's instincts; she wiped her boots on the doormat and warily stepped into a gloomy hall.

On the left was a fine oak staircase that wound up past paired, leaded windows before it disappeared beyond a double-height ceiling. Underneath the stairs' highest sweep was a door, slightly open, revealing a desk covered in papers and envelopes.

'Please wait here.' The housekeeper went through a doorway opposite the staircase.

Cream, linen-fold panelling lined the walls, with oil paintings in heavy gold frames. The picture by the front door featured a glum couple posing in serene countryside. The attention of their dog, a smooth-haired harrier, was on his master, who was wearing a weird, triangle-shaped hat. The woman's straw hat was simple, but her skirt was ridiculously wide, jutting out horizontally from her hips.

Sophie untied her cardigan from her waist, pulled it on, and sank into a deep, high-backed armchair. The air was faintly musty, as if centuries of dust had been brushed out of sight, behind wainscots and floorboards. Charlotte slumped at her feet and Hugo began pacing, oddly in time with a grandfather clock.

Tick-tock, tick-tock. The world shifted. She was back in the headmistress's study: the sound of the clock, the smell of furniture polish and formidable Miss Parncutt, visibly distressed, *I'm so sorry...* Sophie exhaled, like she always did, forcing herself into the present. The day she'd learned her parents were dead was always with her. A part of her.

She focused on Hugo. Why was he even here? Had her brain imagined him because he'd turned up at the university?

The housekeeper returned. 'This way, please.'

Sophie made herself stand and nudged Charlotte out of her doze. 'Come on. Whatever happens next, it's smart to act like we're awake.'

They followed Hugo into a spacious drawing room that was overcrowded with heavy mahogany furniture. A vaguely middle-aged woman in a long cream gown with leg-of-mutton sleeves, stood up from an emerald, damask-covered couch.

'Hello, I am Lady Anne Lacey,' she said, briskly, as if they had an appointment. Her face was bare of makeup and her dark hair was arranged loosely on top of her head.

Charlotte started bouncing.

This woman would go over like a skittle. Sophie pulled on Charlotte's lead and gripped her collar. '*No.*'

Charlotte retreated to lean against Sophie's legs. Dream-bounced but obeyed commands. Good to know.

'You must be tired,' said Lady Lacey. 'Do sit down.' Her voice was unexpectedly high, and her words were clipped, reminiscent of black and white films and *The Crown*.

Sophie sat gingerly on a sofa by a coffee table, keeping Charlotte well away from a large stone fireplace and a flimsy embroidered screen.

Hugo sat beside her. 'I'm Hugo and this is Sophie.'

'And this is Charlotte,' said Sophie, still gripping her collar.

Lady Lacey smiled politely. 'Shall we have tea?'

'You have tea,' Sophie blurted. Reassuring development. But this was her dream. Of course, there'd be tea. Eventually.

'Keeps the Empire going.' Lady Lacey pulled a rope on the wall. A young woman in a dark dress, a white apron and a maid's cap appeared at the door, her eyes wide.

'Afternoon tea for three, please,' said Lady Lacey, 'and a jug of water and two glasses. Oh, and a bowl of water for the dog.'

Lady Lacey sat opposite them and smiled again. 'It is quite a walk.'

The maid returned with a three-tiered plate stand of sandwiches, scones and cake slices and another younger maid came in carrying a silver tray crowded with delicate china cups and saucers, a silver teapot, a porcelain jug of milk, a leaf strainer, sugar cubes and tongs.

Sophie's knotted shoulders relaxed. This dream was getting better.

The maids left, then one returned with a glass water jug and two squat glasses, before putting a bowl in front of Charlotte. Sophie released her collar but kept hold of the lead.

Charlotte drank noisily and lay down.

After the maid poured tea and left, a primeval caution about eating and drinking in a strange place crept into Sophie's head, a residue of half-remembered fairy tales.

Lady Lacey sipped tea and Charlotte began to snore. Hugo drank a lot of water, demolished half the food and also sipped tea. He looked worried but not poisoned.

Sophie drank three glasses of water and a cup of tea. The maid had poured in the milk *after* the tea. Why didn't the maid know she hated that? The sponge cake and scone were warm from the oven, unbelievably delicious. She piled strawberry jam on a scone, tried not to eat too fast and fed Charlotte tiny sandwiches. Charlotte was able to eat while asleep, a useful skill in any circumstances.

Sophie ate the last sandwich, egg and cucumber, and finished her second cup of tea. Used to teabags, she'd forgotten to catch the leaves in the strainer, but it still tasted wonderful.

'This is very kind of you, Lady Lacey,' Hugo was saying. 'I mean, you don't know us or anything.'

'*Anne*, please.' She glanced at the closed drawing room door. 'No, I don't know you, but I know where you are from, and how you got here.'

'You do?' said Sophie, feeling nauseous.

'You came out of the lift and walked along the lane.'

'How do you know? Where is *here*?' Hugo's alarmed face mirrored Sophie's growing panic.

She was going to throw up. This Anne woman was too serene, too calm—

'You are in England, not far from the university, but it hasn't been built yet. And I came here like you, many years ago.' Anne looked directly at Hugo, then at Sophie. 'You will have to make a new life here, like I did.'

Hugo sat bolt upright and Sophie's breathing was shallow, speeding up.

Anne hesitated. 'You see, there's no way back.'

For some British families, sending their children away to a private boarding school at the tender age of eleven is normal. Accepted without fuss, generation after generation.

Sophie's mother was a nurse, her father a poorly paid pastor, so sending their only child to such a school was *not* normal. An opportunity for sure. But a daunting one.

The school had been founded by Henry VIII to educate the deserving poor. By the twenty-first century, the poor — deserving or otherwise — were catered for by the local comprehensive school. But mindful of their charitable status, Hadley still offered one full scholarship a year.

Sophie's regular schoolwork wasn't challenging so she enjoyed writing the essay for the scholarship. But when she opened Hadley's congratulatory letter, she saw in her parents' faces her own feelings: stunned, excited ... but scared.

In the autumn, saying goodbye, Sophie felt a desperate cold feeling in her guts.

'This is a gift from God. Enjoy it.' Her father gave her a proud bear-hug.

And Sophie hugged him back, treasuring the scent of coffee on his jacket and old mints from his pocket.

As he released her, she caught the distress in his eyes and blinked hard. 'I will.'

By Sophie's side, the headmistress waited patiently, used to doting parents and daunted children. But in front of a school that resembled an aristocratic mansion, Sophie was seeing her father anew — his ill-fitting suit, open-toed sandals he wore with socks, regardless of the weather or occasion — and she felt a rush of protective love.

Her mother was dressed for work in spotless green scrubs, her dark blonde hair tied in a neat pony tail. She wore little makeup; with strong eyebrows and a clear complexion, she didn't need to. Her eyes too bright, she enveloped Sophie in a fierce maternal hug.

Martin Arundel was shaking hands with Miss Parncutt. 'Thank you again.'

The headmistress led Sophie into a cavernous hall with oak floorboards and a sixteenth-century hammer beam ceiling, and Sophie told herself to just keep going. Get through every minute, every day.

As the weeks passed, the desperate, empty feeling faded, but the memory of it stayed, sharp and strong.

That same sensation was threatening to overwhelm her now, even in a dream. She willed away the urge to retch and focused on the woman who looked like an extra from a period drama. Not real … a dream, only a dream.

'Are you a prisoner?' Hugo was casting around the room, as if for guards or handcuffs.

'No,' said Anne. 'I don't want to go back. Three other people have come through and they feel the same. But this is the first dog.' As though in response, Charlotte gave a particularly contented snore.

Three other people? It didn't matter. Make small talk, play for time, get to the lift. 'Are you all right with dogs?'

'Absolutely, and you are welcome to stay at the Manor. The Laceys took me in when I arrived. I had cash in my bag, but my money didn't work. Yours won't either.'

No way back and no money. Faint with panic, Sophie tried to steady her breathing.

'Why don't you have an amble around the gardens?' said Anne. 'All will become clear in due course.'

Gardens. Get to the road and keep going, turn this into an escape dream not a nightmare.

'I will have your room made ready. One on the ground floor with French windows would suit Charlotte.'

Room? 'I'm not up for sharing with Hugo.'

'Really?' He sounded disappointed. 'Anne, we're not together. We came through the lift by accident.'

Anne noted Sophie's left hand, bare of rings, including a wedding band. 'The Manor is not short of rooms. You can have one across from Sophie.'

'This really is very kind of you,' repeated Hugo, getting to his feet.

'Not at all. Through that doorway, gardens on your left.'

Sophie stood and gently prodded Charlotte awake. As they walked along a wide corridor, Hugo said, half to himself, 'Going by Anne's dress, it's around the start of the twentieth century.'

'And you know this, how?'

'You didn't do history?'

'Only the Tudors and the Nazis.' Her subconscious must have picked out this time because it lacked relentless death and grimness, well, until 1914 and the First World War. Hugo had been in a higher set. Different topics, better results. She was good at essays but, since her parents' death, crap at exams. Miss Parncutt had ascribed that to trauma — a reasonable theory.

Sophie stepped onto a broad flagstone terrace. Beyond a metal lattice table and chairs and a large parasol, immaculate lawn stretched into the distance, giving way to orchard, the grass murmuring, 'I'm expensively tended.' Mature trees, closer to the house, were in full bloom and below the terrace two men were weeding extensive flowerbeds: fragile waves of pink, blue, yellow and white.

The breeze changed direction, carrying with it a familiar, pine-like aroma. Sophie sniffed, searching for the source. Directly below the terrace was trailing rosemary, cascading down to the lawn in a glorious, violet wave.

Rosemary for remembrance.

Aunty Wendy's voice, rehashing Shakespeare, repeated in her head. Her aunt's casual comment, six months after Sophie had come to live with her, had provoked an unthinking, wounded response. Sophie had shouted, 'I'll never forget them, never. I don't need a stupid herb to help me.' Her aunt's face crumpled, Sophie hugged her and they'd both cried.

Eventually Sophie found some solace in her aunt's neat garden, learning how rosemary — as well as basil, dill, marjoram and tarragon — could enhance mushroom risotto and countless other veggie dishes.

Sophie knelt and reached over the edge of the terrace to pick one of the tremulous, fragile flowers, letting the familiar woodsy aroma calm her. Aunty Wendy's rosemary didn't flower in summer and this shade of intense violet was unfamiliar. She stroked the soft, veined petal.

'The standard lamp in the drawing room … it was plugged into the wall.'

She straightened and turned. Hugo was sitting under the

parasol, drumming on the table with long, unexpectedly delicate fingers, given his height.

Sophie stepped towards the table. 'So?'

'Electricity wasn't installed in homes, even grand ones,
until the 1930s.'

She hadn't noticed the lamp. '*The past is a foreign country:
they do things differently there.*'

'Familiar … poetry?'

'No, a novel. *The Go-Between.* I did it for A level.'

Charlotte yawned. She was sprawled at Hugo's feet, a
sparrow hopping in front of her, pecking for crumbs.

'This place is way too idyllic,' said Sophie, 'and that Anne
woman shows no curiosity about the lift or portal or whatever it is, and she's too unfazed and welcoming.' A perfor-
mance, to charm the unwary — classic nightmare stuff.

'Not a drugs trip.' He shook his head as if not entirely
convinced. '*They* are dangerously mad … psychedelic.'

'I'll take your word for it.'

'Anne might have reasons for not wanting to go home,
but three other people? How likely is that?'

'Not very.' Sophie strode over to the sandy moat encir-
cling the house and a good piece of lawn. Vertical sides and
too wide to jump. The only route out was through the house.

Back on the terrace, she lifted a handbell from the table.
The casing was brass, the handle chestnut. An everyday
object but beautifully made. Seized by an urge to ring it, she
slammed it down.

'That's nice,' said Hugo, pointing.

Half concealed by apple trees, an arched stone bridge
spanned the moat, linking lawn and orchard.

Had her brain just conjured that up? Her heart began
pounding. Cut left beyond the bridge, find the road.

Charlotte was curled on the flagstones, her breathing slow

and soft, her legs already twitching in a different adventure, a dream within a dream. What did she dream about? Were dreams unique or boringly similar? Okay, whatever the trappings, this was a variation on a regular nightmare. Separation-anxiety, maternal worry. Charlotte worn out by the never-ending trek was part of that, an illusion, like her own aching feet.

But despite knowing Charlotte wasn't real, Sophie's instincts screamed against abandoning her. Could this be a quest test? Conquering her greatest fear — losing Charlotte. Sophie knew from movies what to do; *escape as soon as possible, while you're still strong.* She gritted her teeth. 'Got to go.'

'Where?'

'To the lift.'

'Better to stay, Sophie, you must be exhausted. I know I am.' He gestured at the chair beside him. The seat cushion cover was royal blue silk.

'I'll be fine.'

'You can't get there before dark.'

'Want to bet?' She jumped down narrow stone steps onto the lawn and sprinted towards the bridge, but her right foot felt so sore she stopped running. She unlaced her boot and pulled it off. The light grey sock was smeared red; blood from the blister.

Hugo ran past her, blocking entry to the bridge. 'You're only here so I can rescue you.'

This was different. She'd always been exclusively self-rescuing—

'And then I'll wake up.' He grinned.

He'd wake up? If she was in his head, Hugo was the hero. Mad. She was the hero here. Only a blister … she put on the boot and tied the laces. One kick and he'd be on the ground. 'Out of my way.'

'No.' He gestured at the house, his face set. 'Better to face a threat here than in pitch darkness down that lane.'

Had a point.

'If this is a vampire dream,' said Hugo, 'we could barricade ourselves in until dawn.'

'Could be evil people or aliens. Dawn wouldn't help.'

'We should sleep together.'

She arched an eyebrow.

Confusion and doubt showed in his face. 'No funny business.'

He seemed sincere. But even if he wasn't, compared to a nightmare house, Hugo was a trivial risk.

'At least these people speak English.' He shot her a nervous smile.

Real Hugo at school had mostly ignored her. At Uni he'd acted friendly, for the same reason she had. Neither of them knew another soul. In a dream, though, he could be perceptive, sensitive. Hey, they could be friends. She smiled at him and limped to the terrace, every step more painful, adrenalin, or dream equivalent seeping away.

The maid they'd seen earlier with the tea tray was waiting beside Charlotte. 'Sir, Miss, shall I show you the bathrooms?'

'I'm Sophie and this is Hugo.'

The girl looked taken aback.

Sophie persisted. 'And you're…'

'Miss Able.' She blushed.

Her face was vaguely familiar but that figured. Dream people weren't imagined from scratch, but borrowed, mixed up.

'Let's go.' Hugo strode after Miss Able into the house.

CHAPTER 6

Sophie hastily woke Charlotte who snorted her annoyance before reluctantly going with her mistress into the Manor.

But inside, Charlotte sped ahead, reaching Hugo just before he went through a door at the end of a corridor.

Sophie sighed. Bad habit, following Hugo — from now on, Hugo should follow her.

The room beyond was a good-sized bathroom, with a roll-top bath with brass taps and claw feet, a sink, and blue and cream tiles on the walls. The blue was the exact same shade as the terrace seat cushions. Cream towels were folded neatly on a shelf beside the bath.

'Where's the shower?' asked Sophie.

Charlotte immediately lay down on the polished wooden floor. This translated as 'not my problem.'

Miss Able was frowning.

Sophie frowned too. 'What?'

'Domestic showers only came in after the Second World War.' Hugo was fiddling with the bath taps. He straightened.

'Top of the range, but compatible with the period.' He drew a shaky breath.

Sophie touched the taps: metal, smooth and cold. A flicker of uncertainty. She hadn't had more than a couple of baths in her life. Why would she dream of a bathroom without a shower? Could this be real? No. Time travel was fantasy, like pixies or vampires or gods. And there were no showers in *Downton*. She'd known that, just forgotten. Either she was asleep, or she'd hit her head in the students' union. But her head didn't hurt—

Miss Able cleared her throat. 'Lady Lacey had the facilities installed a few years ago. Sir, there's another one upstairs.'

Hugo took the hint and left with Miss Able.

The toilet was in a different room. Sophie went in, squeezed Charlotte inside, turned the key in an old-fashioned lock, and glared at her reflection in a wall mirror. 'What's happened to my hair?' Normally sleek blonde, it had got tangled by the breeze in the lane. And her nose and cheeks were pink from the sun.

The hook fastening of her pendant necklace had slipped around to the front and she moved it back behind her neck. The stone was an unusual swirly blue, like a wondrous galaxy captured by the Hubble Space Telescope; a precious present from her mother. Sophie wore it most days. Logical she'd be wearing it in a dream.

Charlotte was by the door, wanting to go out.

'Give me a minute.' The loo seat was shiny ebony wood and the toilet paper was stiff and scrunchy. She pulled on a chain hanging from a box high on the wall and it flushed fine. The soap bar lathered up fine too. She opened the door and Charlotte raced along the corridor to Hugo who was staring out a window.

He turned, his tanned face tense. 'I'm going to have a bath

upstairs. Mr Watkins here has started running it.' Beside Hugo was an earnest young man with brown hair and prominent blue eyes. Dressed in a dark suit, Mr Watkins was sturdily built but short; standing to attention, his head barely reached Hugo's shoulders.

Miss Able's posture also resembled a soldier on parade. Her auburn hair was neatly arranged in a tight bun. 'Miss, shall I run your bath?'

'That's very kind of you, but I'm fine.' Sophie walked outside again and told Charlotte, 'If there was a state-of-the-art rain shower with jets, I would *not* get undressed in this spooky place.'

Charlotte settled on the terrace, soaking up strong evening sunshine, entirely content. But Sophie wasn't. The possibility that this was real tugged at the edges of her mind, and growing unease turned back to fear. She walked towards a rose bush with rich red petals and sharp thorns. Before she had time to get squeamish, she grabbed at it, and swore. The spikes had torn into her fleshy palm and blood was dripping from her hand, red as the rose. She wrapped her hand in the bottom of her shirt. The stains looked real. And the pain felt too real.

She returned to the terrace, sat down and rested her head on the table. Her hand was stinging but imagined pain could feel real in dreams. She closed her eyes.

She was naked in the students' union, everyone pointing and laughing—

Her arm was being nudged. She blinked. Still here. Could you dream in a dream? Hugo was a vision of old world elegance in a blue silk dressing gown that matched his eyes. Best not to comment. 'How was the bath?'

'Just the right temperature.' But his prompt, easy answer was at odds with his stiff body language.

'Would you care to see your room, Miss?' Miss Able was

holding a pile of folded clothes. She turned to Hugo. 'Sir, your room will be ready shortly.'

Hugo nodded.

Sophie nudged Charlotte, who eventually stood and yawned loudly, and they all followed the maid to a room dominated by a solid, four-poster bed with a wooden canopy; gossamer cream curtains were draped around the bedposts. By an open side window was a dressing table and a tall, free-standing mirror.

'These clothes are for you, Miss. There's a tea dress in the wardrobe, if you feel like a change.'

The dark polished wardrobe was only slightly smaller than Sophie's school dorm and the bedroom wouldn't have fitted inside the ground floor of Aunty Wendy's house. Sunlight refracted through old glass set in floor-to-ceiling French windows, and the air carried a faint lemony scent, as if the room had been freshly scrubbed.

Hugo was scanning the room, finally looking at the ceiling.

Miss Able was watching Charlotte, her eyes wary, and Charlotte had raised her head, sensing disapproval.

Not everybody liked dogs. Sophie got that. She walked to a cast iron fireplace and ran her finger over the slightly puckered wallpaper above it; the colourful design featured blue and yellow silk birds with exotic plumage. Smelled like an old book.

'Lady Lacey thought you might prefer a light supper in your rooms.' Miss Able gestured to a small bellpull on the wall. 'Miss, if you need anything else, please ring.'

'Sir, your room's ready.' Mr Watkins was standing in the doorway.

Hugo walked towards Mr Watkins and Miss Able said, 'Back in a moment, Miss,' and followed Hugo into the corridor.

Sophie sat on a silky blue bedspread and played with the curtains. 'This is grand enough for a princess.' Charlotte tried to jump on the bed and Sophie gently pushed her down.

Miss Able returned with a red tartan blanket and laid it on the floor. 'For your dog, Miss.'

Charlotte, accustomed to sleeping on her mistress's bed, glanced dismissively at the blanket and turned her head towards the French windows. Sophie stared at the floor, illogically embarrassed. Other dogs slept outside and worked all day … guarding the house or rounding up sheep. 'Thank you.'

Miss Able smiled. She'd missed — or forgiven — Charlotte's spoilt-brat impression. She pointed to a cupboard with a bowl and jug on top. 'You've got toiletries in there, Miss. Deodorant powder, soap and moisture cream.'

By the bowl was a toothbrush in a cardboard box; there was no plastic wrapping, but it looked brand new.

'I'll leave you to settle in.'

After Miss Able had gone, Sophie carefully laid the blanket over the delicate bedspread and sat on the edge of the bed.

Two other maids came in and put trays of food on trestle tables.

'My room's like yours. It doesn't feel real.' Hugo was leaning against the door jam, dressed in his shorts again.

Some dreams felt real. At the moment at least, this was surreal. 'That's for one person?'

'Yes, Miss.'

'Could I have supper in here too?' Hugo asked the maid.

'Of course.'

Sophie wanted to tell Hugo to eat in his own room but didn't have the energy. She was dreaming she was tired.

After more trestle tables and food were brought, Hugo closed the door and sat in a Queen Anne armchair, upholstered in a light blue fabric with thick, navy swirls. 'What's the deal with your shirt?'

'Snagged my hand on a rose bush, to see if it had dream thorns. It hurt, the blood looks and smells like blood. But none the wiser.'

Hugo gazed into the empty grate beside his chair. 'I should eat, though I'm not hungry. Finding this a bit overwhelming.'

In the lane she'd wanted Hallucination Hugo to morph into a cool dream friend, but she'd made him *too* sensitive. If this was a trap, she should beef up his action man skills — Jack Reacher or James Bond...

Hugo smiled at Charlotte who was standing like a statue, transfixed by slices of cold beef pie, chicken, lamb and another meat, partridge or pigeon. 'She's being very good. All this on a low table, George would have dived in and eaten the lot.'

'George?'

'My dog at home, typical labrador.'

'Charlotte's always behaved around food but she's more poodle than lab.'

'Labradoodles don't shed, right?'

Sophie grinned. 'Charlotte does. Part of her charm.'

Once Hugo had eaten a beef pie slice with no ill effects, Sophie gave Charlotte a helping and her expressive canine eyes widened. Sophie Arundel had the same face eating chocolate cake. Charlotte enjoyed veggie dogfood well enough, but adored meat. And as this couldn't be real, no animals had been hurt and Charlotte could have exactly what she wanted, except for pigeon or whatever it was — removing the bones would be too fiddly. Sophie examined the chicken and finally gave Charlotte a breast.

'What are you doing?'

'Charlotte can't have cooked bird bones.'

'She's a dog.'

'Bird bones can splinter,' said Sophie, 'cause internal injuries. Honestly, it's well-known.' She didn't want this turning into a Charlotte Fatally Injured nightmare.

'Last Christmas, George stole a whole turkey carcass. He went to the vets but was fine.'

Unwelcome development, Hugo handing out dog advice. 'I won't risk it.'

'Fair enough. You must have a slice of pie. It's delicious.'

'I'm veggie.'

'Since when?'

'Forever.' It had been Isha who'd persuaded her. Quite a step when you're eleven.

'You eat the cheese and most of the bread,' said Hugo, 'and the pudding.' He poured white wine into two glasses and sipped one. 'Sweet but drinkable.'

After they'd picked at the meal, Hugo put the trays with the remaining food in the corridor, returned and closed the door behind him. 'I hope this is the right thing to do. It's what I've done in hotels.'

Sophie didn't reply. She'd never stayed in a hotel with room service. Hugo was rich and spoiled in real life; logical he'd be the same in her head. 'Why are you in my dream?'

'You still think this is a dream?'

'On balance … yes.'

'Then I'm having the same one. Unlikely.'

'You're in my head so you would say that.'

'No, Sophie, this is real. I'm pretty sure.'

'But all this, it's too perfect.'

'That's the point. Dreams make no sense, turn horrible for no reason. You can fly. Dead people live again. Unconnected events get mixed up and change. So far *everything* has been consistent within its own world.' He ran his forefinger down a bedpost, tracing a delicate line of acorn shapes carved into the wood. 'Everyone might dream differently but mine don't have this level of detail.' He sighed. 'Relentless, logical.'

She'd fallen hard in the students' union. She must have hit her head. Was she in a coma? Plugged into opiate painkillers … that would explain this vivid dream. Her stomach clenched. A coma could last for weeks — or years. And if she was in hospital, where was Charlotte? Ignored or kidnapped or hurt or worse. Sophie jumped off the edge of the bed, fighting panic. The real Hugo was a walking encyclopaedia. She must have imagined him to help her wake up. 'What do you know about comas?'

'Only stuff I've read online, people waking when they hear family talking or favourite songs.' He swiped his dark fringe from his eyes. 'Not very scientific.'

He only knew what she did. Figured. Unknown birds were singing outside and if anyone was talking or playing music, she couldn't hear them. Her brain had cocooned her in a rose-tinted period drama. That's why people died. Brain damaged or horribly injured, nobody would want to be forced back to reality. Fear gripped her and she fought the urge to scream.

'There's a big flaw in your coma idea.' Hugo seemed calm, but was tapping his feet, his trainers drumming on an antique Wilton rug depicting a bird of paradise in a tree, spun in muted greys, pinks and yellows. 'How much do you know about this period?'

'As much as anybody.'

His lips curved with scepticism. 'But if this is your coma, I'm not here. But I am.'

'You could be talking to me in hospital.'

'This is getting weird.'

'More than this?' She gestured at the room.

'You can't be certain this isn't real.'

'Listen to yourself, we've magically travelled back in time … ridiculous. Would be like visiting Narnia.'

'Narnia was invented. The past existed or perhaps exists. That's supported by theoretical physics.'

'You've lost me.'

'Einstein believed that the past, present and future exist simultaneously,' said Hugo. 'Time isn't linear, we only think it is.'

Okay, definitely didn't know that.

Charlotte was turning in a circle, so Sophie attached her lead, unlocked the French windows and stepped with her into the dusk.

Save for birdsong, the quiet was absolute, stretching far beyond the gardens, and away from the light of the Manor's windows, the growing dark felt solid and endless.

Hugo was standing a few steps from her, his angular face troubled and curious. 'This could be the proof. The greatest scientific discovery ever.'

No, accidental time travel was the least likely possibility. Dread pooled in her guts. 'I'm dead.' The last few hours could actually have been seconds, her brain spooling down before oblivion.

'If you're dead, so am I.' He frowned. 'I don't remember dying but I could have had an aneurysm. So quick, I didn't realise.'

'What's an aneurysm?'

'Internal bleeding.'

She made a fist, digging her nails into her sore palm and winced. Did dead people feel pain?

'We're not dead.' Now his face was earnest, as if he wasn't entirely sure. 'People who've technically died sometimes see a tunnel with a bright light at the end. And they've stimulated parts of the brain on conscious people and produced the same result.'

'So?'

'No tunnel here.'

Not dead. Progress of a sort. But the dread was spreading, empty and cold, and as she stepped into the house, her limbs felt heavy, and she pictured herself in a hospital bed, her legs angular and immobile under thin sheets.

Charlotte leapt on the bed and stretched, Hugo locked the French windows and turned. His eyes, dark with worry, met hers. 'I know you're frightened, Sophie. I am too. But if anything happened, Charlotte would kick off.'

The real Charlotte would, but this one was happily settling on a strange four-poster bed. Sophie drew a measured, calming breath. She needed to face reality, however horrible. The most likely scenario was a coma. When regular dreams veered off course, waking usually followed. Might be the same with comas? The only grating element was Hugo. Make him go away. 'I really don't like you.'

He shoved his hands in his pockets and glared. 'We hardly spoke at school. You don't know me at all.'

'Only by reputation.'

Charlotte cocked her head, unnerved by the tone change in their voices.

Hugo scowled. 'What's that supposed to mean?'

'Entitled, arrogant posh boy … we've got nothing in common.' She clicked her fingers. 'Hallucination Hugo, disappear.' His face was a picture. Confusion, regret? It didn't matter. 'I'll wake up now.'

'You're a complete bitch. And you are awake.' He turned on his heel. 'Unfortunately, so am I.' He closed the door softly behind him, when she'd expected a slam.

CHAPTER 7

*H*er heart hammering, Sophie locked the bedroom door. No bolt, and Miss Able would have a skeleton key like hotel chambermaids.

I know you're frightened, Sophie. I am too.

Baffled, exhausted — and, yes, frightened. Like pain, fear could feel real in dreams and on waking, fear *was* real. Sweating, rapid heartbeat, even as imagined threats dissolved.

But the bedroom remained stubbornly solid, and outside the unknown birds were still singing, warbling like a mocking chorus. Hugo was right; dreams, including coma dreams, couldn't do detail, not consistently like this. But if she was really in the past, at home she'd inexplicably disappeared. Aunty Wendy and Isha would be distraught. The dread deepened.

The counterpane under the bed canopy was shadowed, despite the light provided by a heavy bedside lamp, and the rest of the room was entirely dark, but she made herself inspect every inch, closing the side window and tapping on panelling for hollow sounds. Raised on fantasy and sci-fi boxsets, she didn't rule out monsters hiding behind walls.

She wedged a spindly Windsor chair under the door handle, searched the toiletries cupboard and found a nail file, identical to one languishing in her suitcase. Shoving it in someone's eye might give her time to escape.

But she had to sleep. Keeping on the lamp, she ignored a nightdress and dressing gown that Miss Able had left folded on the bed and took off her boots. She put the nail file on a bedside table, slid under the heavy bedclothes and pulled them up to her chin. Charlotte's soft breathing sounded loud in the silence as Sophie closed her eyes. If this was a century ago, she'd die before she was born. Born and repeat, in an endless loop. She should leave her parents a note. *Don't leave the house on Friday, November 18th, 2011.* Worked in movies. No. They'd tell themselves it was 'God's will.' And the future had already happened, so was it preordained? Her heart started hammering again. No, this couldn't be the past. A delusion, a psychotic episode…

The next morning, dawning memory and light from a narrow gap between long, thick curtains snapped Sophie awake. Charlotte wasn't beside her. Sophie's heart missed a beat and she leaped out of bed and stumbled, misjudging the drop to the floor.

Charlotte was a few feet away, her head between the curtains, gazing out the window. Sophie sagged with relief and winced. The blister on her foot was bleeding again. She stepped hastily off the bird rug.

She opened the cream curtains, took in lawn, trees and flowerbeds and drew a long, relieved breath. Nothing had happened in the night because this really was a stately home — a century ago.

Knocking.

'Miss, can I come in?'

Familiar from TV shows and visiting National Trust houses, yet the real past was something else. Strange, alien, unknowable. But she took the nail file from the table and returned it to the toiletries cupboard. 'Miss Able?'

'Yes, Miss.'

Sophie moved the chair, unlocked the door and stepped back.

Miss Able was holding a wooden tray laid with tea and toast. 'Good morning, Miss.' She put the tray on the bed, fully opened the curtains and arranged the tiebacks.

Charlotte was pawing the French windows.

'Shall I take him out, Miss?'

'No, don't worry.' Sophie put on her boots, attached Charlotte's lead to her collar and went into the garden. She didn't trust this maid.

Outside, Charlotte busied herself in a flower bed. Her plastic bag was miles away by the lift, tied to an oak branch, so Sophie pushed soil over the evidence with her boot.

When they returned, Miss Able said, 'No sugar, with milk, is that right, Miss?'

Her preferences during afternoon tea had been noted … written down? Creepy.

'It'll go cold, Miss.'

Tea and toast couldn't be creepy, not in themselves. And instinct was now telling her this girl was exactly what she seemed. Sophie got into bed and Miss Able put the tray on her lap. The tea was mighty fine, and the toast was crunchy and buttery. She sneezed. Duck feathers in the pillows?

'Interesting dog, Miss. What's he called?'

'She's a girl dog. Her name's Charlotte.'

Miss Able's face went blank. 'Pretty name, Miss.'

Sophie got out of bed and Miss Able knelt by the

toiletries cupboard and took out a roll of bandages. 'I can help with your foot, Miss.'

'I only need a sticking plaster.'

'Haven't any sticky plasters. This will do it.' Sophie sat on the bed, took off her socks and Miss Able wound material around Sophie's foot with practised ease, cut it to fit and attached a safety pin. 'There.'

Miss Able went to a drawer and handed Sophie clean cream socks.

'Thank you.' Sophie put them on and stepped into her boots again, tying the laces looser so the pin on top of her foot didn't rub. 'Could I have a bandage for this?' She turned her right hand over to show the wound.

'Goodness.' Miss Able poured water from the jug on top of the cupboard into the bowl and tipped in a tiny drop from a small, chunky bottle. The plain brown glass had no label.

'What's that?' Sophie peered at the bottle.

'*Milton*, Miss. Good for cuts as well as cleaning.'

Miss Able dunked a handkerchief into the water mixture and pressed it against Sophie's palm.

Sophie gasped. It stung like hell. Doing its job.

Once the dressing was secure, Miss Able gave a pleased nod.

Sophie smiled back. This would always have taken a while to accept. Magic and gods weren't real, any more than happy endings, but time travel was like invisible molecules and genes, extraordinary *and* real. Scientists would eventually study it. Hey, there'd be degrees and PhD's. Her priority, though, was less abstract. Get to the lift.

She'd apologise for last night; couldn't just bail and leave Hugo. 'Do you have a couple of bikes? To borrow, so we can go down the lane, get home?'

Charlotte tossed her head. This usually translated as 'No.'

Mental note: don't trust Charlotte's instincts in complex

situations. Charlotte didn't realise they'd time travelled. To her, this was just a cool place.

'Being a fish out of water isn't nice, Miss. I can leave a couple outside the French windows before lunch.' Miss Able paused. 'But you must be careful.'

'Why?'

'There's vagrants and all sorts, looking for work.'

Job hunting was hard — and stressful. Months of unemployment before Aunty Wendy started her dog breeding business had accelerated her Parkinson's disease. And now her niece disappearing without trace ... that could kill her. Miss Able might have info that could help with getting home. 'What do you know about the lift?'

Scepticism flared in the maid's eyes before she bent down to cautiously pat Charlotte. 'I've never seen it, Miss, and I've never heard of anyone going back, but if you do, can you leave the bicycles on the verge? The gardeners can collect them.' Miss Able picked up the tray. 'Is that all, Miss?'

'Er, yes.'

Miss Able left, closing the door quietly behind her.

That girl had grown up here. If she didn't believe in the lift, had never seen it, maybe it had disappeared? Ignoring a fresh ripple of fear, Sophie rummaged in her bag, holding her breath against the mouldy apple smell.

Her mobile was sleek and smooth and dead. And that was nonsensical. Travelled back a century, but they were only in the lift for seconds and the battery had been fully charged.

The phone lead was in her suitcase — far away in the future. Despite the tea, her mouth had gone dry. Phone separation anxiety. She focused on breathing. In out, in out. This would pass. Given the situation, it was small beer. In, out. In, out.

After finally managing to calm herself, she hauled off her blood-stained shirt, leaving it folded on the bed, and put on a pink camisole with delicate straps that Miss Able had left out. It showed off her toned arms, a side effect of gym work. 'Come on, time to mend fences.' Charlotte joined her as she stepped into the corridor.

Hugo opened the door wearing his splendid dressing gown; he looked more like a duke than a student.

'I'm really sorry about last night.'

He gestured for her to go in.

She sat uncomfortably on a leather armchair beside a fireplace. There was a slight tang of tobacco and something rich and alcoholic … whisky. Sunlight from mullioned windows on two sides of the room was dancing, soft and golden, on the bed, illuminating cream embroidery on a lighter counterpane. The bedstead was rosewood, with no canopy, and the room felt airy and light, despite plush red curtains and a navy rug on the floor. And there was a stand-alone mirror, like hers.

'You called me a bitch and you were right,' said Sophie. 'What I said was crass.'

He sat on the edge of the bed. 'In seven years, I think we've exchanged, what, around twenty words?'

'I thought if I could make you disappear, I'd wake up. Well, not *you*, imaginary Hugo.'

His lips thinned into a hard, cynical line. 'You thought I wasn't real so when you kicked off you meant every word.'

'I didn't. It's just … you're one of the rich kids.'

'How do you make that out? Yegor's family has a superyacht.'

'I don't mean the foreign students,' said Sophie. 'I just said the first thing that came into my head.' He couldn't help being posh and annoying. 'Wish I could take it back.'

He looked thoughtful.

'Can we start again?' She shot him a cautious smile. 'Friends?'

'Okay.'

'You'd studied this period,' said Sophie, 'realised this was real.'

'Actually, it was you that made me sure I wasn't dreaming.'

'Sorry?'

He shot her a self-deprecating grin. 'When you didn't want to sleep with me.'

'Right.' Boys often wanted to jump on anything vaguely presentable, in their dreams or otherwise. 'I'm not sure of anything anymore, half expecting to see fairies.'

'The jury's out on supernatural friends but I'm converted to time travel. What a fantastic experience.'

'I thought you were scared witless? I bloody am.'

Recognition flared in his eyes. 'I'm still in shock, I guess.' He ran his hand over the silky bedspread. 'I've been studying this period for years, done an A level and chosen a degree in it … this is a safe, ordered society, Sophie. We can live every detail as it happens, watch history unfolding.'

'What if we can't get home?'

He swallowed.

'Did you ever wish you could experience it for real?'

'I thought about how it would have been,' said Hugo. '*Actual* time travel … no. You?'

'Never.'

'Yet here we are.' He gestured at the room, but his eyes were on her.

And he was flesh and blood, seeing and feeling. Her face felt hot. 'About the lane—'

'I thought I was dreaming.' He was embarrassed. 'Clean slate?'

'Yes.' Good, she hadn't given him the wrong idea.

'And I won't turn to the dark side, start seducing maids.' He gave her a different smile, lopsided, mischievous.

'Good to know.' Her heart flipped. Indigestion. Eaten that toast too fast.

She stroked Charlotte who was leaning against her legs. 'But you'll be spared the temptation. Miss Able's getting us bikes.'

'I'm not sure.'

'About bikes or going back?'

He hesitated.

'Seriously?'

'John says a chauffeur could take us.'

'John?'

'Mr Watkins,' said Hugo. 'I couldn't go on calling him by his surname. It felt weird.'

'He could be lying.'

'Why would he?'

'Miss Able suggested the lane isn't safe,' said Sophie, 'to put us off.'

'Hardly handcuffs and a locked room, and John doesn't believe in the lift, has never seen it.'

'Neither has Miss Able.' And that was creeping her out.

'I don't believe *nobody* wanted to go home. More likely they couldn't, so made the best of it.' He sighed. 'And we need more info *before* cycling twenty miles there and twenty miles back.'

'I'm not waiting.'

'It might be a door but what if it's a time machine, like the *DeLorean* in *Back to the Future*? If we don't know how it works, we could be eaten by dinosaurs or burned alive when the planet was forming.'

She hadn't thought of that. 'I'll go see but not touch. Just suss it out. And this afternoon I'll meet you here and we can make a plan.'

'In the meantime, we shouldn't tell anyone about the future, or we'll mess up the timeline.'

'Good point.' But then a selfish idea formed, and it made her heart race. *Everything* she did here could change the future, affecting countless people, for good or ill, but she didn't care, as long as her parents didn't die in a stupid car crash.

Hugo took his phone from a bedside table and turned it over in his hand. 'If we are stranded, I could write instructions for my great, great grandchildren. They could charge this, reverse-engineer it and start a company called Melon or Banana.' His tone wasn't light-hearted, more gallows-humour.

'Founding a billionaire dynasty would be some compensation for being trapped here.' She wanted to sound sarcastic, but the words came out flat.

Charlotte was snuffling at Hugo's dressing gown. He patted her head. 'John says we don't need to attend short prayers before breakfast.'

Her brain was still full of her parents and she struggled to focus. 'Okay...'

'That's when the servants are told about events or problems. They're being told about us, so they don't gawp. Things like your jeans make you stand out.'

'And your shorts.'

He shrugged. 'I'd better get dressed. Breakfast's at nine-thirty.'

'No idea what time it is.'

'I'll knock on your door in...' He checked his watch. 'Five minutes.'

CHAPTER 8

*J*ohn led the way to the dining room.

Hugo was now wearing grey twill trousers and a cream long-sleeved shirt.

'John's clothes?' Sophie whispered.

'I don't think so,' said Hugo, 'but it felt rude to ask.'

Charlotte sprinted ahead, smelling food. Oblivious to the awesomeness of time travel, she was still Miss Mindfulness, living in the moment, enjoying eating, sleeping and snuggles.

Through a maze of blue-carpeted corridors, they finally reached a stately dining room. Anne was chatting with a slim, distinguished-looking man at a table big enough to host a banquet. A rectangular carpet — the same royal blue as in the corridors — was positioned under the table, the rest of the room's expansive, oak-planked floor left uncovered. On wood-panelled walls were oil paintings, mostly portraits, darkened and cracked with age.

A comforting, rich coffee aroma swirled from a silver jug on the sideboard but then Sophie was assailed by a cooked bacon smell. As usual, it made her feel slightly sick.

By her legs, Charlotte tensed. A black retriever was

bounding towards them. Sophie tensed too, fearing an unpleasant incident, but the dogs began a friendly doggy greeting ritual, sniffing and wagging tails.

Anne's companion stood up. Wearing a baggy brown suit, his hair was grey-flecked, but his face held traces of the handsome young man he'd once been. 'Sir Richard Lacey, how do you do?' He had the same clipped accent as Anne.

'Very pleased to meet you. I'm Hugo Harrington and this is Sophie Arundel.' Hugo was still wearing his trainers and, despite the borrowed clothes, looked as out of place as Sophie did. Like backpackers invited into Buckingham Palace.

Sophie's palms were clammy and before they all shook hands, she wiped them on her jeans. She'd never been good at meeting new people, let alone aristocrats that were long dead.

'It's very good of you, Sir Richard, to let us join you,' said Hugo.

'Please call me Richard.'

'This is Charlotte.' Sophie pointed.

'And this is Jack.' Richard's smile didn't quite reach his clear brown eyes. He bore a remarkable resemblance to the man in the pastoral picture in his hall.

Two tall young men, dressed in black suits, white shirts and gloves, were standing by a heavy sideboard laid with lidded breakfast dishes on silver trays. One footman was fair, with rosy cheeks; the other had shiny, ebony hair, dark eyes and a generous mouth. An imposing, older man — the butler — was issuing quiet instructions.

'Shorten has a tradition of welcoming unusual visitors,' said Richard. 'Do sit down.'

Shorten. Connected to the photo in the students' union?

'Is someone else joining us?' asked Hugo, indicating an extra place setting.

'Freddy doesn't usually have breakfast. He might be awake by lunchtime.' Anne exchanged an indulgent look with Richard. 'He acquired bad habits at Cambridge.'

'The university?' said Hugo.

'Yes,' said Anne. 'He's a similar age to you.'

'He passed the entrance exam early and read maths,' said Richard. 'He went up when he was seventeen.'

'I hope you'll become friends.' Anne smiled.

A fresh lurch of unease. Making friends took days, weeks. Focus. She'd see the lift today, suss it out, and get home tomorrow. The fair-haired footman put a thick linen napkin on her lap and Charlotte slid under the table with Jack. She wasn't usually so relaxed with a strange dog but since this started, she'd been unpredictable.

The same footman was at Sophie's elbow again, offering tea or freshly ground coffee. He was avoiding her eyes, as if embarrassed.

'Coffee, please.' Sophie turned to Anne and Richard. 'This is very kind of you.'

'Our pleasure,' said Richard, his face expressionless.

Anne sipped her coffee. 'I know how apprehensive you are feeling. When I arrived, there were many differences to get used to.'

'What year is it?' asked Sophie.

Anne put down her cup. '1925.'

'Oh.' Hugo's guess — the beginning of the twentieth century — was way out. 1920's ... *The Great Gatsby*, glamorous parties and skimpy knee-length dresses. But Anne's gown was floor length and Amish modest. Definitely not a party dress.

'What year have you come from?' asked Richard.

'2017.' The date was a fact. Solid and provable. But it echoed oddly in Sophie's head, sounding futuristic. Unreal.

Richard glanced at his wife. 'Anne has told me men have visited the moon. Have we colonised Mars yet?'

'No,' said Hugo. 'That's some way off.'

Anne gestured at the sideboard. 'As you can see, our breakfast habits aren't that different.'

If you lived in a five-star hotel. Sophie's place setting had a sapphire mat with delicate gold leaf around the edges, silver cutlery and an individual dish of butter, pressed in the middle with a delicate L. At Aunty Wendy's house, they ate in the kitchen or slobbed in front of the TV. Napkins were occasionally put out for guests but only if they asked.

Sophie had kedgeree and toast, and two sausages for Charlotte. A fan of kedgeree, except the fish bits, she tucked into the rice, eggs and cream; they were as yummy as on a long-ago holiday in Scotland. The toast was fresh white bread, like the rolls the previous night. She carefully put her cutlery together on her plate to signal she'd finished eating. 'Anne, can I ask, do you remember what lift you got into, before you arrived in Shorten?' Anne might be lying about coming through the lift or there might be other portals. Nothing was certain.

'In the student's union. It had been painted gold.'

Hugo was frowning but Anne's prompt answer rang true. And if they'd all stepped out of the same lift, likely there was only one portal. 'Did you ever want to travel back a century?'

'No,' said Anne, smiling at her husband. 'Never gave it a thought.'

Sophie stared miserably at her clean plate. This idea was going nowhere.

Hugo was still eating kedgeree and a suspicious item that might be devilled kidneys. After Richard had given Jack bacon, Sophie covertly fed Charlotte sausages.

'I suppose I should be used to unexpected visitors,' said

Richard, 'but it still comes as a surprise, a welcome one, of course.'

The slightest jarring note but, hey, they had just turned up at his house.

'Visitors,' said Anne. 'That's what the locals call us.'

'You said there were others,' said Hugo.

'Mr Parkes runs the pub in the village,' said Anne. 'He arrived in 1902. And Miss Hemmings, the head gardener now, she came through with another girl in 1911, Miss Alderman. I'm afraid Miss Alderman died in 1913. She was working in the gardens and had a scratch. Nothing unusual, but it became infected. She's buried in the estate graveyard, by the small chapel.'

'How old was she?' asked Hugo.

'Nineteen,' said Anne.

Sophie turned over her bandaged hand, her heart sinking. Antibiotics hadn't been invented yet—

'The year after Mr Parkes arrived, there was a great deal of interest from the scientific community,' said Anne, trying to lighten the mood. 'An earnest young man interviewed us. What was his name?'

'Mr Eddington,' said Richard.

'Initially, he was very excited,' said Anne, 'but he never found anything.'

Sophie smiled at the fair-haired footman who was topping up her coffee. Only six visitors — had to have some-thing in common? If she couldn't find the lift this morning, figuring that out could help them get back.

'How long was Mr Eddington here?' asked Hugo.

'We had a stream of scientists coming and going in 1903 and 1904.' Anne wiped her lips delicately with her napkin.

Sophie sipped her coffee, then returned the cup to its saucer. All the cups here were tiny. Mugs must be a modern thing.

Richard dropped his napkin on the table and got to his feet. 'If you will excuse me, I have things to attend to. I hope you have a pleasant day.'

Jack dutifully followed his master.

Anne seemed flustered. 'Our estate manager died unexpectedly last week. Apart from the shock of losing the poor man, Richard is running the estate single-handedly.'

'Anne, I'll understand if this question is too blunt or personal,' said Hugo, 'but you mentioned yesterday you didn't want to go back?'

'Richard and I were married within a year of me coming here. Shorten has been my home for nearly thirty years.'

Sophie finished her coffee. 'That's *so* romantic.'

'I should get going too.' Anne got to her feet. 'I have an appointment with the dressmaker in a few minutes. You can never have enough day dresses.' This latter remark was directed at Sophie. 'Have a wander round the estate. It's a lovely day.'

As Sophie went with Charlotte and Hugo out of the room, the dark-haired footman's eyes followed her, his lips curved in amusement, and Sophie was glad to get outside. Not long before she could collect that bike.

She relished the fresh air and ambled, conscious of her sore foot.

Hugo sat on a stone seat by an ancient sundial in a bower and she sat beside him, keeping Charlotte on the lead. She briefly closed her eyes, breathing in sweet flowery scents.

'Anne's told him about the moon landings, likely she's told him other stuff too. That could have changed who knows what at home ... *before* we left.'

The idea gave her goose bumps. Maybe her parents weren't supposed to die? 'Whatever was different, we — or anybody — wouldn't have known that it had been changed.'

'Worrying but logical.' Hugo frowned. 'I didn't notice the lift had been painted.'

'Your eyes were glued to your phone.' Sophie patted Charlotte. 'But you must have noticed the pictures.'

'Pictures?'

She told him about the artwork on the doors.

'That makes no sense.'

'And there's stuff here that makes no sense.' Sophie ruffled Charlotte's head, the caress reassuring, familiar.

'Like what?'

'If Anne arrived thirty years ago, when she was at the university in the 1980s, that would have been the early 1890s. She married Richard a year later but Freddy's only our age, so she waited nearly a decade to have him. Why would she do that?'

'There may be other children before Freddy, who've flown the nest or … and this affects you.'

'What does?'

'Having a baby at this time was risky,' said Hugo, 'even if you were well off. Perhaps that's why she waited?'

'I'm not staying for another week, never mind thirty years. And I'm certainly not going to have a baby.' She tapped her fingers on the cool stone of the seat. 'I'll find out everything I can today, and sort this.'

He had that pensive look again, a slight crease between his strong brows.

'You don't want to go home.'

'Of course, I do. I don't want to die here. But it can't be straightforward or at least one of the visitors would have gone back.' He stared at the sundial. 'And none of them did.'

CHAPTER 9

Ten minutes later, when Sophie walked into the bedroom, Miss Able was there, putting away something in a drawer. She turned, her eyes narrowing. 'Miss, that camisole is underwear.'

Explained the footman's embarrassment. 'Sorry, I didn't realise.'

'The bicycles are outside, Miss.' Miss Able unlocked the French windows and opened one door.

'Thank you for this.' Sophie self-consciously pulled on her cardigan, stepped into soft drizzle and called for Charlotte to follow her.

The bikes were propped against a wall; they had baskets, shiny bells but no gears. That was okay, wasn't as if the lane had steep bits. Doing about ten mph, she'd be there in a couple of hours, a bit longer if Charlotte tired and slowed to walking pace.

'The shortest way to the lane is by the office.' Miss Able pointed from the doorway, before stepping back and shutting the door.

Charlotte was jumping about, ready for action. Sophie

put her lead in the basket and cycled along an alley between the main house and a much smaller brick building, over a rickety wooden bridge straddling the moat, then onto the drive.

A boy around her age was strolling towards the house, exuding the confidence of carefree youth, humming under his breath. He was as slender as Hugo and almost as tall. His navy trousers were loose with a sharply ironed, straight crease down the front and his long-sleeved, white shirt was buttoned to the top. His jacket matched his trousers and around his neck was a yellow bow tie that was slightly askew. Hugo's clothes must have been borrowed from this boy.

When he saw her, he stopped and offered his hand. 'Freddy Lacey, how do you do?'

His sandy hair, straight nose and easy smile were attractive in a boy-next-door sort of way. Ironic for a boy living in a stately home.

'Hello.' Sophie jammed on the brakes and put her feet down. Still astride the bike, she shook his hand.

The handshake was formal, his hand warm and smooth, but her skin faintly prickled, as if with static electricity, and at the edge of her mind something stirred. Recognition? No, imagination fuelled by stress—

'I've heard all about you. The servants are buzzing with it.' Freddy was looking at her camisole and jeans. 'Those ... trousers are pukka.'

'Sorry?'

'Top rate.' His accent was less clipped than his parents, more Prince Harry than *The Crown*. 'I love your dog by the way. He's massive.'

'*She* is quite big. Bigger than Jack.'

'I'd say. That's why I thought she was a boy.' Freddy's face was lightly tanned, as if he played tennis every day or enjoyed long country walks. 'Wonderful curly coat, and that red collar is wacky.'

'She doesn't have any pink stuff.'

'Pardon?'

'Pink for a girl.'

Freddy looked puzzled.

The drizzle was turning into rain. 'Nice to meet you but I need to get going.'

Freddy frowned, seemed conflicted. 'Righty ho,' he said finally, and turned towards the house.

Sophie cycled onto the deserted lane and pedalled steadily, getting into a rhythm, ignoring her aching legs; they were still sore from yesterday's trek. Her split palm hurt from gripping the handlebars but didn't feel weird. Hopefully sorted by the *Milton* stuff.

Charlotte was keeping up with ease, rushing through puddles, but she'd tire in an hour or so. 'This is a real-life quest,' Sophie told her, 'so pain and suffering's part of the gig.'

Dark clouds and rain made it night-gloomy and the road turned into a grey snake, winding between silent, brooding hedges. 'When we get closer,' she told Charlotte, 'that fancy light will be a welcoming beacon.'

Charlotte ran ahead, graceful and fast, relishing the exercise, and disappeared around a bend.

Sophie's jeans were wet through, but the rain was pleasantly cool on her head and shoulders and the sound of the bike's rubber tyres sliding over sodden tarmac was repetitive and soothing. Whoosh, whoosh, whoosh—

A movement to her right, a jumping blur. Something shoved her sideways and she landed with a thwack, painfully banging into the angular bike as it thumped against the ground.

She lay winded, her face on the tarmac and rain splattering on her back, but someone pulled her roughly to her feet. A hand clamped over her mouth and a sharp pain seared her neck.

'Don't move.' The voice was male and brusque.

Sickly body odour and the stench of nicotine invaded her nostrils and she gagged, her heart beating loud in her ears, blotting out coherent thought.

'This knife can gut you like a fish. Understand?'

Held fast by a hand on her face and a knife at her throat, she managed a grunt.

In front of her was another man, with a filthy unkempt beard. His determined eyes were crawling from her boots to her face.

Think. Focus.

But her brain was frozen in panic. Beard Man's trousers and shirt were caked in grime. He reeked worse than the man holding her, and she gagged again.

'Nice necklace.' Beard Man ran his hands over her jeans' pockets and explored her camisole under her cardigan.

She writhed.

'Keep. Still.' The knife point went further into her neck, layering pain on pain. 'Or I'll cut you up.'

She stopped moving, paralysed with horror. Time slowed, captured in slow motion, unfurling like smoke from a dying fire. If he slashed her throat, would she drown in her own blood or bleed out into nothingness? She closed her eyes and saw her parents' faces behind her lids. Were they waiting, feeling her terror, would they comfort her after—

'No purse,' said Beard Man.

The hold on her head tightened. 'We'll get something for the jewellery.'

Sophie forced herself to open her eyes.

Beard Man was peering at her jeans. 'Odd sort of get up.

Perhaps she's from a circus?' He smiled, revealing gap-ridden brown teeth. 'Or a loony bin … won't be missed.'

The other man stiffened. 'She's nobody, no risk to us.'

'She'll remember my face. Do it quick.'

Adrenaline surged and Sophie's brain raced through the options. Backwards head butt? No, the grip on her mouth and head was too strong. She was still holding Charlotte's sturdy lead handle. Hit out with that? No, a glancing blow at best.

The rough hand released her mouth to break off the pendant.

'No!' Her shout sounded shrill and feeble, and Sophie braced for a slash across her throat. But the hand came back, so hard, she bit her tongue.

She had surprise on her side. Kick—

Barking.

Charlotte was hurtling along the lane. In a heartbeat she was on Beard Man, sinking her jaws into his leg. Then she mauled him like a toy.

The hard hand left Sophie's mouth but gripped her forehead, pulling her head back, exposing her throat, and the knife point pushed in.

A metallic taste spread across her tongue. Fear or blood or both. 'She's my dog.' Her voice came out as a squeak. 'If you let me go, I'll call her off.'

Charlotte had left her quarry whimpering on the verge and was now circling, her eyes fixed on Sophie and the man who held her. Charlotte's gaze was unwavering, her soft golden irises eclipsed by huge, intense-black pupils. The gentle pet had gone. This was a wolf who'd tasted blood and was eyeing her next prey.

The hand tightened on Sophie's temple but the man's foul breathing near her ear was quick with fear.

Charlotte snarled, exposing teeth dripping with blood, and the sight gave Sophie hope. 'If I die, she'll tear you apart.'

Beard Man was trying to stand. Groaning and panting, he was clutching at his leg, now a gory tangle of blood, rags and shredded flesh.

Sophie was free. She stumbled and fell.

Her captor reached his friend in two strides and hauled him over his shoulder in a single heave. Tall and muscled, he sprinted off like an athlete, his mate's head banging like a metronome against his back. In moments, they'd passed a bend down the lane. Lost to sight.

Dazed, Sophie watched the turning for movement. Nothing.

She touched her neck and her fingers came away sticky with blood.

Sophie stayed on her knees on the rough tarmac, too numb to feel anything, even relief. Charlotte had moved close and Sophie hugged her, beyond grateful for superior canine hearing. No human would have heard that cry of distress.

Charlotte sniffed at Sophie's legs, checking her mistress was okay, and Sophie staggered to her feet, holding a scraped elbow. Her narrow escape hit home again like a thudding arrow and she drew a deep breath. Then another one.

Charlotte stepped back and stared at the bend in the road where the vagrants had gone, then snarled and pawed the ground, her blood up. Sophie grabbed her collar and attached the lead, her fingers clumsy with exhaustion. Charlotte wanted those men dead, but she might get stabbed.

It was darker now and the rain heavier, and the bike lay twisted, the handlebars and front wheel badly bent. She wouldn't be able to push it, never mind ride. And those men hadn't gone far, would be on the road… Despair threatened to overwhelm her.

Water hit her in a cold spray. Charlotte was furiously writhing, spinning off rain from her sturdy frame.

Sophie wiped her face with her hand. 'Back to the house.' She turned around. 'Even a kickass knight would bail.'

But Charlotte didn't move, still watching for the men.

Sophie pulled on her lead. 'Come on.'

Charlotte followed reluctantly, then ran, rushing through puddles on the extended lead.

The rain stopped, the clouds parted, and a mocking sun shone on the wet road. Sophie's left hip was aching from the bike fall, but adrenaline kicked in and she sped up.

When she reached the putrid pool near the house, she paused, gathering the strength to carry on.

Someone was walking around the bend towards them and Sophie's grip strengthened on the lead handle.

But it was Hugo.

When he saw her, he froze.

She reached him and, in fits and starts, told him what happened.

He exhaled, fighting to control himself. 'Breathe.'

'Trying to.' She swayed.

'You're safe.' He caught her by the shoulders and hugged her.

She buried her head in his chest for a long moment before stepping away.

Charlotte was standing proprietorially close and Sophie unfastened her lead, trying to focus. Houses in the 1920s had phones. 'Call the police.'

'You need to think this through.'

'What?'

'You can't report it, your reputation will be toast. Asking for it, all that bollocks.'

'He had a knife to my throat.' Her voice cracked.

'We're nobody here, Sophie … strange visitors. Those

skinny jeans, two men, *you* would be on trial as much as the muggers. What happened would get sexed up.'

'Hugo, they didn't rape me—'

'Listen. If we're stuck here and there's a trial, you'll have *no* chance of a good marriage.'

She had no intention of marrying anyone, but she got it. In this nuts time, she needed to preserve her mythical virginal reputation. Couldn't ID the man with the knife anyway. Hadn't seen his face.

'Where's the bike?'

'Trashed. Never got near the lift.'

'The lift can wait,' said Hugo. 'We need a downplayed mugging story with no discrepancies. Tell Miss Able that a boy snatched your necklace and you fell off your bike. End of. And that story will do the rounds.'

'She gossips?'

'Tells John everything.'

Sophie took a steadying breath. 'What sort of things?'

'After breakfast, John mentioned how nasty your hand injury looked.'

Miss Able was Gossip Central. Uncomfortable thought. Note to self: not just the mugging story — *no* sharing.

'Gardeners are working by the drive. I'll distract them and the housekeeper so you can get cleaned up. You're in no state to fob off concerned questions.'

She was shaking now, as well as soaked and smeared with mud.

'Ready?'

'Yes.' She linked arms with him and stumbled around the corner.

They passed gardeners weeding by the Manor gates. Hugo ruffled Charlotte's head and said amiably, 'Sophie came off her bike.'

In the hall, he talked to the housekeeper about nothing, and Sophie hurried by with Charlotte.

Fortunately, the corridor leading to her room was deserted. She found the bathroom, stepped inside and locked the door. Then she peeled off her clothes, dropping them in a sodden heap on the wooden floor.

She ran the bath and Charlotte watched her mistress with solemn eyes.

Sophie pulled off the hand bandage that was now a muddy mess and dropped it in a small wicker bin. The cut on her palm didn't look too bad. She examined her neck in the mirror. A shallow puncture wound, a finger-width across and not too much blood. Might leave a scar … but she didn't care.

Losing her mother's necklace though was the *worst* feeling. She gave in briefly to angry, bitter tears then sniffed, took a cream soap bar from a cardboard box on a shelf by the sink, thoroughly washed her hands and cleaned her neck.

Sitting on a wooden stool, she tested the bath water; any hotter and her elbow would really sting. It was awkward, climbing into the high-sided roll-top bath, but she managed it. As she washed her injuries, the pain merged together, but the physical cleaning felt good. Dulled the feeling of violation that was lodged in her brain like a splinter.

She hadn't found shampoo or conditioner so just rinsed her hair.

After the bath, she put the soap bar in its box and took a towel from the shelf. It was scratchy, not fluffy. As she dried herself, she was careful to avoid getting blood on the towel from her elbow, and left the towel on the side of the bath.

Her cardigan had a rough, scarlet-framed hole in one sleeve, the camisole was splattered red from her neck and her jeans were rain-sodden and stiff with mud. She wiped Charlotte's jaws with the camisole, turning the pink fabric ruby, then soaked it in cold water. Unless Miss Able was a secret Miss Marple, she'd attribute the remaining faint splodges to the fall from the bike.

Sophie slipped on the cardigan, closed it, took the rest of her clothes and stood by the door. Hearing nothing, she ran with Charlotte down the passage to the bedroom and shut the door behind her. She took off the cardigan, draped it over the spindly chair with the other ruined clothes to dry and, rummaging in a drawer, found the dressing gown. She put it on, fastened a few buttons, got into bed and cuddled a damp and muddy Charlotte, keeping her mostly on the tartan blanket; lifting her into that high-sided bath would have been impossible.

She wanted to hurt those men, *really* hurt them. But the instinct didn't feel natural or normal. Only shameful. A betrayal of the fragment of her parents' faith she still followed, and believed in. Her mother's long ago bedtime stories — heroes turning the other cheek — were wrapped up in precious memories: the feel and smell of strawberry bubble baths, her feet on a furry, hot water bottle in bed, and the comforting sound of her mother's voice, reading the same words so often, Sophie knew them by heart.

Sophie pulled the heavy bedcovers to her shoulders. After their car accident, she'd managed to park a cold need for revenge. She could do that again.

She'd been almost sure this strange place was real, but near death had clinched it. She wished, willed herself away to her bedroom at Aunty Wendy's, picturing the photo of her parents and her posters, a mishmash of fit actors and sports flyers: a fresh-faced Robert Pattinson in *Harry Potter and the Goblet of Fire*, a kickboxing female silhouette proclaiming *Kick Like A Girl*. Her mind meandered to a special memory — cradling a milk-scented, helpless bundle of fur. Charlotte, no bigger than her palm. Her mind drifted further: her parents' voices floating up the stairs from the kitchen, glasses chinking as they cleared away dinner, her mother's kiss on her forehead, the aroma of red wine and dark chocolate—

A light knock and the door opened.

'Are you ill, Miss?' Miss Able seemed curious, not concerned.

The housekeeper must have told her Sophie Arundel was back. 'Yes, caught a cold from the rain.'

Miss Able went over to the French windows. 'Where's the bicycle?'

'A boy snatched my necklace and the bike wobbled and I fell off and the handlebars are really bent.' Sophie pulled the bedclothes right up to her chin.

Miss Able turned. 'I did warn you, Miss.'

'I couldn't push it, so I left it where you said, at the roadside.'

'One of the gardeners can carry it on a wheelbarrow.' Miss Able's face was carefully blank but her stiff body language indicated irritation, annoyance. She took Sophie's bloody cardigan from the chair and examined it at arm's length, her lips twisting in distaste, then let it drop.

'I scraped my elbow.'

'You need a hot cup of tea, Miss.' Miss Able bustled out the door.

'I just want to sleep,' Sophie confided to Charlotte.

But when Miss Able returned, Sophie took a sip.

'You do look washed out, Miss.'

Sophie drank the tea and slept.

CHAPTER 10

Three hours later, Sophie was woken by another knock on the door.

Miss Able came in with a tray. 'Tea and a nice beef sandwich, Miss.'

Sophie smiled her thanks and sat up. She'd stopped shaking but her neck and elbow were throbbing like neon lights. Miss Alderman's fate still might be hers, if soap wasn't enough and she couldn't get home and source antibiotics.

She ate the bread and butter, gave the beef to Charlotte, and drank more tea. Aside from the buzz of pain, she felt oddly normal. The memory of the assault was vivid but seemed unreal because the Manor was so ... civilised.

'You'll feel better after a bath, Miss.'

Sophie didn't want to move but declined to mention this would be bath number two. Miss Able would ask more questions and — Hugo had been right — Sophie Arundel was in no state to invent answers.

'We'll get your hair nicely washed. Lady Lacey has her hair done once a fortnight.'

'I wash mine every day.'

'You'd get fed up with that, Miss. Takes a couple of hours and if you wash it more than once a week, it'll dry out something dreadful.'

Washing her hair would take *hours*? Unlikely.

'I can wash your hair, Miss.'

That would be too much. 'Don't worry, I'll do it. Is there any shampoo and conditioner?'

'We haven't got what you said.' Miss Able opened the toiletries cupboard and took out a cream soap bar like the one in the bathroom. 'This breaks down in water, Miss.'

No clue how that would work. The bar in the bathroom hadn't 'broken down' in the bath. Sophie got out of bed and saw her knotted, damp locks in an oval wall mirror above the cupboard. So matted, the comb in her bag would be useless. 'Do you have a detangler brush?'

Miss Able looked blank.

Charlotte was wagging her tail, keen for another outing.

Surprising. Did dogs and other mammals' brains just move on from stressful events? Hopefully, Sophie Arundel could too. She padded barefoot towards the door.

'Miss!'

'What?'

'You can't go into the corridor like that. Would be … indecent.' Miss Able busied herself fastening every one of the dressing gown's many buttons. 'There.' She opened the door and scanned the passage.

Were male servants loitering, hoping to catch illicit glimpses of a girl in a maid outfit or her in a lacy robe? Unlikely such people would be employed in the Manor. Or had Miss Able grown up in a religious cult obsessed with female modesty?

In the bathroom, Miss Able locked the door and began filling the sink.

There was no sign of the wet towel. 'Shall I run the bath?'

'Oh no, Miss. We need to wash your hair first.'

'Surely, it would be easier in the bath?'

'Not really, Miss. It takes as long as it takes, and the water would go cold. You'd catch your death.'

Two hours later, Miss Able was still combing Sophie's tangled hair. Miss Able had the patience of a saint. She'd rinsed Sophie's hair, before patting in soap flakes that she'd scraped off the bar with a knife. Subsequent rinsing had involved lots of sink filling, draining and refilling. Charlotte had been fascinated, watching intently.

Sophie shifted slightly on the wooden stool and smiled at Miss Able. 'When did you start working here?'

'When I was twelve, Miss.'

'How come you didn't carry on at school?'

'That's when everyone leaves, Miss.'

Not everyone. Freddy had done a degree. Sophie Arundel was in a house that did child labour ... shouldn't judge. 1925 was a long time ago.

Miss Able wrapped a towel around Sophie's hair and began drawing the bath.

After what seemed like another hour, Miss Able tested the water with her elbow. 'Just right.'

'Thanks for this, but I can take it from here.'

Miss Able seemed puzzled.

A misunderstanding. 'Um, I'm fine having a bath by myself.'

'It's not safe, Miss. Suppose you slipped.'

She'd been lucky not to fall before. Hugo had bathed with John in tow but men used urinals with strangers. So for him, no big deal.

Sophie unbuttoned her dressing gown and Miss Able waited patiently.

A slip of a thing, barely five foot tall. A vision of Miss Able pushing her under water popped into Sophie's head.

She'd never liked horror films so had watched hardly any, but they'd wormed into her subconscious.

Charlotte was now lying on the floor, half napping.

If Miss Able tried any funny business, Charlotte would bite her. Rip her apart. Don't think about it.

Sophie got in the bath and winced as the hot water predictably stung the raw skin on her elbow and hand, but the pain quickly faded.

'That's a bad bruise on your hip, Miss.'

But only a bruise. Or she couldn't have sprinted to the Manor.

Miss Able handed her a sponge and the cream soap bar from the shelf and peered at Sophie's neck. 'And those cuts are nasty.'

'Scrapes from the tarmac.' Distract her. 'Would you mind if I called you by your first name?' This formal surname business *was* weird.

For a moment, worry showed in Miss Able's face, but she said, 'My Christian name is Maud, Miss.'

'And please call me Sophie.'

'Absolutely not, Miss.' Maud sat stiffly on the stool. 'That would be ... disrespectful.'

While Sophie soaked, Maud talked. Her voice was soothing, like reverse therapy — a shrink making small talk — not probing, raking up bad thoughts.

'When you travelled though time, Miss, did it hurt?'

Interesting question. People felt grotty after flights with too many time zones; after travelling back a century, she should feel like pants. 'Actually, didn't hurt at all.'

'What's the future like?'

Keep it vague. 'Women can train for any job they want.'

'Like what, Miss?'

'What are you good at?'

'Being a lady's maid.'

'Apart from that. What if you could do anything?'

'Anything … would be lovely to work in an office, Miss. Be one of those secretaries, taking notes and typing.'

Sophie had never wanted to work in an office or be somebody's secretary, even if it had been renamed 'personal assistant.' But she should react positively. No point in Maud aspiring to be the boss … women bosses were a modern thing. 'My grandmother started out as a secretary but later went into teaching. She's in her eighties now, does private tuition.'

'That's sad.'

'No, she loves it. Says it keeps her young.' Sophie wiggled her toes in the bath water.

'Well I never. She's lucky to have her health.'

'Yes,' said Sophie. 'She'll live to be a hundred.'

'That's *very* old.'

Sophie made lazy water patterns with her fingers. 'Is it hard, being a lady's maid?'

'It's mostly common sense, Miss, but I've watched Miss Jefferson, Lady Lacey's maid. I'm not good at hair styling though. I need more practice.'

Maud chatted about over-worked kitchen staff and the travails of other maids, and Sophie let herself relax. She could be converted to baths. Showers woke you up, got you going, but if you had no deadlines, no place to go, lying in a bath was heavenly.

'… anyway, a few years ago, Mr Hunter, he's number one footman now, he tried to interfere with Miss Blackmore. She slapped him so hard, it made his eyes run. Handsome devil but he knows it.'

'He has very dark hair and eyes?'

'Yes, Miss.'

He'd been amused when she'd worn that skimpy top to breakfast … mentally undressed her.

'He'll be butler one day.' Maud stood and reached for another towel. 'The water's going cold, Miss.'

Sophie climbed out and Maud wrapped her in the towel.

After Sophie had dried herself, she put on the dressing gown. 'Can we put in more hot water?'

'Miss?'

'For Charlotte, she's splattered with mud.'

Maud's lips parted but she didn't speak.

'She loves being washed. For her, it's like a doggie spa.'

Maud's mouth was now an inelegant O.

Sophie ran the hot tap. 'If you could help me … she's quite heavy.'

Between them, they lowered Charlotte in. The cream soap was as effective as doggie shampoo and with Charlotte blissing out, Sophie got her spotless in five minutes. She wrapped Charlotte in her own damp towel to prevent messy writhing and Maud insisted again on completely fastening Sophie's dressing gown.

Once in the bedroom, Maud leaned against the door. 'Washing a dog in the bath.' She shook her head.

Sophie sat in the blue armchair. 'How else could we have cleaned her?'

Maud started rolling her eyes but stopped herself and removed the towel around Sophie's hair. 'One last comb through.'

After sorting a particularly stubborn knot, Maud said, 'You were lucky, Miss. You could have broken something, would have had to go to Derby.'

'Why?'

'To have an X-ray. They have a machine there.' Maud returned the comb to the toiletries cupboard. 'All done.'

Sophie felt her hair. Smooth, sleek, normal. 'I am grateful for your help.'

'And I'm glad to be your lady's maid, Miss.'

Really? She hadn't looked thrilled when Sophie Arundel had boomeranged back to the Manor.

'My parents would have been proud. I'm only twenty.'

Sophie picked up on the 'would.' 'I'm so sorry about your parents.'

Maud acknowledged Sophie's words with a polite nod.

She didn't seem upset. Perhaps they'd died many years ago? 'Were they very strict with you, when you were younger?'

'Not especially, Miss. We always had chores to do and knew to finish our plates.' Maud smiled, remembering.

'You weren't restricted on where you could go with other children, including boys?'

'No. I still go walking with Mr Watkins by the river. Done that since before I started at the Manor. It's beautiful there, had some lovely times.'

'Are you and Mr Watkins together?'

'Pardon?' Maud blinked, puzzled.

'Is he your boyfriend?'

'We're courting, Miss, is that what you mean?'

'I guess.' Good. Maud hadn't been born into a scary cult. Sophie stood up to get dressed and froze. 'Where are my clothes?'

CHAPTER 11

*A*ll gone. Even her knickers. She scanned the bedroom in a panic.

'Sent to the laundry, Miss.'

Sophie felt foolish. 'Of course.'

But that cashmere cardigan had been a lucky charity shop find. Wouldn't be the same darned, and now a shrunken vision of it danced in her head. 'This is awkward … I've nothing to wear.'

Maud opened the wardrobe with an air of triumph, lifted out a long, cream dress and laid it carefully on the bed. 'This is much better than those trousers, Miss.'

'Do you have any clean underwear?'

Maud opened a drawer and held up loose, white Bermuda shorts; near the bottom of the cotton legs were delicate pink bows.

Sophie gaped. Pretty in their own way but if these were knickers, they were truly vast.

Maud took a bodice from a drawer. 'And you can wear this, Miss.'

The vest was cute. White, with narrow straps, it fastened at the front.

Sophie pulled on the shorts, baffled but resigned, put on the bodice and began doing it up. 'This is too small.' She took it off. 'I don't need it.'

Maud's eyes widened. 'If you're sure, Miss.'

'Quite sure.' Sophie stepped into the dress. With an empire waistline, high collar and three-quarter sleeves, it was way over the top, like a stage costume. Lace was the dominant theme, from the neckline to the hem. Anne could have worn this when she'd first arrived. They were around the same height. Sophie examined the silky material under the lace. 'Posh.'

'It's a tea dress.' Maud fussed until the fastenings at the back were closed.

The collar was irritating the cuts on her neck. Sophie tugged at it. 'Sorry, could you undo the top buttons?'

Maud frowned but unfastened them, then handed Sophie a sleeveless, filigree cape. Once on, its length exactly matched the gown's ankle-length skirt. Charlotte licked its hem in approval.

Sophie pulled on a fresh pair of socks, stepped into her scruffy boots and tied the laces. She turned around in front of the long mirror. The boots looked fine with the dress. Maud would take a different view; her flat black shoes were impeccably polished.

'Now I need to dress your hair, Miss.'

'What?'

'It needs to go up, be fixed with pins.'

'Please don't worry. I'm happy with it like this.'

Maud gave a disapproving sniff. She wore her hair like Anne and the housekeeper so expected Miss Arundel to conform. After a moment, she gestured at Sophie's bag beside the wardrobe. 'Shall I give the inside a good wash?'

'That's really kind of you. An apple went off.' Having a lady's maid was odd but cool.

Someone knocked on the door and Maud opened it.

Hugo paused in the doorway, taken aback at Sophie's transformation. 'It's a lovely day now. Come to the terrace.'

Maud went to the wardrobe and took out a straw hat with a huge, floppy brim. Around the crown was a broad, cream ribbon. 'Informal, Miss, but better than nothing.'

It was Ascot posh. 'I'll pass,' said Sophie. Her dress was theatrical. Adding a hat would be comical.

Maud seemed confused.

Sophie smiled at her, ruffled Charlotte's head, picked up her lead and stepped into the corridor.

Before they reached the terrace, Hugo said quietly, 'Are you okay?'

'Yes.' And she was. Hopefully. 'It was lucky you were in the lane when I got back.'

He nodded. 'I just fancied a walk.'

Outside, the recent heavy rain had left a sheen on the lawn and the terrace's stone flagstones were damp, but the air tasted fresh, and the sun was warm on her face and on her shoulders through the thin dress.

Freddy was there, drinking what she presumed was tea. Cakes and sandwiches were arranged like before on a three-tier stand.

Sitting at Freddy's feet, Jack's attention was on the nearby food, but when he heard Charlotte approaching, he raced off with her across the lawn.

Hugo sat at the table. But before Sophie could take a seat, Freddy stood and drew out a chair for her.

If a boy had done that at home, it would have jarred, a false display of charm to get her into bed. But Freddy was just … charming.

'Sophie's gone native.' Hugo gestured at her dress, his flippancy at odds with his eyes, serious and careful.

'You are *so* politically incorrect,' said Sophie, sitting down and playing along with acting nonchalant.

'Politically what?' Freddy rang the handbell.

'In the future, you have to be careful what you say, to avoid giving offence.' Hugo went into a long explanation, with examples, that he also had to explain.

A hundred years ago — one long lifetime — but a huge culture gap. Sophie pulled at her collar. Still chafing.

A maid came out and Freddy ordered more tea.

'Apparently, there's an X-ray machine in Derby,' said Sophie. 'I thought they were a modern thing.'

'No,' said Hugo. 'Invented in the nineteenth century.'

'That machine only arrived last year,' said Freddy. 'When I fell out of a tree, Dr Griffiths pressed and poked my arm to find the break.'

Sophie winced. 'Were you reading in the tree?'

'Just climbing,' said Freddy, 'down by the river, like you do when you're young.'

'You don't anymore?'

He laughed. 'No.'

'I still climb,' said Sophie. 'There's an old apple tree in my aunt's garden. In the holidays, I sit in it and read for hours.'

Freddy seemed surprised.

The maid returned, poured tea for Sophie and Hugo, and topped up Freddy's cup.

'Freddy was saying they employ so many servants because people are starving,' said Hugo. 'I thought it was hard to recruit in the 1920s, with better wages and hours in factories. The history books have it wrong.'

'The passage of time could soften the memory of poverty,' said Sophie, 'like Caribbean pirates, sanitised, diluted?'

'What is history, but a fable agreed upon?' said Hugo.

'Very poetic,' said Freddy.

'The man who said it was more into war than poetry,' said Hugo. 'Napoleon.'

With Hugo, who needed Google?

Freddy sipped his tea and turned to Sophie. 'How are you settling in?'

'The Manor's lovely … but in the lane, this young lad snatched my necklace and I fell off the bike.' Her tone was pitch-perfect casual.

But Freddy looked shocked. 'Good gracious. Are you all right?'

'Absolutely fine.' She took a ladylike sip, glad the annoying collar hid her neck.

'I should have dissuaded you from travelling alone,' said Freddy. 'Was the necklace valuable?'

Worth about ten quid but priceless to her. Sophie made herself shrug.

'I'll tell the groundsmen to keep an eye out,' said Freddy. 'Could you describe him?'

Beard Man's features loomed up in her mind, clear and sharp. 'No, happened too fast.'

'I was mugged last month. Or a century from now.' Hugo gave Freddy a tense glance. 'Sorry, still coming to terms with being here.' He put his cup down. 'Someone nicked a phone from my pocket. Wimbledon High Street, in broad daylight. Annoying, but no big deal.'

If Hugo had hoped his story would lend credibility to her blasé attitude, it hadn't worked; Freddy was watching them as if they were aliens. Sophie focused on keeping her face impassive.

'Miss Hemmings arrived with a tiny telephone, but it didn't work,' said Freddy, 'and I don't understand why anyone would carry one. You'd have to answer it all the time.' He looked at his place setting, then at Sophie. 'I'm so sorry about your necklace.'

She shot Freddy her grade one smile, hoping to distract him. 'It's very warm. Almost tropical.'

He gave her a nervy smile back.

Freddy seemed uncomplicated but something was going on with him.

'Last year was a washout,' said Freddy. 'This year's been the opposite. Hardly rained at all. Miss Hemmings is tearing her hair out.'

If they couldn't get home soon, she should quiz Miss Hemmings. The head gardener might have crucial info. So could the guy who ran the pub.

'Would you care for a scone or a slice of cake?' Freddy asked Sophie.

She shook her head. She'd missed lunch but after eating bread and butter, she wasn't hungry. 'Freddy, tell me about the visitors.'

'I was saying to Hugo, I've heard the stories since I was little, about Mummy and the others.'

'Did they all come through a lift?' asked Sophie.

'I'm not sure. I've never asked Miss Hemmings or Mr Parkes.' Freddy selected a sandwich from the plate stand. 'Mummy thinks it only looked like a lift, so that may be a red herring. I wrote to Mr Eddington last year, asking if he had a theory and whether I could assist with calculations, but he said he was too busy.'

'Well, they didn't find anything,' said Sophie.

'That's where maths comes in,' said Freddy, his boyish face animated. 'You can prove or disprove a theory without physical evidence.' He looked at her hands. 'Your nails are … intriguing.'

'Baby pink.' Now a peeling mess. When was remover invented?

Barking, loud and angry, erupted from below the terrace.

Charlotte was snarling, her lips right back, exposing her teeth, and Jack was responding in kind.

'What's up with them?' asked Hugo.

'No idea.' Sophie grabbed the lead and ran onto the lawn.

Jack was climbing on top of Charlotte and being repulsed with fearsome barking.

But Sophie kept her distance. Too dangerous to physically force them apart. 'Charlotte, *off*.'

This wasn't the predator who'd lunged in the lane. Charlotte's eyes were golden, not black. '*Off*.'

Jack backed away and when Charlotte reluctantly went quiet, Sophie stepped forward, attached the lead and returned with her to the terrace.

Freddy took Jack by the collar and dragged him off the lawn.

Sophie sat at the table, keeping Charlotte close. 'I'm really sorry about this.' Jack wasn't to blame. This was fallout from the lane. Charlotte was stressed and shaken and taking it out on Jack.

'They're deciding who's top dog.' Freddy sat down, still holding Jack's collar, and rang the handbell.

Sophie inspected Charlotte. 'No blood drawn. Is Jack all right?'

Freddy checked him over. 'Seems so. Only play-fighting.'

'Yes.' Sophie gave Charlotte a calm, relieved pat.

A different maid came onto the terrace. 'Can you fetch a lead for Jack, please?' said Freddy.

As the maid went inside, Freddy turned to Sophie. 'This evening, how about a picnic? There's some lovely spots. It's not far but after what happened in the lane … if you like, we could go by car?'

Car. They'd be at the lift in no time. 'I'd like that.'

The maid returned with a lead and Freddy attached it to Jack's collar. 'My parents love picnics.' He glanced at his watch and stood up. 'If you'll excuse me, I need to finish an analysis of crop yields. See you at the picnic.' He strolled off, Jack trotting at his side like nothing had happened.

'I like Freddy. He's got an enquiring mind.' Hugo smiled. 'John told me about washing Charlotte. I could tell he thought it beyond eccentric.'

'So, Maud *does* tell him everything.'

'Miss Able?'

'Yes, I ditched the surname thing.'

'They're thick as thieves those two.' Hugo reached for a tiny, crust-free sandwich.

'Did you really have your phone nicked?'

'Yes.' His eyes were on her face. 'Freddy's asked if we'd like to go riding tomorrow. Would you be up for that?'

'We might be home by then, driven safely along the lane.'

'What do you mean?'

'I'm going to steal their car.'

He looked shocked. 'I understand why you want to get home ASAP, what happened in the lane was horrific, but—'

'Didn't endear me to the place.' She managed to sound glib though a haunted, helpless feeling was as raw as her elbow. 'I'll need your help.' Aunty Wendy's driving lessons had barely covered the basics.

'Freddy's assured me one of their chauffeurs can take us.'

'And you believe him?'

'Actually, I do.'

She got it. Stealing a car would mess with him staying at the Manor, doing nice-to-have research.

'Richard's apparently convinced it would be a waste of time, but he's fine about it.'

'Freddy's hiding something. So is his father, and they're not going to help. We need to suss out the lift *now*.'

'You're still upset. I understand.'

She rolled her eyes. 'Why would Richard lay on transport if he thinks it pointless?'

'He doesn't want permanent house guests,' said Hugo, 'or the opposite. He's a gracious host.'

Or pretending to be. A trickster.

CHAPTER 12

*D*uring the school holidays, Sophie used to ride Floss, a nervous rescue pony. Aunty Wendy's home was less of a house, more a scruffy refuge for waifs and strays. Sophie was the only human waif. Apart from Floss, there were chickens, cats and a goat. When Aunty Wendy's health deteriorated, she wound down her dog breeding business and sold all her beloved animals — apart from Charlotte. Barely able to care for herself, but kind and stubborn, her aunt had insisted Sophie take up her university place. *It's only a few hours on the train and you'll be back for Christmas.*

A century away, her niece thought about those words as she walked out of the Manor and onto the drive, gravel crunching under her boots. She'd assured Hugo that she'd just assess the lift but now was resolved to go much further than that. It would always be a risk — today, or in a week or a month.

Keeping Charlotte on a short lead, Sophie approached an olive green, immaculately polished open car and with her free hand adjusted the hat that Maud had insisted she wear. It was surprisingly heavy. No wonder women in old sepia photos looked so grumpy. More elaborate and even larger than the floppy brimmed hat, it had silk flowers around the brim and was secured by two long — potentially lethal — pins. If the vagrants were still in the lane, she'd got mean weapons.

Anne and Hugo were chatting on the front steps. A chauffeur wearing a smart suit, peaked cap and leather gloves was holding the front passenger door open for Anne. The car engine was running and the driver's door was ajar.

Now or never. Sophie opened the rear door behind the driver's seat, unclipped Charlotte's lead and dropped it into the seat well. Charlotte jumped in and Sophie closed the door.

Then Sophie jumped behind the wheel. She felt for the pedals with her feet, but an instant later someone was wrestling her out, their fingers digging painfully into her arms.

'You are *not* doing this.' Hugo's voice was quiet and even.

She was too close to kick and he was holding her in a clinch to stop her punching. Her hat brim tipped up; Anne and the chauffeur were staring.

'Let me *go.*'

Hugo swore under his breath and frogmarched her, his arms like a vice. 'Sophie wanted to see how the car worked.' His tone was convincingly cheery.

He opened the rear door and she punched, but he saw it coming, dodged and shoved her in beside a startled Charlotte. Sophie tried to scramble over the seat, but Hugo climbed in and grabbed her arm.

'Don't even think about it.' He glared.

She glared back. 'Get *off.*'

Anne sat in the front passenger seat. The chauffeur closed her door and Hugo's, then got in.

As the car moved off, Hugo cautiously released Sophie

and sat back against the half-height door, his mouth a resolute line.

The chauffeur was watching Sophie in the rear-view
mirror, his young, moustached face expressionless. And
Sophie seethed, so angry she wanted to spit.

The car speeded up and Anne chatted with the chauffeur,
but Hugo remained silent, his mouth set, determined.

Charlotte began barking at Sophie's hat. You didn't have
to be a dog whisperer to translate, 'Take it off,' and, unused to
a car without a roof, Charlotte was standing, tongue out,
about to leap. Sophie grabbed her collar and clipped on the
lead. A harness wouldn't have helped; no seatbelts to attach
it. She pushed Charlotte half into the seat well.

The car floor was carpeted, the seats made of soft brown
leather; in other circumstances, with a warm breeze on her
face, Sophie would have enjoyed the ride.

They stopped beside a river and another old-fashioned
car — this one bright red — with a chauffeur, two maids and
a footman, arrived from the Manor and parked behind them.
Freddy and Richard were already there; they'd ridden on
horseback, with Jack running.

Sophie climbed out, keeping Charlotte on the lead.

Maud had wound Sophie's hair around scrunched balls of
paper called 'rats,' making her hair fuller, wavier and heavier
at the back, but they felt scratchy. 'Only little girls wear their
hair down, Miss,' Maud had said, with the gravitas of Isaac
Newton, as if it was a provable fact, like gravity or the laws
of motion.

Folding chairs and tables were being set out, tartan blankets arranged on the grass and crisp white tablecloths,
glasses and plates being laid with practised ease. Sophie's
mouth was open, so she hastily shut it. These people organised a picnic with military precision.

She sat down, adjusting her hat to better see the river. A

grassy bank sloped gently to the water and, further away, ash trees and weeping willows grew to the water's edge. Narrow enough to swim across, the river was calm and languid, moving with a gentle *swoosh*.

Sophie accepted a glass of white wine and a cucumber sandwich and tried to calm down. Riding tomorrow, she'd get to the lift.

Much later, she was still sipping white wine. She ate a small slice of Victoria sponge cake and fed Charlotte pork pie. Picnics at home involved too much prep and you were always too cold or hot or attacked by insects. But with help, picnics were just fine. She'd only reached for her non-existent phone twice and *not* having it, she'd taken more notice of nature — the gentle gurgle of the river, bird song amidst the quiet. If this was social media cold turkey, she might be through the worst?

Hugo and Freddy were sitting on the grass, either side of her chair and Anne's.

'There's no annoying insects here,' said Hugo.

'The vicar says it's because last winter was so cold,' said Anne. 'He collects insects.'

'We should do this more often,' said Richard, 'make the most of the good weather.'

'You can't work every day,' said Anne.

'I'll need to work on Saturday,' said Richard, 'and Sunday, after church.'

Charlotte was straining against the extendable lead, lying on the grass, her head close to Jack's. Sophie blinked. Their noses were touching, as if they were kissing. That would make an awesome *YouTube* video. Jack must have conceded that Charlotte was 'top dog.' Sophie unclipped her lead.

'Do dogs fall in love?' Hugo shot her a cautious smile.

He was annoying, and naïve, but she shouldn't ignore

him. If the lift had disappeared, she'd need an ally. 'It's a pack thing.'

'Don't animals just…' Freddy's face flushed. '…mate?'

The servants were standing around the cars, talking in low voices. One of the maids was scowling, staring in Sophie's direction. When Sophie didn't break eye contact, the maid turned away. What was that about? She was conventionally dressed, though not up to wearing anything approaching Anne's outfit. It was hot in the shade and Anne's dress was close fitting. Wearing a corset and sitting very straight, she'd kept the same posture throughout the picnic, occasionally waving her fan.

The river looked clean and invitingly safe. Sophie tugged out the two gigantic hatpins, put them on the ground with the hat and removed the lace cape. At home she'd have stripped to her undies but mindful of the maid's judgmental stare, she pulled off her boots and socks but kept on the dress. She caught Freddy's eye. 'Fancy a dip?'

He gave her a wicked grin, rapidly took off his shoes, socks and tie, and they waded together into the river. The bed was sandy and soft.

'Freddy.' Anne had stood up and was shaking her head.

Freddy ignored his mother and slid completely in and Sophie sighed with pleasure as she did the same. Beside her, Freddy was still grinning. 'This is wonderful. I'm so glad you're here.'

And at that moment, she was glad too. Sunlight was sparkling on the water and on Freddy, giving his hair blond highlights. He treaded water and splashed, soaking her face and she laughed and splashed him back. She'd miss Freddy.

The dogs had followed them in and were swimming near the sweeping branches of a willow tree. Freddy turned and waved. 'Come on, Hugo, it's fabulous.'

Hugo didn't return the wave. He was standing beside

Anne, his face inscrutable. Freddy did breaststroke and Sophie lazily floated. The delicate material of her dress was floating as well, the lacy skirt gliding just below the surface as she moved in the water. With the sun on her face, Sophie was gloriously glad to be alive.

'We'd better get out,' said Freddy. 'As it is, we're going to get it in the neck.'

'I don't understand.'

'Not really the done thing.'

When she reached the bank, the servants' faces were either blank or screwed up, like they were chewing lemons. Richard's face was blank, but Anne looked angry. Baffling.

As Sophie stood to follow Freddy out, he froze, his eyes on her breasts.

The front of her dress had turned transparent, like a wet T-shirt. Awkward.

'Shall we go to the house?' said Anne. It was an order, not a suggestion.

Freddy slipped on his shoes, picked up his socks and tie from the grass, and went with his father towards the horses. Jack, after an impressive writhe to dry himself, ran after them.

The servants packed up the picnic and Sophie sheepishly put on her hat, careful not to stab herself. She retrieved her cape, boots and socks, reattached Charlotte's lead and walked towards the car in bare feet.

But by the open passenger door, she paused. She was soaking wet and, despite some determined shakes, so was Charlotte. Anne obviously wanted Sophie Arundel and her see-through dress out of sight fast, but they'd permanently water-stain the seats.

'Excuse me, Miss.' The chauffeur was carrying two picnic rugs. He laid them one on top of the other over the back seats and gestured for Sophie to get in.

'Thank you.' Sophie's voice was low enough to carry only to him.

Unexpectedly, he winked, before turning and getting into the driver's cab. A gesture of support? Or her wet dress parade had made his day, and he was laughing at her.

The car set off across the grass, Anne silent in the front passenger seat, looking fixedly ahead and Hugo, on the other side of Charlotte, silent too, staring out at fields and trees.

Sophie's foot bandage was wet but somehow still firmly attached. She put on her socks and boots as they drove in uncomfortable silence back to the house and Sophie was glad to retreat with Charlotte to her room.

Glimpsing herself in the long mirror she winced; her nipples and the swell of her breasts were graphically clear.

She hung the cape over the spindly chair, gingerly removed the hatpins and put them on the floor with the hat, then tried to undo the buttons of the dress. But located on the centre of her back, it was impossible to undo even one. Finally, she lay on the bed in her wet dress with an equally wet Charlotte. 'Maud was right. I'm a human fish out of water and it's horrible.'

A knock on the door. How did Maud sense when she was needed? Was telepathy part of her job spec? 'Come in.'

But it wasn't Maud. It was Hugo.

He closed the door behind him and turned to face her. 'I can't believe you're this stupid. If you had stolen the car, gone down the lane and found nothing, what would have happened? You wouldn't be prancing around playing Lady of the Manor. You'd have been chucked out. And so would I.' He frowned. 'And we will be now, after your swimming stunt.'

She sat up, swung her legs over the side of the bed and folded her arms defensively across her chest. 'I didn't know my dress would go transparent.'

'I thought Anne was going to faint.'

'Freddy went in too.'

'He's not a grace and favour guest,' said Hugo. 'Look, like when we didn't say what really happened in the lane, we *have* to play by their rules.'

'What rules?'

'Ladies don't lark about in rivers, at least not in full view of their hosts and servants. You can't behave like … a man.'

'I'm wearing a long dress and my hair's in weird rolls.' Not to mention ludicrous underwear.

'Forget what you're wearing, you need to act smart.' He sat, without asking, in the armchair. 'If we can't get home and they chuck us out, what the hell would we do?'

'Get to the lift.'

'What if there's nothing there?'

'We'll keep searching. I'm not giving up.'

'I've talked with three gardeners who regularly walk the lane,' said Hugo, 'and, unless they're professional actors, they've *never* seen it.'

'Maybe it's only visible to certain people?'

'According to Freddy, each visitor only sees it on this side when they step out. Anne looked for it for months when she arrived and found nothing. That farmer bloke has never seen it. A whole team of scientists found nothing.' He put his head in his hands. 'I'm struggling with all of this, but we need to face facts.' His voice cracked. 'We may be here for the rest of our lives.'

The rest of our lives echoed ominously in her head. No, she wouldn't accept she was stuck here.

'Anyway, tomorrow we'll know for sure. Reynolds is taking us after lunch.'

'Reynolds?'

'The guy who drove us to the picnic.'

'They could have said that to fob us off.'

'Sophie, the Laceys are exactly what they seem, not ruthless gangsters holding us to ransom.'

'You want to stay.' She'd been right before.

He sighed. 'A few days, perhaps a week, but you're in denial. Anne coming through all those years ago, she's given us a sort of respectability. But we're precarious guests. If we are stranded, you'll need to marry well. Get a dodgy reputation and you'll be stuffed.'

'I'm not marrying anyone. This is ridiculous.'

'You're not listening. We'll go with Reynolds but if the lift's gone, we need a fall-back plan.'

'And mine is finding a husband.'

'I have no idea what I can do either,' said Hugo. 'My mind's full of questions and no answers.'

'We could go to the nearest town, get a job?'

He raised his eyebrows, like she'd suggested pole dancing. 'Unemployment around here is bad, there's 'unrest' in Derby, which I think translates as riots.' He paused. 'If the lift's there, we should get in. We have no way of minimising the risk. Nobody knows how it works.'

'Agreed.'

'We might have already been reported missing.'

Her insides clenched. No 'might' about it. With no phone call two days running and her mobile mysteriously out of action, Aunty Wendy would have called the university and then the police.

'My mother will be beside herself.' His lips were pressed thin with worry. 'But in the meantime, we need to fit in.' He stood up and managed a rueful smile. 'And keep safe.'

CHAPTER 13

*D*ay two in the bonkers past had gone badly. Day three had to be better.

Sophie finished her tea and toast and pushed back the bedding. It was bulky as well as heavy. When were duvets invented? She'd Google it when she got home.

She slipped out of bed and put on the dressing gown over the matching ankle-length nightdress she'd slept in. The empire waistline and short lacy sleeves were familiar, if not exactly modern; her mother could have worn it.

In the bathroom, Sophie twisted the lid off a round white and pink tin labelled *EUCRYL Tooth Powder,* coated the head of the toothbrush and rigorously brushed. Last night, she'd yearned for an electric toothbrush and dental floss after brushing for two minutes, and today was no different. Might as well have used a twig. And the tooth powder tasted chalky and gritty.

Back in the bedroom, Maud produced a bigger bodice and Sophie sheepishly put it on. Fitting snugly, it was more comfortable than her underwired bra.

Maud laid out a pink dress, the same style as the previous one. 'You mustn't worry about the picnic, Miss.'

'Sorry?'

'Lady Lacey understands.'

'She does?'

'Master Freddy went swimming and children play in the river all the time.' Maud's round face softened. 'Mr Harrington told Lady Lacey you were upset about your necklace, and you're not mad.'

Some servant must have repeated to Maud the entire conversation. 'You've got to be kidding.'

'Kidding?'

'It's not your fault.' Sophie picked up the dressing gown again and put it on over her underwear. 'Back in a minute.'

Hugo was trying to gaslight her, but very cleverly, telling people she *wasn't* mad, so they'd think she was. Luckily, she was ferociously sane. Leaving Charlotte dozing on the bed, she padded barefoot across the corridor and banged on Hugo's door.

John opened it, his eyes wide with surprise.

'I need a word with Mr Harrington.'

She stepped past and John left, closing the door behind him.

Hugo stood up from a regency writing desk beside an arched, diamond-paned window and put a cap on a fountain pen. His hands were dotted with indigo ink stains.

'How dare you go behind my back, telling people I'm not mad, so they think I am.' She folded her arms. At least he had the grace to look guilty. 'Well?'

'I didn't want to disturb you in case you were asleep.' He put the pen carefully on the desk. 'So, I couldn't tell you.'

Tell, not ask. She was struggling to keep her temper.

'You'd had a stressful day and I had to do something. Necessary damage control. Anne was upset, but fine about it, and so was Richard. He made a joke about Anne finding it hard to adapt to their customs. And Freddy…'

'Yes?'

'Thought it a jolly jape.' He turned and gazed out the window. 'I couldn't sleep last night, trying to get my head round … everything.'

She'd slept like the dead, beyond exhausted.

He faced her. 'I get it, Sophie. The way this society treats women … if we are stuck here, this is going to be harder for you.' He distractedly swept his hand through his hair, so his fringe stood up. 'This may blow over, though the servants are beyond scandalised.'

'Maud seems more protective than shocked.'

'There you are, then.' He averted his eyes from her chest.

Her dressing gown was open, giving him an eyeful of old-fashioned underwear. She closed it.

'I should have consulted you *before* discussing the picnic. Am I forgiven?'

Most people would have bought the contrite expression. 'I guess.' She sat in his leather armchair.

'Every time I think I'm handling this … it hits me worse. I'll never see my family again, I've just disappeared, they'll think I'm dead, in four years there's the great depression, then the Second World War—'

'I still think we'll get home. We have to.'

He sat on the bed, his face tense. 'If you want to talk about the lane—'

'I'm fine.' She never wanted to think about it, let alone talk, but appreciated the offer. 'All we can do is take it one day at a time.'

'You're right.' He flexed his ink-stained fingers. 'Shall I call for you when it's time for breakfast?'

As entitled posh boys went … he was okay. She stood up and nodded.

Back in her room, Charlotte was lying on the bed snoring, legs akimbo, and Maud was making quiet clucking noises. Maud might be sympathetic about the picnic, but she'd never approve of Charlotte. Sophie kissed Charlotte's head. 'Let sleeping dogs lie' had never applied to Charlotte; even sound asleep, she could be safely petted.

Maud stopped clucking, Sophie took off the dressing gown and Maud slipped the pink gown over Sophie's head.

Waiting for Maud to finish fastening the dress felt unreal, as if she were a princess or very, very rich. 'Where are my boots?' They weren't where she'd left them by the bed.

Maud went to the wardrobe and brought them over. They were still battered but now clean and polished. Sophie stared.

'Haven't I cleaned them properly?'

'You have,' said Sophie. 'Thank you.' The faux leather looked amazing. Billionaires must live like this, so why were they always getting divorced? Perhaps they got bored and took crazy risks—

There was a gentle knock at the door and Maud opened it.

'Ready?' said Hugo, his face inscrutable.

Breakfast meant facing Anne and Richard, the snooty butler and nosy footmen. Brazen it out.

In the corridor, Charlotte led the way jauntily like before, guided by her nose.

'Are you up for riding?' asked Hugo.

'Definitely.' After yesterday's debacle, Richard might lay on a car just to be rid of her, but he definitely had an agenda … so might not. This ride could be her last chance to get home.

In the dining room, Freddy was sitting at the long table, talking with the butler who was standing by the sideboard. The butler's black suit with matching waistcoat was immaculate, as were his black bow tie and white shirt with winged collar.

As Sophie and Hugo approached the table, the butler gave a slight nod in their direction, his face expressionless.

Freddy stood, pulled out a chair and she acknowledged him as she sat down and breathed in the aroma of coffee. And today the juicy, salty scent of bacon wasn't making her sick.

Charlotte settled by Sophie, her nose twitching, and the two footmen filed in and stood to attention.

Richard came in with Jack. No Anne. Good. Anne's face at the picnic had been more chainsaw massacre than ill-advised swim.

When Mr Hunter offered Sophie coffee, his handsome face was a picture of exaggerated — and false — respect, but she looked him in the eye. 'Thank you.'

'Anne is keen to hear about home,' said Richard.

'Do you think we'll ever get back?' asked Sophie, watching the fair-haired footman give her a steaming helping of kedgeree.

'No one ever has.' Richard gave her a kind and under-standing smile.

Hugo's attention was on his breakfast, his expression glum.

Breathe … nerves about what she'd find in the lane — or not — were jangling like a warning bell; never seeing Aunty Wendy or Isha again and no way ever to communicate. No. Too awful to accept.

After breakfast, back in the bedroom, Maud had hung a dark brown dress on the wardrobe door. The skirt was open on one side, like a wrap-around apron.

'What's that for?'

'Stops you getting tangled with the saddle, Miss, if you

fall off.' Maud laid it on the bed and took out from a drawer what was unmistakably a corset.

'I'm sorry, I'm not wearing that.'

Maud set her mouth but fastened the riding habit over Sophie's bodice.

The disapproval in Maud's face was becoming familiar. And wearing. But it wasn't worth an argument. She crossed her fingers. Within hours she'd be out of here.

Maud handed her a black, boxy hat. It fitted snugly, had a small peak at the front but no straps.

Sophie walked to the stables with Hugo who was carrying a hat like hers. Charlotte was predictably excited, bouncing a little as she walked; she'd spent a lot of time watching Sophie ride Floss around Aunty Wendy's tatty paddock, and always ran alongside when Sophie had ridden further afield, trotting and galloping.

The Shorten grooms — all male — were saddling up and patting interested-looking horses. The horses' faces were like Floss's before an outing and mirrored Charlotte's now: anticipation, excitement.

And despite her fears about the lift, Sophie felt the same. The smell of horse sweat, edged with straw and manure, evoked happy memories: frosty exhilarating gallops in the Christmas holidays, and more leisurely outings in the long months of summer, along secluded footpaths and hushed fields. For Sophie, though, riding horses was a guilty pleasure. She might believe in animal rights, but she was still using horses, just not as horribly as some of her fellow humans had over millennia: neglecting them, turning them into food or glue, or taking them into countless battles to get wounded or killed.

'If we can get home, I'll never forget this,' said Hugo. 'The beautiful house, Freddy and John.'

'Do you think rich people get divorced so much because they're bored?'

He giggled in a very un-Hugo way. 'They don't get divorced more than anyone else, but because they have money, you get to read about it. Anyway, in this time, the only way to divorce was to prove adultery. Social suicide.'

She hadn't thought about that. Marriage with no get-out-of-jail clause… Why would anyone sign up? Regular marriage had incentives — one of the few things she remembered from English law lessons at school. Cohabitants weren't entitled to anything if their name wasn't on the house deeds or bank accounts. But whatever the practical benefits, marriage didn't appeal. Her father had seen himself as head of the family in line with his religious beliefs and her mother had gone along with the fiction, at least in public. Why was a mystery.

'We ride every day, depending on the weather,' Freddy was saying to Hugo. 'The river has excellent salmon. In September we go shooting and in winter we hunt.' He adjusted a shotgun strapped across his chest.

Richard had one too.

Freddy surely didn't actually *kill* animals? He seemed so kind. She wouldn't kill an innocent animal if she were starving to death. Not that going hungry was an issue, even combing through meat-heavy meals.

'Is Anne not coming?' asked Hugo.

'Thrown, years ago,' said Richard. 'Put her off.' He turned to a groom who was standing by a large black horse and said to Hugo, 'Prince here will suit you.'

Jack was staying close to Richard and, after a moment's hesitation, Charlotte walked on with Sophie. Freddy followed, avoiding eye contact.

He surely hadn't been embarrassed by her wet dress? At home, boys would have filmed it. Well, the straight ones.

Freddy paused by a brown horse. 'I thought you could ride Molly.'

He strode off and Sophie cautiously stroked Molly's nose. Molly tilted her head but didn't object. On her saddle were what looked like rabbit ears, about a hand high; they were hard and firmly attached. An extra strap was on the other side to keep the saddle secure.

Freddy had mounted another horse. His saddle hadn't got funny ears. Neither had Hugo's.

'Miss?' A young man was offering his hand to help her up.

'Can I have a normal saddle, please?'

He straightened. 'It's a side-saddle. You've never ridden before?'

'Not with a trick saddle.'

'It's straightforward.'

'Do you ride like this?'

'Of course not, but I'll show you.' He jumped onto Molly with a practised air and turned around, so he was half facing forward and half towards Sophie. 'You put your right leg on the first pommel and your left leg hard under the lower one. Use it as an anchor. You can jump gates with that.'

No. Jumping or galloping while precariously perched on one side would be very difficult — and beyond crazy.

The boy was handing her a cane. 'You can control her with this.'

'I'm not going to hit her.' She scowled at him. 'I want a regular saddle.'

'What's wrong?' Freddy had dismounted and was walking towards them.

'I can't ride with this ... crap saddle.'

'I don't understand.'

'Apart from anything else, it's got to be seriously dangerous.'

Hugo was watching them, worried and embarrassed, and

Freddy was nonplussed. Sophie put on her best doe eyes. That always worked on boys so would work on Freddy.

He held her gaze for only a moment. 'I'm sorry, it would be entirely inappropriate.'

'What would?'

'If you sat … astride. Perhaps you should stay at the Manor?'

Charlotte barked, confused by the delay.

Sophie sucked her teeth. 'I'll figure it out.'

Freddy gave her a relieved smile.

She unwrapped the apron skirt, put her foot on the stable boy's offered hand and hauled herself onto Molly.

The boy's face had gone bright red, like he'd chewed on a bonnet pepper. She shuffled around like he had and ensured she wasn't sitting on her skirt.

As she gathered up the reins, Hugo wasn't looking in her direction but Freddy was staring, a stunned-shocked stare. He must have seen her Bermuda shorts. Get over it.

Hugo's horse was tossing his head. Even with a trick saddle, Molly seemed safer and Sophie embraced the nourishing sensation of horsey companionship. An equine earthy smell was mingling with the whiff of polished leather from the saddle and as Molly started to walk, the saddle made a creaking sound, just like Floss's saddle. The reins felt smooth and supple in Sophie's hands and she smiled. She'd enjoy this *and* get to the lift.

Richard led the way into a tilled field, the dry summer earth muffling the sound of his horse's hooves. Jack ran happily alongside, Charlotte was staying close to Molly, and in front of them, Hugo's horse was still skittish. Freddy brought up the rear.

They passed through a copse of sturdy hornbeam trees into wild meadows. Yellow, bell-shaped cowslip flowers waved gently beside buttercups open to the sun, and under a cluster of pear trees, heavy with white blossom, swathes of bluebells rustled, their scent sweet on the warm breeze. Bluebells in the summer … didn't they only flower in spring?

Insects buzzed and, high above them, a lark was singing its heart out. But despite nature's best efforts, Sophie was jittery. She had no idea where they were — in relation to the Manor or the lift.

Beyond the meadows was fallow pasture, bordering a field of barley. Sophie's heart thudded. Ahead was a familiar wooden gate and its twin across a lane. They'd been out for a while but following a roundabout route. Not far from the Manor.

Freddy dismounted and walked forward to open both gates, then Richard crossed the lane into another field. As Molly reached the tarmac behind Hugo's horse, Sophie gently pulled on Molly's left rein and pushed both her knees into Molly's left side. Riding side-saddle, to get a horse to turn right, you could only use the reins or that horrid cane. She said to Hugo. 'See you at the lift.'

Molly trotted, stretched her legs and galloped.

Taken by surprise, Sophie swore, pushed her left leg harder under the lower pommel attached to the saddle and leaned forward, but she was barely clinging on. Couldn't do this for long. Pulling as hard as she could on the reins, she yelled. 'Whoa.' Molly slowed around a bend but then sped up again.

Charlotte wouldn't match this pace. Sophie fought the urge to glance back and focused on not falling off. Underneath her, Molly's muscles flexed and rolled, and Sophie's legs burned with the effort of keeping her grip on the saddle. Increasingly desperate, she repeatedly pulled on the reins and yelled, but Molly ignored her.

Hugo was shouting.

Around a bend, and another one. Sophie was shaking now, sweating with exertion and panic.

Molly gave a whinnying scream and reared, throwing Sophie off.

Sophie hit the ground with body-shattering impact and rolled through shallow water. Molly was stamping, terrified of something. Get away from her hooves, keep rolling, rolling…

Still.

Pain. In her spine and in her head. But it was muffled, like a hazy shape discerned through warped glass. Hardly able to move, the pain grew nearer, sharper and sharper, second by second, and she cried out.

Long seconds passed or time stopped, but the sky stayed surreally blue, crisp and perfect.

And right beside her, someone else was in agony, whimpering in despair.

Sophie managed to turn her head. In a looming dark thicket, a huge brown deer was tangled and trapped, its eyes huge, front legs oddly bent.

'It's too far gone,' said Freddy's voice.

Bang. The deer's head exploded, raining slippery skin, blood and bone.

CHAPTER 14

Sophie sprinted around campus, an invisible phantom, passing through people and walls. Charlotte was lost, in danger, in pain.

Hugo was sitting outside a café. He pointed with a vaping cigarette and spoke in a lilting Irish accent. 'You've just missed your parents and you should take better care of Charlotte. She's over there.'

But she wasn't.

'It's too far gone.' *Bang.* Molly was writhing on the ground, head bloody, nostrils foaming…

Gliding above school like a human eagle, Sophie circled lazily, relishing the uplifts and air currents, seeing the crenellated tops of the buildings and the people below with a sweeping avian clarity; she zoomed into the old hall and the Leaving Ball. Her parents were there in their usual casual trousers and tops, drinking Prosecco and talking to Hugo, who was sitting on the floor, wearing his shorts and hoodie … in Cornwall on the beach, she stood on the poisonous spines of a weaver fish, agony, but not her foot, her head, unbearable pain … hot sun, but she was cold, strapped to a hospital trolley, fluorescent lights moving faster and faster … Charlotte by the lifts, out of reach—

Sophie vomited. A bowl was in front of her face and she vomited again.

The four-poster bed swam then steadied, but bitter in her nostrils was a lingering, powerful smell like boiled metal, hard and tangy. She grabbed someone's arm. Her spine ached but her head felt as if it had been cleaved apart. She wanted to die.

A hand on her chin tipped her head back and a bitter-sweet cordial flooded her mouth. As it slid along her throat, voices murmured but made no sense.

Miraculously, the pain fell away and she surrendered to a serene, bath-warm embrace.

Sophie was swimming in a glorious, sparkly ocean.

Her eyelids were being forced open. Panic. She pushed at hard fingers and blinked furiously.

'That's a good girl. Get your bearings.' A balding man with a stethoscope around his neck was smiling down at her.

No pain. And its absence was unbelievably wonderful.

Her mouth tasted of spices, edged with something acrid, and she registered the tangy smell again. It was vaguely familiar, like intense disinfectant.

'You have mild concussion and some bruises,' said the doctor, 'but otherwise you're well.'

Well? She'd been off with the fairies.

The man leaned in, disturbingly close, staring into her eyes.

'How long was I … unconscious?'

Anne came into view, her face set and serious. 'About

fifteen minutes. It was fortunate Dr Griffiths was doing house calls nearby and you were so close to the Manor.'

Sophie frowned. Close to the Manor … that made no sense.

'You were galloping towards the house,' said Anne, 'and fell off just around the corner, by the stagnant pool.'

Bloody idiot. She should have turned right in the lane, not left. No. Understandable mistake. The gates looked the same, as did the lane.

'She can take the bandage off and get out of bed tomorrow, but no riding for a month.' The doctor collected his battered leather bag and left.

Sophie sat up slowly and sipped water from a glass on her bedside table. Near the bottom of the bed under the bedclothes was an odd lump. She pointed. 'What's that?'

Anne pulled back the blankets, revealing something rectangular wrapped in a cloth. 'Hot brick.' She moved it up the bed and Sophie cautiously put her feet on it. Hard and angular, but comfortingly warm.

Sophie reached out to Charlotte lying beside her and touched her muzzle. Charlotte regarded her solemnly, her golden eyes wide in her earnest brown face. Her expression meant, 'It's okay, you're okay.'

Charlotte was right. Trapped in an alien past but alive.

Anne rearranged the blanket neatly, adjusted pillows behind Sophie's back and helped her put on a silky, short jacket over her nightdress.

'A matinee jacket's better than a dressing gown when you're poorly.' Anne sat on the spindly chair by the bed.

'Why is it called a matinee jacket?'

'I have no idea.'

'I'm sorry to be so much trouble.' Sophie's voice sounded detached, as if the words were being spoken by someone else. And she felt aftermathy — slow and calm.

'You are our guest. You need to make a proper recovery.'

'What was that horrible drink?'

'Laudanum. Morphine and alcohol.'

Explained the sparkly ocean. 'And that smell is rank.'

Anne sniffed. 'Iodine. In your head bandage.'

Sophie touched her temple. A thick dressing was wrapped around her head like a turban.

Anne took a small medicine bottle from Sophie's bedside table and put it in her skirt pocket.

'Laudanum?'

'No. *Fowlers Solution.* Dr Griffiths sets great store by it but it's going down the sink.'

'But if the doctor thinks it's good—'

'It has arsenic in it.'

She'd ingested poison. Sophie's mouth dried. She'd tried her best; the odd, calm feeling came back.

'You've only had one teaspoon and you probably lost that being sick.'

'Molly.'

'What about her?'

'She's dead.' Sophie's heart compressed into a tight, hard knot; her reckless dash towards the lift had cost Molly her life.

'No, Sophie. She's not.'

'I thought she'd been injured so—'

'Freddy shot a deer. It wasn't going to recover. Molly's fine.'

Sophie drew a long, relieved breath.

'Richard and Freddy always carry guns on the estate,' said Anne. 'It's not only deer that get into trouble. So do sheep and cows. Richard's having the stagnant pool drained and that thicket removed. No animal should die in agony.'

'No.'

'And Reynolds can take you to the lift spot tomorrow. *Not* finding the portal helped me focus on my life here.'

Her certainty that the lift had gone forever sent a chill into Sophie's core, but she sensed Anne wanted to protect her, recognised an ally from a familiar future.

'Before I married, I tried to find the lift and Richard worried if I did, I wouldn't come back.' Anne smiled to herself. 'Of course, I would.'

'Could you have mistaken the place?'

'A room-size square of light? I couldn't have missed it.'

Tears pricked behind Sophie's eyes.

'You were lucky to come through in summer. It was November when I arrived, cold and wet, and when I finally reached the Manor it was dark.'

Sophie shivered. 'Sounds awful.'

'I was terribly frightened, but the old housekeeper was kind. She gave me fresh clothes and a room in the attic.'

'Anne, I have to get home. Everyone will assume I've been kidnapped or murdered.'

'You need a new hot brick and some tea.' Anne rang the bellpull.

Sophie wiped her damp eyes with her hand. When were hot water bottles invented? They lasted for hours.

'I know this is hard, but I adapted. I'm sure you will.' Anne smoothed out the bedcovers. 'My parents travelled a lot and I hardly saw them, so after I arrived here, it was my old nanny that I really missed. Nanny Wilson always wore a crisp brown uniform that smelled of soap.' Anne smiled, remembering.

A nanny ... Anne's family must have been posh. Sophie pictured a horrified Mary Poppins being shown into the tiny box room in her parents' house. 'But having a nanny must have been fun. You had brothers and sisters?'

'No.'

Interesting. They had that in common.

'And I was packed off to boarding school when I was seven.'

'I boarded, but I was older.' So, they had that in common too. But little else. Most of the children at Hadley, like Hugo, had been from wealthy families. 'What was your house like, at home?'

'Victorian. Not as big as the Manor and falling down around our ears.'

Yes, Anne was posh. 'I grew up in an ugly shoebox.' Sophie had inherited it but hadn't seen it for years. Aunty Wendy rented it out.

'Well, whatever home is like, it's familiar, comforting.'

'There was a picture of a big house on the lift.'

'I remember,' said Anne. 'Straddling both doors, quite splendid.'

'It was the same size as the other pictures.'

'What other pictures?'

'A girl with a sword,' said Sophie, 'and a man rocking a cot, and a cottage on fire.'

'I don't remember that.'

Maud came in with a new hot brick, but it was too hot. Sophie moved her feet to just beside it. Another maid handed her a cup of tea.

Sophie sipped, relishing the familiar taste.

Anne got to her feet, her face resolute. 'Bedrest today.' She walked towards the door.

'Thank you.'

Anne turned and smiled. 'I'll be back at teatime.'

Sophie finished her tea and Charlotte dozed beside her.

'Hey.' Hugo was in the doorway wearing a boxy brown suit and clutching a book.

She smiled. 'Hey.'

He came in and sat beside the bed. His cheekbones looked incredible, high-angled and symmetrical.

She blinked. 'I'm concussed.'

'You're lucky you're not dead.' He took off his jacket and hung it on the back of the chair.

'What's with the Newt Scamander tie?' He was sporting a grey bow tie, a subdued accompaniment to his pink shirt.

'Freddy wears a suit and tie, and I need to blend in,' said Hugo. 'And Freddy does have a passing resemblance to Eddie Redmayne in *Fantastic Beasts*.'

'Taking off your jacket is as casual as it gets?'

'I've given the fashion a name. Shorten Male Casual.' He shot her a dry smile. 'Only really acceptable at weekends, so I'm pushing it today.'

'Sorry?'

'It's Wednesday.' His gaze shifted to the doorway.

Freddy was standing there, his formal suit at odds with his hair. It was tousled and messy, as if he'd randomly dragged his fingers through it. 'You gave us quite a shock.' He was smiling but Sophie sensed he'd been seriously spooked.

'What were you shouting on the ride?' she asked Hugo.

'You're going the wrong way.'

'How did you know?'

'I didn't. You'd said you were going to the lift but Richard thought you'd just lost control. Molly was going hell for leather for home.'

Freddy disappeared from view.

'"Hell for leather" is right.' She'd never given a thought to that cliché before. The side-saddle in this case was probably unscathed but her legs ached from holding onto it for dear life.

'You should see their library.' Hugo was holding a small hardback, bound in emerald green leather. 'It's quite something.'

'What's the book?'

'A short story.'

'Not up for reading.' Sophie wriggled down the bed and put her head on the pillow.

'I could read it out loud?'

'I'd like that.' She pushed along the hot brick to put her feet on it. 'What's it about?'

'A man searching for a supernatural green door.'

'Appropriate.' She turned on her side, facing him.

As he read, his voice surrounded her in a comforting rhythm, melodious and soothing, but when he finished, she made a face. 'Hate the ending. He spends years searching for the door, finally finds it but plunges to his death...'

'I should have chosen something more light-hearted.' He closed the book. His hands were still blotchy with ink.

Following her gaze, he glanced down self-consciously. 'Fountain pens are tricky. If you lose concentration, you get ink everywhere. But I need to persist. Necessary basic skill.'

'History notes?'

'More of a diary, with ideas about the lift.'

She'd ask Maud for a notebook to record theories. She explained her idea about the visitors, and what she and Anne had in common.

'I didn't have a nanny,' said Hugo, 'and I've got three sisters. And thousands of people go to boarding school. It must be something more unusual than that or there'd be loads of visitors.'

'So, we ID the unusual thing to figure out why the door opened, and find it again.' She frowned. 'And hopefully avoid plunging to our deaths.'

'Assuming it's not random.'

'That would suck.'

Hugo bit his lip. 'My sisters will be a huge support to my parents.'

Aunty Wendy had her church friends. And her faith. That had helped her when her sister died. Now her niece was missing, assumed dead, hopefully she'd find comfort there again.

'We arrived on Monday, 20th July 1925. We've been here three days and…' He checked his watch. 'About four hours.' He tapped his fingers on the book. 'Not that I'm counting.'

'Seems like longer.' She turned onto her back, adjusting the pillow under her neck.

'Everyone speaks very properly here,' said Hugo, 'particularly Anne and Richard.'

He was trying to distract her, but she went with it. 'Do you think Anne spoke like that when she arrived, or picked it up?'

'Perhaps a bit of both.'

Sunlight was rippling on the underside of the bed's canopy, on a cream coat of arms, faded with age. Brown stags with noble expressions and craggy antlers were leaping around intertwining tree branches and a stylised blue L. She pointed at the frieze. 'The stags on the lift and on the Lacey coat of arms — they're identical, except on the lift the stags were just outlined.'

He stood and peered at it.

'What if the stags and the mansion depicted Shorten Manor?' said Sophie. 'A destination name, like on a bus?'

'But the other pictures you saw… How can someone rocking a cot or holding a sword be a geographical location?'

'They could be symbols? There were maths signs too.'

Hugo rubbed his eyes.

'Anne only saw the mansion.'

'Maybe she was in a hurry,' said Hugo, 'so didn't notice—'

'Or,' said Sophie, 'there's more than one lift.'

CHAPTER 15

Sophie was woken the next morning by someone ominously clearing their throat. She sat up in confusion, hastily wiping sleep from her eyes.

'I'm afraid Charlotte's had an accident, Miss.' Maud was standing in the doorway, holding a tea tray.

Snatched out of an anxious dream about Charlotte and thrust too fast into reality, Sophie's heart lurched. 'What's happened?' She scanned the bedroom in a panic.

Charlotte was stretching contentedly in front of the French windows.

'She was sick in the night, Miss. I think she ate your hair ribbon when it came back from the laundry. From what I could tell, it was blue.'

'I'm so sorry. I'll sort it.' Sophie steadied her breathing as Maud put the tray across her lap.

'Oh, it's already cleared up, Miss. It wasn't nice.'

'Thank you for that,' said Sophie, inwardly mortified.

Charlotte had form in this regard, though her preference was for socks. She liked to swallow such garments whole, two or three at a time, and regurgitate them. For a mere human such behaviour would mean at the very least an unpleasant stay in hospital, plus sessions with a behavioural therapist specialising in sock issues. Even for Charlotte, such behaviour wasn't risk-free. Usually, such temptations were tidied away.

But Sophie didn't have any ribbons, blue or otherwise. Right … Charlotte had eaten her thong. Maud wouldn't imagine it being worn as knickers, or, as Maud would see it, *barely* worn.

'I can get you a new one, Miss.'

'Please don't worry.'

After Sophie had finished her tea and toast, Maud removed Sophie's head bandage and Sophie got out of bed and peered in the oval mirror — a small cut near her hairline and a big angry bruise but otherwise unscathed.

In a neat pile on the armchair were her jeans, shirt, bra and cardigan. She examined the cardigan. Soft … good as new. And Maud's darning was miraculous, near invisible.

Sophie stepped into clean cotton drawers and put on her jeans, ignoring Maud's disapproving expression. The zip only went halfway. She tugged and jigged about but it made no difference. She hauled them off. 'They've shrunk.'

'Must have been washed too hot. They were very dirty, Miss.'

Only bought a week ago, but cheap as chips. Likely would have shrunk at home.

Sophie put on her wired bra.

'It's like part of a corset,' Maud ventured. 'Is it comfortable, Miss?'

'Sort of, but I take it off when I dress casual at home, in jogging bottoms and a T-shirt.'

Maud looked puzzled.

No way was she explaining jogging bottoms. Maud would regard them as outrageously slovenly.

Maud serenely consigned the vanquished jeans to a drawer, fetched a tin from the cupboard, unscrewed the lid and frowned. 'I thought this was full.'

Sophie put on her innocent face. Hugo had decanted half the deodorant powder into another tin for himself; men here didn't use it, too 'unmanly.' In return, rather than ask Maud, she'd asked Hugo to get her a razor to shave her legs; hadn't wanted her request doing the rounds. She now had smooth legs and last night at bath time, Maud hadn't noticed. Win, win.

After accepting the tin with a smile, Sophie put on a pale blue gown; it was like the others but with a shorter cape. There were matching, kitten-heeled shoes too but Sophie pulled on new walking boots. Anne had noticed the state of Sophie's old ones and a cobbler had dropped off a range of footwear, including beaded court shoes and slippers.

Maud took a curvy straw hat from the wardrobe, smaller than the usual. 'Lady Lacey thought this would be easier for everyday, when you're out and about in the gardens.'

It was just a regular hat, with no pins.

Sophie asked about a notebook and pen.

'Of course, Miss.' Maud returned the hat to the wardrobe. 'It's nearly nine-thirty.'

Asking Anne for a watch would have been a request too far, given all the trouble she'd caused. 'Come on, Charlotte — breakfast.'

In the corridor, Charlotte jumped about in excitement and Sophie knocked on Hugo's door.

Hugo opened it wearing his brown suit, a cream shirt and a regular, long tie. The tie was unexpectedly colourful — a lurid mix of red and azure shapes. But no one at home would have given him a second glance. Unlike her, in this lacy dress. Not to mention her enormous drawers. What was male underwear like here? A glossy cologne advert came to mind, featuring Hugo posing in black trunks. She rubbed her temple. Still concussed.

As they walked along the corridor, Hugo said, 'We could get home today.' His tone was hopeful rather than confident.

'Fingers crossed.' Reynolds was driving them down the lane after breakfast.

When Sophie came into the dining room, the butler turned towards her, his expression enigmatic as usual, but the fair-haired footman stared and Mr Hunter smirked.

She was appropriately dressed … likely her swim with Freddy was still ruffling feathers.

Only Richard joined them, seeming genuinely pleased she'd recovered.

After the meal, back in the bedroom, Sophie picked up her cardigan, folded her shirt into her bag, hoisted the bag over her shoulder and went with Charlotte to meet Hugo on the front drive.

He turned up a few minutes later, wearing his shorts and T-shirt and carrying his hoodie. 'You're going back in that dress?'

'Have to. Jeans shrunk in the wash.'

Reynolds was waiting with the green car, the engine running. Hugo took the front passenger seat and Sophie got in the back with Charlotte and gripped her collar.

As they drove off, Sophie leaned towards Hugo. 'If it's there, and 'home' is written on the doors, will you get in?'

'Yes, I've plenty of notes.' He shot her a tense smile. 'But I'll check before I do, in case it's a bottomless shaft.'

'So will I.' Her mind raced ahead, picturing the square outline and fancy light. 'How long before we get there?' she asked Reynolds.

'Depends how far it is, Miss.'

'About twenty miles,' said Hugo.

'Not far off an hour, then.' In his rear-view mirror, Reynolds gave her a respectful nod.

Perhaps he hadn't been mocking her at the picnic? 'Have you worked as a driver for long?'

'Only a few months, Miss. But my family used to have a garage, so I grew up with cars.'

He'd been the boss's son so working as a servant must be hard. Like her, he didn't quite fit in. Neither fish nor fowl.

A thickset man was walking on the verge and Sophie's stomach dropped. But he waved, and Reynolds waved back.

Just a gardener.

Beyond the field gates, mile after mile, every bend and all the trees and shrubs looked the same; lucky they'd marked the lift spot. She tapped her feet, her palms sweaty. Please let the lift be there. She didn't do praying but the voice in her head repeated, defying logic.

'Here,' said Hugo, and Reynolds stopped the car.

Charlotte's small green bag was still hanging from the branch, the thin plastic swaying in a gentle breeze.

Sophie jumped out and ran towards the oak, searching beyond it for an almost invisible, unnatural straight line or tell-tale corner. Nothing. She stopped and slowly scanned the space above the verge in front of a dense bay hedge. Still nothing. If the lift was there, it was entirely invisible.

She walked cautiously forward, hoping to feel the lip of the threshold or to be stopped by unyielding doors, but she just ended up by the hedge. She sneezed; the air was teeming with heady oak and birch pollen. She turned and retraced her steps, standing in the middle of where the lift should have been. The grass beneath her feet was overgrown. 'Why isn't this flattened?'

'Four days … vegetation would have recovered.' Hugo was kneeling, moving his hands along the ground to find metal, not soil and flora. Despite thinking it unlikely, he'd still hoped to find the lift waiting for them.

He stood and squared his shoulders, but looked devastated, drained.

Sophie gestured at Charlotte's bag, consumed with a wearying, hollow disappointment. 'The lift *was* here. This is proof.'

'Yes.' His voice was flat. 'It's unsightly, but we should leave it.' He checked it was securely tied.

'It's biodegradable,' said Sophie, out of habit, her mind still on the lift.

'I know I should care but, at this moment, I really don't.' He put his hand tiredly through his hair. 'We should search the area.'

'In narrow sweeps.' She tried to sound upbeat, but the last dregs of hope were draining away.

They combed the ground like a forensic team, examining blades of grass, wildflowers, nettles. The oak's canopy cast the verge into sun-dappled shade and as they toiled, above them in the tree, pigeons were cooing.

The sound should have been soothing but Sophie wanted to throw something at them. 'We should have worn gloves.' She turned over yet another prickly thorn with her foot and sneezed again.

'If it's random, we'd need to set up camp, for months, maybe years.'

'Didn't work for Eddington.' And camping was hard. Her friend Lily had returned from a Combined Cadet Force exercise at school with hypothermia. 'Let's focus on the visitors.' Sophie straightened and stretched. In the meantime, she'd do nothing that would shock the servants, embarrass herself or Anne. Act smart ... demure and dignified.

Reynolds had turned the car around, ready for the return journey, and was on his haunches by the driver's door, polishing a wheel arch with a yellow cloth. Charlotte hadn't moved from the back seat and was snoozing, stretched out in the sunshine. Sophie despondently shoved her over to make room as she climbed in.

Hugo sat in the front again and Reynolds faffed around, adjusted the brake, then got out and fiddled with something at the front of the car before turning over a crank. He leaned into the driver's seat, pulled at a knob and turned a key on the dashboard, went to the front again, adjusted something else, and flicked over the crank in one decisive movement. The engine rattled into life and Reynolds climbed into the driver's seat.

'Starting this car is complicated,' said Hugo, displaying his capacity for understatement.

Reynolds nodded. 'And every car's different.'

When they turned into the drive, Richard was waiting on the front steps. 'Anything there?' He was asking Reynolds.

'Nothing, sir,' said the chauffeur, opening Sophie's door.

'Now you can relax, enjoy this wonderful weather.' Richard smiled and disappeared inside the house.

As Reynolds drove to wherever the cars were kept, Hugo said quietly, 'This was a one-off. If we study the visitors and work out how to find the lift, Richard won't let us drive there.' He shook his head. 'I don't understand why he doesn't want us to find it.'

Sophie recalled Anne's remark, almost an aside. *Before I married, I tried to find it and Richard worried if I did, I wouldn't come back.* 'This isn't about us. He thinks if she could, Anne might go home.'

'They seem happy,' said Hugo, 'and I can't believe she'd abandon Freddy.'

Anne is keen to hear about home. 'Faced with a real choice, I'm not sure what she'd do.' Anne's understanding and kindness in hosting two strange visitors suggested she still valued any connection with her old life. 'Richard wouldn't take the risk.'

Charlotte dashed off towards the alley and the gardens and Hugo gave Sophie a worried glance. 'Even if another visitor turned up tomorrow, by the time they reached the Manor the lift might be long gone.' He paused at the start of the alley. 'But if it was still there, finding out where the drivers keep the keys wouldn't be hard…'

'Can you remember what Reynolds did to start the car?' She couldn't.

'No.' Hugo frowned. 'And if we can't start it, we can't steal it.'

CHAPTER 16

'It wasn't there.' Hugo sat beside Freddy on the terrace.

'That's a shame,' said Freddy, standing and drawing out a chair for Sophie. But his eyes betrayed him. Like his father, he was relieved they'd found nothing.

Sophie sat down and Freddy rang the handbell.

'We'd like to meet Miss Hemmings,' Hugo announced, as if quizzing the visitors had been his idea.

'Should we just go find her or make an appointment?' Sophie had no idea of the protocol and wanted to suss that out *before* she put her foot in it.

'I'd go for an amble,' said Freddy, 'see if you run into her.'

The maid came out with coffee and Freddy stood up again. 'Enjoy elevenses. Back to the mill.'

'Sorry?'

'Things to do.' Freddy gave a mock salute and walked towards the brick building by the alley.

'He mentioned he was analysing something before the picnic,' said Sophie.

'Crop yields. They haven't found a new manager yet so apparently paperwork's piling up.'

She'd thought families like the Laceys socialised all day, but this was evidently a business.

'Anne works too,' said Hugo, 'visiting new families on the estate, checking they're okay.'

Lady Bountiful stuff.

After coffee, Hugo went off to change into his suit and Sophie returned to her bedroom.

Charlotte climbed on the bed, keen for another snooze, but Sophie dropped her bag and cardigan and stared out of the French windows, too consumed with misery to see the view. She traced her forefinger along a line of lead framing a diamond-shaped panel of glass and drew a calming breath. Just Keep Going.

After a few minutes, someone knocked on the door.

It was Hugo, dapper in his suit but looking weary.

Sophie put on her resolute face and prodded Charlotte awake.

Outside, a gardener directed them over the moat bridge and beyond the orchard to three large greenhouses.

The only similarity to Aunty Wendy's rickety lean-to greenhouse was the name. Nineteenth century or older, all identical in size and shape — an elongated oval — each had a high, domed glass roof. In the nearest one, a short, wiry woman was standing by rows of tomatoes, giving confident instructions to a group of young men. Her brown hair was cut into a neat bob and her loose black trousers and dark long-sleeved shirt matched her colleagues' attire. Gardening in a tight-fitting, floor-length gown like Anne's would have been impractical at any time of year, but in here in July, it was sweltering.

The woman looked up, surprised to be interrupted.

'Miss Hemmings?' said Hugo, politely.

'Ah, the new visitors. I wondered when I'd meet you.' The head gardener had a faint cockney accent.

'Would you be free to chat in a few minutes?' asked Sophie. The young men were staring curiously, mostly at her.

Miss Hemmings checked her watch. 'Now is a good time.' She turned to the group. 'It's nearly noon. Go for lunch. Start again at one.' The gardeners dutifully filed through the building towards a back entrance and Miss Hemmings opened a side door. Charlotte rudely sniffed at her trousers, but Miss Hemmings patted her.

Distracted by the smells in the greenhouse, Charlotte had forgotten to bounce. A disturbing vision of Shorten's head gardener being knocked to the ground in her workplace appeared in Sophie's head and happily dissolved.

As Miss Hemmings led the way past the other greenhouses, Sophie did introductions, leaving out 'Miss' and 'Mr,' and including Charlotte.

Miss Hemmings smiled. 'You must know that everyone knows your names.'

Sophie didn't know and the idea made her uncomfortable, though it was entirely logical that time-travelling guests would be hot gossip, even if they weren't the first.

'Please call me Lucy. You must be more used to Christian names.' Lucy pointed to an archway in a high brick wall. 'We grow vegetables, fruit, and herbs in the walled garden, and on the estate, we have cows, sheep and pigs, as well as chickens, so the Manor's self-sufficient, except for sugar, and salt and pepper.'

Sophie was sort of interested, but Hugo was listening with rapt attention. If they never got home, his existing knowledge and curiosity would serve him well. The thought didn't cheer her.

Not far from the walled garden was a small cottage. Lucy opened the front door and they trooped into a dim room, sparsely furnished with a tatty armchair and side table.

'I don't use the parlour. North-facing, so too gloomy.' Lucy led them into a more welcoming kitchen.

On the left was an oak dresser. To the right, against the internal wall, was a rectangular stone sink above a plain wooden cupboard. Lucy ran water into a bowl from the sink tap and put the bowl on the tiled floor.

As Charlotte happily slurped, Sophie walked towards a timber-framed window, subdivided into four square panes. Outside was a surprisingly colourful garden. Tall and short plants jostled for space, primary shades squashed in with softer hues of violets, limes, yellows and pinks. She turned to Lucy. 'So many beautiful flowers.'

'Dog Rose, Honeysuckle, Enchanter's Nightshade, Columbine, Forget-Me-Nots, Kingcup.' Lucy counted them off on her fingers. 'And that's just for starters.' She wrapped a thick tea towel around her hand and lifted a battered kettle from a hook that hung above a cast iron stove near the basin. She put the kettle on top of the stove. 'They're all wildflowers. I never have time to make it tidy.'

The stove was narrow and free-standing, its sturdy surfaces scarred and worn with age. Lucy opened a door at the front and, with a small shovel, transferred coal from a bucket into the oven.

'The garden is wonderful,' said Hugo. 'It would be shame to change anything.'

'All down to Mother Nature.' Lucy shut the oven door with a clang.

'Does the stove keep hot for long?' Hugo walked over to examine it.

Lucy put the towel aside. 'I put in coal every morning and just top it up later.'

'Not that different from our old Aga,' said Hugo.

Hugo's family had an Aga. Those old-fashioned cookers were eye-wateringly expensive, even second-hand. How entirely predictable.

Lucy gestured towards a square table and two upright chairs by the window. 'Make yourselves at home.'

Charlotte was now happily mooching about, determinedly sniffing the floor, and Sophie sat opposite Hugo and tried to relax. But disappointment from the lane was still lingering, an ache in her guts.

The air carried the same faint, musty smell as the Manor's grand entrance hall, with its intriguing portrait of Richard's glum ancestors and their dog. Sophie tapped her fingers on the grooved, wooden table. These humbler walls had also sheltered untold generations. If they couldn't get home for weeks or months, she should ask for a cottage. She imagined slow mornings making breakfast, Charlotte snoozing by the stove.

'This kitchen is so cosy.' Hugo looked around, planning his own pied-a-terre. 'The house comes with the job?'

'I moved in after Mr Devon died. His widow could have stayed on, but she went to live with her grown up children.'

'She could have kept the cottage…' Hugo seemed puzzled. 'Is that usual?'

'It is in Shorten.' Lucy took cups and matching saucers from the dresser.

'What happens in other places?' asked Sophie.

'They get chucked out.' Lucy set the crockery on the table. 'Richard changed that before we arrived.' She straightened. 'But it was unheard of for a house to be allocated to a single woman. I only got it because Anne weighed in behind the scenes.'

Right. Zero chance of a cottage. 'How long have you lived here?'

'Three years.'

'But to start with, you lived at the Manor,' said Hugo, 'with the girl who came through the lift with you?'

'We did, but if we'd stayed on as guests, we'd have ended up in corsets, sitting around all day, bored witless.'

Sophie nodded in recognition. If they didn't find the lift, that would happen to her.

Lucy steadied a cup on a wobbly saucer. 'When we both started working in the gardens, we moved to the attic. There's a whole warren of rooms up there.'

'For how many people?' asked Hugo.

'Twenty or so. The men live in the basement.' Lucy grinned. 'As far from the women as physically possible.'

'Was it easier,' said Sophie, 'not being a guest?'

'No frills, but more privacy. Once you close your door, nobody barges in first thing to give you tea and toast.'

Lucy was right about privacy, or the lack of it; she and Maud might as well be cohabiting — just without the sex. If she was stranded for a while, she should move to the attic, get a job. 'Are servants allowed to keep dogs?'

Lucy raised her eyebrows. 'No. The gamekeepers' dogs are kept in kennels by the stables.'

She couldn't handle that. Neither would Charlotte.

The kettle on the stove was making a busy, singing sound, but Lucy ignored it. She opened a tall cupboard beyond the stove by a back door and took out a small milk bottle. 'I've no fridge, of course, but the larder works fine.'

'How does it keep cold?' asked Sophie.

'Thick walls, and a grille open to the outside.'

Sophie turned to Hugo. 'When were fridges invented?'

'Nineteenth century … but they didn't catch on in Britain until the 1960s.'

'Why did it take so long?' Lucy took a jug from the dresser and poured milk into it.

'Life was tough in Britain after the war,' said Hugo. 'Rationing didn't even end until 1954.'

'Really?' Sophie's tone was sceptical. 'Nine years after the war?'

'Like I said, life was tough,' said Hugo. 'We didn't pay off the huge war loan from the States until after the turn of the century.'

Lucy looked impressed.

Sophie was too, but not surprised. Hugo's brain was crammed with all sorts of trivia, not just dates. He'd won the Christmas quiz in their final year at school, narrowly beating his friend Alex, who'd won the previous two. She glanced at him, trying not to think about bleak post-war Britain; if they were stuck here, they'd likely experience it first-hand.

'It's good to finally meet you.' Lucy put the jug on the table. 'Ridge and Walker didn't stop talking when they got back with the garlic. Your jeans, Sophie, they caused quite a commotion.'

'They're supposed to be tight fitting,' said Sophie, feeling awkward. She poured milk into her china cup and passed the jug to Hugo.

Lucy shrugged. 'Everybody gossips about everything and anything.'

'Sorry, you've lost me,' said Hugo, putting milk into his cup. 'Garlic?'

'Wild garlic. Grows on the roadside. At home it flowers for a few weeks in the spring but here it carries on till August.'

Like the bluebells. 'Do you know why it might flower differently in the 1920s?'

'It's a mystery. But it's heavenly in sauces and soups.' Lucy placed an outlandish teapot on the table. With a shiny blue ceramic body and grey pewter lid, it resembled an Aladdin's lamp. 'This came with the house. I've tried rubbing it, but no genie appeared.'

'That's a shame,' said Sophie, smiling at Hugo. 'We could have wished ourselves home.'

He returned the smile, but with an effort. 'We searched the lift spot this morning.'

'We spent hours there the first few weeks,' said Lucy.

Hugo leaned forward. 'Did you find anything?'

'Nothing. As if we'd imagined it.'

CHAPTER 17

'We even tried once at night,' said Lucy, 'because we'd arrived in the dark.'

Sophie gave thanks they'd landed in daylight. 'You came through the lift in the students' union?'

'We did,' said Lucy, 'going to the accommodation block, like we had a hundred times before.'

'Did your lift have gold doors?' asked Sophie.

Lucy spooned loose tea into the pot from a battered green tin with a gilt '2' on the front. 'Bright gold, with a drawing of a posh house.'

'Were there any other pictures?'

'No.' Lucy seemed bemused. 'Not that I remember.'

Lucy had come through the same lift as Anne.

'Janet had drunk so much Chardonnay, she didn't notice the paint job.' Lucy's lips twisted in a poignant smile. 'But she sobered up fast when the doors opened.'

Knowing Miss Alderman's first name made her more real. And more dead. Don't think about it.

'What happened then?' Hugo couldn't keep the urgency out of his voice, hoping for a vital clue.

'I realised that the lift had a pretty chandelier.' Lucy took teaspoons from a drawer in the dresser. 'The space was bigger and there were mirrors on the walls and ceiling, but outside there was just blackness.' Lucy's breezy manner faltered. 'Janet was muttering, "not real," and though it wasn't cold, my teeth were chattering. The overhead light dimmed, and we could make out trees. Eventually we got out and sat on the road. After a while, the clouds parted and there was moonlight. The lift doors were still open, and the chandelier was shining bright again.' She put a teaspoon carefully on each saucer. 'It began to get light, so we decided to explore. Walking away, I remember thinking, if push comes to shove, we can turn around.' Lucy tipped sugar cubes into a bowl from a cardboard packet.

'I thought the same,' said Hugo.

Lucy placed a small strainer on a saucer on the table and removed the teapot lid. 'Janet bucked me up.' Lucy's lips softened. 'Said it was an adventure.'

The kettle had stopped singing on the stove and steam was rising from the spout. Lucy wrapped the tea towel round her hands, took the kettle and carefully poured boiling water into the teapot, conscious that Charlotte was again snuffling her trousers, the fabric scented with interesting garden smells.

Lucy hung the kettle on the sturdy hook above the stove and draped the towel over a handle on the front of the oven.

'Why do you keep the kettle on that hanger?' asked Sophie.

'If you leave it on the stove, it boils dry.' Lucy fetched a three-legged stool from beside the larder and sat on it at the table. 'So, how are you finding the Manor?'

'Daunting,' said Sophie. 'At first I thought I was dreaming.'

'We did too.' Lucy stirred the teapot with a spoon.

'When did you realise you weren't?' said Hugo.

'That first morning. We'd expected to wake up in the tower block, but we were still in the ridiculously grand bedroom. It was the details, the carving on the bedstead, the heavy blankets, that made us realise it was real.'

Hugo gave Sophie a knowing glance and she avoided eye contact, regretting anew how mean she'd been to him on their first day.

'Within hours, Janet was planning to go down the lane,' said Lucy, 'but I can remember staring at the door in the loo, trying to wish us home by the sheer force of wanting.'

All the visitors had experienced the same gamut of emotions when they'd arrived; but these weren't unusual — wouldn't explain why there were so few visitors.

'Do you have a loo here?' asked Hugo.

'Outside.' Lucy gestured to the back door.

'I was just curious,' said Hugo, in no hurry to check it out.

'You're spoiled at the Manor,' said Lucy, but her tone was good-natured. She replaced the pewter lid and, using the strainer, poured tea into the cups.

'How did you end up as head gardener?' Sophie took a sip of tea.

'I'd been studying the history of domestic horticulture.' Lucy added milk to her cup. 'I'd always wanted to work in the gardens of a grand house and suddenly here I was. I asked to help with the gardening and Janet did too.'

'Be careful what you wish for.' Hugo gave a soft whistle.

Sophie caught her breath. 'This was your dream job. Why you stepped through the portal?'

Lucy shook her head. 'Gardening's my passion but it wasn't Janet's. She wasn't an outdoor person at all. When winter set in, she hated it. Even with lots of layers, 1920s clothing isn't warm.'

And now Janet was lying in the cold earth. Despite the pleasant temperature of the room, Sophie shivered.

'And the greenhouses had no electricity.' Lucy dropped three sugar lumps into her tea. 'Two are built into the ground, warmed by south facing windows, but one was heated by a furnace. Very hard work.'

Sophie took another sip of tea. 'But people were friendly, your workmates?'

'*No*. Downright hostile. Lady gardeners ... we caused quite a fuss. But they gradually got used to us — with Anne's support.' Lucy paused for breath, as if she'd been storing her experiences for years and been waiting to share them.

Had she made many close friends? No. Too intimate a question. 'We think the visitors might be the key to finding the lift,' said Sophie.

Hugo fished out a pad and pen from his jacket pocket. 'Do you mind if I make notes?'

'Fill your boots,' said Lucy.

Maud had left Sophie a notebook and pen after breakfast but, fixated with the trip down the lane, she'd forgotten them. She'd write this up later — if necessary, copy from Hugo's pad. 'You and Anne only saw a picture of a mansion, but I saw three other pictures.' She described them.

'That might be important,' said Lucy.

Hugo scribbled in his pad. 'And we're trying to figure out what the visitors have in common.'

'Because there are so few of us,' said Lucy, quickly understanding. 'But we're all very different.'

'How do you mean?' Sophie took another sip of tea.

'Alan Parkes is an odd man.' Lucy stood, went to the dresser and took a blue tin from a low cupboard. The tin depicted doves, a fat naked cherub and an idealised country girl gazing at Cupid's arrow. 'I haven't any food for lunch. I usually eat in the servants' hall, but I've plenty of Mrs Ferris's finest.' She removed the lid. 'Help yourself.'

'Mrs Ferris is the cook,' said Hugo, addressing Sophie. He reached for a chunky chocolate biscuit.

Knowing Hugo, he'd memorised all the servants' names.

'You'd go home if you could?' Hugo asked Lucy.

'Nope, nothing to go back to.' Lucy sipped her tea. 'And it's nice being the boss.'

Sophie picked out a biscuit and took a bite. The crunchy chocolate tasted like a hand-made artisan confection. 'Did you ever wish you could travel in time?'

'No.'

'Did Janet?' asked Hugo.

Lucy swallowed. 'She was a computer scientist. I don't think it ever entered her head.'

Okay, five out of six visitors *hadn't* fantasised about time travel, and after a decade, Lucy obviously still missed her friend.

'Can you remember the date you stepped into the lift?' Hugo asked.

'I can't remember the day,' said Lucy, 'but it was July 2003.'

Hugo made a note.

'Did your phones stop working?' asked Sophie.

'Yes.' Lucy took a biscuit. 'All we had was the clothes we were wearing, keys, a five pound note and two dead mobiles.'

'So, you lost your photos too.' Sophie's pictures, mostly of Charlotte, had been recently stored in a digital cloud. If she was stuck here, she should make a will, include the password.

'What do you mean? Photos?' Lucy finished her biscuit.

'Ones you'd taken on your phone,' said Sophie.

Lucy frowned, nonplussed. 'Phones that took photos cost a fortune. We just had regular Nokias.'

Of course. Lucy had left in 2003, from a time before smart phones.

Charlotte was sniffing the air near the tin and Sophie

moved it in from the table edge. The biscuits were yummy, but chocolate was poisonous for dogs.

'You'd used the lift many times,' said Hugo, 'so it was your second or third year?'

'Second,' said Lucy. 'We were volunteer counsellors, so didn't have to move off campus like everyone else did after the first year.'

'And when you stepped through the portal, it was July,' said Sophie. 'Out of term time.'

'I lived there all year round and Janet only went home some weekends.' Lucy took another sip of tea. 'When I finished school, I'd thought long and hard about getting a job. Nearly didn't take up my place.'

'My grades were so bad,' said Hugo, 'I didn't think anywhere would take me.'

'What happened?' Sophie asked him.

'Glandular fever.'

'My A levels passed in a blur,' said Lucy. 'My mother died two months before the exams. I had no other family. I only went to university because it had been important to her. But I never settled, depressed probably.'

'That's awful,' said Sophie, trying not to think of her parents.

Hugo was frowning into his cup.

Time to steer the conversation to a less upsetting topic. 'Do you get reasonable pay?'

Lucy snorted. 'The pay's terrible, but the cottage is mine until I keel over.' She took another sip of tea. 'There's a handyman who does repairs if I can't manage them, and all my food is free.' She pushed the tin further from Charlotte's questing nose. 'I could take days off, but I don't. Everything has a set time to be done, depending on the season. I love the work. And most people are happy to be here, being paid ...

even if it is a pittance. The servants don't get drunk and disgrace themselves. Well, not often.'

It wasn't entirely clear if Lucy was joking, though her brown eyes were twinkling as she stroked Charlotte, who had reluctantly abandoned her biscuit mission. 'It's quite difficult at the moment, with no estate manager.' Lucy chewed thoughtfully on another biscuit. 'But the office is swamped with applications. We should get a replacement soon.'

'Anne said you arrived in 1911,' said Hugo, also eating his second biscuit. 'Can you remember the date?'

'Not exactly, but it was May,' said Lucy. 'And like Anne, we weren't looking forward to the end of the world. I persuaded Mr Devon to take on two female gardeners, but they didn't work out.'

Charlotte was now leaning against Sophie's legs. 'What *are* you talking about?'

'You really don't know, do you? Anne hasn't told you.' Lucy hesitated. 'The First World War, it didn't happen.' Her voice, quiet and calmly certain, reverberated around the kitchen.

Hugo was staring at Lucy, his eyes wide. And the words repeated themselves in Sophie's head.

The First World War, it didn't happen.

CHAPTER 18

*L*ucy placed her cup carefully on its saucer and frowned into the silence. 'If Anne felt she couldn't discuss this, I'm out of line telling you. She was embarrassed about worrying Richard, but after all this time...'

Comprehension and shock paled Hugo's face and he also put down his cup, less carefully than Lucy. 'Why? How?'

'I spent a while talking it through with Anne,' said Lucy. 'We were glad, obviously. No trenches, no mass casualties, no patriotic sacrifice. No Spanish 'flu either. Everything carried on the same. There was talk of war for a while, then the Kaiser died in Germany and it just went away. Britain stationed troops in Belgium, so did the French. That may have stopped it.' Lucy paused. 'I think they're still there.'

'Was Archduke Franz Ferdinand assassinated?' asked Hugo.

'No,' said Lucy. 'He died in a shooting accident, here in England in 1913, at a weekend party. Lots of families round here do them.' She rolled her eyes. 'Not my cup of tea. The men kill pheasants and the women watch or stay indoors.'

Hugo got abruptly to his feet, the legs of his chair scraping on the wooden floor. 'Lucy, it's been really good to meet you, but I suppose we'd better let you get on.'

'I'd be happy to chat again.'

'Thank you,' said Hugo, taking Sophie's arm.

In a daze, Sophie allowed Hugo to hurry her out, with Charlotte in their wake. They passed the walled garden and the greenhouses, and Hugo released her arm. He sat on the lawn by the moat, visibly shaken.

'It's a good thing, isn't it?' Sophie gathered Charlotte to her. 'All those men not killed in the trenches, not to mention the horses that died.'

Hugo gave a snort, or it could have been a cough. '*Millions* of men died, Sophie, all over the world. In Britain, it was as if a whole generation was wiped out. But with no Great War, other things will be different and that's not good news.'

She must have misheard. All those men and horses not being killed had to be good.

'Why didn't Anne tell us? It's not like it's a little thing.' He sounded angry. 'This will need thinking through but I'm sure we're in a more dangerous place.'

'I can't see why.'

Hugo determinedly cuddled Charlotte. She stilled, unaccustomed to his unsolicited attention, but then licked his chin. After a minute's snuggling, Hugo regained his composure and stood up. 'Don't ask anyone about this yet. I need time to think.' He checked his watch. 'It's nearly one but I can't face lunch. Can you tell Freddy I've got a headache?'

'Of course.'

Hugo went to his room and Sophie walked slowly to the dining room, her mind still reeling. As she crossed the threshold, the butler and footmen stood straighter and she managed a friendly nod, but was glad when the Laceys came in, diverting the servants' attention.

Charlotte adopted her beguiling food-begging expression and Freddy flopped into his allotted place. 'Where's Hugo?'

Sophie gave Hugo's excuse and concern registered on Freddy's face. Despite growing up a century apart, Freddy and Hugo were standard-issue posh boys; enough in common to become friends.

Lunch was more formal than breakfast, not served from the sideboard: poached eggs, hot beef pie, other meats, soft cabbage, steam puddings and cheeses. Sophie had two eggs, a wedge of soft cheese and resisted a helping of treacle sponge, all the while ruminating on the possible causes and consequences of a war that didn't happen.

Back in her room, Sophie closed the door and said to Charlotte, 'The timeline's been contaminated.'

Charlotte looked only mildly interested.

'So, home may be different, maybe a lot. Which could be a good thing.' But even as Sophie fantasised about seeing her parents, sci-fi plots ran through her head. 'This might never have been *our* past at all, but a parallel universe, a century behind.' She sat on the blue chair, her mind racing. 'Enough like home that Mum and Dad could still be born in the 1970s. Okay, not *my* mum and dad but close enough. And if I make it to ninety-two and another Sophie Arundel's born in 1998, I could meet myself as a baby. Well, a different me.' Would she ever understand this 'parallel worlds' stuff? Did anybody?

Uninterested in multiverse theory, Charlotte yawned and stretched in front of the French windows. Her fur needed proper brushing and de-knotting, but dog grooming was a modern thing...

On the dressing table was a stack of notebooks with stiff, plain cardboard covers, small enough to fit in a pocket. Sophie stood, walked over and took a silver fountain pen, carefully removed the cap and opened a notebook, intending to write *Lift Puzzle* on the first page. She moved the nib on the paper.

Nothing. Just a wince-making scrape.

She shook the pen. Indigo ink sprayed across the golden walnut dressing table and onto Sophie's pale blue skirt and the priceless bird carpet. Mortified, she replaced the pen cap, found a linen handkerchief in a drawer and wiped the ink from the table. The wood was highly polished, so the liquid came off. The carpet was a different matter.

Sophie ran to the bathroom, collected two towels and, in the bedroom, pressed one onto the stained rug, soaking up the ink. She poured water from the toiletries cupboard jug on to the other towel and scrubbed at the carpet. This only made the stains larger.

Leaving the towel over the blots, she sat on the bed. She was worn out by the attack in the lane and the lift disappearing and Lucy. And the trick pen was the last straw.

She lay down and closed her eyes.

Somewhere a gong sounded.

A brief knock on the door and Maud bustled in. 'Time to dress for dinner, Miss.'

Sophie braced herself and confessed about the ink.

Maud took the towel from the floor and struggled not to cringe.

'I'm so sorry. Is it ruined?'

'I'm not sure, Miss.' Maud glanced at Sophie's stained skirt and at the carpet again.

'Is there a pencil I can borrow?' She'd get home soon, didn't need to master ink-juggling.

'Yes, Miss.' Maud dragged her eyes from the carpet. 'You forgot your hat today.'

'Sorry?'

'Down the lane and with Miss Hemmings. Ladies wear hats outside, and on visits.'

Maud received regular movement updates. 'But not in the Manor?'

'No, Miss. And not if you're staying at another house.'

Too many rules…

Maud took a comb from the dressing table drawer. 'Let's dress your hair.'

Sophie didn't have to check in a mirror to know she had bed hair. Not attractively askew. A tangled mess. 'Could you cut it into a bob?'

Maud looked stunned. Cartoon stunned, as if she'd suggested stealing the silver or having sex. 'Absolutely not, Miss. It's your crowning glory.'

'It could be nice.'

Maud smiled. 'You're joking.'

Sophie smiled too. She could always cut it herself but, on balance, the risk of a hideous outcome outweighed the benefit.

After a painful twenty minutes detangling Sophie's hair and putting it up in a loose bun, Maud opened the wardrobe and brought out a ruby red gown with exaggerated puff sleeves and a short train.

Might be appropriate on Oscar night, but a teensy bit over the top for home dining. 'I'll stick with my regular dress.'

Maud returned the gown to its place, her lips compressed in disapproval.

Sophie hastily called on Hugo. When he opened his door, Charlotte dashed past him and launched herself onto his bed, pushing her luck. But Hugo was unfazed, and gestured for Sophie to come in.

His fine wool jacket matched his black trousers and bow tie and was scallop-shaped and longer at the back, reaching his knees.

Sophie raised an eyebrow. 'Nice tux.'

'It's acceptable to wear black tie, not white tie.'

'White tie?'

'More formal. Not sure what it involves, apart from the tie.'

His fringe was shorter. 'You've had your hair cut.'

'John did it this afternoon. Only took five minutes.'

Refraining from making a face was hard but she managed it. She sat in his armchair. 'Are you okay?'

'Got to be. Anne and Richard must have their reasons for not giving us chapter and verse, but I should have guessed.'

'You're not Sherlock Holmes.'

'Anne's dresses, vagrants wandering the roads, rioting in Derby … he'd have realised in hours.' Hugo sat on the bed and cuddled Charlotte. 'In *our* 1920s, the crime rate was low. Most potential criminals had died in the trenches. There were race riots in the ports in 1919, but they were linked to the war. Soldiers coming home resented foreign men taking their jobs. People died.' He tapped his fingers on the pale silk bedspread. 'By Freddy's account, whole streets in Derby – *this* Derby – have been gutted. Hundreds of people have been killed or injured.'

Tiny goosebumps rose on Sophie's arms, but she willed herself to keep calm. 'There could have been visitors over thousands of years, so a huge change, like stopping a world war, could be inevitable? The butterfly thing … it's from a 1950s sci-fi book, *The Sound of Thunder*. The hero steps on a butterfly in dinosaur times and comes back to find the present changed.'

'A bit like Chaos Theory.'

'Which is?'

'A butterfly beating its tiny wings on one continent eventually causes a massive storm on another.'

'We've done way more than that,' said Sophie, 'interacted with all these people…'

'My great, great grandmother married my great, great grandfather because her previous fiancé was killed in the Great War. This means my parents and my sisters were never born. And I shouldn't exist.' He sounded at the end of his tether.

'You do exist. Right now, right here. And, so do I.'

'You're handling this surprisingly well.'

'I'm a good bluffer.'

'On the other hand, my family might be alive,' said Hugo, 'if this isn't our past. A parallel universe.'

'I'm way ahead of you.'

For a moment, he seemed to lose his train of thought. 'Whatever this is … before, we knew roughly what our future would be. Now we don't.'

Sophie wrinkled her nose. 'So? Everybody lives with not knowing the future.'

Hugo sighed, more to himself than at her. 'The twentieth century was horrendously violent. If the Great War never happened, the future here, *our* future, is a complete lottery. Could be even worse. Will the Second World War happen? If it does, we could lose it.'

She'd studied the Nazis to death at school. She really didn't want to experience them first-hand. 'Anne seems pretty straight. We should ask her about this over dinner.'

'Yes.' He stood up, his eyes apprehensive.

Sophie got to her feet too, straightening her stained skirt with equally stained hands.

'Fighting with an old-fashioned pen?'

'The pen won.'

Hugo opened the door, Charlotte ran past him into the corridor and they followed. By the time they reached the anteroom by the dining room, the dogs were excitedly wagging their tails.

At least Charlotte was having a good time.

Freddy and Richard were wearing the same black tie outfits as Hugo. Anne smiled in their direction. Her cream gown had a longer train than Sophie's rejected dress.

Sophie accepted a small glass of amber liquid from the fair-haired footman, sipped and nearly gagged. Toe-curlingly sweet. She felt awkward when he whisked away her full glass, but no one noticed.

In the dining room, five places had been laid at the huge table like before, but the table settings were more elaborate. Each setting had forks of various sizes to the left and knives to the right. Above the table mats were a small spoon and fork, three stemmed glasses of different sizes, a squat glass and a handwritten menu card listing six courses, held upright in a slim, silver holder.

When Sophie sat at the table, like before, the footman placed a large linen napkin across her knees.

'The biggest glass is for red wine,' said Anne, 'smaller for white, and smallest for pudding wine. The tumbler is for water.' As if on cue, the butler poured water into Anne's glass. 'Use the cutlery, starting from the outside, except the first knife which is for bread. After that, cutlery on both sides matches each course.' Anne lowered her voice, her twinkling eyes at odds with her deadpan expression. 'The main thing is not to panic.'

Sophie resolved to copy her hosts.

The starter course arrived and she peered at the menu card. *Mushroom vol-au-vent sautéed with wild garlic.*

She ate every morsel. Delicious.

Freddy shot her a shy smile. 'I'd love to know how the lift works, the real nuts and bolts.'

She smiled back. Freddy was too posh and buttoned up but he was genuinely curious about the portal; had a maths degree so must be clever.

'You have a beautiful house and estate,' said Hugo, 'and in weather like this, it's heavenly.'

'It can be cold and draughty,' said Anne. 'Even with big fireplaces, it's never warm enough during most of the year. But you get used to it.'

Sophie accepted a token piece of lamb, ate soft carrots with potatoes cut into tiny, narrow sticks and sipped a crisp white wine. Each course was quite small and came with a different wine. She only sampled each glass, keen to stay dignified and demure, not wasted.

'I was thinking,' said Richard, 'we should install central heating. My brother has it in his house in New York. The American Radiator Company has a sister company in Hull.'

When was central heating introduced in their England? Perhaps it caught on earlier in the States? But with no Great War, there'd surely be loads of differences—

'Wouldn't it be very expensive?' said Anne. 'I grew up in a house without it. I'm happy to put on more clothes.'

'I'd like to at least start,' said Richard, 'in a few rooms.'

'My parents put in underfloor heating last year,' said Hugo.

Irritation flickered for an instant in Richard's eyes, thinking Hugo's remark one-upmanship.

'Only for an old coach house,' Hugo added. 'We're renovating it.'

Coach house? Grand enough to store one like the Queen's, brought out for royal weddings and opening parliament... Sophie sipped her water. In some ways, Hugo was as mysterious as Anne and Richard. She liked him but he could be annoying. The downside of being clever? But Freddy wasn't annoying—

'Like the Romans?' asked Anne.

'I'm not sure.' Hugo acknowledged Mr Hunter, taking his clean plate. 'You use electric cabling or water pipes.'

The next course was wild duck, with thinly sliced pota-toes like hot crisps. After that, apple pie with strawberries in brine was served, and hard and soft cheeses.

'We met Lucy Hemmings today,' said Hugo, 'had a really good chat.'

The footmen put out more glasses and cutlery, and bowls that were very cold to the touch.

Vanilla ice cream. It looked wonderfully creamy, but nerves had stolen Sophie's appetite. *If Anne felt she couldn't discuss this, I'm out of line telling you.* Exploring a mystifying, alternate history could be interesting, but questioning why their hosts had concealed it could get them thrown out — or worse.

Sophie shook her head slightly at Hugo. Yes, everyone was feeling mellow after a nice meal, but without more info, they should put this off.

But Hugo's attention was on Anne and Richard.

'She mentioned the First World War never happened.' Hugo was trying to sound casual but failing.

Anne blinked, her eyes over-bright, and Richard nodded at the butler who promptly left the room, followed by the footmen, closing a side door behind them.

Sophie's nerves, already stretched, pulled even tighter.

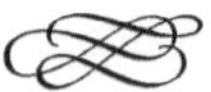

CHAPTER 19

'I don't know why the Great War didn't happen.' Anne sounded as if she was being blamed for something.

'We have some ideas that could explain it but they're only theoretical,' said Hugo.

Keeping her voice cautious and respectful, Sophie said, 'People coming through the lift must have changed history.'

'The visitors obviously affect decisions people make, including important ones.' Richard smiled at Anne, his expression so genuine and fond that Sophie looked at her place setting, embarrassed.

'There may be other portals,' said Hugo, 'at the bottom of oceans or in remote mountains, but not many accessible ones, or they'd have been studied and monitored.'

Freddy made a face. 'Mr Eddington gave up.'

'Are there any folk tales about portals in other parts of the country or abroad?' asked Sophie.

'Not as far as I know,' said Richard.

'Any local ghost stories,' asked Hugo, 'or warning nursery rhymes?'

'There's the green-eyed barmaid,' said Anne. 'Eighteenth century, I think. She disappeared on New Year's Eve, supposedly taken by fairies, jealous of her beauty.'

'Did she vanish from the lane?' asked Sophie.

'No. Spirited away from the village pub while fairies danced in the moonlight,' said Anne. 'I think alcohol was involved.'

'If the portal is unique and opens infrequently,' said Hugo, 'I don't think the occasional visitor in Derbyshire, even over millennia, would be enough to change enormous events, like a world war.'

'And all the visitors have come from the future in chronological order,' said Sophie. 'Anne, you came from the 1980s, Lucy from 2003, and we arrived from 2017. Time travellers would surely arrive randomly, from the past and future.'

Hugo glanced at her. 'Good point.' He turned back to Anne. 'At home, there's a rough consensus amongst scientists, well, theoretical physicists, which may explain why your Great War never happened. The theory was around in the 1980s but was more obscure and not widely accepted.'

Anne's eyes were still bright, her hands trembling, while her husband just seemed intrigued.

Definitely missing something here.

'I don't understand the maths,' said Hugo, 'but scientists believe there are many parallel universes. Multiverses. There might be eleven. No idea why. Or there are millions, billions, possibly trillions. Some universes are similar, others a bit different or totally different. If you accept that idea, we've come from a different universe, but this world is very similar. Well, apart from the Great War.'

Silence.

Charlotte and Jack, sitting side by side on the floor on the other side of the table, were watching Hugo, troubled by his serious tone.

'Can you explain *any* of the maths underpinning this?' Freddy asked Hugo.

'No.'

Freddy's lips pressed together in frustration.

'I can't either,' said Sophie.

'Few people could.' Hugo turned to her. 'Have you read *A Brief History of Time*?'

'Only the first chapter … if I ever get home, I'll have more motivation to finish it.' She'd struggled to understand Hawking's book.

'I got to the end, but forgot what I'd read,' said Hugo. 'It's complex.'

'In seventy years,' said Sophie, 'it might be that a version of me and Hugo will be born here but make different choices, live different lives.' Stephen Hawking was awesome, but *Star Trek* was an easier source of ideas.

'Multiverses are bound up with something called string theory,' said Hugo, 'but I can't remember why.'

'How does the lift fit in with multiverses?' asked Freddy.

'Sorry,' said Hugo, 'I've no idea.'

'Your watch is working,' Sophie said to Hugo, 'so time is passing at the same rate as at home. How come it's 1925?'

'Time here could be passing slower, but because my watch still works I'm guessing the difference is very small.'

'And the time lag increases over the decades?' said Richard, his eyes riveted on Hugo.

'Exactly,' said Hugo.

Sophie took another sip of water. For someone born in the nineteenth century and not familiar with string theory, Richard was a quick study.

'Does this mean the Second World War won't happen?' Richard squeezed his wife's hand. 'In many ways it sounds worse.'

'It was for civilians,' said Sophie. 'Let's hope Adolf Hitler has already been run over by a car in Vienna.'

Anne made a face, reminding Sophie of Freddy.

Hugo hurried on. 'Lucy told us that Archduke Ferdinand died in a shooting accident. Is that right?'

'Yes,' said Anne. 'He was over here attending a shooting party. The shoot went ahead although the weather was dreadful, deep snow. One of his loaders slipped and shot him by accident. The article in *The Times* confirmed my doubts.'

'You'd already noticed other differences?' asked Sophie.

Anne and Richard exchanged smiles, enjoying a shared joke. 'There was the holiday we never had,' said Richard, 'staying with James.'

'Richard dearly wanted to visit his brother in New York,' said Anne, 'by way of the latest and best liner. When I heard it was the Titanic, I flatly refused to go and wouldn't let him go either.'

'Good decision.' Sophie had seen the movie when she was way too young; nightmares about drowning toddlers had lingered for a while.

'But the Titanic did not sink,' said Anne. 'It got safely to New York and is still in service.'

'It didn't hit the iceberg?' Hugo was all rapt attention now.

'Not long after leaving Dublin, many of the passengers and crew went down with food poisoning,' said Anne, 'including the bigwigs and the chap who was keen to show how fast the ship could go. A lower chap was put in charge and he was nervous about making a mistake. They did hit an iceberg — it was recorded in an obscure shipping report — but no damage was done because they weren't going too fast.'

'*So* lucky,' said Sophie.

'But if other ships have used the same hull design,' said Hugo, 'it's a disaster waiting to happen.'

Anne frowned. 'You're right.'

'I am curious,' said Richard. 'Why, after more than a century, do you know so much about the Titanic? It's a splendid ship, but one of many. Did you study it in school?'

'No,' said Sophie, 'most people know about it from the movie.'

'*A Night to Remember*,' said Anne. 'Very moving.'

'When was that made?' asked Sophie.

'Before I was born,' said Anne. '1950s, I think.'

'The Titanic was infamous before that,' said Hugo, addressing Richard. 'Everyone knew that it had been dubbed unsinkable and sank on its maiden voyage. On the positive side, it's also remembered for chivalry and bravery. Most women and children survived, even those travelling third class, because they were put on the limited number of lifeboats.'

Hugo knew about this stuff ... the Kate Winslet movie might not have been *entirely* accurate. 'Do you have films yet?'

'We went to the cinema in London last year,' said Richard. 'Anne found the silent film boring.'

Anne looked sheepish. 'Only a little.'

'Have you noticed other differences?' Hugo asked Anne.

'I haven't, but I was never taught much history, at least the domestic sort, so may not have noticed.'

'Have you got the vote?' Sophie asked her.

'No, despite all the suffragette marches.'

'Women don't,' said Freddy, as if it was immutable, like being born or dying.

Sophie turned to him. 'But you can vote?'

'Now I'm twenty-one.'

'I voted in the last election,' said Sophie. She'd registered online, hadn't taken long.

'All this fuss about votes for women,' said Freddy, 'it's

quite peculiar. You're not going to start chaining yourself to railings, are you?' He was watching her, unsure.

'Of course not.'

'Fortunately, we agree about most things,' said Richard, glancing at his wife, 'including politics.'

Emboldened by Richard's relaxed body language, Sophie said, 'But why should it be the husband who votes? And what about unmarried women?'

'You mean nuns?' asked Freddy.

'No,' said Sophie, 'just women who don't want to get married.'

'Who would choose to be a spinster?' said Freddy.

'Me,' said Sophie, 'and singleton's a better word.' Freddy was staring at her as if she'd gone bald.

'I'm almost certain this isn't our past,' said Hugo. 'And the upside of that, is that we can tell you about the future and not mess with history.'

Richard smiled at his wife. 'It was thanks to Anne that we invested in indoor plumbing.'

'And you're ahead of the curve with electric lighting,' said Sophie.

Feeling more relaxed, Hugo took a sip of wine. 'Who knows what might be different? You might not get hammered with inheritance taxes.'

'You didn't think to mention the taxes, dear,' Richard said, lightly, squeezing Anne's hand. She was on the verge of tears.

Hugo cleared his throat. 'I hope we haven't trespassed too much into your family's private affairs.'

'You may have solved a mystery, at least in part.' Richard stood and rang a bellpull. 'But I'd be obliged if you didn't discuss this further. It unsettles the servants.'

Hugo nodded so Sophie did too, though she was unclear why anyone in the 1920s would be 'unsettled' by a scientific theory explaining the visitors.

'Freddy, shouldn't we write to Mr Eddington again?' Anne still seemed uncomfortable.

'We should. Tempt him away from relativity and stars.'

The footmen and butler came back, fruit and nuts were offered and a decanter of port was passed around, but Sophie demurred, as did Hugo.

'This is when we leave the chaps to it,' said Anne, standing decisively, addressing Sophie.

Bizarre.

Hugo gave her a reassuring smile; okay, not bizarre. And it would be rude not to follow house rules. She got to her feet and nudged Charlotte. 'Come on, you're a girl too.' Charlotte resisted and determinedly stayed on her stomach facing Jack, who was settled by Richard's chair. Sophie put on her firm voice. 'Come on.' Finally, with an annoyed shake of her head, Charlotte hauled herself up.

Sophie followed Anne into the drawing room. The low table that had been laid for afternoon tea when they'd arrived was now set for coffee.

Charlotte snorted, still put out by her forced departure from the dining room.

'What are they going to do in there?' asked Sophie.

'Smoke cigars and drink whisky.'

Sophie had never smoked, so couldn't imagine puffing on a cigar like a rich old man, and she wasn't curious about the whisky. Too much like yucky medicine.

'I usually enjoy reading the paper after dinner, but I'm a little tired.' Anne walked to the door. 'But do stay and have coffee.'

'Thank you.'

Anne seemed on the brink of tears again. 'Goodnight.'

As Anne left, Sophie addressed the young maid waiting to pour. 'I think I'll call it a night too.'

CHAPTER 20

'I picked up more info at the cigar and whisky session,' said Hugo, as they walked to breakfast the next morning.

When he didn't elaborate, Sophie said, 'Do I get to play with the big boys tonight?'

'Women 'withdrawing' at the end of dinner is the norm. Will be for decades.' A sheepish expression showed briefly on his face. 'But the upside is, with no servants, Richard's more relaxed. He's got a problem with us finding the lift but otherwise, he's on the level.'

Sophie stopped walking. 'So, everything's fine, apart from that one, small thing.' Hugo stopped too. A maid walked past them, and Sophie lowered her voice. 'Are you going to tell me what you learned, or do I have to guess?'

'The rioting isn't just in Derby. It's happening all over the north and getting worse.'

'So?' At home, there was always trouble; here was no different.

'If this spreads to Shorten, Sophie, we'll have to choose a side.'

'What do you mean?'

'The haves or have-nots.'

He'd drunk too much whisky last night. 'Bit dramatic.'

He frowned. 'The Laceys have been very kind.'

'They have,' said Sophie, 'but if there's injustice, I'm not going to side with the richest family in the neighbourhood.'

They resumed walking and as they reached the dining room, Hugo whispered, 'Let's hope it doesn't come to that.'

Anne wasn't at breakfast and, as usual, neither was Freddy.

Since she'd arrived, Sophie had eaten generous helpings of kedgeree — that could turn into a bad, weight-gaining habit. So, she ate just toast with thick sticky marmalade.

Towards the end of the meal, Richard said to Hugo. 'Would you like to go riding this morning?'

'Absolutely.'

Richard gave Sophie a genuine smile and she smiled back. She'd follow Dr Griffiths' advice and avoid riding; despite not believing in fate, she'd never been one for tempting it.

In the corridor out of earshot of the dining room, she said to Hugo, 'Can I borrow your notes from yesterday?'

'No problem.'

'Anne was upset last night. That's why she didn't make breakfast.'

'Not necessarily,' said Hugo. 'At home, there was a convention that married women could have breakfast in bed.'

'What's that about?'

'If she's tired after a night of passion.'

'You're winding me up.'

'I'm not, scout's honour.' His face was deadpan.

'Were you a scout?'

'No.' He retrieved his notepad from his room and handed it to her, then went to change into riding gear.

'*No* idea if he's serious.' Sophie ruffled Charlotte's head. 'Let's explore.'

They wandered along a maze of hushed corridors with random pictures on the walls: a faded sepia photo of two farmhands sitting on a hay bale, another of an old woman in a frilly cap, and a framed sampler with a perfectly embroidered alphabet, together with numbers and animals, including two stylised peacocks.

A door was ajar, creaking on ancient hinges, taller than a regular door. Sophie stepped over the threshold. Books lined the walls, neatly sorted by size, the largest at the bottom. The smallest books were high up under a vaulted ceiling, their titles too far away to read. Intermingled scents, familiar from the library at school, lingered in the air: brittle paper, leather and very old ink. 'Hugo was right about their library,' she said to Charlotte. 'So many worlds within one room.'

Charlotte lay down on an oak floor, stretching contentedly in beams of sunlight streaming through an arched leaded window, and Sophie peered at a burgundy leather-bound volume with peeling gold letters on the spine. *Philosophiae Naturalis Principia Mathematica.*

She reached out to touch it but stopped. Mega-valuable and not light reading, even if she could read Latin. She stepped back and scanned the bookshelves. Once she'd copied Hugo's notes, she'd let the info simmer in her brain, but in the meantime, she'd lose herself in a novel.

Ladders attached to the bookcases were just tall enough to reach the highest shelves. Sophie stepped on a bottom rung. It seemed solid. She took a few steps up and leaned to take a slim, blue-bound volume, but the ladder glided sideways, alarmingly fast. She stopped leaning, regained her balance and coaxed out the nearest book.

Once back on solid ground, she blew off the dust, the particles dancing in the air. She gave a soft whistle. A posh edition of *Sir Gawain and the Green Knight* — the pre-reading for her degree. Crazy coincidence. She put it back and searched for something less familiar.

Cautiously ascending again, she picked out a shiny green book, imprinted with gilt lettering. *Far From The Madding Crowd.* This world wasn't quite the same as home so some classic novels could be different. But with this story she wouldn't know. She'd never read it.

She climbed down, sat in a wingback red chair and opened the book. *Volume 1.* So long, they'd split it in two. She went up the ladder for the second half.

The story drew her in until Charlotte pawed the door. Keeping the books, Sophie took Charlotte outside, then returned to the bedroom.

Putting the books aside, she examined the carpet. The stains were still there, but really faint.

The ink-stained blue dress had gone to the laundry. Hopefully, the stains would come out; all of these dresses looked expensive.

On the dressing table, Maud had left a rectangular, black box, with *EVERSHARP* printed on the top. Sophie sat at the dressing table and opened it. Inside was a gold pen and folded paper. She unfolded the pamphlet.

Not a pen. A fancy pencil.

A picture showed the different parts, labelled A through to E. An American invention, going by the word *eraser.*

She read the dense text. *To write: Propel lead from point by turning cap E to right, clockwise. To repel lead: Turn cap E to left and push lead back at Tip A. To release plunger...* she skimmed to the end. *Eraser is under cap E. To use pull cap straight off. Do not unscrew.*

She registered the familiar, heavy feeling associated with exams. Unnecessarily complicated instructions. What was wrong with a regular pencil and rubber?

But she'd already blotted her copybook — literally. She carefully read the directions again. You extended the lead with the cap at the bottom of the pencil and when it ran out, you replaced it. Four were supplied. She gently turned the cap at the bottom clockwise and the lead poked out. She made a nonsense scribble in a notebook. Success. She pulled off the cap she'd turned and there was the rubber. She wrote *Lift Puzzle* on the first page and managed to copy Hugo's notes, despite his atrocious writing, then noticed her nails. Polish was mostly gone. None of the women here painted their nails — or wore make up. Considered too racy...

Sophie returned the pencil to its box and registered a different heavy feeling. Rummaging in a zipped compartment in her bag, she found a single tampon. She was stuffed.

A light knock and the door opened. 'Miss?'

How did Maud do that? Appear on cue, when she had a problem? Unnerving. 'Have you any more of these?'

Maud squinted at the tampon. 'What is it, Miss?'

Really stuffed. 'Um, it's my time of the month...'

'It's all in here, Miss.' Maud took out a pad of material and two safety pins from the chest of drawers.

Half a lifetime ago, Sophie had used a smaller item at primary school but without safety pins.

'There's plenty, Miss.'

'Thank you. And thank you for rescuing the carpet.'

Maud smiled and bustled out.

Sophie sorted her underwear, then sat glumly back at the dressing table.

'There are many things I will never take for granted, ever, ever again,' she told Charlotte.

Sophie took the pencil and underlined, *We're all very different*. 'I can't see how the parallel universe thing helps.' She turned the page. 'But I'll have a page for each visitor.' She wrote their names at the top of each one: *Anne, Lucy, Janet, Alan, Hugo, Me.*

On the last page she wrote, *Friday, 24 July 1925* and *Day Five.* 'Better than scratching lines on a wall.' Then she shut the notebook and wrote *PRIVATE* in big letters on the cover.

Never write or post anything that could bite you in the ass. Her straight-talking history teacher, born and bred in New York, had drummed that into her. *Mary Queen of Scots, those letters sealed her fate. Don't make the same mistake.* Miss Berkowitz's unflinching account of Mary's botched beheading, along with others betrayed by nonsense spell books and burned alive at the stake, had given Sophie nightmares. So, she'd taken on board the need for caution; yes, Charlotte's pictures were in a cloud, but only shared with Aunty Wendy and Isha.

Sophie went over to the wardrobe and, standing on tiptoe, put the notebook flat on the top. Good, invisible. She'd keep it there overnight.

She took down the notebook and put it with the pencil in her roomy dress pocket. 'If inspiration strikes, I can instantly record it.'

Charlotte ignored her and pawed the door again.

'I know, another sunny day. We should go to the terrace.'

She picked up *Volume 1*, went outside, and sat in the shade of the umbrella. But she'd barely read a page before Anne came out and joined her.

Sophie closed the book. 'I'm sorry if what we said last night was rude or presumptuous. We didn't mean to be.'

'It brought up matters that Richard and I decided long ago not to speak about, but we have formally told the servants about your many universes theory.'

Charlotte made a sympathetic snorting noise and Anne stroked her but then looked straight at Sophie. 'We need to talk.'

CHAPTER 21

'When I came through the lift,' said Anne, 'no one except Richard believed I'd come from the future. The servants thought I was barking mad. At their best, they humoured me. His mother asked whether I was part of a particular Scottish clan. I wasn't, of course. There are a lot of Camerons. She wanted her eldest son to marry someone from a respected local family. I was *not* what she had in mind.'

'What did Richard's father think?' Sophie was playing along but baffled as to why Anne was sharing this.

'He'd died, years before I arrived. Richard and his mother argued about how to run the estate, and he'd usually let her have her way, but he refused to compromise about me. When we finally married, I was able to think about the future, plan for the family and Shorten.'

'The servants must have realised you weren't mad when Alan and Lucy came through?'

'Some were less sceptical, and Mr Eddington and his team generated a great deal of interest and speculation. But when I was wrong about the Titanic, I started to question my sanity. The whole household was geared up to deal with the Great War and when it didn't happen, I was a laughing stock. I lost their respect.'

She'd got this wrong. The servants were borderline obsequious. 'Honestly, Anne, as an outsider, I can only tell you that this household respects you, loves you.'

'Richard does. He loved me even when he thought I might be mad.' Anne gazed out at the gardens. 'The passage of time has helped. Most of the servants weren't born when we married.' Anne gave Sophie a tired smile. 'Mr Crawford was a young footman.'

'Sorry, who?'

'The butler. I think he practises his poker face in the mirror every morning.'

Anne had taken them in, fed and clothed them, and now was baring her soul. What did she want in return? Sophie said, quietly, 'Couldn't you have sacked them and hired new ones?'

'In theory, but Richard's mother was in charge and fond of the senior servants. Anyway, she shared their opinion.'

'I can't believe you've lived with this, all these years.'

'It is a dreadful thing to say,' said Anne, 'but it improved once Richard's mother passed away. Without her pointed remarks, the atmosphere did change. Or the servants confined their smirking to downstairs.'

'Downstairs?'

'Their rooms and the servants' hall.'

'When the war didn't happen,' said Sophie, 'Lucy's reputation must have been trashed too.'

'She'd made changes, anticipating a shortage of gardeners, but I was responsible for the whole household.'

No wonder Anne had been so pleased to see them. She'd

been lonely, even with Richard and Freddy, and living with secretly sneering servants 24/7 would have sent anyone crackers. Richard's request not to blab made sense now; Anne wanted to control the narrative, squash ill-informed gossip. And another penny dropped. 'You waited to have Freddy because you thought he'd die in the war.'

'Yes.' Anne's voice faltered. 'For Richard's mother, that was the last straw. She was convinced I was insane when she died.'

For a moment, Sophie was lost for words. Anne did want something, but it wasn't onerous or sinister. She wanted friendship. 'But you'd sack anyone now who thinks you're mad?'

'If Mr Crawford found anyone speaking disrespectfully, he'd dismiss them, but there are still whispers and innuendoes.' Anne looked Sophie in the eye. 'When you arrived, I should have told you about the Great War ... everything. But I couldn't face dredging it all up again.'

'Anne, I completely understand.'

'And I knew how you were both feeling, thought you had enough to cope with.'

'You said you didn't want to go home—'

'That's true, but at the beginning it was a case of getting through each day. Richard always supported me. My lowest point was years later when I was having Freddy. I had chloroform, but if anything had gone seriously wrong ... of course, by then I was in no state to find the lift, even if I could have persuaded Richard to have me driven there.'

Anne Cameron still missed home. Just as Sophie Arundel would, if she couldn't reopen the portal.

'But it turned out all right.' Anne was smiling — a contented smile — directed beyond Sophie towards the garden.

Freddy and Hugo were walking across the lawn with Jack. When they reached the terrace, Jack raced off with Charlotte, Hugo and Freddy flopped into nearby chairs and Freddy beamed at Sophie.

Sophie beamed back. She and Hugo owed a lot to Anne's fortitude. All the visitors did. She'd be Anne's ally *and* lady-like *and* figure out the lift. She was a girl; she could do three impossible things. All at the same time.

After lunch, Sophie took Charlotte for a walk and Hugo came with her.

'Freddy gave me this.' He took a ball from his pocket and threw it high. Charlotte saw it and scampered in the opposite direction.

'Charlotte doesn't catch balls,' said Sophie, hurrying to pick it up. 'She doesn't get it or thinks it's silly. Not sure which.'

'How odd,' said Hugo, 'George will run after balls for hours.'

'I think it's the poodle part of her.' She gave him back the ball. 'Is Freddy in the office?'

'No, walking the estate boundary. Reluctantly. He'd much rather be working on a maths problem.'

'Freddy doesn't want to take over ... in due course?'

'He does. Just thinks there's no harm in putting off the hard work part.'

'Understandable,' said Sophie. 'He's very laid-back.'

'About some things.'

'You spend a lot of time with him.'

'He's good company.' They'd reached the bower. 'Shall we sit for a minute?'

The flower scents were intoxicating, and the dell was

hushed, slumbering in the heat. Charlotte ran in and lay panting in the shade of a crab apple tree that was thick with pale pink blossom.

'I'll stop walking her if it gets much hotter.' Sophie reached down and gave Charlotte a reassuring pat.

'I had a long talk with Richard on our ride,' said Hugo. 'When the Great War didn't happen … Anne must be a strong person to have survived that, psychologically I mean.'

'Without Richard's support, she might not have done.'

'It's strange. Everyone spends their childhood learning, planning careers. But if you get the most important relationship right, everything else is detail.'

Depressing thought. 'Don't half of marriages end in divorce?'

'That means fifty per cent succeed. Anyway, I'm not sure what the real failure rate is.' He gave her his lop-sided smile.

Sophie's heart flipped. Okay, not indigestion. She fancied him. Isha would die laughing. Actually, wouldn't believe it. Less likely than if she'd come out and dated Madison, Hugo's bitchy pal at school. She pretended to examine an impressive column of pink hollyhock flowers near her seat. Focus on practical matters. 'Let's quiz this Alan bloke.'

'According to Freddy, the pub's only two miles away.'

'Not keen on walking.'

'Reynolds is taking us this afternoon. I asked Richard last night.'

'Surprising.'

'He doesn't think Alan will be any help,' said Hugo, 'and there was an assault near the pub last week.'

'The same men?' The heavy hand on her mouth and Beard Man's hard face was a too-clear memory.

'Richard didn't go into detail.' Hugo avoided her eyes. 'But the upshot is, he's not keen on Freddy — or us — walking.'

'I'll go with that.'

He rested his head against the back of the stone seat. 'We were bloody lucky to get taken in.'

'So why do I feel…'

'Trapped?' Bitter recognition showed in his face.

'And bored, like I'm wasting my life.'

'Missing friends and entertainment on tap?'

'Yes, but mostly trapped.'

He traced his finger over the sundial. 'I keep telling myself this is a unique opportunity to experience history. Well, a different history.'

'I love their library and being able to do nothing except read should be wonderful, but *forever*? It sucks.'

'My leisurely days are at an end.'

'What do you mean?'

'Richard wants me to learn about the estate, with a view to becoming manager, though that would be years down the line. My family have a farming background. I could make a good fist of it.'

'I didn't make the shortlist?'

He frowned. 'Female estate managers have yet to catch on.'

'You don't seem exactly thrilled.'

'Learning about the estate feels like a big step, like I've given up.'

'*Not* giving up,' said Sophie. 'This is your fallback plan.'

He shot her a resigned smile.

'If we are stuck here, I could be a teacher.' Victorian novels might feature doughty governesses and mysterious, handsome fathers but the reality would be far worse. And she was no Jane Eyre, dignified in the face of adversity. Sophie Arundel would swear or hit someone. 'In a village school—'

'Fulfilling, but hard.'

'Sorry?'

'Poor,' said Hugo, his eyes on the sundial again. 'If this is the same as home, salaries for schoolmarms were a pittance.'

Okay, independence in poverty didn't appeal.

'I know you're not keen, but you'd be better off marrying.'

'I'd be completely dependent on my husband.'

'You might find someone decent. My only option is helping out here.'

Most people at school had planned to work in London. She gave him a mischievous grin. 'You could send out a clever CV, land a lucrative job in the city.'

'*No family, no education or skills acquired in this universe …* they'll not exactly be beating a path to Derbyshire. But on the upside, I get time off to practise cricket.'

'Why?'

'For the Manor versus the Village match on 6th August. The Manor's lost the previous two, so honour's at stake.'

Sophie chewed her lip. 'You could have come here to play cricket, on a proper pitch?'

'A reason to cross universes? A bit extreme.'

'You do love cricket.'

'Even so.'

Charlotte launched herself at Sophie's knees and Sophie gently pushed her down.

'Why does she try to sit on you when she's obviously too big?'

'She used to sleep on my lap when she was a puppy, so in her mind she's toy dog size. It's teenage body image distortion syndrome but in reverse. On a sofa, she can still half lie on me.'

Hugo brushed his fringe from his forehead, though it wasn't long enough to cover his eyes. 'She's a lovely dog.'

'She acted up at Uni. That day was stressful before we stepped into the lift.' Sophie patted Charlotte's head, conscious of a growing desperation. 'If we are stuck here, I don't know how long I can carry on … pretending.'

'Pretending?'

'You know, acting demure, not doing regular girly things.'

'Like?'

'Running, kickboxing, throwing the javelin…'

'Snogging in country lanes.'

'Or that.' She traced her finger along the edge of the sundial. 'I'm really missing kickboxing but I was a bit obsessive.'

'My father thinks I have the opposite problem,' said Hugo. 'That I get bored too quickly, so I'm always searching for the next challenge.'

A lifetime in estate management would be tough. And with a low boredom threshold, any future wife had better watch out.

He checked his watch and stood up. 'I start properly on Monday, wading through a paperwork mountain, but I've got a briefing at three.'

Sophie put on her sympathy face but felt excluded, and so bored that filing seemed attractive.

'We're meeting Reynolds on the driveway at six.'

Hugo strode to the house and Sophie strode too, feeling stupid in her pantomime dress and curvy straw hat.

Back in her room, she put the hat on the blue chair, and lay down to think about the lift puzzle.

She woke to find Maud pointedly removing the formal, red gown from the wardrobe to remove imaginary fluff. 'It's nearly six, Miss. Enough time to change. And this is still a tea dress.'

This was code for *no corset required.*

'You can wear it to dinner because this counts as your home, when we haven't got guests.' Maud adjusted the dress on the hanger.

'But aren't we guests? Me and Hu— Mr Harrington?'

'Not really, Miss, local families sometimes stay.' Maud hung the dress on the wardrobe door.

Ridiculously grand, but more to the point, dressing up for dinner would mean dressing up every night — forever.

'Lord Lacey says you're from a different universe, Miss.'

'That's our best guess.'

'I couldn't understand it.'

What had Hugo said? 'It involves string.'

'String?'

'I don't think it's real string.' Go for the basic summary. 'My England's pretty much the same but on a different planet.'

Maud nodded vaguely.

Sophie didn't need to be telepathic to guess what Maud was thinking. *From a different planet. Explains a lot.* She attached the lead to Charlotte's collar. 'I'll be back before dinner.' Sophie picked up her hat and stepped towards the door.

'She does love her walks, Miss.'

'And she'll love the pub. She's a sucker for new people.'

Maud's intake of breath made Sophie turn around.

'Ladies don't go to pubs, Miss.'

'Why on earth not?'

'It's not respectable,' said Maud, as if it was obvious.

'It's a rough pub?'

'Like every pub, Miss, with fights and all sorts. Only last week, Mr Parkes had to break one up.'

Right, a rough pub. 'I'm going with Mr Harrington and Master Freddy. I'll be fine.'

Maud gave her the curt smile that meant resigned disapproval. 'You should wear a proper hat, Miss.' She fixed the hat with the flowers on Sophie's head.

It was crazy big. But she needed to learn about this

etiquette stuff — to seduce a gullible, kind person into marriage. If necessary. Eventually. Was this the moment to give a little? It wasn't as though the scarlet gown involved a corset and a long train like Anne's, and it would look incredible. 'Could you help me with the red dress tonight?'

Maud allowed herself a triumphant smirk.

CHAPTER 22

'I could have driven us,' said Freddy, as Reynolds parked the splendid olive-green car carefully beside the village green. The journey along a deserted road had taken less than five minutes.

Sophie leaned forward to Freddy in the front passenger seat. 'When did you pass your test?'

'Test? I haven't done a test. Reynolds showed me the basics. It's really easy.'

Reynolds was staring straight ahead, a muscle flexing in his jaw with the effort of holding his tongue.

Mental note: don't get into any vehicle with Freddy at the wheel.

Despite the sultry temperature, Freddy hadn't removed his jacket. Hugo hadn't either. Male Shorten Casual was strictly confined to the Manor.

'I'd really like to drive this,' said Hugo.

Freddy opened his door. 'It's wizard fun.'

After Sophie climbed out with Charlotte, Hugo went and stood outside the driver's cab, talking to Reynolds about how the car started. This took so long they didn't get to discuss the braking system.

Mental note: ditto with Hugo.

Sophie glanced over the driver's door at the dashboard. A shiny wood veneer was crowded with round dials and raised knobs, like the cockpit of an old-fashioned plane. In the seat well were two pedals and long, unfamiliar levers rising out of the floor. If — no, *when* the lift appeared — she'd need to get there fast. If only arriving visitors saw it, the lift didn't stick around for long.

Stealing this would require written instructions. With diagrams. She turned her best doe eyes on Freddy. 'Could you teach me to drive?'

Freddy's smile was indulgent. 'With Reynolds here, you don't need to.'

Reynolds met Freddy's eyes, male superiority bridging social status as easily as logic. Hugo's expression was suspiciously bland.

Sophie wanted to swear but held her tongue and turned towards the green. The open space was ringed with pretty cottages. Women in long shapeless dresses and bonnets were chatting in doorways and by a shabby timbered building, tough men in loose trousers and jackets were unloading barrels from a cart.

Hugo scanned the village. 'No war memorial,' he said, half to himself.

The villagers were acknowledging Freddy but gawping at her and Hugo, and at Charlotte, who was exploring the green on her extendable lead.

'Do you have problems with your eyes?' asked Freddy, addressing Hugo.

'Sorry?'

'The glasses,' said Freddy.

Hugo was wearing his shades. 'No. Eyes are fine. They help you see better when the sun's bright.'

'Can I try them on?' asked Freddy.

Hugo handed them over.

'These are excellent, just excellent. You're right, it is easier to see everything.' Freddy reluctantly returned the glasses. 'Let's go to the church. You can see for miles from there.'

They walked up a steep path towards a picturesque chapel.

'How was the work briefing?' Sophie asked Hugo.

'Daunting. A lot to learn.'

She stifled a nagging, bitter feeling. Job envy…

As the ground levelled out, she stopped to admire the view. Stretching into the distance was a valley with neat green fields.

'The church is fourteenth century.' A warm breeze ruffled Freddy's sandy hair and he brushed it from his eyes. 'We come here at Christmas and Easter. The chapel on the estate is too small.'

'Sophie, you need to see this.' Hugo was standing at the side of the church, examining a stained-glass window.

Hearing an urgent note in his voice, she hurried towards him.

Above the window, partly concealed by a buttress, was a carving of two young faces staring in opposite directions, the back of their heads touching. Her breath came out in a whoosh. 'Identical to the university chapel.'

Hugo gestured. 'Is this the same window? A man on a horse?'

'I don't know.' She hadn't noticed the stained-glass design.

He gave a low whistle. 'So unusual, it must be the same building.'

'It can't be. We're miles from the lift spot and the Uni chapel was only a stone's throw from the lift.'

Freddy was beside them. 'That carving looks like the symbol of Janus.'

'The Roman god of doorways and thresholds.' Hugo reached out and touched it. 'Hell of a coincidence.'

Now Sophie held her breath. A god of doorways … and maybe portals?

Charlotte was circling and sniffing. Sophie knew the signs, and a few moments later said to no one in particular, 'I'll bury it.'

'You don't need to, it's off the path,' said Freddy. 'We have a boy who picks up after Jack and the hounds. He should take on Charlotte.'

'You *employ* him to do that?' Sophie couldn't keep disbelief out of her voice.

Hugo shot her an ironic smile. 'We're not in Kansas anymore.'

'Kansas?' asked Freddy.

'A reference to an old film,' said Sophie, not up for explaining the entire plot of *The Wizard of Oz*.

'I see,' said Freddy, politely. 'The boy's only twelve but does a good job.'

'Shouldn't he be at school?'

'He's simple. School wouldn't do him any good.'

Now Hugo had his, 'I'm not going to be fazed' expression, last seen when she'd told him about the lift pictures.

They walked down to the village and Sophie sat on a bench by the green, with Charlotte at her feet. Skinny children were playing with a big wooden hoop, rolling it along the grass. The boys wore scruffy shorts and shirts, the girls calf-length dresses with heavily darned, white pinafores. 'Freddy, what's this village called?'

'Little Shorten.'

The picture in the students' union ... the feeling she was being watched. Had someone known she'd come here? Had *she* somehow known? She breathed in clean country air. No. That was bonkers.

'There's the school,' said Freddy, pointing at a village hall.

Her teaching idea was a non-starter. She'd be rubbish at it anyway.

'And that's the pub.' Freddy gestured across the green. 'Used to be a travellers' inn.'

Half-timbered with square leaded windows, the building's upstairs floor jutted out at the front, like a half-opened drawer.

'I've heard all Mr Parkes' funny stories.' Freddy turned to Sophie. 'I'll wait with you.'

He assumed she wasn't going in. Freddy had the same views about pubs as Maud.

Sophie shook her head. 'I need to ask about the lift.'

Freddy glanced at Hugo, as if for confirmation.

'We'll be at least half an hour,' said Hugo. 'If you go back, you could finish that bookkeeping.'

'Are you sure?' Freddy was addressing Hugo but looking at her.

'We'll be fine,' said Hugo.

Freddy gave Hugo a coin. 'You might be from the same universe, but Mr Parkes doesn't do free drinks.'

Hugo turned the coin over. 'What is it?'

'A shilling,' said Freddy. 'Reynolds can pick you up in, say, forty minutes.' He turned back to the car.

'Don't make a scene,' whispered Hugo.

'I wasn't going to.' She was just surprised. But given Maud's attitude, she shouldn't have been.

Hugo took off his shades. 'Come on.'

Creaking in the breeze was a battered sign. In faded black letters, above a picture of a farm door, was the pub's name: *The Crooked Gate.*

Near the sign, a man and woman were talking in low voices. The man had a rough beard and flinty eyes, and an instinctive alarm went off in Sophie's brain.

The couple were eyeing Charlotte, their body language wary, though Charlotte was wagging her tail. Sophie shortened her lead.

'We're looking for work.' The man's tone was half defiant, half apologetic.

'No harm in asking at the pub,' said Hugo, affably, pocketing his sunglasses. He gestured for the couple to go in first.

The man's thin coat was too big for him and swayed as he walked, and the hems of his trousers were ragged. His companion followed him wearily across the threshold. Her wrist-length gloves were torn and she was carrying a threadbare shawl. Patches of material on the bodice of her dress were also threadbare, showing part of a grubby corset.

Sophie looked away, ashamed; the assault in the lane had blunted her natural empathy.

The dim interior of the pub was a sharp contrast to the bright day outside and it took a moment for Sophie's eyes to adjust.

Beyond the shabbily-dressed couple and Hugo near the bar, the only other person in the pub was a skinny man in gardener's clothes, sitting by a window smoking and drinking beer; the place stank of both.

Okay, not a gastro pub. She shivered. Cold as well as dark.

Hugo addressed the drinker. 'Is the landlord around?'

'Should be. E's not the sort to be rushed.'

Might be why the place was full to bursting. Actually,

there could be another reason. The boys' scruffy shorts, the girls' darned pinafores … nobody in Little Shorten had any money. Not for clothes or beer.

Sophie smiled at the woman. 'I'm Soph … um Miss Arundel, by the way.'

'Mrs Fletcher. How do you do?' Her thin face was sallow, save for marked shadows under her eyes.

They shook hands.

As Hugo introduced himself to Mr Fletcher, a man walked through a door behind the bar. Fifty or older, he was thick set, balding and unshaven, the sort of unshaven that made no effort to be cultivated stubble. It jarred with his smart dark shirt and navy tie. He scowled at Sophie, then Hugo. 'Wondered when you'd show up.'

'You're Alan?' asked Hugo.

'That's right.'

Charlotte stiffened and growled.

Alan's scowl deepened. 'Keep that dog under control.'

Sophie made Charlotte sit, pushing her down. Not worth asking for a water bowl.

Alan shifted his scowl to the Fletchers. 'Who are you?' His pronounced northern accent made the words sound overly blunt. 'We don't often get women in here.'

Mr Fletcher took his wife's arm, then addressed Alan. 'Do you need any help? We used to run a pub in Derby.'

Alan looked them over. 'I won't have riffraff in here. *Out.*'

Sophie's jaw dropped and she turned her back on the bar. 'There might be work on the estate. A car's coming to pick us up. We'll take you to the Manor.'

'Absolutely, no problem.' Hugo's face reflected Sophie's feelings — embarrassed and angry.

Mr Fletcher stood straighter. 'I appreciate the offer, but we'll make our own way. Come on, my dear. Just a couple of miles.'

Sophie stepped towards them. 'But the roads aren't safe.'

Mrs Fletcher's face hardened. 'Nowhere is.' She gave Alan a defiant stare, turned on her heel and left with her husband.

Sophie gave Charlotte's lead to Hugo and darted after them.

Outside, she shielded her eyes from the sun with her hand. 'I think the barman's just odd.'

Mrs Fletcher regarded her curiously. 'Rude, but not odd, we get that reaction in most places.'

'You won't at the Manor.' Sophie mentally crossed her fingers. She had no idea how they'd be treated. 'Visitors' were a special case… She'd ask Anne to talk to the butler. He was in charge of booze, might appreciate skilled help.

Mr and Mrs Fletcher walked off and Sophie returned to the bar.

Hugo was sitting on a stool and she sat on one beside him.

'Beer?' asked Alan.

'Two half pints would be good.' Hugo's tone was studiedly neutral. He gave Sophie Charlotte's lead.

'You were students at home.' Alan made it sound like a crime.

'Yes.' Sophie couldn't keep a hard edge from her voice.

'Enjoying yourselves at the Manor?'

Alan made it sound like Sex Party HQ, but she said, 'Everyone's been very kind. When you arrived, did you live there?'

'I did and, yes, they were kind, given they didn't know me from Adam.' Alan took two glasses from a rack behind the bar and carefully examined them before putting one under a beer tap and pulling down a brass handle. 'I told the Laceys, I didn't like people lording it, thinking they're better than everyone else.' He put a beer on the bar. 'They took it too personal.'

His view of the Laceys was understandable but the way he'd treated the Fletchers ... worse than 'lording it.' She wanted to call him out but followed Hugo's lead, controlled her temper, and said, 'The Manor is intimidating.'

Alan pulled the tap handle, pouring another beer. 'I only needed to stay a few days, get on my feet. I moved here, worked as a barman and when the landlord left, I took over.'

'You enjoy it?' said Hugo.

'I do, but it's hard work.' Alan put the second beer on the bar. 'Not that you'd understand.' He didn't seem to be joking.

Hugo didn't reply.

This man didn't know them, had no idea of their background. Hugo spoke posh, but his reputation at school had been for awesome general knowledge, not laziness.

'You don't get on with the Laceys?' Hugo's tone was carefully polite.

'We get along well enough.'

Charlotte was staring meaningfully at her mistress, wanting to leave. Sophie patted her, silently conveying that they wouldn't stay long. 'I presume you came through the same way we did, the students' union lift?'

'I did.'

'There's only six of us,' said Hugo. 'We might be able to reopen the portal, if we can work out what makes us unusual. Do you mind if we make notes?'

Alan turned his back, taking another glass from the rack and fishing out a grey cloth from a drawer.

Hugo took out his pad and pen, taking Alan's silence for agreement. 'You were a student?'

Alan turned to face them. 'No, full-time barman.'

Sophie fished out her notebook and pencil. 'The big house on the lift doors might depict Shorten Manor.'

'I hope not,' said Alan. 'It was on fire.'

'Wasn't that a much smaller house,' said Sophie, 'a different sketch?'

'No.' Alan frowned. 'The other picture was a road or river that forked. Nonsense modern art.'

This wasn't clear cut. She wrote on Alan's page, *Big house on fire and forked road. More than one lift.* But then added, *Or do the doors change?*

CHAPTER 23

Sophie took a cautious sip of beer. It was warm and weak and tasted of soap.

Hugo was scribbling on his pad. 'Alan, at home, did you ever wish you could travel in time?'

'No.'

Scratch that idea. Nil out of six.

'Five pence,' said Alan, 'old money.'

Hugo handed over the shilling and, as Alan reached into a drawer for change, Hugo said, 'When did you get in the lift?'

Alan hesitated. '1994, autumn … October.'

Sophie wrote that down.

'Did you ever try to get home?' asked Hugo, pocketing his change without checking it and writing on his pad.

Alan wiped the bar with the cloth. 'Not long after I arrived, I cycled there. No trace of it. Like I'd dreamt it.'

Hugo looked tiredly at his drink, defeated.

'Only went out of curiosity.' Alan poured himself a beer. 'Why would I have gone back to that dump? Stupid kids getting drunk, expecting me to clean up after them. I'd had enough after a term. Been planning to get myself a nice little country pub. When that lift opened, I thought I'd had a heart attack and died.'

Hugo caught her eye.

Whatever his grumbles, this was Alan's dream job. Like Lucy. 'We've heard the story of the green-eyed barmaid and the fairies.' Sophie made her comment light-hearted, hoping Alan would warm to them.

Alan settled himself on a stool and took a sip of beer. 'I reckon the poor lass was murdered. Her killer invented the dancing fairies to cover his tracks and gullible people bought it.'

Freddy had mentioned Alan's stories. This one wasn't funny.

'I'll give you some advice,' said Alan. 'People here don't like change or newcomers. You'll never fit in at the big house. You'd be better off leaving, making your own life. The servants never took to Anne, still talk behind her back.'

Sophie sipped her beer, Alan's words resonating. If Anne had never been accepted, what chance did Sophie Arundel have?

'Anne's full of airs and graces, but she's no better than she should be.' Alan leaned forward, as if sharing a confidence. 'By all accounts, she set out to seduce Richard Lacey. Under all those fine clothes, she's just a harlot.'

Sophie registered Hugo's intake of breath and put her glass aside. Anne had shown them nothing but kindness, hadn't been snobby or patronising. And *harlot*. Perhaps in every universe there were such words: slut, tramp, whore ... and the rarer male equivalents — playboy, playing the field — weren't equivalents at all, barely insults. She gazed into her beer. In a different universe, during the Christmas holidays, she'd slept with the hottest boy in the school. So, by Alan's yardstick, she was a harlot. Good-time girls should stick together. She stood up. 'Anne's done good and I will too. After I marry Freddy, I'll bear in mind what you've said, decide which servants should stay on.' The shock on Alan's face was gratifying. 'Are you coming, Hugo?'

Hugo hastily put down his glass and beer splashed on the bar. The skinny man was staring, and his startled expression followed them to the door.

Outside, they stepped into a wall of humid heat. There was no sign of the Fletchers. 'That told him.' She let out Charlotte's lead.

'Have you learned *nothing* from the picnic? Within hours your crass boast will be all over the village. Freddy will be mortified.'

'It was only a joke.' Maybe it had been a stupid thing to say, but Alan's jibe about Anne had hit a nerve.

Hugo hauled off his jacket, exasperated. 'Would you marry Freddy, if he asked?'

She rolled her eyes. 'I only met him four days ago.' She fished out a linen handkerchief from her skirt pocket and wiped her temple. 'So ... *no.*'

'You need to be really careful how you tell him about this.'

'Alan insulted his mother. He'll understand.'

'That's not the problem.' Hugo hesitated. 'Freddy really fancies you.'

'No.'

'I can't believe you haven't noticed.'

Freddy acted interested when she talked, but she'd put that down to good manners, gallantry — how a posh boy would behave in 1925. 'I like Freddy and don't want to hurt him, but...'

'But what?'

'If we are stuck here for years, I'm not closing any doors.' She set her mouth. 'Even if that means behaving like a harlot.'

Hugo sighed. 'Reynolds won't be long.' He dropped his jacket on the grass and sat under an elder tree by the pub sign, and Sophie flopped beside him with Charlotte, who was panting, already too hot.

'In the meantime,' said Hugo, evenly, 'you need to act smarter.'

Like a broken record. 'I'll bear that in mind, Mr Perfect.'

'You weren't like this at school.'

'Like what?'

'Such a rebel.'

At Hadley she had kept her head down. Never smoked dope or fallen off the roof on a cider binge. The dope and cider kids had wealthy parents, had all got into other schools. Eventually. Expulsion for her would have been a disaster. Fully funded scholarships to private schools were as rare as second chances, and the state school near Aunty Wendy was in 'special measures,' which was official speak for crap. 'I snuck out with Isha to a club on the Paris trip and before that I tried to buy wine once. Okay … pathetic. But the rules were the same for everyone. I read a whole book of them on the first day.' She glared. 'Here the rules are invisible and mad.'

'You read *all* the school rules… Why?'

'So, I didn't mess up. Obviously.'

'You didn't already know not to do drugs, alcohol or have sex on the premises?'

'I was eleven. Trying to suss stuff out.'

Hugo shook his head, as if what she'd said was nonsensical.

He hadn't needed to read the rules because the school was a clone of his previous one.

Sweat was trickling between her breasts under the cotton bodice and, though her hat provided shade, the prickly straw only made her feel hotter. Oh, to slob with full-on air-conditioning. 'We need to focus on the lift puzzle.'

'The lift puzzle… Agreed.' He exhaled. 'I hope I'm wrong

but being an estate manager isn't my dream job, so that idea's pants.'

'What did you want to do?'

'Hadn't decided.'

'Me neither.' Sophie waved her hand in front of her face as an improvised fan.

'The churches aren't the same building, but the Janus symbol might be a clue that the scientists didn't pick up?'

'The pub name — *The Crooked Gate* — could be a coincidence, but what if the barmaid wasn't murdered? There could be another portal here?'

'So why didn't we step out into the pub?' He loosened his tie. 'We've marked the spot in the lane. We should focus on that.'

Hugo was never defeated for long. If your family was rich and successful, confidence was part of the inheritance package. She fanned her face again. 'If there was a portal at the pub, it could have malfunctioned. Or got blocked or buried.'

'Like in *Stargate?*'

'Whatever's happened, the portal on this side came out the nearest place it could, in the lane, where the universe has another weak spot or tear?'

'You said you didn't finish Hawking's book.'

'I didn't,' said Sophie. 'It's sci-fi stuff.'

'If portals are rare, tears or weak spots are too. The odds of one being twenty miles away are crazy.'

She was melting in this stupid humidity now, struggling to think.

'But not impossible.' He stood slowly and looked back at the green and the church. 'The physical location of the portal may change, but parallel universes are supposed to occupy the same space.'

Same space. She got to her feet, remembering the church on campus shimmering and the rush of different, fresher air.

The same geography, but here a previous portal: the Uni chapel in place of the church on the hill, boxy buildings filling the green and the lift in the same location as the pub. 'Hugo, if we're standing on campus, that *is* the same church.' Students could be right beside her or passing *through* her. Don't think about it.

'The students' union must have been built over *The Crooked Gate*. It fits.' He grinned. 'We're getting somewhere.'

'But villages were destroyed to make way for airports, not universities.'

'Yes, that doesn't make sense.' He wiped his damp forehead with his hand. 'But the Janus symbol does. Scary gargoyles were put on churches as a reminder that sinners go to hell, but also to ward off evil spirits. The carving's old. Could have been put there to warn the locals about the portal.'

Sophie peered down the road. The green car was a dot in the distance, coming towards them. Charlotte got to her feet.

'The sculptor could have come through himself?' Hugo picked up his jacket from the grass.

'It might have been a *she* who carved it. This way to find a better life in the future — not a warning but an exit sign.'

Hugo's mouth twisted in what could have been a smile. 'We should ask Anne if the Janus symbol's a local tradition or a one-off and, for Richard's benefit, play down its significance.'

'Oh, we definitely need to play it down.' Sophie waved at Reynolds as the car drew nearer. 'If the gargoyle is a warning or a signpost, that means the portal *can* be opened from this side.'

CHAPTER 24

Back in the bedroom at the Manor, Maud removed Sophie's hat.

'The pub was rough.' Sophie ruffled Charlotte's head.

Smoothing her features to avoid looking smug, Maud returned the hat to the wardrobe and put the hat pins carefully in a drawer.

Half an hour later, despite a cool bath, Sophie regretted agreeing to wear the scarlet dress. The material was heavy — and hot. But the bodice wasn't too fitted, and the skirt swayed with an expensive *swish*.

Charlotte gave a short bark, which could mean approval.

Maud was holding silk stockings.

No. That would be too much. 'At home, when it's this hot, bare legs are fine.'

Maud frowned.

This type of frown would be followed by Maud's Determined face. After that it was her Game-On face and finally Open Hostilities. At that level of escalation, there could only be one outcome: surrender, humiliation and stocking torture. Stall her. 'At home, a princess called Diana went to

Ascot and wore no stockings. From that moment, bare legs became socially acceptable, although ordinary people had been doing it for years.'

'Did you know the princess, Miss?'

'She died in a car accident before I was born.' Maud's view of her social status was way out.

'That's awful, Miss.' Maud was still holding the stockings. 'Have you been to, um, Ascot?'

'No.' Horse racing was cruel; she'd have turned down an invite to the Royal Enclosure even if it had been personally signed by the Queen. 'But some girls at my school went last year.'

Maud grudgingly folded the stockings and put them away.

'What time is it?'

'Nearly eight, Miss.'

Sophie knocked on Hugo's door and Charlotte — connecting calling for Hugo with mealtimes — stared ahead, willing the door to open.

Hugo came out, dressed in his black tie. 'That's a nice dress. I heard you were wearing it.'

'What?'

'Maud mentioned it to John when we were in Little Shorten.'

Given Anne's servant nightmare, she wouldn't confront Maud about her loose tongue. If they really fell out, Sophie Arundel's name would be mud downstairs.

Hugo adjusted his bow tie as he walked. 'If we ever do get home, you should ask Anne if you could take that dress with you.'

'When would I be able to wear it?'

'A diplomatic bash or charity ball, or to dinner parties.'

She was getting to know him now ... he wasn't taking the mick. Not in a nasty way. She was Scholarship Girl, so he believed if they ever got home, she'd be successful. That thought, and his voice and sense of humour, were giving her a new, fuzzy feeling, or it could be the first sign of heatstroke. 'If we *are* stuck here, dressing for dinner every night, I'll be exhausted. Anne and Richard never seem to relax—'

'Sit on the sofa and watch TV ... well they can't, can they? I think it's a frame of mind. Richard relaxes when he's out riding.' Hugo adjusted his bow tie again.

'Your tie's fine.'

'I wore pre-tied ones at home. These are much trickier.'

Unnecessarily checking his clothing was a tell-tale sign that he was nervous or worried. Like when he put his hand through his hair.

'When you tell Freddy about the pub,' said Hugo, 'get in early it was a joke.'

'Oh, okay.'

The Laceys were already in the anteroom enjoying pre-dinner drinks. Anne was wearing a flattering midnight-blue gown; the colour suited her pale complexion and dark hair.

But Freddy was watching Sophie Arundel. 'You look smashing.'

She smiled automatically. 'Freddy, I need to tell you something.' He immediately sauntered over. 'I've done something stupid.'

Freddy made a mock, unbelieving face.

She told him what Alan had said and how she'd said the stupid thing. Freddy hooted with laughter, so loudly that Anne and Richard turned around. Hugo turned too, his face carefully blank.

'I thought you didn't want to marry,' said Freddy, still laughing.

'I shouldn't have taken your name in vain,' said Sophie. 'It was only a joke.'

'You didn't mean it?' Freddy glanced beyond her to Hugo and his parents.

'Of course not. I just wanted to take the wind out of his sails. I hope it doesn't embarrass you or your parents.'

'I won't tell Mummy what he said.' Freddy's eyes were serious now. 'So, where you're from, ladies do the proposing?'

She guessed that sometimes they did. It wasn't something she'd thought about. But she didn't like where this was going. 'Always boys.'

'At home, it's still the done thing to ask a girl's father first.' Hugo was beside them, his voice loud enough to carry to Anne and Richard.

'Thanks for being so nice about this,' said Sophie to Freddy.

Freddy smiled, though his eyes were on Hugo. He had his father's eyes.

'What's this about?' asked Anne.

'I've messed up,' said Sophie. 'I'll tell you about it after dinner.'

'All right,' said Anne, her eyes shifting back to Freddy.

Sophie told Anne about the Fletchers. Hopefully, the couple had arrived safely at the Manor and were still here. 'I didn't make any promises, obviously.'

'Mr Fletcher might be useful to Mr Crawford.' Anne went over to the butler, who was standing to attention beside the dining room's open double doors, and she briefly spoke with him. He nodded and left through a side door.

Ten minutes later, when Sophie and Hugo filed into the dining room with the family, Mr Crawford was in his usual place by the sideboard, directing the footmen.

Dinner that evening reflected the weather.

'Gazpacho,' Anne pronounced slowly when the first

course was served. 'I think it's Spanish. It only works if you have reliable iceboxes. Lukewarm, it's horrid.'

The tomato consommé had subtle flavours, onions and peppers, and tasted complicated, like soup rarely did from cans or cartons made by robots.

'Did you have any career planned after university?' Hugo was asking Anne.

'My degree was in psychology, but I had no fixed ideas.'

Four big holes in their Dream Job Theory. Sophie finished her soup, hoping the Janus clue would prove more promising. 'There's an intriguing gargoyle on the church in the village.'

Hugo put down his water glass and described the young faces, omitting that they gazed out in opposite directions. Freddy had recognised the carving as a classical symbol for doorways and thresholds. Likely his father would too.

Freddy was sipping his wine, didn't elaborate, and Richard seemed relaxed.

'Is it a local tradition?' Sophie's tone was just the right side of casual.

'I don't think so,' said Richard.

'I'll ask the vicar,' said Anne. 'He'll know.'

Sophie hid a tiny portion of fish under squidgy vegetables, and the boys and Richard talked about cricket.

After the main course, Anne turned to her. 'We hold a ball every summer. I always enjoy it. I think you will too.'

'When's it being held?'

'18th of August. We invite the whole county.'

'Will Alan be invited?'

Anne looked pained. 'He made it clear he dislikes those sort of events.'

'Hugo, how did you get on with him?' said Freddy, interested enough to pause exhaustive cricket analysis.

'He was hard to talk to.' Hugo was Mr Tactful; should have been a diplomat.

'I didn't like him,' said Sophie.

'I used to think he was funny but perhaps he's just a bad sort.' Freddy slowly twirled his wine glass and addressed Hugo. 'Tell us about your England.'

Hugo smiled at Anne. 'I've told Freddy about washing machines and dishwashers. Even done drawings.'

'I know how they work in principle,' said Anne, 'but not well enough to make them from scratch. A shame. I could have made a fortune.'

'Machines do a lot of work that servants do here,' said Freddy, oblivious to the footmen and Mr Crawford listening to every word.

'More people are better off,' said Hugo, 'working in offices or from home. But it's not all good. You can spend your life checking messages, not talking to people right next to you.'

'Our phones are really mini-computers, connected all over the planet.' Sophie ate the last morsel of her summer pudding. Faithful to its name, fresh raspberries and straw-berries were piled on soft pink bread, soaked in the fruits' juices. Too messy for Charlotte but she'd already had fish and potatoes.

'You can sit in your bedroom or a café,' said Hugo, 'see and talk to people in New York or Australia, listen to music or watch a film.'

'But *how* does it work?' asked Freddy.

'Your computer sends a request to a web server...' said Sophie. 'Actually, I don't know.'

Freddy turned to Hugo.

'Sorry,' said Hugo, 'I don't either.'

Freddy shook his head. '*So* frustrating.'

A rumbling directly overhead heralded a much-needed

thunderstorm and a lightning flash lit up the dining room: the people, the silverware and the cut glass. Richard was watching his wife, Hugo was sipping his wine and Freddy's gaze was on his place setting, his expression wistful. Then the scene was gone, a shutter snapped shut.

Despite the humidity, Sophie felt suddenly cold and she shivered. She longed for home, a physical ache for her aunt and Isha — and for laid-back modernity.

When Anne stood up a few minutes later and Sophie followed her out, dragging a reluctant Charlotte, all Sophie wanted was to lose herself in sleep. But she sat on the familiar sofa and geared up for small talk.

Anne sat down opposite her. 'This is the small drawing room. The large drawing room will be used as a ballroom in August.'

How had she missed a room vast enough to be a ballroom?

As the maid poured coffee, Sophie recounted what she'd said in the pub, omitting Alan's spiteful observation. But Anne cut her short, shooed away the maid, making dismissive hand gestures, and the maid hastily closed the door behind her.

Odd. She hadn't seen Anne shoo a maid before.

'This could be dreadful. Really dreadful.'

'Freddy was fine about it.'

'I made many mistakes when I arrived, but this?' When Sophie didn't respond, Anne said, 'Do I have to spell it out? Everyone will presume you are secretly engaged. If the engagement is not publicly acknowledged, you will be gossiped about, have *no* chance of a decent marriage.'

'What about Freddy?'

'What about him? Sophie, the rules here aren't fair. This won't affect Freddy in the slightest. If you don't get engaged, it will finish you.'

CHAPTER 25

*D*ating at home had been straightforward, almost rule-free.

Sophie was flattered when Pete Watson showed an interest. Known universally as Pete Whatsisface, he was so fit, he did modelling in the holidays. She did the responsible thing — went on the pill — and in year twelve, just before Christmas, she stayed over at his parents' house. Not in a spare room; his mother had assumed they were sleeping together.

But Sophie felt awkward and inadequate, and dumped him soon afterwards, dressing it up with 'needing her own space.'

'He's self-obsessed,' she told Isha, 'and a humour-free zone.'

'He's *gorgeous.*' Isha pushed out her bottom lip, baffled. 'I hope you don't regret it.'

And Sophie didn't. Not the sex or the dumping. Just one of those things.

But in this universe, it seemed that one careless remark could ruin her life.

'You've just met.' Anne's eyes were narrowed, suspicious.

'I only said it to put Alan down.' Freddy hadn't been fazed because it didn't affect him. It only affected her. Should have kept her mouth shut, acted smart. 'Could we deny I said it, that I was misunderstood?'

'You said there was a witness in the pub.' Anne's face was set, hard. 'We need to start a counter-rumour. You must tell Miss Able, in the strictest confidence, that you make these jokes in your world and Freddy understands.'

'Sorry?'

'Within hours it will be common knowledge, here and in the village. You need to use the assumption that visitors can act strangely to your advantage.'

Clever media spin but using servants—

'And no more swanning about in tea dresses. Restrict them to teatime, between three and five-thirty.'

Had she been swanning? Hadn't felt like swanning. Only wear a tea dress at teatime. Logical.

'Fortunately, as soon as you arrived, I ordered appropriate day dresses.' Anne's face was still stony.

That night, Sophie told Maud about the new clothing regime and shared the edited pub boast, urging Maud to secrecy.

The following morning, Maud draped a corset over the spindly chair and Sophie's gaze was unwillingly drawn to it. Forget resting after sex, *this* was why Anne put off getting up.

The white, dead bones of a murdered whale were protruding under the thin cotton and nausea rose in Sophie's throat. How long had that whale swum in the ocean, free, glad to be alive? She could explain to Maud in gruesome detail how whales were killed, but what would that achieve? Nothing for Maud. Her uniform, including her underwear, was mandatory. Not wearing a corset would get her sacked.

But Sophie Arundel had supported whale charities for years. How could she wear one?

Anne's determined face materialised like a spectre in her head, clear and grim.

Deep breath. 'I'm ready.'

Maud put it over Sophie's head, then tightened the laces as if hauling rigging on a whaling ship. 'It's the latest style, for the new woman.'

Sophie gulped. The corset pinched her hips not her waist and was longer than she'd expected. She tried to sit down and stood hastily.

'Don't be afraid of breaking it,' said Maud. 'It's very strong.'

'How do you fasten yours? You couldn't do this by yourself.'

'Oh, I don't, Miss. I share a room with Miss Parry. She does mine and I do hers.'

Once the corset was immovable, on went a thin chemise, petticoat, delicate silk stockings and — finally — a formal day dress. The mahogany wardrobe now housed four such dresses, in varying styles and colours. The one Maud had selected was dusky teal blue with a round neckline and close-fitting, elbow-length sleeves, ending with lace flourishes; more lace overlaid a high-waisted, plain bodice. The skirt draped normally over the hips but gathered in below the knees before reaching the floor, making it difficult to walk. Pockets were cleverly hidden in the skirt's folds. The look was elegant, but complicated, and fastening it took Maud a while.

From start to finish, the whole procedure had been akin to a squire arming up a knight, but this armour didn't deflect blows, just prevented her being dressed by anyone other than

Maud, who'd done some special training course. 'Why is it so narrow at the bottom?'

'Hobble skirt, Miss. Very fashionable.'

Once Sophie's hair was in a loose bun, Maud left, and Sophie retrieved the notebook from the wardrobe, put it in her pocket with the pencil, and called on Hugo.

He opened his door wearing grey trousers and his colourful tie, but the sleeves of his pale pink shirt were neatly folded up to the elbows. He took in her outfit. 'The full Monty?'

'With bells on.'

'Can you breathe?'

'Just about.'

He shut his door behind him.

'You've forgotten your jacket.'

'Saturday.' He smiled. 'Don't need it.'

'This is *so* unfair.'

'You get to dress down at teatime.' His accent was exaggerated silly-posh and clipped. *'Every day.'*

Her annoyance dissolved and she giggled. 'I guess.'

As usual, Freddy wasn't at breakfast. Towards the end of the meal, Richard said to Anne, 'I need to work this morning, just for a few hours.'

Anne made a face, the informal gesture at variance with her gown, a hobble-skirt design in light blue silk.

'It's cooler today.' Sophie glanced at Hugo. 'We could take both dogs for a walk.'

Charlotte and Jack came out from under the table, expectant, alerted by the word 'walk.'

'That would be kind,' said Richard. 'Jack gets very bored in the office.'

'I'm happy to mind him.' And Jack's attachment to Charlotte was entirely reciprocated, though there could be no puppies.

After breakfast, Anne took Sophie aside. 'I know these clothes feel peculiar. If it's any comfort, a few years ago, the fashionable silhouette was much more extreme.'

The mind boggled. But Sophie nodded, as if she understood.

Outside, the dogs raced across the moat bridge and Sophie followed, taking frustrating half steps. As she tottered, Hugo slowed to her pace, and when she told him about Anne's grilling and the PR campaign, he made sympathetic noises.

Surprising, given how appalled he'd been. She managed to throw a ball for Jack, despite her tight bodice and sleeves, but Jack lost sight of it. He eventually rooted it out and dropped it at her feet, before racing after Charlotte and staying at her side like a determined shadow.

Shame she couldn't swap souls with Charlotte, like a dog and human *Freaky Friday*, just for a day. It would be wonderful to run and leap so fast, but Charlotte would be even more prone to social gaffs... 'All this fuss about Freddy and my reputation really sucks. At home, if I'd bonked the whole school rugby team, it wouldn't have ruined my life.'

Hugo stopped walking. 'You'd have been filmed and eaten alive by trolls.' He was managing to keep a straight face but only just, imagining sordid pictures...

'Yuck. Not helping.'

'Everyone's reputation is precious, but women suffer more.'

Sophie turned to face him. 'Since when have you been a feminist?'

'Since birth. If I'd ever suggested I was better than my sisters, they'd have beaten me senseless.'

'Sounds rough.'

'I'm exaggerating, but not much. I was convinced my

parents loved them more. I wasn't allowed out by myself, but they came and went as they pleased.'

Didn't seem likely. 'How old were you when this was happening?'

'Three, or four. They were quite a bit older.'

'I knew you weren't serious.' She began walking again, conscious of her corset digging into her hips.

'It never occurred to me that women could be regarded as less than men until I went to school.' He kept to her snail's pace. 'Other boys had different opinions.'

'That figures.'

'Anyway, it's not rocket science. Only a moron would assume a person is less intelligent because of their gender.'

He was serious. Another surprise.

Charlotte was hurtling back from the tree line, her legs stretching in joyful, easy motion. Sophie smiled. 'Charlotte's a feminist.'

'And you know this, how?'

'She's not ground down by gender stereotypes. Just does what she wants.'

Charlotte was now sprinting towards a pigeon lingering on the ground, but Sophie was relaxed. Charlotte wouldn't hurt it.

'Why did you call her Charlotte?'

'A few reasons,' said Sophie. 'After Charlotte Bronte who wrote *Jane Eyre*.'

'Okay.'

'She's like Jane in the story. Determined and strong, with a complicated inner life. But Jane wouldn't have suited her. Too plain. Even when she was a tiny puppy, she looked like a princess. Anyway, not long after she was born, Kate Middleton had Charlotte, so that confirmed the name.'

Hugo seemed interested in the view. 'Do you think you tend to over analyse things?'

'Possibly.'

'Charlotte had the fluorescent jacket…' He turned to look at her. 'If you don't mind me asking, what condition do you have?'

Sophie took in his earnest expression and laughed, so much that her ribs ached against the corset and she had to stop walking. 'Hugo, the condition I had was a mixture of desperation and low cunning.'

He stopped too. 'I don't understand.'

'While I was at school, my aunt minded Charlotte. But she's ill and a couple of months ago she got worse and couldn't dog sit. I didn't want to miss out on Uni, so I had two options. Dump Charlotte in kennels or bring her with me.'

'Couldn't your parents have taken her?'

Hated explaining. 'No. They died in my second year at Hadley.' She registered the shock on his face and turned away.

'I'm sorry, Sophie, I had no idea.'

'I kept it private, didn't want people feeling sorry for me.' Charlotte was leaning into her skirt, and Sophie patted her and exhaled, consciously pushing away the familiar smell of furniture polish. It was indelibly woven into her brain, wrenching her back to Miss Parncutt's study, to that moment she'd learned her parents were dead. Even in a different universe, the imaginary scent smelled real… Think about something else. 'I couldn't afford a decent kennel.'

Hugo looked dazed, still processing about her parents. 'And you wouldn't have sold her—'

'No. So, I winged it. With the fluorescent coat, I had no problems. Like you, people were too embarrassed to ask.'

Now he was staring, literally open-mouthed. After a moment, he said, 'You're outrageous.'

She allowed herself a wicked grin.

'How ever did you cope at Hadley without her?'

'The long holidays helped.'

They started walking again.

Completely rational that school was in a different universe. Unreal. All her old life felt like that. Helplessness ran through her, hollow and bitter.

'What school did you go to,' asked Hugo, 'before Hadley?'

'Local primary school.'

'Small and friendly?'

'Not exactly. Lots of fights but I learned how to handle myself.' After being beaten up on the first day, she'd quickly figured out punching and, on one occasion, biting. Within a term, she was an awesome bully deterrent.

Hugo frowned. 'So, you learned to react fast and think later.'

Recognition. 'Maybe.' Despite taking such small strides, she was sweating from too many layers of underwear beneath the close-fitting dress. 'Let's turn around.'

'My first school was quite intense,' said Hugo, as they retraced their steps. 'Geared to passing entrance exams to the best schools. I was up for that, but my parents wanted a place that could see beyond grades.' He watched the dogs as they ran towards the house.

'I loved the extra curricular stuff.'

'So did I,' said Hugo. 'The cricket, the fencing, the CCF.'

He'd played soldiers for years in the Combined Cadet Force. Like Lily, who was now a soldier for real. The hollow feeling returned, the reality of the situation hitting Sophie anew. She might never see Lily again. Anyone again.

'And I loved the acting,' said Hugo.

'Must have been fun.' She should have persuaded Isha to do drama with her, ignored Hugo's stuck-up friends.

'You did athletics,' said Hugo, 'and kickboxing.'

No need to mention winning the county kickboxing

championship — Hugo had watched it in Hadley's gym, along with the whole school.

'Did your parents choose Hadley for all the extras?'

She managed not to snort. Only rich people could *choose* a prestigious boarding school. 'The essay scholarship was a one off. I got lucky.' She grimaced. 'And then we got in the lift and our luck ran out.'

'This business with Freddy will blow over.'

Sophie crossed her fingers and focused on Charlotte waiting on the terrace, wagging her tail, Jack at her side.

Back in her room, Sophie didn't see the sumptuous bed or pretty curtains, only endless days of corsets, social gaffes and humiliating husband-hunting. Her silk stockings had wrinkled annoyingly around the ankles and she hitched them up before fishing out her notebook. Brain freeze wouldn't stop her cracking this; the lift puzzle was a research project, not an exam.

She read through her notes and numbers leapt out. *Dates.* 'We know when the visitors left home. It shouldn't be too hard to find the days and times we all arrived, and if there's a pattern, we can predict when the portal opens again. *Yes.*'

Charlotte yawned and Jack closed his eyes.

'Well, *I* think it's a good idea.'

When she called on Hugo to go to lunch, she outlined the theory. 'But if the pattern's not obvious … my maths skills are pretty basic.'

'Mine too.'

'We'll need Freddy,' said Sophie, 'so Richard will know.'

'Yes, but like with Janus, we can play it down.'

Over lunch Sophie explained her dates idea and Anne said, promptly, 'I got into the lift on Monday, 20th January 1986. I'm not sure what date it was here.'

'24th November 1893,' said Richard, smiling at his wife. 'I remember it well, but surely it wouldn't be that simple?'

'Almost certainly not.' Hugo turned to Freddy. 'We'd appreciate your help.'

Freddy's whole face lit up. He really was maths obsessed.

'We know when Miss Hemmings left and arrived, but only when Mr Parkes left,' said Sophie. 'Do you know the date he came through?'

'June 1902,' said Anne, 'the year before Mr Eddington started his investigations.'

'What a fascinating problem,' said Freddy, 'but it might be an impossible one. If we do find a pattern or number of patterns, you came from a different universe.'

'And your point is?' said Sophie.

'There will be variables … incredibly difficult to calculate.' Freddy took a sip of water. 'You measure the calendar year like we do, based on the time it takes the earth to rotate around the sun?'

'Yes,' said Hugo.

'And time here runs slightly slower,' said Freddy. 'Perhaps your earth is rotating at a different rate? The sun could be a different size, so could your earth. And what about the stars? Do you have the same constellations? Your world developed differently so why shouldn't your universe?'

Sophie's brain was hurting. Why had she thought this would be straightforward?

CHAPTER 26

'We could study the constellations tonight,' said Hugo. 'No, actually, we shouldn't.'

'Why not?' asked Freddy.

'I wouldn't know if the sky was different unless it was *really* different. I never did astronomy.'

'Me neither,' said Sophie.

Hugo turned to her. 'And if we're going all *Star Trek* … even if we could predict the portal opening, how do we get to the right universe? We might end up in a really strange one, or a world that seems like home but is crucially different.'

'What's *Star Trek*?' asked Freddy.

'I'll tell you all about it,' said Sophie, 'but let's find a pattern, *then* worry about impossible stuff.'

'Impossible stuff,' repeated Freddy.

'James T. Kirk.' Anne's lips curved in a nostalgic smile as she looked at her husband. 'Where to start?'

That afternoon, Sophie tore a blank page from the notebook, drew a small table, put in the visitors' dates and made copies for the boys to study. And after dinner, in her room, she read and reread the dates. But inspiration proved elusive.

The next morning, when she went to the terrace as arranged, Freddy was back from church, sitting at the table with Hugo. The Laceys hadn't suggested she and Hugo attend Sunday services, and Sophie was grateful.

The dogs zoomed under the table and as Freddy stood and pulled out a chair for her, Sophie noticed his hair. Slicked, flat and shiny, as if he'd emptied a bucket of grease onto his head.

Hugo put his fingers on his lips, meaning, 'Don't mention his hair.'

Sophie sat down and secured her sheet of paper on the table by setting the handbell on one corner. 'Let's check my copying was accurate.'

She glanced over at Freddy. 'Your mother left on Monday, 20th January 1986, Mr Parkes left in October 1994, Miss Hemmings in July 2003 and we left on 25th September 2017.'

'Mummy arrived on 24th November 1893,' said Freddy, 'Mr Parkes in June 1902, Miss Hemmings in May 1911, and you came through on 20th July 1925, at around eleven in the morning.'

'Good,' said Sophie. 'All our figures are the same.'

'Miss Hemmings and Miss Alderman arrived during the night,' said Hugo.

'Anne came through in the afternoon,' said Sophie. 'We don't know what time of day Mr Parkes got here.'

'That won't make any difference, given how vague some of the dates are.' Freddy rang the handbell then set it back on Sophie's paper.

'I confess,' said Hugo, 'I got nowhere with this last night.'

'The same,' said Sophie.

Freddy ran his finger along the figures on his sheet. 'Mr Parkes doesn't fit. The difference between departure and arrival dates for everyone else is 92 years, 2 months. For Mr Parkes it's 92 years, 4 months. Too large a variable, if time passes here only a little more slowly.'

'He could have misremembered when he left? He wasn't very sure,' said Sophie.

A young maid arrived with a laden tray and poured coffee.

'The real problem is there's no obvious pattern *between* arrivals.' Freddy took a thoughtful sip from his cup. 'Mr Parkes arrived eight years, seven months after Mummy. Miss Hemmings came through eight years, eleven months after him. And you arrived thirteen years and eleven months later. Differences of 103, 107 and 167 months. All prime numbers but, given the lack of accuracy, that has to be a coincidence.'

Freddy wasn't reading from notes. This was all in his head.

Hugo put down his cup. 'We need an Enigma machine.'

'Shame we're stuck with Alan *Parkes*,' said Sophie, 'not Alan Turing.'

'Alan who?'

Hugo and Sophie gave Freddy a potted history of code breaking.

'I'll be able to help with that, if there's a Second World War,' said Freddy. 'I suppose here it would be the First War.'

'You mustn't repeat what we've told you about code breaking,' said Sophie. 'Keeping all that secret was crucial to us winning.'

'Right you are,' said Freddy. 'Tell me about *Star Trek*.'

Sophie gave a short summary of the franchise.

'Real scientists have managed to transfer molecules a very short distance,' said Hugo, 'but we're a while off beaming objects, let alone people.'

'Have you any more crazy stories?' asked Freddy.

'Let's crack this puzzle first,' said Hugo.

When they stopped for lunch, Anne related what the vicar had told her about the carving.

'We chatted after the service and he told me all about it.' Mr Hunter topped up her glass of water. 'It's a pagan symbol and there's nothing like it in the county. There are stone carvings of similar heads in Rome, but not on a church.'

Richard smiled at his wife, unworried.

'That's interesting,' said Sophie, keeping her face blank. Good. The same church. A solid, verifiable fact.

That afternoon, she and the boys interrogated the visitor dates for three hours and found nothing. But Freddy's hair looked fine. The Grease Fest must have been a one-off.

They met again before dinner, worked on more calculations and theories, but came up empty.

Afterwards, Sophie took Hugo aside. 'What was the deal with Freddy's hair?'

'It's the height of fashion.'

'What did he use? Butter?'

'No. *Brilliantine*. Manly grease in a tin.'

The following morning, Sophie was surprised and relieved to see the pale blue tea dress back from the laundry; according to Maud, it had been soaked in milk for twelve hours before being washed. And, miraculously, the dress was now ink-stain free.

After breakfast, instead of studying the visitor dates, Sophie started Volume 2 of *Far From The Madding Crowd*. Her brain would benefit from a maths break.

She met up with the boys at five after they'd finished work. Initially, as they studied the dates in the small drawing room, Sophie's mind did feel fresher, but Freddy's rapid reasoning soon made her head spin.

When Freddy left to think through a new calculation in his room, Sophie folded up her paper to put it in her pocket and asked Hugo about his first day at work. She imagined the office like a World War Two war room, with wall charts and a mini replica of Shorten, and maids rearranging miniature servants with tiny shovels. Unlikely she'd ever get to check it out for real.

'Richard's trying to run an efficient farm, manage hundreds of employees and their families, including those who've retired and need hospital visits,' said Hugo. 'Without a manager, he's drowning.'

'Why hasn't he appointed one?'

'No shortage of candidates, but it takes years to get to know an estate, so good guys don't move.'

The next afternoon, she met up with the boys again. Freddy's calculation looked impressive but didn't work. The following day, he wrote incomprehensible formulas. They didn't work either.

'Because there's no obvious pattern,' said Freddy, 'we need the exact dates and...'

'What?' asked Sophie.

'The variables between universes factored in *before* doing the analysis.'

'And there could be billions or none,' said Hugo.

Freddy nodded. 'If your multiverse theory is correct.'

Weary and frustrated, they gave up.

After breakfast the next morning, with no meeting with the boys to look forward to, Sophie's day stretched out like an endless, solitary road: reading for hours, dozing in her room in the afternoon, and walks that felt like slow-pacing in an enormous cage.

At home, a good run always cheered her up. But nobody in Shorten ran, or even walked fast.

The boys were practising cricket in a field behind the greenhouses. Absorbing for them but boring to watch. A daring thought. Anne might know of a lockable room to practise kickboxing? Couldn't hurt to ask.

Sophie set off across the lawn, walking slower than a centenarian, while the dogs played their favourite game. Like frantic instructions in American football, they put their heads close together, then sprinted in different directions before rushing to consult again.

She'd just crossed the moat bridge when she heard Freddy calling her name. He was wearing a suit, not cricket whites.

'Have nets been cancelled?' She walked back across the bridge.

'No, strained my shoulder,' said Freddy. 'May I join you?'

She wanted to laugh at his formality but restrained herself.

Freddy matched her slower pace. 'Hugo told me Charlotte doesn't fetch. It's strange.'

'She's okay just running.'

'You and Hugo say that a lot.'

'What?'

'Okay,' said Freddy. 'It means all right?'

'Or I understand, or I'll do what you're suggesting. It means a lot of things. Maybe that's why we use it so much? I've never thought about it.'

'Okay,' said Freddy. 'It's an okay day today.'

'That can mean a good day, but it can also mean an average day or not a brilliant day.' Sophie smiled at him. 'This is making my head hurt.'

'You and Hugo have an interesting accent,' said Freddy. 'I can't place it. Londonish, but not quite.'

'Hugo is much posher.'

Freddy seemed bemused. 'You sound the same.'

Did they? Her accent must have changed at Hadley. Gradually, subtly, subconsciously. Surprise mingled with irritation. She was proud of her family, her regular background.

'Is Charlotte a mixture of breeds?' Freddy patted Charlotte's head as she rushed by.

'Poodle and lab. Originally bred in Australia as guide dogs for people with allergies. But they were hard to train.' She knew her labradoodle history.

'Allergies?' said Freddy.

'Some people are allergic to dogs. That's a problem if they need their help.'

'Like with the hunt.'

'Sorry?'

'They kill and retrieve.'

Of course in 1925 there'd be fox hunting. Think about good things. 'If you're partially sighted or have medical conditions, you can take a dog to Uni.'

'What's a Uni?'

'Oh, sorry, university.' The familiar knot of misery tightened. They'd been gone eleven days now. Aunty Wendy and Isha would be going through hell. And with no bodies to find, there would never be closure.

Charlotte launched herself towards a pigeon, maybe the one she'd pursued before. At the last moment, the pigeon rose into the air, avoiding capture. Again. But Charlotte was never downhearted by failure. Did that mean she was determined or just stubborn?

A few moments later, Charlotte began exploring a shrub near the moat, brushing against the leaves and collecting unfamiliar, delicate flowers on her fur. The pink petal tips raggedly lightened towards the bottom, resembling a tie-dyed T-shirt.

Sophie knew little about plants. Lucy might know whether this was unique to here, though impressive plant lore wouldn't help find the portal.

Charlotte emerged onto the lawn, her head dotted pink and green like a fairy headband, and Sophie set about picking it all off.

'Is she trained to help people?' asked Freddy.

'No, but many dogs at home sniff out explosives or find people buried after earthquakes.'

'Remarkable.'

'I think dogs are remarkable, but I'm biased.' She finished gleaning flowers from Charlotte and tried to be positive. 'I love how quiet it is here.'

'When I was at Cambridge, I missed that. But now I miss my friends. Phil Hall will be a professor one day… I should write to him about the visitor dates. If there's only a few variables between universes and there's a pattern, he'll find it.'

'Could you have been a professor?' She threw a ball for Jack.

'No, had to pick up the reins here.' Freddy sighed. 'Such a shame Hugo doesn't know the maths behind the multiverse theory. I'd have loved to study it.'

'You could have discovered it a century early.'

'But I'd have cheated,' said Freddy. 'Not much fun in that.'

Jack dropped the ball at Sophie's feet, and she threw it again. 'Isha, my friend at home, she's good at maths.'

'Odd name,' said Freddy. 'Is she foreign?'

'She's from India.'

'Gosh,' said Freddy. 'You're missing her.'

'Very much.' At Hadley, the Russian students had stuck together, like the Chinese and those with parents in the forces. And the rest — Brits from elite families, in politics or the media or business — they'd been schooled from birth to seek out their own. Scholarship Girl and Indian Girl had been natural allies.

'You'll get on famously with Kate … Miss Gilbert. I haven't seen her since Cambridge. We should visit.'

'She's not coming to the ball?'

Freddy shook his head. 'She's too young.'

'How old is she?'

'Fifteen … she'll be invited next year.' Freddy smiled. 'She could climb a tree really quickly, but I was a better swimmer.'

'In the river?'

'Yes, she stuck to the edges.'

'I wish we could go swimming again.'

'It's a shame,' said Freddy, his face sombre. 'But Mr Farrow was very sniffy about it.'

'Who?'

'My valet.'

The rulebook for Freddy might be shorter but his valet sounded as prim as Maud.

'I'd *so* like to,' said Freddy.

Even tiny transgressions here were risky and she'd vowed not to rock the boat to help Anne — not to mention her own marriage prospects — but she couldn't resist. 'When you're in charge, Freddy, you could change the rules?'

He gave her a subversive grin. 'I just might.'

CHAPTER 27

'If we can't go swimming, there's something else we can do.' Freddy walked towards a wicket gate flanked by a tall box hedge, the topiary reaching high over the gate in an arch.

He opened the gate, Sophie stepped through and smiled.

Outlined in chalk was a tennis court.

She walked to the baseline, imagining serving and volleying. The neat grass was a glorious vivid green.

The court was right beside the greenhouses but invisible behind the hedge.

'The net's in there?' Sophie pointed to a leather steamer trunk under an elevated umpire's chair.

'With the rackets and balls,' said Freddy. 'I need to rest this shoulder, but you and Hugo could play on Saturday. I'll referee.'

Two days later, it was too hot and humid for tennis, but Sophie and Hugo still played for over an hour in the afternoon, Sophie in a tea dress and Hugo in his cricket whites. Lacking trainers, Sophie went barefoot while Freddy — dapper in Shorten Casual — presided in the umpire's chair.

Sophie had watched Wimbledon more than she'd played and Hugo wasn't very good, so that worked fine. The boy who normally collected hound poo fetched balls and stopped Jack running off with them, and maids brought out cold drinks.

'We should do this every week,' said Sophie, when they took a break between sets.

She won the next game by sprinting and getting a lucky drop shot. As they changed ends, one of the maids scowled at her, muttering — nothing good. Sophie stared back but the maid didn't look away. Uncomfortable, Sophie tried to focus on the tennis.

Afterwards, during Sophie's cool bath, Maud was unusually quiet, and as soon as she was dressed, Sophie hurried off with the dogs to the small drawing room and read the paper.

The front page mostly featured soap and medicine adverts; there was only one news story. *Manchester Unrest Under Control. Forty streets destroyed by fire, five hundred people killed or missing, martial law and curfew imposed by emergency order.* The article continued inside, with a photo of a gutted street and a list of ruined homes and shops, with quotes from residents, but it was the last paragraph, with no attached comments, that so shocked Sophie, she read it again, unable or unwilling to believe it. *The bodies of two adults, five children and a baby were recovered from an undamaged house. Starvation presumed cause of death.*

Anne came in wearing a violet tea dress with minimal lace. 'It's too hot to sit on the terrace.' Usually at this time Anne rested in her room, but Sophie was glad she enjoyed her company enough to make the odd exception.

Sophie put down the paper. 'This is horrible.'

'I know, I read it this morning.' Anne rang the bellpull.

'There's no benefit system?'

'Not like at home.' Anne sat elegantly on the sofa.

Sophie straightened up from her slouch. 'Are people starving in Little Shorten?' The village children had been very skinny.

'No, everyone works on the estate, and first-time mothers, older people, all get support. Oh, I meant to tell you, Mr Crawford's training up Mr Fletcher, and Mrs Fletcher did the pub accounts so has taken on bookkeeping.'

'Doesn't Freddy do that?'

'He did. And he hated it, found it boring.'

Sophie glanced again at the paper, glad the chance encounter outside *The Crooked Gate* had done some good. 'How far is Manchester?'

'About a hundred miles.'

'How far is Derby?'

'Far enough. The trouble there won't affect us.'

Good to know. The Manor was a prison but also a sanctuary. She'd never gone hungry. Actually, had never thought about it.

The young maid came in with the tea tray, set everything out on the table, poured the tea and left, carefully closing the door behind her. Maud had mentioned her roommate's duties involved serving elevenses and afternoon tea ... so that maid must be Miss Parry. Five years younger than Maud, she was meticulously turned out and never spilled a drop of milk or tea.

At home a century ago, Sophie Arundel would have been a maid, but Hugo was way too posh to be a servant. Had Anne sensed that? 'Why didn't you send us downstairs?'

'When I woke up here that first morning, the housekeeper wanted to do just that, but Richard's mother took me aside and examined my hands. She turned them over and ran her fingers over my palms. For a mad moment, I thought she was telling my fortune.'

Sophie finished spreading strawberry jam on her scone. 'What was she doing?'

'Seeing if I'd lived a life of toil. Girls in the 1970s and 80s didn't work in the fields or domestic service, so my hands were as soft as hers. Because of that, she decided I should stay on as a guest.'

A whole life, thirty years of marriage, hingeing on a moment. If Anne had been a maid, Richard would never have noticed her, let alone proposed.

'But in the present climate, it would have been difficult to send you downstairs.'

'Why?'

'There would have been resentment, if you and Hugo had taken jobs that others had worked for.'

She hadn't thought of that.

'Fate gave me a chance for a good life. I wanted you and Hugo to have that too.' Anne smiled. 'And Charlotte.'

A silly vision of Charlotte wearing a white apron and hat, following her mistress around a busy kitchen, materialised then vanished. 'I'd have been okay serving drinks but I'm a terrible cook.'

Anne laughed. 'So, I made the right decision.'

'Yes.' Like with Anne three decades ago, the die was cast. On the upside, she'd got through a whole week without making a single mistake. Sophie ate her scone, relishing the freshly baked aroma as well as the taste.

'Sophie, when you're wearing a tea dress, you *must* stay indoors and certainly not play tennis.'

'Why?'

'It's scandalous to be seen exerting yourself, and more so, without proper underwear.'

Explained the rude maid's staring. And Maud's silence while Sophie Arundel had guilelessly wittered on about the match... But Maud had never been slow to hand out advice.

The tennis faux pas must be serious if Anne was telling her off—

'Tea dresses … they're also called teagies … have a risqué reputation.'

Really? They were as modest as a weird handmaid's outfit.

'How can I put this delicately? They can be put on and off relatively easily, without a maid's assistance. Fewer fastenings.'

'I have tried to take it off myself, but all the buttons are on the back.'

Anne's cheeks turned a delicate shade of pink. 'The point is…' She checked the door was closed. 'A man for instance, who was not your husband, could easily undo them.'

Her Freddy boast… 'The servants think me and Freddy are together?'

Anne's lips thinned. 'They like to gossip.'

So it wasn't just Maud. 'But Freddy refereed. He never said anything about my dress.'

'Freddy's head is full of maths and equations, not ladies' clothing etiquette. But now you're here, he needs to be more careful. I've already spoken to him.'

A light knock, the door opened, and Mr Hunter came in carrying a silver tray, his dark eyes inscrutable. On the tray was a cream envelope addressed in dark blue ink: *Mr Hugo Harrington and Miss Sophie Arundel.* 'Apologies, Miss. This arrived last night but was overlooked.'

After she picked it up, he gave a curt nod and left.

Inside was a small note, scrawled in the same ink. *STAY AWAY FROM THE LIFT.*

Or what? A threat? Nobody here cared if they got home or not — except Richard. A twinge of unease. She showed the note to Anne. 'Do you recognise the writing, or the ink?'

'No.'

'You've never been sent a letter like this?'

Anne shook her head. She took the note and envelope and examined them. 'Worrying.' She handed them back. 'It could be a threat but perhaps the person's worried the lift could be dangerous?'

'Then why not say so, or sign the letter?' Sophie returned the note to the envelope.

'It could be someone with mental health problems, and treatment … I don't think there is any. Perhaps in London, but it would be very expensive.'

'They either recover or get worse?'

'Or are locked away. I had a good friend here who became depressed after her daughter was born. Her husband put her in the county asylum. She died in there. Kate was basically brought up by the governess.'

'When you say her husband…'

'Two doctors signed the paperwork on his say so. I visited her many times,' said Anne. 'A cold clinical place.'

Sounded like a horror film.

'But Kate's a jolly soul.'

'Freddy's friend?'

Anne nodded. 'And Charles didn't marry again.'

'He wasn't trying to get rid of her?'

'I don't think so, but other men abuse the system, lock women up because they can.'

Sophie shuddered. Anyone having that much power over her … made her skin crawl. She glanced back at the envelope. Mental illness could involve irrational obsessions, stalking … violence. She put the envelope in her pocket, out of sight, but the sense of unease remained, settling like a canker.

'Don't worry, I'll find out who wrote that.'

She had no reason to doubt Anne's sincerity, but she and Hugo would sort this.

Ten minutes later, when she called on him, he seemed embarrassed, though he was fully dressed.

The dogs rushed in and Sophie sat awkwardly in the leather armchair, bemused by his body language.

He made to close the door but left it ajar. 'Freddy told me about the tennis fallout. I should have realised a tea dress was inappropriate. I'm sorry.'

'No worries.' She smiled. 'I'm guessing A level history didn't cover Tea Dress Shame. Not exactly a mainstream fact.'

'No, but I'm still sorry.' He glanced at the door. 'And you shouldn't be in here, Sophie … in that dress.'

'Getting changed takes forever and this can't wait.'

'I know.' He gestured towards his bed. *The Times* was spread out on the coverlet, open at the page with the photo of the burnt-out street. 'These riots are turning into an uprising. The walls of this estate won't protect us from that.'

'We've a more pressing problem, right here.' She fished out the envelope and handed it to him.

He removed the note and frowned.

'Could this be Richard?'

Hugo sat on the bed, his eyes still on the note. 'Unlikely. It's not like we've solved the puzzle and will be strolling home tomorrow.'

'Mr Hunter said it arrived last night but been "overlooked." Maybe he made that up and he wrote it?'

'Why invent a story that could be checked out in minutes by Mrs Rawlings?'

'Who?'

'The housekeeper,' said Hugo. 'She deals with all the mail. And our being here doesn't affect Hunter in the slightest.'

Sophie hesitated. 'Maud and John have loads more stuff to do because of us.'

'But that's all good. Both promoted.' Hugo scanned the note again. 'We should show this to Freddy. I trust him.'

Before dinner, in the anteroom, Freddy read the note and showed it to his father who raised his eyebrows. 'Odd.'

Richard seemed genuinely intrigued, but then he would in front of Anne.

'Should we call the police?' said Hugo.

'The nearest station is in the market town,' said Richard, 'but giving advice isn't a crime.'

'Do you recognise the handwriting?' Anne asked Freddy.

'No, but whoever wrote this would disguise their hand.'

'Someone may have seen who delivered it,' said Anne. 'I've asked Mrs Rawlings to make enquiries.'

Freddy returned the note to Sophie.

After dinner, Sophie showed it to Maud.

'Peculiar.' Maud examined the note and envelope in the light of the heavy lamp. 'Good letters, Miss. Not your run of the mill person.'

'You don't recognise the writing?' A long shot but worth asking.

'No.' Maud left the note and envelope on the bedside table. 'But I wouldn't worry, Miss. No one sees the lift again.'

Her casual certainty made Sophie want to swear, but she sat in the blue chair and thought about the note. She wanted to believe it was a joke but instinct told her it wasn't.

'Perhaps the person's worried about something else in the lane.'

'Like what?'

'An animal trap could have been left on the verge,' said Maud. 'Made of iron.' She clapped her hands together. 'Takes your leg off and then you die.'

Sophie winced. She and Hugo had walked every inch of the lift spot, but such a thing could be hidden in the longer grass. 'Are they on the estate?'

'No, Miss, they don't use them nowadays.'

'That's a relief.'

The next morning, when Sophie called for Hugo to go to breakfast, she gave him the envelope with the note inside. 'Maud doesn't recognise the writing but John might.'

He folded it in half, slipping it into his trouser pocket.

Later, at coffee, he handed it back. He was wearing his cricket whites, as was Freddy.

'John's baffled,' said Hugo, 'but Mrs Rawlings might recognise the writing or the ink.'

'She could have sent it,' said Sophie.

Freddy shrugged. 'Why would she?'

When the boys went off to nets, Sophie went to the small study by the hall.

The door was open, revealing a rickety bookcase full of dog-eared files and, beside it, Mrs Rawlings sitting at a battered desk, slitting an envelope with a lethal-looking letter opener.

Sophie stood on the threshold with the dogs in tow, nerves fluttering. The housekeeper's respect was important, like Maud's. 'Mrs Rawlings, could I speak with you? If you're busy I can come back?'

The housekeeper stood up, her hazel eyes friendly. 'I'm happy to chat now.'

Sophie put the envelope on the desk. 'I wondered if you might recognise the writing.'

Mrs Rawlings examined the envelope and then the note. 'This is like a clue in the book I'm reading. *The Murder on the Links.*'

'Agatha Christie?'

'Yes, I've read her other one too.'

'If she's like the author at home, she'll write at least fifty.' The stories made for feel-good TV but this note made her feel queasy. 'It could be a threat.'

Mrs Rawlings' wrinkled brow creased more. 'I don't recognise the hand or the ink and the paper's thin, no watermark.' She peered at the envelope again. 'This writing is careful but the message in capitals is more slap dash. Would you mind if I showed this to Mr Crawford? I'll leave it for Miss Able to collect.'

'Thank you.' Mrs Rawlings was concerned, not running scared.

Before dinner, Maud gave Sophie back the envelope. 'Everyone's talking about it.'

'What did Mr Crawford say?'

'It could be anyone here or in the village.'

Not very helpful.

Over pre-dinner drinks, Anne said, 'Mrs Rawlings has no record of the time the anonymous letter arrived. It must have been delivered after everyone had retired.'

Richard looked mildly curious.

'I could burn it?' said Freddy.

'No, I'll keep it.' The note was safe in Sophie's linen drawer.

Freddy frowned. 'For what?'

'In case,' said Sophie, 'the implied threat is real.'

'You should take up a hobby,' said Anne, as she and Sophie sat in the small drawing room after dinner.

'Yes.' Cabin fever was getting worse.

'Painting and embroidery are socially acceptable.'

Couldn't draw and never sewn a button, let alone a masterpiece of tiny stitches. Despite the tennis debacle and the anonymous letter, Anne seemed relaxed. Now was the time. 'I was wondering if there was a spare room where I could do kickboxing? Nobody would see.'

Anne's eyes widened. 'Like Kung Fu in that *Karate Kid* film?'

'Um, I'm not sure. It's good for general fitness, co-ordination and muscle strength. You can train on your own with a punch bag, like boxers.'

'That would put off potential suitors.'

'Oh.' But Anne's reaction wasn't entirely bad news. She thought Sophie Arundel might attract some.

'Archery is considered ladylike, because you only move your arms,' said Anne. 'Is this kickboxing important to you?'

'I was good at it at school, and I'd love some private me-time. I feel like I'm always on show.'

'The Manor can be quite claustrophobic … I think I know a way you could do this.'

'Really?'

'Mini archery. There's plenty of lockable rooms on the ground floor and you could do it in all weathers.'

'With a mini board and bow?'

'No, silly, your kickboxing.' Anne gave her a conspiratorial smile, enjoying getting one over on the system. 'I do have some idea how difficult it is to adapt to life here. You need to work off surplus energy. I'll ask Lucy to make a punch bag. She won't tell anyone. She hates gossip.'

With the shock of the Great War revelation, the pub debacle and wrestling with the lift puzzle, Sophie had forgotten how much she'd liked Lucy. 'The bags are made of leather or canvas, filled with sand and rags. You hang them from a hook in the ceiling, but they're quite heavy. They can go on a stand. Would Lucy mind if I borrowed one of her tops and trousers? She's a bit shorter but we're similar build.'

'I'll ask Lucy about that too,' said Anne, 'on one condition.'

'What?'

'We *really* need to keep this to ourselves. I cannot imagine what the servants would think.'

'Understood.' Forget Marriage Joke Visitor and Tea Dress Shame, the gossip mill would explode. And Maud would start an anti-kickboxing campaign, involving a Shorten version of hybrid warfare. Instead of cyber hacking, fake news and stirring up the locals, she'd begin small. Kickboxing harmed feminine health, fuelled suffragette violence and, most effectively, she'd use pained expressions. A single glance usually sufficed. More than one, delivered relentlessly every day, and Sophie Arundel would be a gibbering wreck.

Selling this would require cunning.

The following morning before lunch, Maud was in a good mood, humming to herself as she bustled about the bedroom.

'Lady Lacey's suggested I do mini archery.' Sophie's voice was borderline bored. 'She's put aside a room so I can practise in private until I get the hang of it.' Anne had given her a key — the only one, as the room hadn't been used in years.

Maud's eyes narrowed. 'Whereabouts is this room?'

'At the back of the house.' Anne had also given her one of Lucy's tops and a pair of trousers and Sophie had put them in a drawer. She took them out. 'My dress wouldn't be practical, so Miss Hemmings has lent me these.'

'Ladies do archery in day dresses, Miss.'

She'd anticipated this. 'I know, but I haven't done it before, and my regular sleeves are so tight. Lady Lacey approved because I'll be practising in private.'

'I'll need to come with you. Wouldn't be right, Miss, wandering around in those clothes.'

This, she hadn't anticipated. 'Why not?'

'Wouldn't be respectable, Miss.'

And she'd underestimated Maud. She'd gone straight for the open verbal assault. 'I don't need a chaperone. It'll just be me in the room.'

'I'll go with you, Miss, wait outside.'

Sophie rolled her eyes. 'I'll be practising for an hour.' Exaggerating, but not much.

'I'll sit and do my mending chores.' Maud had on her determined face.

When Sophie saw Hugo in the anteroom at lunch, she repeated the mini archery fiction.

'A private gym. Brilliant.'

He was thinking about joining her. 'It's me-time.'

Hugo shrugged. 'Okay.'

After lunch, Sophie took Anne aside. 'Miss Able's acting like a bodyguard, wants to sit outside while I practise.'

'She takes her duties seriously, that's all.'

'And she disapproves of the clothes, but that's what Lucy wears.'

'It's taken a long time,' said Anne, 'but Lucy has managed to become an honorary man.'

'If I could dress and undress normally, it would give Miss Able a break.'

Anne made a face.

Sophie was reminded again of Freddy.

Anne lowered her voice. 'But if you were seeing … someone, those clothes would be easier to take off than a tea dress.'

Chance would be a fine thing. An entire sex life confined to Pete Whatsisface and eventually some chinless wonder from a parallel universe... 'I'll get Miss Able to sit at the end of the corridor. Right outside, she'll realise I'm not delicately shooting arrows.'

'That would be sensible,' said Anne. 'When I saw Lucy, she was intrigued. She's making the punch bag today.'

'I'm keeping the key in here.' Sophie patted her skirt. 'I love that all my dresses have pockets.'

Anne's lips curved into a smug smile. 'I insisted on them when I married, though they weren't fashionable. Of course, men have them routinely.'

The next morning, Sophie put on Lucy's trousers and top and set off to the 'gym,' with Maud and the dogs in tow. Sophie had helped Lucy smuggle in the punch bag overnight, using wheelbarrows, and enjoyed her company so much, she'd invited her to the first workout. And the head gardener taking on 'mini archery' had placated Maud; Lucy's presence made it more respectable.

In the corridor, they passed a maid, her striking red hair barely confined in a large bun. After two weeks, Sophie knew all the maids by sight, except the most junior. According to Maud, scullery maids cleaned the public rooms hours before the family came down for breakfast.

This girl wasn't familiar, must have been promoted — or recently hired. Apprehension slid along Sophie's backbone. The anonymous note writer could be her…

No. None of the servants, old or new, had a motive.

Lucy was sitting on a wooden chair up the corridor from the designated room. She got to her feet and exchanged a respectful nod with Maud.

Sophie gave Maud the dogs' leads and as Maud sat on the tatty chair, Jack lay on the wooden floor beside her. Charlotte, annoyed at being left behind, remained standing, watching Sophie and Lucy walk away.

Sophie unlocked the door, she and Lucy stepped inside, and Sophie relocked the door.

The room was the size of a large classroom, with chairs stacked in a corner.

Sophie walked over to a diamond-paned window framed by heavy curtains. Outside, not far from the house, was a dense line of elm trees. 'It's good we're not overlooked.' The carpet under her feet was grey and fraying. 'We should move this.'

They rolled it against the wall but were enveloped in a choking dust cloud.

When it finally settled, Sophie drained half her canteen. 'Glad I brought supplies.' When she'd asked for two water flasks, she'd allayed Maud's suspicions with an unnecessarily convoluted explanation about the benefits of sufficient hydration. She'd also asserted that stout walking boots were more comfortable for 'standing about.'

Lucy took a long swig from the other flask. 'You've been doing this for how long?'

'Eight years.' Sophie began warm-up stretches. 'And doing it here might just keep me sane.'

Lucy copied her stretching. 'The fallout from your Freddy joke won't last forever.'

'Who knew a one-liner could be such a big deal?'

'It's because they don't have television, so they make up soap operas.'

'I suppose it's like school,' said Sophie, 'everyone living so close together.'

'Except we're all dependent on one family.'

'Except that.'

Lucy put her hand on the wall and stretched one leg, then the other. 'And that anonymous note…'

'Anne suggested the writer could be looking out for us, that the lift could be dangerous.'

'So why didn't they warn her? Or me and Janet? We searched for it often enough.'

'Perhaps they weren't born or really young when you and Anne arrived?'

'Or the writer thinks you're on to something. The visitor dates were a good idea.' Lucy stopped stretching and grinned. 'Or someone stayed too long at the pub.'

The note had been delivered on a Friday night. But the author — presumably the same person who carried it — had been careful to remain unseen. Someone was collecting snatches of gossip, logging their theories. But Sophie returned Lucy's grin, reassuring her; Lucy was worried too.

'Stand like this, one foot in front of the other, and follow through, using your body as well as your arm.' Sophie punched the bag in slow motion. 'Keep your thumb wrapped outside your first and second knuckles.' Sophie demonstrated.

Lucy copied her.

'That's it.'

'Complicated,' said Lucy, stepping back from the bag.

'Understand the basics and, with practice, it'll be instinctive.' Sophie ran on the spot. 'Near the moat, there's this beautiful, pink-tipped flower I've never seen at home.' She described it.

'Sounds like Saxifraga Rosacea. Went extinct in the 1960s.'

'Are there plants unique to this world?'

'There are, as well as familiar ones that react differently to soil type and weather. Consistent with the parallel worlds idea.' Lucy grimaced. 'Like that wretched Virginia Creeper.'

'Sorry?'

'The monstrous vine spreading over the main house at the front. Grows faster than at home.'

'Why haven't you cut it back?'

Lucy shrugged. 'Anne likes it...'

Sophie stopped running on the spot. 'Use your legs to put weight behind the punch, like this.'

Lucy gave the bag a stronger punch, and another one.

'I'm *so* glad you're here. Anne and I get on but you're closer to my age.'

'Not really. In six years, I'll be forty.'

'You don't look anything like forty.' And she didn't. Whippet-thin but with a smooth complexion. 'Late twenties.'

Lucy acknowledged her compliment with a sceptical shrug and concentrated on punching.

When Lucy stopped, Sophie threw herself into the familiar workout, happily focused, relishing the 'boof' sound as her feet and fists hit the bag.

Finally, Sophie wiped sweat from her temple and stretched, tired but energised. She smiled at Lucy. 'Another session in a few days?'

Lucy returned the smile. 'Definitely.'

Sophie opened the door and locked it behind them.

Up the corridor, Maud stood up, judging but resigned. The dogs were alert, guarding the corridor. And *not* judging.

Lucy went off to work and as Sophie returned to the bedroom, Maud said, 'You were shooting arrows really quick, Miss. Bang, bang.'

Maud must have been listening at the door, perhaps peering through the keyhole. Mental note: always keep the key in the lock. 'Miss Hemmings is pretty good at hitting the target, but I need to practise every day.'

Hugo and Freddy came around a turn in the passage. And gawped.

It wasn't only her clothes … her face was pink and sweaty. She hurried past. She'd tell Freddy mini archery was gruelling. Hugo, though, wouldn't be fooled.

When she saw Hugo again before lunch, she fessed up. 'If word got out, everyone will think it's seriously weird. You won't say anything to Freddy, or John?'

'I won't, but if I were you, I'd explain to Freddy.'

'Bad idea, Hugo, he wouldn't understand.'

'He's bursting with curiosity, thinks you're doing some-thing else in that room.'

'Like what?'

'He didn't actually say what he thought, just wondered why you were red in the face. Maud's already given John chapter and verse, so Freddy's valet will have heard, and by Freddy's account, Mr Farrow's still wary of us. Bolster the mini archery fiction, get Freddy on side.'

'Okay.' He knew Freddy better than her.

After lunch, Sophie persuaded Freddy to join her alone on the terrace and confided about kickboxing.

'You're practising how to fight people. Why on earth would you do that?'

'It's not about hurting anyone. It's a way of toning muscles and keeping fit.'

'Sounds unladylike.'

How entirely predictable. Maybe if Freddy saw the practical reality, he'd understand. 'Why don't you join me tomorrow after breakfast?'

'Righty ho,' said Freddy. 'We can go to the office later.'

The following morning, Freddy wasn't at breakfast, but when she reached the corridor by the gym with Maud and the dogs, he was already there — with Hugo. He hadn't mentioned he was coming.

She gave Hugo an amused smile. 'You too?'

He shrugged.

'I can't be in a locked room with you by myself,' said Freddy, avoiding her eyes. 'Not with you dressed like that.'

Hugo was pressing his lips together, trying not to laugh.

Sophie acknowledged Lucy, walking briskly along the corridor. 'Miss Hemmings is coming too.' Lucy had been busy at work, but Maud had been adamant. No chaperone, not happening.

Freddy stood straighter, as if he'd been caught doing something untoward. Lucy might technically be a servant, but Freddy respected her.

Sophie unlocked the door, and inside the boys took chairs from the stack and sat down. So did Lucy; the head gardener wasn't up for training with an audience.

After hastily relocking the door, Sophie did routine stretches. 'You see, like you do before cricket.'

'I don't do that,' said Freddy.

'It's so you don't pull a muscle before intense exercise.' Hugo crossed his legs, his face expressionless.

Lucy was relaxed but Freddy was hunched, his face contorted as if he'd swallowed a wasp.

Sophie finished stretching. She'd take it easy and do a

short session; she didn't want to alarm Freddy. Well, more than he was already. Sophie began punching, raised the intensity and interspersed with kicks. 'See, it's not rocket science.'

Freddy was shaking his head. 'Rocket science?'

'It's more difficult than it looks,' said Lucy.

Sophie lay on the floor using half bricks wrapped in cloth to strengthen her arms.

'You could join a circus,' said Freddy.

Sophie put down the bricks. This had been a very bad idea.

'Honestly, Freddy, in our world, people do this every day,' said Hugo.

Freddy frowned. 'I think I'll stick to cricket.'

If she put kickboxing in context, Freddy might see it as more normal? 'I used to compete against other girls. I wasn't the tallest, so had to train hard.'

'Not the tallest?' said Freddy. 'You're tall for a girl.'

Freddy couldn't know many girls. 'I'm only five foot, five. I usually won my kickboxing bouts but the girl who beat me in javelin last summer was nearly six foot.'

'A girl as tall as me? No.'

'Most girls are taller than me,' said Sophie.

'In our Great War, officers were generally taller than the men,' said Hugo, 'and with better nutrition, the average height has gone up quite a bit.'

Sophie squared her shoulders. 'I need your help, Freddy, to support the idea of "mini archery."' Her quotation gesture was lost on him.

'Do you really want to keep on with this … oddness?'

'It makes me feel more relaxed,' said Sophie, deploying her best doe eyes. 'More at peace with the world.'

Freddy dropped his gaze. 'All right.'

As they opened the door to leave, Lucy said, 'Such a tiny target, it makes it really hard to hit.'

'Absolutely,' said Freddy.

'I'll keep practising,' said Sophie.

Afterwards, during her bath, she said to Maud, 'Standing shooting arrows … stops me putting on weight.'

Maud's brow creased, more of a question than a frown.

But Maud was a tough nut to crack.

'In the mornings, I'm ever so busy, Miss, and by the evening I just want to sit down.'

She got it. Maud thought shooting arrows into a toy target was pointless. Actually, Maud had a point. Working out was a first world luxury. 'I've never seen you out of breath. Your work keeps you active and you've got a very trim figure.'

'Thank you, Miss.' Maud collected a fresh towel from the shelf. 'I thought you wouldn't do your mini archery today.'

'Why?'

'Being your time of the month again, Miss.'

'I feel fine.' Her monthly cycle, previously kept regular by the contraceptive pill, was now unpredictable and chaotic. And her relationship with Maud was way too intimate, yet they weren't exactly friends … and memories of privacy and independence were already fading, like career options she'd taken for granted.

In the bedroom, after Maud left, Sophie opened her notebook, turned to the last page and wrote *Wednesday, 5 August 1925, Day 17,* then scanned the visitors' pages.

If she couldn't find a real clue soon, hope would fade too.

CHAPTER 29

*S*ophie put the notebook in her pocket with the pencil and went out to the terrace; she'd sit in the shade and draw the lift pictures. In her mind's eye, they were still clear.

But the boys were there, drinking coffee and sharing some hilarious joke. The dogs zoomed under the table to lie in the shade and Freddy pulled out a chair.

Sophie smiled at him as she sat down. 'What happened to slaving in the office?'

'Elevenses, *then* back to work.'

'Right, elevenses...' said Sophie. 'I never know what time it is.'

'You haven't a watch?' asked Freddy.

Sophie shook her head and Freddy rang the handbell for more coffee.

Hugo giggled. 'What are the odds?'

'What's so funny?' asked Sophie, worrying she was the butt of the joke.

'Freddy and me share the same birthday,' said Hugo. '23rd June.'

'Really?' said Sophie. 'How bizarre.'

'I'm three years older,' said Freddy, as if that made it less bizarre. 'When's your birthday, Sophie?'

'Not till the autumn.' Just as well. All of them sharing a birthday would be creepy. On 29th October, she'd be nineteen, or was it twenty? Her nineteenth birthday would have been a month after she got in the lift, but in Shorten it had been 20th July. Had she gone back two months or forward ten? If she was still here in October, celebrating a birthday would feel like giving in — like Hugo working for the estate.

'In point of fact, it's not much of a coincidence,' said Freddy. 'It's called the Birthday Paradox.'

'What is?' said Sophie.

'You might think it unlikely that two people have the same birthday,' said Freddy, 'but it isn't. If you have a room of only 23 people, there's a 50-50 chance two of them will share a birthday. In a room of 75 people, there's a 99% chance.'

Miss Parry poured Sophie's coffee and Hugo said, 'Come again?'

'That's why maths is so fascinating,' said Freddy. 'I worked it out in my last term. Phil thought of the name.'

'Freddy, there are 365 days in a year,' said Sophie. '75 people in a room almost guaranteed to share a birthday … that can't be right.'

'It seems wrong, but it's true. Imagine you're in a room with 22 people, all with different birthdays. You'd assume the chance of you having a unique birthday is high. Only 22 days have been taken and 343 days are free. But what if you work out the *probability* that everyone in your group of 23 has a unique birthday?'

Sophie frowned. 'No idea what you're talking about.'

'For person one, the probability is 100%, because every date is clear,' said Freddy. 'For person two, there's one day they would share with person one, but the other 364 are clear, so their chance of a unique birthday is 364 divided by 365. For person three, it's 363 divided by 365, and so on through to person 23, whose probability of having a unique birthday is 343 divided by 365. To find the probability of everyone in the group having unique birthdays, we multiply all the 23 probabilities together, and get a probability of 0.509, or 50.9%.'

'Only sort of following.'

Hugo was frowning now.

'If that's the probability that any two people share a birthday,' said Freddy, 'what about the probability that *you* will share a birthday with at least one other person? For that to be greater than 50%, you'd need to be in a group of 23 people.'

'So why,' said Sophie, slowly, 'isn't it 100% with double the number, 46 people?'

'As each person is added, the odds curve up rapidly,' said Freddy, 'but when the curve hits 50%, the rate of increase goes down. Goes virtually flat when 57 people are measured, and the odds rest at 99%.

'You mean 75 people,' said Hugo.

'No, 57. I could draw you a graph—'

'It's no good, Freddy, this is beyond me,' said Sophie.

'Me too,' said Hugo.

When he wasn't giving out social advice, she really liked Hugo, as well as fancying him. What were the odds?

'I was born on a Thursday,' said Freddy. 'Do you have the same rhyme?'

'*Thursday's child has far to go,*' quoted Hugo. 'But I was born on a Wednesday and I'm not full of woe. Well, not usually.'

'You've lost me again,' said Sophie.

'It's a nursery rhyme,' said Freddy. 'And in our version, it's

Friday's child that's full of woe. Wednesday's child is loving and giving.'

Hugo smiled. 'I'll take that.'

'I was born on a Thursday too,' said Sophie. 'So was Charlotte.'

'The rhyme's just tosh,' said Freddy.

'So, it's not such a coincidence,' said Hugo, 'that you, Sophie and Charlotte were born on a Thursday?'

'No. Probability again.'

'Okay,' said Hugo, 'what are the chances of having the same middle name?'

'Low,' said Freddy. 'Mine are Cameron and Richard.'

'Edward, Peter, Strickland,' said Hugo.

The boys turned to her. 'Deborah Ellen.'

'Pretty names,' said Freddy.

When the boys returned to the office, Sophie went to the library and drew the lift pictures. The mansion and the cottage on fire didn't take long but recreating the man rocking the cot and the girl holding the sword required numerous rubbings out and tweaks. But Alan's pictures were easier. Just curls of fire on the mansion and a line for the forked road.

She stood and stretched. She'd been fiercely holding on to those images and now she felt unburdened, lighter.

She scanned the bookshelves. She'd finished *Far From the Madding Crowd* and was looking for a shorter story.

Climbing almost to the top of the nearest ladder, she picked out a slim hardback bound in brown cloth: *The Time Machine*. The title and author's name on the spine and cover were printed plainly in darker brown and the only picture on the front was of a small, winged sphinx, outlined in the same dull colour as the lettering. Recumbent on its belly, its fore-arms jutting out in front, it resembled the famous statue in

Egypt except the face was softer, its mouth curved in a slight smirk.

Sophie settled in the red chair and finished it before teatime — and felt seriously creeped out.

She waylaid Hugo in the corridor when he came back from work.

'H. G. Wells wrote the green door story and also wrote this. It's about the far future, pretty weird. He never names the time traveller but I'm guessing it's the author.' She handed him the book. 'I think he stepped through our portal.'

'I've read this and some of his other work. This was published in…' He opened the cover and turned a page. '1895. Around the same time it was written at home.'

He went into his room, Sophie followed with the dogs, leaving the door ajar though she was wearing the full Monty. If Hugo wanted to seduce her, he'd need to put aside at least an hour — unless he'd stolen a bolt cutter that would make short work of whalebone.

She put her hand to her temple. *The Time Machine* really had knocked her sideways.

Hugo sat on the edge of the bed, the book still open in his hand. 'If Wells went through our portal, why write about a man who builds a time machine? Why not just describe the lift?'

'Better for the plot, the hero gets to decide where he goes?' Sophie perched on his armchair. 'The sphinx on the cover is outlined in exactly the same style as the scenes on the lift doors. Maybe Wells saw a sphinx?'

'Go on.'

'But the meaning of the sphinx in the story isn't clear.'

'No, it isn't.' Hugo bit his lip. 'Perhaps power, enduring over eons, or the opposite. Inevitability of decay, death … and why have a green door in a wall in the other story?'

'No idea.'

'Wells at home was scarily accurate about the future. Predicted aircraft, tanks, nuclear weapons, space travel. And in *The Shape of Things to Come,* published in the early 1930s, he has the Second World War starting in January 1940.'

Sophie swallowed. Germany had invaded Poland on 1st September 1939. 'A few months' difference. I'm not sure what Freddy would make of that with his probability stuff—'

'The narrative was so confident, like it had already happened.'

'But if the Wells at home came through our portal to Shorten,' said Sophie, 'he had no way of learning about the future, only an alternate past.'

Hugo frowned.

'Let's focus on the H.G. Wells here,' said Sophie. 'If he went through the portal to the students' union, believed he'd travelled ninety years into the future, *not* across universes ... he learned about twentieth century history, thought it set in stone—'

'If the H. G. Wells here is like the one at home, that's not what he concluded. In *A Modern Utopia,* our Wells describes a parallel world with an alternate future, and in his *Shape of Things to Come,* World War Two lasts for a decade and the Brits stay neutral.' Hugo ran his hand through his hair, messing up his fringe. 'The Wells at home could have visited other universes where time passes faster?'

'And saw different, contradictory, futures... When was *Utopia* published?'

'I can't remember,' said Hugo, 'but after *The Time Machine.* I really hope *The War of the Worlds* came from his imagination, not field trips.'

'Yes.' She'd seen the Tom Cruise movie.

'*The Shape of Things to Come* was published at home in the early 1930s. That Wells must have gone through the portal more than once. Perhaps many times? If he figured out how it works, the version of Wells here has too.'

Sophie shook her head. 'So why couldn't Eddington?'

'I don't know.'

'How did the Wells *here* come across the portal in the first place?' said Sophie. 'The lane's out in the sticks.'

'The portal had moved to the lane by 1893, when Anne came through.' Hugo closed the book. '*The Time Machine* was published after that…'

'In 1895, but books take a while to write and get published. Wells could have found the portal *before* Anne arrived, maybe years before, when it was still in *The Crooked Gate?*'

'And at home, the portal location never moved from the pub.' Hugo shot her a rueful smile. 'Perhaps both versions of Wells heard about the missing barmaid and found a lift in the cellar?' He sounded flippant, not serious.

But Sophie stood up, her brain whirring. In the lane, when she'd looked back, the lift had acquired the colours of the trees and hedges, like camouflage. 'The portal adapts to its surroundings … became a lift in the students' union. Wells at home, and here, went to the pub and found a door.'

'A green door.' Hugo's eyes widened.

'And in 1903, when Eddington's research team were in the lane, the Wells here realised where the portal had moved to.'

Hugo gave her the book. 'Wells spent decades travelling between universes…'

'We can write to him here, visit—'

'That would be a risk.'

'Why?'

'In *The Time Machine,* he's coy about whether the story is true,' said Hugo. 'And in *A Modern Utopia,* he asserts emphatically that the narrator isn't him. He won't want to admit how he got the ideas. We've already got one writer sending us threats. If Wells thought his reputation and livelihood were threatened—'

'We sign a gagging order, whatever. Hugo, he can tell us how to get home.'

He smiled. 'Yes.'

'I'll ask Anne how to word the letter, use the correct form of address…' Sophie beamed at him. '*Yes.*' Inevitable that Anne would tell Richard, but worth the risk.

That night, after dinner, Sophie and Charlotte went with Anne as usual to the small drawing room. After Miss Parry had poured coffee and left, Sophie said, 'Why do we leave and sit here by ourselves?'

'Women aren't supposed to drink whisky or smoke, and it protects our delicate ears from worrying talk about politics.'

When Sophie snorted, Anne added, 'The custom fails miserably to keep the outside world at bay. I read the paper every day and last year I persuaded Richard to have a telephone installed.'

'He didn't want one?'

'He thinks it's uncivilised, an invasion of privacy. I didn't understand at first, but everyone is used to social occasions being arranged in advance. The idea that a friend might call unexpectedly, and you'd have to speak to them, interrupting your routine … it is quite a change.'

'Do you get nuisance calls, like at home?'

Anne seemed puzzled.

'Trying to con you out of money.'

'I don't remember that. Anyway, even if we did, Mrs Rawlings would deal with it.' Anne's mouth twitched. She was trying not to laugh. 'Obviously, if the call was a personal one, from a known acquaintance, I'd speak to them, or call them back.'

'Now, that *is* civilised.'

Anne leaned forward. 'Tell me about the twenty-first century.'

Yes, Anne still missed home. Sophie told her about huge TVs and tiny phones.

'Do you have flying cars?'

'No.'

'That's a shame.' Anne sipped her coffee. 'Are there still wars?'

Sophie told her about 9/11, Iraq and Afghanistan.

'Religious fanatics?' said Anne, trying to take it in. 'What happened to the Cold War?'

'The Berlin wall came down years ago. Russia's not friendly but eastern European countries are in NATO.'

'That's incredible,' said Anne. 'You'll be telling me next there's a British Wimbledon tennis champion.'

'There is. He's won it twice.'

'Now you're teasing.' Anne placed her cup and saucer on the table. 'The cricket match tomorrow will be fun.'

Sophie was actually looking forward to it, just to get out of the Manor.

She told Anne about their H. G. Wells theory, playing it down like they had about Janus.

'I'm afraid you can't write to him,' said Anne. 'He died on a visit to Russia, in a traffic accident. In 1920, if I remember right.' Seeing Sophie's face fall, Anne added, 'You could read his *Times* obituary. The library in the market town has all the previous editions.'

Sophie put her cup aside. The coffee tasted bitter. How would Wells' obituary help? A tribute to his novels before an untimely death...

Their best lead had died with him.

CHAPTER 30

The Laceys' green car came to a gentle halt in a leafy lane near Little Shorten.

Reynolds opened Sophie's door and, restricted by her narrow skirt, she turned slowly around in her seat and placed both feet on the ground at the same time. She'd never thought about the mechanics of exiting a car. Now she had to.

Keeping the dogs' leads short, Sophie followed Anne through an open gate towards a small pavilion beside a cricket pitch.

Sophie's corset was pinching her hips, her cream skirt was even more tapered than usual, the bodice was uncompromisingly fitted, and the whole sweaty combo was topped off with silk stockings and wrist-length linen gloves. Her huge hat — a millinery masterpiece of intricate wired cloth adorned with the feathers of dead birds — shielded her face from the curious but compromised her field of vision.

Anne was wearing an almost identical outfit.

Chairs and tables were set out by the pavilion. Anne sat stiffly on an upright chair at the front and Sophie sat beside her. Nearby, on a small round table, was a jug of water and two glasses. Half under the jug was a damp piece of paper the size of a saucer with *Lady Lacey* written on it in smudged blue ink.

Across from them, by a tea tent, three young women in loose-fitting dresses and small straw hats were giggling and gossiping, their voices clear and shrill across the open space. Hobble skirt torture and giant hats were evidently a privilege thing.

One of the girls was moving her hand in a slow circle over her stomach, staring at Sophie and smiling. What was that about? Sophie tilted her head, so her hat brim obscured the girls, and took off her gloves; Anne had insisted that gloves were always removed before drinking or eating, unimpressed by Sophie's certainty that ladies in *Downton* kept them on.

Sophie put the gloves on her lap, poured water into the glasses and handed a glass to Anne.

'In previous years, we walked here and back,' said Anne. 'But it's so warm today, I'm happy to use the cars.'

The roads aren't safe remained unspoken, and Sophie sipped the tepid water and focused on the men in cricket whites walking onto the pitch. 'When the boys were talking tactics last night, it was so detailed. All that stuff about left arm orthodox spin and yips.' Freddy had been worried about the yips — losing confidence when he bowled.

'I have to confess,' said Anne, 'I stopped listening after the earnest discussion about anchors.'

Anchors played defensively so could bat until the end of time. 'My friend Lily loves cricket. She was captain of our house's mixed team.'

'I don't remember women playing,' said Anne, squinting to see if a distant fielder had caught the ball.

Fielding, bowling, batting — *anything* — would be better

than being trussed up like a chicken in an oven. 'It's not as popular as men's cricket.' Sophie pulled a linen handkerchief from her sleeve and wiped her moist face. Years ago, at another cricket match, cheering on Lily, she'd drunk chilled canned drinks and read an entire book on her phone, in between chatting with Isha and clapping. Should have brought a book today. No, Anne would have confiscated it. Conspicuous visitors had to be riveted to the action. 'How many hours until tea?' The Manor had organised refreshments.

'Around three,' said Anne.

Sophie finished her water and pictured the fridge in Isha's house in London, particularly the bit that pushed out ice in different shapes. Yes, it helped to think about ice.

The kitchen staff had put a water bowl under the table and the dogs were lying beside it in the blissful shade. Shame there wasn't room for her.

'When I arrived at the Manor,' said Anne, 'day dresses had high, very stiff collars. Quite uncomfortable.'

She couldn't imagine being *more* uncomfortable.

The soporific heat went on and on.

No sign of the boys. Must be waiting to bat. She'd told Hugo about Wells before breakfast and his face had crumbled.

Her thoughts shifted to the lift pictures. She'd hoped committing them to paper would trigger an idea, but it hadn't. She closed her eyes, trying to ignore the corset pressing against her ribcage. Breathe, try to relax.

She looked the part but was secretly an alien on a strange planet. If E.T. landed here, would they put it in boy's clothes or a complicated gown and hat? Or a child's midi dress with a white pinafore? The faint buzz of insects and the fresh smell of recently-cut lawn faded... She was on a beach, wading into a wonderfully cold sea—

Her arm was being pinched.

'Wake up,' said Anne. 'Hugo's been bowled. You must tell him you saw the whole thing.'

'Oh, I will.' It would have been the same at school, if she'd missed a vital moment. That had happened quite a lot. If she couldn't get home, there would be more cricket matches. Every year. For the rest of her life.

Hugo was walking towards them, slightly red-faced. 'Fifty odd runs, not bad, considering.'

'You were unlucky not to get more,' said Sophie, with smooth, plausible authority.

'A good innings.' Anne turned her attention back to the pitch where Freddy was at the crease.

'I'll get water,' said Hugo, and headed to the tea tent.

When he reappeared with three glasses, the water wasn't cold but Sophie dearly wanted to pour it over her head. No, a sodden hat would add Mad Visitor to her reputation. She put her fingers in the water and sprinkled it on her face.

'I don't envy you that getup,' Hugo whispered.

'The hat's the worst. I'd feel cooler without it.'

'Good afternoon.' An elderly, portly man, in a dog collar and dark suit, was peering at them quizzically through thick glasses.

'Hello, vicar,' said Anne, cheerily.

Hugo stood and shook hands. 'Hugo Harrington.'

'The Reverend Alfred Wetherby.'

Should she stand? Anne had stayed seated, so Sophie did too. 'Hello.'

'Do you mind if I join you?'

The dogs were wagging their tails against Sophie's legs and his question was a formality; Anne gestured at a chair beside Sophie.

'So,' said the vicar, once he'd sat down, 'you're the new

visitors. Anne's told me all about you.' He smiled, his eyes twinkling. 'You must come to a service when you can.'

'Do you have carols at Christmas?' Sophie had been a confirmed atheist since her parents' death, but she'd enjoyed Hadley's carol services. She'd even sung in the choir.

'We certainly do. You'd be very welcome, though it's a long way off.'

'I'd like that,' said Sophie, 'if we're still here.'

'You're going travelling?' asked the vicar.

Hugo glanced at Anne. 'The Laceys have been very kind but we'd like to go home.' He turned to the vicar and paused. This would get back to Richard. 'We think there might be a way, because of your gargoyle.'

'Ah, yes, Janus. The workmanship is very fine.' The vicar lowered his voice. 'When I arrived forty years ago, the departing vicar was thinking about having it removed.'

'Why?' said Sophie, shifting her legs. Charlotte's head was resting on her feet, threatening her circulation.

'Pagan symbol. Worried the bishop would find out and disapprove. He wanted to replace it with Saint Brigit. She's associated with doorways and thresholds.'

'Why didn't it happen?' asked Hugo.

The vicar wiped his glistening forehead with a large white handkerchief. 'Saint Brigit also has pagan origins. I managed to persuade him that Janus wasn't incompatible with Christian theology.'

'How did you do that?' Hugo sounded impressed.

'In my youth, I did the Grand Tour, spent many wonderful weeks in Rome. One of the highlights was the arch of Janus. Very impressive, built by Constantine the First or Second. It's at a crossroads and if you stand in front, it frames a Christian church, Saint George's.'

Sophie moved her legs again. The vicar was very knowledgeable.

'I said if Janus was good enough for Constantine,' added the vicar, 'he should be good enough for us.'

'We think the lift can also appear as a door,' said Sophie. 'The arch in Rome could be another portal?'

'An intriguing idea.' The vicar seemed downcast. 'It's unfortunate I can't return.'

Italy was on Sophie's long, bucket list. In a few years, if she persuaded some kind sucker into marrying her, they could do this grand tour thing? 'If you don't mind me asking, why can't you go back?'

'There is … unrest, all over Europe.'

'I've read about it in *The Times*.' Hugo glanced over at Sophie, his eyes serious.

From now on, she needed to keep informed, read the paper every day, cover to cover. If chaos theory operated in this universe, trouble on the continent would find its way here.

'On a happier note,' said the vicar, 'there are splendid examples of Janus heads in the Vatican Museum. Most are of the same man with a beard, some are different heads looking in opposite directions, male and female. But it may be that ours is unique. No obvious gender and so young.' He looked at Hugo and Sophie in turn. 'Have you tried to get home?'

'We have,' said Hugo, 'but if the portal only does random appearances, the chances of catching it are miniscule.'

'Are there any church records in Little Shorten about visitors?' asked Sophie.

'None that I know of.' The vicar smiled. 'But in previous centuries, life for most people wasn't so different a hundred years earlier, or later. Visitors might have crossed over without realising what had happened. And if they did realise, claiming such a thing could have landed them in hot water.'

'Or tied to a hot stake,' said Anne.

'Indeed.' The vicar mopped his brow again.

A tall, rangy young man was walking purposefully towards them. He was dressed like the vicar but had a neat, black goatee. The vicar got to his feet. 'May I present Mr Herbert Clutterbuck?'

Herbert had a slight stoop, like he spent too long talking to short people, and his face was deeply flushed, as if he'd been running.

The vicar accepted a glass of water from Herbert, and said, 'Mr Clutterbuck has been assisting at services.'

Hugo stood up. 'How do you do? I'm Hugo Harrington.'

The dogs were growling under the table. It was very hot.

'How do you do?' said Herbert, and turned to Sophie.

Okay, this greeting wasn't a question that required an answer, only an echo. 'Sophie Arundel. How do you do?'

Everyone shook hands, their palms sweaty.

'I'm staying at the Old Rectory until September.' Herbert sat beside Hugo, but his eyes were on Sophie, his gaze intense.

She tilted her hat to obscure her face.

Herbert cleared his throat. 'The vicar mentioned your many worlds theory. God created only one world. For us. Everyone knows that.' He had a sing song voice, as if he were giving a sermon.

The Laceys' decision to share the multiverse theory meant new acquaintances would inevitably be sceptical.

'The idea is as outrageous as spiritualism.' Herbert cleared his throat again. 'You must have come from an obscure part of the empire. It is very large.'

Spiritualism? Sophie briefly tilted her hat to see Herbert's expression. It matched his voice — squeakily earnest.

Alan was walking by, towards the tea tent, and Sophie lowered her hat brim again, shutting him out. Giant hats had their uses.

'We haven't come from anywhere abroad,' said Hugo.

'And the multiverse idea is quite old. Isaac Newton wrote about it.'

'Really?' said Sophie.

'In his book, *Opticks*, published at the beginning of the eighteenth century.'

Herbert rolled his eyes. He had slight bags, as if he didn't get enough sleep. 'Wicked, possibly blasphemy.'

'Mr Clutterbuck did theology at Oxford,' said the vicar, as if this explained Herbert's views.

Herbert cleared his throat yet again and sipped his water.

Perhaps he had an obscure medical condition?

'We're a broad church.' The vicar seemed embarrassed. 'I'm an evolution man, myself, though it took me some time to embrace it. Ingenious process, beautiful and cruel, but consistent with a wonderful creator, caring for a whole world, don't you think?'

'If our theory is right, more than one,' said Hugo. 'At home, quite a few clergy came to believe that religion and evolution could rub along together. That God guided natural selection.'

The vicar chuckled. 'Quite so.' He wiped his moist forehead again. 'I confess, I was sceptical when Lady Lacey arrived, but then we had Mr Parkes and Miss Hemmings and now your good selves, so there's obviously some kind of door.'

Herbert's face was getting redder.

He thought them oddballs, with an even odder story. Understandable.

Herbert took a small book from his pocket and wrote in it with a simple, stubby pencil — looked like a modern one. 'I record ideas for sermons as they come to me.'

'Mr Clutterbuck is taking over a living in Derby in the autumn,' said the vicar. 'I'm trying to prepare him. It can be quite daunting, guiding one's parishioners.'

A suspicion began to form in Sophie's mind. 'How far is the Old Rectory from the Manor?'

'A couple of miles,' said the vicar. 'We're just outside the village.'

Sophie leaned forward. 'Mr Clutterbuck, when did you move here?'

'Two months ago.' He gave her an interested smile.

The uneasy feeling whenever she thought about the anonymous note would stop if they found the culprit. Reasoned with them. 'Would you mind if I read your sermon notes?'

'Not at all.' He handed her the book.

Wickedness. The need for vigilance. His script was spiky and business-like, the beginning of the words slightly darker, as if he'd pushed harder with the pencil. Nothing like the anonymous envelope. She returned the book.

'How is religion in your world?' asked the vicar. 'Going strong?'

'It is,' said Hugo.

'The Church of England's much the same as here,' said Sophie, 'except for female vicars.'

Astonished silence.

'But not many female bishops,' Sophie added.

'Heresy,' said Herbert, sounding more like a nutter from the Middle Ages than an Anglican curate.

Hugo cleared his throat. 'At home, religion is mostly a force for good, but a tiny minority use it as an excuse to wage war. But then that's happened throughout history.'

Sophie vowed to clear her throat soon, for extra gravitas.

The vicar's eyebrows had shot up. 'In England?'

'Mostly abroad,' said Hugo. 'In Britain, it tends to be isolated events, though the police are stretched, trying to stop them.'

From under her hat, Sophie glanced again at Herbert. He was tapping his feet, staring into space. What an odd man.

'Are people in the Church of England involved?' The vicar sounded worried.

'No,' said Hugo. 'People have disagreements, like over female vicars, but it doesn't go beyond polite debate.'

'That *is* a relief.' The vicar sat back in his chair and addressed Hugo. 'Are you enjoying learning about the estate?'

'Very much.'

The vicar lowered his voice and said to Sophie, 'I was sorry to hear we won't be having a wedding.'

Telling Maud in confidence had worked. 'It was only a joke.'

'Indeed,' said the vicar. 'Quite so.'

Anne must have heard every word, but her attention remained on the pitch. Freddy was walking towards them in his usual languid manner, amid scattered clapping.

Herbert stood up. 'I believe it is time for tea.'

The vicar and Herbert strolled off and Sophie watched them, glad to literally see the back of Mr Clutterbuck.

'He's had some difficulties,' said Anne, getting to her feet. 'A scandal in his last parish. This is a fresh start.'

Sophie stood up too, hopefully in time to avoid a blood clot or heat exhaustion, and thought again about Herbert. As Freddy had observed, anyone could disguise their writing. Her gloves had fallen onto the grass and she put them on the chair. 'Anne, do you think Mr Clutterbuck sent that letter?'

'He's only just met you.'

But if not Herbert, then who?

Freddy was by her chair and she smiled at him. 'Well played.'

His answering grin gave her a warm glow, unconnected with the sultry temperature.

In the tea queue, as the boys stood behind Sophie

discussing the bowling action that had put Freddy out, the man in front of her turned around.

'Shame about the wedding.' Alan's face was deadpan. 'I hope that hasn't left you with too much of a problem.'

What did he mean? 'No.'

'I presumed you *needed* to marry so when people asked, I told them.' He didn't lower his voice. 'And gossip here … it's unstoppable.'

Telling Maud in confidence hadn't worked, and Alan was fanning the flames.

CHAPTER 31

For an insane moment, Sophie thought about shouting, *'I'm not pregnant.'* But anyone who hadn't heard would be memorably informed and, anyway, ladies didn't shout.

Now the mocking girls made sense. No one decent would marry her. Forever dependent on the Laceys, or life-long poverty... She'd redeploy Maud, who could authoritatively deny it, but fake news had a life of its own. When her stomach didn't swell, the gossip mill might think of a worse lie. If terminations were illegal, could the police make her have a medical examination, a virginity test—

'I was sorry to hear about the visitor dates,' said Alan, 'that you couldn't find a pattern.'

She blinked, momentarily thrown by his abrupt change of subject. Gossip flowed fast between the Manor and the village. Discussing the visitor dates over lunch with the footmen there had been stupid, and Freddy must have told his valet the dates hadn't panned out and Mr Farrow had blabbed...

She wanted to swear. No, act smart. 'A dead end, but we're not giving up.'

'Best brains in the land couldn't work it out. Don't rate your chances.'

Sophie shrugged.

'But if you do find the answer, I'd really like to know.' Alan took a cup of tea and a plate of Victoria sponge. 'It's not so bad here. Enough like home.' He headed towards an empty table.

Sophie helped herself to tea and cake. The tent interior was even hotter than outside, so she went to her old seat by the pitch. Hugo followed her out and sat beside her. The dogs hadn't moved from under the table.

She looked towards the tent. 'Where's Freddy?'

'Deep in cricket analysis with Mr Farrow. What was Alan saying?'

'Asking to be kept in the loop with the lift puzzle.' She sipped her tea and chewed a piece of chocolate cake that tasted like cardboard. 'And sticking the knife in, wondering if I had a "problem," not marrying Freddy.'

Hugo was touching her arm. 'You weren't pregnant when we came through the lift?'

'Of course not.' Her throat felt parched and she took another sip of tea. Plan for the worst. 'This must be damaging the family's reputation, Hugo. I'll have to leave.'

His tea went down the wrong way and he spluttered. After he'd recovered, he said, 'You'll starve.'

A murmur of fear … she shoved it away. She'd survive, the way young women always had. To avoid actual prostitution, she could seduce someone in Little Shorten or Derby—

'And what would happen to Charlotte?'

She couldn't take Charlotte with her, wouldn't let her go hungry. Sophie briefly shut her eyes, hurting as if her heart was being torn in half. 'Could I leave her with you, until I get myself sorted?'

'I'd stay at the Manor while you're begging, sleeping in ditches? Get real.'

He was searching her face and she found herself smiling, immensely glad of his friendship. She trusted him, believed he'd come with her. She'd never trusted a boy. Not even Pete. Not with the sort of trust that involved real risk.

'I don't know how long Anne will protect you, but Freddy wouldn't let you end up on the street.'

'What's it to him?'

Hugo took a judicious sip of tea. 'He's thoroughly decent. He just wouldn't.'

'How can you know that?'

'It's a fair assumption.'

She wasn't reassured. That mocking girl... Why did anybody want to be famous? It was vile. Strangers talking and laughing, thinking they knew her. 'I appreciate your support.' The words sounded oddly formal. The restrained manners here were infectious.

'No problem.'

'You're okay for a posh boy.'

'I'm no posher than Isha,' said Hugo. 'Isn't her father an ambassador?'

'Something high up.'

'Why did you write me off as an entitled loser? I don't get it.'

She avoided his eyes, feeling foolish. 'I fell out with Madison and thought anyone who was her friend was ... like her.' Madison had acted friendly in a science lesson when they'd been paired up for an experiment, but afterwards blanked her. It took a while for Sophie to get it. There was no question of actually *socialising*.

'When did you fall out?'

'About seven years ago.'

'You were, what, *twelve?*'

'Like I said, a while ago.' She'd coined 'A Madison,' to mean anyone who was snobby and two-faced, and her friends had used it to mock the rich kids for bragging about exotic holidays and later on, for driving expensive cars. It had felt good, joking around. 'And all that stuff you said about climate change in the debate at school, you were so ... adamant.'

'I was allocated the more difficult argument. The point was to persuade, not what I personally believed.'

She felt foolish again. The competitors hadn't *chosen* a side. She finished her tea. 'Maybe it's a school thing but for the whole time, lots of stuff felt like a big deal.'

'I know.'

'Do you? You were good at everything.'

'I struggled with maths and physics.' He seemed bemused. 'And for all their talk about underplaying exams, producing a rounded person, it was remorselessly competitive. When I didn't get the grades for Oxford, the logical thing to do was retake my A levels. But I couldn't face it.'

He must have been gutted. 'I'm really sorry I was so horrible the first day here. But we had nothing in common. You had your friends. I had mine.'

He gave her a tight smile and gazed out at the pitch.

She registered his blue eyes and long black lashes, the angular chin and firm mouth, and inside her, butterflies did a happy, illogical dance. He was gorgeous. During that thought, or because of it, a delicious tingling began, and lingered in her core. He'd kissed her when he thought he was dreaming. Must mean something? But she'd once dreamed she'd snogged Isha. Seriously weird. If the kiss in the lane for Hugo had been just a generic wet dream ... explained his lack of interest now. The tantalising tingling dissolved, leaving a nagging void.

Jack was nuzzling into Hugo's legs and Charlotte was leaning into hers. If only people were more like dogs. You knew exactly where you stood with them. Charlotte could read her mind, adored Sophie Arundel and didn't care who knew it.

Across the cricket pitch, the mocking girl was making pregnancy gestures again and so was her friend. Deference was ingrained here, so Alan's lie must be common knowledge — and accepted. One disrespectful person might fear retribution but not ten or a hundred. Sophie pretended to sip from her empty cup. Act dignified.

Hugo stood and walked briskly towards the girls, his young patrician face as cold as a medusa stare. He'd only taken a few steps when they scuttled into the tea tent.

When he sat beside her again, she said, 'I should have done that, but thank you.'

'We're in this together, Sophie.'

She smiled, buoyed up by his support. 'I know.'

But by the time she was in the car, Sophie's insides had shrivelled into a tight, stress ball. The Manor had narrowly won the match but as the boys relived their victory, she couldn't feign enthusiasm. The fallout from *The Crooked Gate* was radioactive dust, long lasting and lethal. How long before Alan's poison reached the Manor?

That evening, she asked Maud if she'd heard any stupid gossip and the answer showed in Maud's face.

'I heard it from Mr Watkins, Miss, who heard it from Mr Farrow, who heard it from—'

'It's bonkers.'

'I know, Miss.' Maud's face was set, serious.

As Maud finished fastening Sophie's dress before dinner, Sophie registered in the mirror an unflattering worry line between her brows. She *really* hoped Mr Farrow wasn't talking about this with Freddy. 'Feel free to tell people I'm not pregnant, Maud. You don't have to go into detail.'

'They'll look silly, Miss, when it's obvious you're not … enceinte.'

'Er, what?'

Maud was gritting her teeth. 'Pregnant.'

'I didn't realise you spoke French.'

'I don't, Miss. It's just a politer word.'

CHAPTER 32

'I just wish Anne would say something.' Sophie hit the bag with a ferocious punch in an attempt to clear her head.

At ten in the morning in the gym, she shouldn't have been bleary eyed, but since the cricket match — two nights running — she'd slept badly. '*Not* knowing what she's planning is worse than knowing.'

'I can't see Anne chucking you out,' said Lucy. 'More likely, she'll send you to stay with a friend until the heat's off.'

Sophie aimed a skilful kick. 'And after a decent interval, I'll *marry well*.'

'It's not compulsory.'

'You did good, dodging that bullet.'

'Exception that proves the rule.' Lucy steadied the swinging punch bag. 'I've never liked dressing up, making small talk.'

'Tell me about it.' Sophie unleashed an explosive kick. 'That's how I feel when I need to act *ladylike*.'

An hour later, Anne sought out Sophie in the library.

This was it. Sophie closed her book and stood up from the red chair.

Anne shut the tall door behind her.

Meet this head on. 'This gossip is damaging the family's reputation.'

'Miss Able is blazing a trail of outrage on your behalf.' Anne settled herself in another chair and gestured Sophie to sit down again. 'As is Miss Jefferson.'

Right, Anne's maid... 'The cricket match—'

'The situation was untenable well before that. I wrote to Kate's father a week ago, asking if you could stay for a short while. I received his reply today. The letter is polite, apologetic and explains that Dereham Hall is being extensively renovated, so it's not practical for you to stay.'

'Okay.'

'No, Sophie, it's not. Dereham Hall is larger than the Manor. No renovation work would be so disruptive as to preclude guests. Word of your ... difficulty has made its way across the county.'

'Oh,' said Sophie. 'How?'

'Servants write letters too. Mrs Rawlings is friendly with their housekeeper and, with some reluctance, Mrs Rawlings confirmed my suspicion. Charles believes you would be a pernicious influence on Kate and your presence in the household would destroy her reputation.'

Sophie's hands tensed around the book in her lap. Every day she stayed here was trashing the Lacey's reputation...

'This will be difficult to get past, Sophie, but you have two things in your favour. Class and community.'

'I don't understand.'

'Class is a strong shield. Yes, our servants gossip and enjoy our discomforts, but when people in the village spread lies, that's different. I suppose deference comes into it but it's more about solidarity. The Manor folk protect their own.'

'Even me.'

'Even you,' said Anne. 'And you're doing the right thing, keeping a low profile. If you carry on acting like other girls—'

'Dignified and demure.'

'Exactly. This will run out of steam.'

'You really think so?'

'Yes.'

Relief coursed through Sophie's veins, sweet and euphoric.

'You'll make friends at the ball and scotch the gossip, you'll see. If *this* visitor can marry well, you can too.' Anne sighed. 'But you need to grow a thick skin. When I was first married, "mad gold digger" was one of the politer things people whispered. Gradually though, Richard's friends accepted me. We had jolly dinner parties where we talked about inventions and changing tastes in food and fashion. The women flatly refused to believe in mini skirts, but the men were very interested.'

Predictable.

'The idea of time travel is familiar, but your theory is more outlandish and, frankly, impossible to imagine.'

Ironic. Given it was a reputable scientific theory.

'But the scepticism about the multiverse idea is quite strange,' said Anne, 'given people believe the most ludicrous things.'

'Like what?'

'Spiritualism, for instance.'

Herbert had mentioned that at the cricket match. 'Belief in spirits?'

'Sort of,' said Anne. 'Mediums speaking to the dead.'

'Creepy.'

'Belief in the supernatural is very widespread. Have you heard of the Cottingley Fairies?'

Sophie shook her head.

'Taken in 1920, photographs of children, apparently with fairies. Caused a sensation at home. The pictures were debunked in the 1970s, but before that numerous so-called experts had declared them genuine. It was the same here. When I told Richard and Freddy the fairies were paper drawings, they were so disappointed. I half wished I hadn't told them.' Anne smiled. 'People here are generally more deferential, so unless you act oddly, in time you'll be accepted.'

Alan's sneering about Anne resurfaced and Sophie chewed her lip.

'And your knowledge from home could be an asset. You could make a killing on the stock market.'

Sophie tried to smile.

An hour later, when she walked with Hugo towards the dining room for lunch, he was uncharacteristically quiet.

'Are you okay?'

'Just knackered.'

'You should take it easy,' said Sophie. 'It's Saturday.'

'I had to go into the office this morning,' said Hugo, 'still not on top of things.'

'But you'll be paid soon.'

'No. Indefinite unpaid internship.'

'That's rough,' said Sophie. 'But worth it, if you make manager.'

'That's decades down the line, and only if I prove myself, become useful.'

She'd never be useful, only a liability. She told him about the letter from Kate's father, keeping her voice low. 'So I can't even get shipped off.'

Emotion showed in his face and was gone. Surprise? Relief?

'But acting like a posh girl may protect my reputation.'

'The class thing works up to a point,' said Hugo, 'for me as well, but...'

'What?'

'If there's a full-blown revolution, that shield will become a target. A death sentence ... guillotines come to mind.'

'England's not France.'

'True, but Richard's told me so often he's not worried, I know he is.'

After lunch, Sophie fetched *The Times* from the small drawing room, went to the terrace and read it from cover to cover, including the foreign news.

Saturday 8th August 1925. Overwhelmed by refugees, Switzerland closes its borders...

Much the same as yesterday. A civil war was raging in Italy and Germany, the death toll in the millions. Bolsheviks had overthrown the government in France; how many people had been executed or imprisoned was unclear.

If she met Prince Charming tomorrow, she wouldn't be honeymooning in Europe.

'May I join you?' Freddy was standing on the terrace wearing Shorten Casual and — unusually — his bow tie wasn't wonky.

'Of course.' It was his terrace. Actually, everything she was wearing was Lacey property, even her preposterous underwear.

He rang the handbell and sat down. 'You're still missing home.'

Aunty Wendy's face materialised in her head, then Isha's. 'I had my whole life in front of me. Travelling, working.'

'Working ... you're in reduced circumstances?'

'No. *Not* working would be weird.'

Miss Parry came out, put down a plate of biscuits and poured tea. Freddy smiled at her, but she didn't notice and hurried indoors.

Sophie sipped her tea, the longing for home still a physical ache. 'Isha's studying to be a doctor.'

'But no one would let her treat them.'

Sophie snorted. 'They will. One of the girls in the year above me, her mother's a heart surgeon. Gives talks at conferences all over the world. When she's not doing heart surgery.'

'Gosh,' said Freddy. 'It would be wonderful to do anything, but it's not realistic.'

'I know. It would be much easier if I were a boy.'

'Not really, I've got no choice at all. I'll run the estate.'

'Oh.' In some ways, Freddy was just as trapped as her. And he was a lovely guy, not a mean bone in his tall, lanky body.

'All my friends are in the same boat. The oldest have to run their places and the others have to go into the army or navy, or the church.' Freddy munched contemplatively on a bourbon biscuit. 'Everyone has to do their best with the cards they're dealt.'

'You should have done philosophy, not maths.'

'Far too difficult.'

'Most people find maths too difficult,' said Sophie, 'including me.'

Hugo was walking towards them.

'You haven't been in the office?' Freddy rang the handbell again. 'Slogging away this morning was bad enough.'

Hugo sat opposite Sophie. 'Only half an hour.' He looked sheepishly at Freddy. 'Grappling with your crop yields graph … the detailed numbers.'

'I wish I was good at maths,' said Sophie.

'I've always found mathematics fascinating.' Freddy sipped his tea. 'No idea why.'

'It's your genes,' said Hugo.

'How do you mean?'

'You've inherited it,' said Sophie.

'Mummy enjoyed the statistics part of her degree,' said Freddy, 'and she's talked about genes.'

Miss Parry came out wearing a new disapproving frown, poured Hugo's tea and left.

'Since the 1980s, genetic research has really taken off,' said Hugo.

'Tell me all about it,' said Freddy, 'but start from the beginning.'

Hugo summarised: Rosalind Franklin and the double helix X-ray, Crick and Watson, and finished with the Genome Project.

'Genome,' repeated Freddy, slowly. 'Odd name.'

'Like a type of gnome.' Sophie giggled. 'It deserves a grander name.'

Freddy stood up. 'I'm going for a well-deserved lie down.'

Sophie watched him stroll away. 'Freddy's like nobody I've ever met.' She finished her tea. 'And Lucy was right about Alan and her and Anne. As different as we are.'

Hugo seemed taken aback. 'We're not so different.'

'Mr Perfect and Miss Gossip Magnet?'

'We have similar values, share … a dry sense of humour.'

'Hadley conditioning. Nurture not nature.'

He hit his head with his hand. 'Why didn't I think of it before? It's got to be linked to DNA.'

'What is?'

'Why so few people step through the portal.' He grinned. 'Sophie, that's it. We share a rare gene. Inherited from beings who built the lift, when they visited our universe.'

'That's wacky.'

'We don't have anything obvious in common because it's invisible … and the portal *isn't* a natural phenomenon. And it's not a portal.'

'So, what is it?'

'A vehicle.' He finished his tea. 'Only available to those with the right DNA.'

'You mean ... a spaceship?'

'Yes, one that travels between universes.'

'*Really* wacky.' Sophie rubbed her eyes, irrationally hoping that would make her brain work better. 'I could imagine sharing an unusual gene with you or Anne or Lucy, but *Alan?*'

'I think genes determine personality, but not completely.'

She frowned. 'Isn't personality part of your soul?'

'Who knows...'

'And I thought the Genome Project ID'd all the genes?'

'No. When they mapped it, they used a small number of people, then assembled the findings to get an overview. The genome is a mosaic, doesn't represent any one individual. Everyone's genome is unique.'

She must have looked impressed because he added, 'I understand the principle, not the detail.'

'H. G. Wells ... the one at home and here might not have figured out how it worked. Both versions are the same person, with the rare gene. They were just able to travel, like us.'

Hugo tapped his fingers on the table. 'We can't research DNA here.'

'And it can't be the only trigger. Lucy said she'd used the lift loads of times.'

Miss Parry was back, collecting crockery and Hugo stayed quiet, keen to keep their discussion private.

The following morning, Sophie met up with Lucy in the gym and told her about the DNA idea.

But she already knew.

'Miss Parry overheard.' Lucy started her stretching routine.

Before she'd cleared up, Miss Parry must have been loitering.

'But she had no idea what Hugo was talking about,' said Lucy, 'so I ended up fielding questions. It was quite awkward.'

'Why?'

'Explaining how DNA's passed on? Sexual reproduction?'

'Right, sorry.' Sophie stretched. 'We were hoping to keep this confidential. Richard isn't keen on us finding the lift. He worries Anne might leave.'

'He was twitchy when we arrived.'

So, Richard had always been paranoid.

Later, when Sophie called for Hugo to go to lunch, he handed her an envelope. *Mr Hugo Harrington and Miss Sophie Arundel* was written in familiar, dark blue ink. 'Delivered by hand last night.'

The uneasy feeling was back. She pulled out the note. *IF YOU OPEN THE LIFT, GOD WILL SMITE YOU DOWN.*

She followed Hugo into his room and sat in his armchair.

'This definitely isn't Richard.' Hugo began to close the door to the passage but left it slightly ajar. 'He's religious, but his god is the friendly Church of England non-smiting kind. If it got to the wire, I suspect he'd do anything to keep Anne in Shorten, but this … it's not his style.'

'Agreed.' Richard was shrewd and smart. These letters were just crass.

'The first note arrives after we analyse visitor dates.' Hugo paced in front of the bed. 'This one lands right after we talk about DNA.'

'Your gene idea is common knowledge downstairs.' Sophie told him what Lucy had said.

'So by now, it'll be all round the village.' He stopped pacing. 'No more lift puzzle chats with servants around.'

'They're stealthy,' said Sophie. 'Probably do special stealthy training as part of their induction.'

'And not just servants. Freddy doesn't need to know.'

'He was brilliant with the visitor dates. If you asked him not to discuss it with his valet, anyone—'

'I still trust Freddy ... but not with this, not anymore.' Hugo rolled his eyes. 'He'd be sorry if you left.'

'Oh.' That was why he'd been relieved when they'd found nothing in the lane. '*He*'d try to stop us leaving?'

'I don't know.' Hugo sat on the edge of the bed. 'But he didn't write the letters, I'm sure of that.'

Charlotte was leaning against her legs and Sophie reached down and patted her. 'Lucy's a good sounding board and never gossips.'

'But if the gossip mill picks up *anything*, she'll be in the frame.'

'It won't,' said Sophie. 'Lucy thought the first note could have been a drunken weekend prank. That was left on a Friday. This was delivered on a Saturday.'

'One might have been, but not two.'

'It has to be Herbert sending them.'

'Both letters were delivered very late,' said Hugo. 'Easy for someone living in the Manor.'

'But Herbert's the only person with a motive. *Wicked, possibly blasphemy.* He really doesn't like the idea of other worlds.'

'It's not far to walk ... and last night there was a clear sky and moonlight.'

'And you know this, how?'

'I was drinking whisky on the terrace, with Richard and Freddy.'

Her exclusion from their cosy chats still rankled. She

stood up. 'If Richard could lend us Reynolds, we could go to the Old Rectory this afternoon. Confront him.'

'No, talk nice.' Hugo opened his door. 'Catch him off guard.'

CHAPTER 33

The Old Rectory was a Victorian, red-brick building, with solid gables and stone-framed gothic windows. In front of the house was a circular gravel drive bordered by neat lawn and mature apple trees. Small compared to the Manor, but still an impressive home.

The late afternoon air was stale and humid and as Sophie unfolded herself out of the car, a slick bead of sweat appeared on her temple. She wiped it off with her fingers and adjusted the prickly inner band of the straw hat away from her forehead.

'We'll only be ten minutes or so,' Hugo said to Reynolds, shutting the car door and stepping towards the house.

Sophie caught up with him. 'Anne still believes it's someone with mental health issues. *Not* Herbert.'

'Richard and Freddy think the same.' Hugo closed a button on his suit jacket.

'Herbert and the vicar must rattle around in here.'

Hugo tugged on a bellpull by the front door and the ring echoed inside.

'Definitely space for rattling.' Sophie shot Hugo a nervy

glance, wishing she'd brought Charlotte along to deter strange behaviour. Herbert was a strange guy.

The housekeeper answered the door. 'I'm afraid the vicar's at church.'

Hugo explained they'd come to see Herbert and she asked them to wait in the hall.

The barely furnished space was dominated by an enormous fern in a planter. Green draping leaves, fully four feet across, stole most of the light from a window. Belonged in a posh greenhouse.

'This is a pleasant surprise.' Herbert smiled at Sophie as he walked through a doorway. He was already dressed for dinner in black tie. 'Please come this way.'

They followed him into a small sitting room crowded with furniture upholstered in dark gothic colours: purple, black, burgundy and vermillion.

'This reflects the taste of the vicar's late wife,' said Herbert. 'Do sit down.'

Sophie sat beside Hugo on a burgundy sofa; white crochet antimacassars protected the back and arms, like fancy versions of the covers put on headrests in trains. She registered a faint trace of lavender, but the familiar scent only heightened her nerves.

'Would you care for tea,' asked Herbert, 'or an aperitif?'

'Thank you, no,' said Hugo. 'We won't take up much of your time.'

Herbert settled himself in a purple baroque chair, took a small glass of amber sherry from a side table and took a sip. 'How can I help you?'

Sophie handed him the envelopes.

Herbert took out the notes, read them and pursed his lips. 'I heard about the first letter but not the second. How curious.' He returned the notes to the envelopes.

Okay, a good actor. And their short wait in the hall had

given him time to get his act together. Sophie pocketed the envelopes.

'We understand your concerns,' said Hugo. 'We'd like to talk things through, reassure you, if we can.'

'You think … *I* wrote those letters?' Herbert seemed genuinely taken aback.

'If we did find the lift and go home, the lift would then vanish from the lane,' said Sophie. 'That's what it does, why your scientists found no evidence. And with no proof, there'd be nothing to undermine people's faith. You're worrying unnecessarily.'

Herbert raised thin eyebrows. 'I'm not worried about *proof*. It's your theory about different worlds that could undermine faith.' He put his sherry glass on the table. 'Whoever wrote those letters must be simple-minded. You can't find the lift because it doesn't exist. You invented it to ingratiate yourself into the Manor and society.' He cleared his throat. 'My apologies, that was … rude.' He smiled at Sophie again. 'Actually, if you disappeared tomorrow, I'd be sorry.' His gaze lingered on her face.

He thought her a gold-digger, but he was *flirting*?

Hugo stood up. 'We should be on our way.'

Disappointment bitter in her mouth, Sophie got to her feet. She'd hoped for a stammering denial or defiant confession, not a masterclass in acting.

Herbert stood and escorted them to the front door, his pale face bland. 'I'm sorry I couldn't be of more assistance.'

Out of earshot outside, Hugo said, 'We can catch up later.'

Sophie nodded. Reynolds was holding open the car door, would likely repeat downstairs everything he heard.

Back at the Manor, despite the dogs barking a greeting chorus from her room, Sophie went with Hugo into his.

She left the door ajar, mindful of propriety, even as her

brain replayed Herbert's reaction. 'He seemed baffled, but who else could it be?' She sat in the armchair.

'I don't think it's him.' Hugo regarded her glumly. 'But once Herbert's a fully-fledged vicar and preaching, he could finish us. Destroy our reputation—'

'Trash my marriage chances … I know.'

'It's more than that, Sophie. If we're regarded as subversives or loonies, we'll be dependent on the Laceys forever.'

'We could move, emigrate?'

'That would take money.'

'Your tie's crooked.' She stood and stepped forward.

'Thanks, I'll sort it.' He walked over to his long mirror.

She returned to her seat and tapped her fingers on the arm of the chair. '*IF YOU OPEN THE LIFT, GOD WILL SMITE YOU DOWN.* There's more than one threat in that. If we exclude a vengeful god getting involved, it could mean that somehow … during *the process* of opening the lift, we'll die.'

Hugo finished adjusting his tie and turned around. 'We'll have to assess the risk if we get that far.'

'The other threat is—'

'The writer plans to kill us.'

'Yes.' Sophie ignored a cold, tight feeling. 'Whoever the writer is, whatever their deal, we need to sort this a different way.'

'How?'

She went over to the door and checked the corridor was empty. 'We make him — or her — lose interest. Over dinner, so the footmen hear, we say we've run out of ideas and given up. But secretly keep trying.' She watched him, assessing his reaction. 'Cunning plan … or too obvious?'

'Giving up so quickly wouldn't be credible, but if we can keep lift ideas *entirely* secret … over time, the decision will seem more convincing. Logical, inevitable.' He nodded, half to himself. 'Clever.'

Brainbox Hugo thought her clever. Way to go.

'Quantum mechanics.'

'What?'

'Illogical, unpredictable,' said Hugo, 'I should have realised before.'

'Another lift theory?'

'Yes, but this one *won't* help us find it, so reinforces your plan. It's quite complicated.'

Of course, it was complicated. This was Hugo.

An hour later, when they met up again and went to the anteroom for drinks, the Laceys were already there.

'How did you get on at the Old Rectory?' asked Anne.

'I don't think he sent the notes,' said Hugo.

Richard frowned. 'So still a mystery. Unsettling.'

Unsettling. No. Someone watching, waiting, threatening to kill them… Way beyond unsettling.

At dinner, Mr Crawford was his normal, inscrutable self but the footmen were restless, whispering more than usual. And Mr Hunter wasn't there, replaced by a shorter, stocky lad.

Between the starter and main course, Hugo said, flatly, 'I've given up trying to find the lift.'

Anne put down her wine glass. 'Whoever the writer is, whatever their motive, you shouldn't let them intimidate you.'

'My change of heart has nothing to do with the notes.' Hugo glanced at Sophie, his expression apologetic, resigned. 'Our DNA theory is just that, a theory. And I realised this afternoon … even if we'd found a pattern in the visitor dates, it wouldn't have helped.'

'I meant to tell you,' said Freddy, 'Phil thinks it could take years.'

'Any more analysis would be a waste of time,' said Hugo. 'I think it's a device someone *built*. If that's right, it's so advanced, it's likely got subatomic software. We're talking quantum mechanics.'

'What's that?' asked Richard.

'Particles at the subatomic level,' said Hugo. 'They don't obey the normal laws of physics. At home, that's been tested and studied for decades. *Not* just a theory.'

Freddy grinned. 'It's fascinating.'

'Subatomic?' said Richard.

'Smaller than an atom,' said Freddy.

'Around this time at home, Einstein knew about it,' said Hugo. 'Do you have Einstein?'

'Definitely,' said Freddy.

'*God does not play dice with the universe*,' quoted Hugo. 'Even Einstein found it baffling.'

'What's this got to do with the visitor dates?' said Sophie.

'Any observed pattern would only be coincidence,' said Hugo, 'and wouldn't enable us to predict future dates.'

'You're right,' said Freddy. 'I should have realised.'

'Please explain,' said Anne, looking at Hugo.

'Normal physics, if you have enough information, you can predict the way a dice falls, from the angle and momentum of the throw, the weight, shape and size of the dice. But in quantum mechanics, particles are random *and* unpredictable.'

'You said you'd struggled with physics,' said Sophie to Hugo.

'This is Discovery Channel stuff.' He looked sheepish. 'Science for dummies.'

'I want to forget about the lift,' said Sophie, 'concentrate on life here.'

Freddy smiled, Sophie smiled back and embraced a surge of relief. If they ever got home, she should audition for RADA, take up acting.

After dinner, Sophie went to her room but Maud wasn't there. Odd.

Sophie tugged the bellpull but it didn't ring. Maud was always around when she was needed, so Sophie hadn't used it before. Was it broken? Wouldn't try again. Didn't want to seem needy.

A knock on the door. 'You rang, Miss?'

Yes, Maud actually said that. Had she somehow forgotten the time?

'I'm so sorry I'm late, Miss.'

'No worries.'

But Maud's face was strained as she moved behind Sophie to undo her scarlet dress.

Sophie Arundel must have committed another faux pas. 'Maud, if I've messed up, please tell me.'

Maud shook her head, as if Sophie was talking gibberish. 'It's awful, Miss, just awful.' She continued determinedly undoing buttons, as if that could somehow help with what was awful. 'Mr Hunter's been dismissed. He's been stealing from the butler's pantry, more than ten guineas.'

'What are guineas?' Sounded like a type of bird.

'A guinea is twenty-one shillings. He spent it on cigarettes and whisky.' Maud rolled her eyes.

'So, ten guineas … is a lot?'

'Nearly half my wages for a year.'

Sophie stepped out of the dress. 'Are the police involved?'

'They're too busy with the trouble in Derby. Mr Hunter's gone back to Little Shorten. Very hard on his family. Goodness knows how long it's been going on. I can hardly believe it.' Maud sucked her teeth. 'And Miss Parry's been dismissed too.'

'Why?'

'She stole sixpence, Miss, from the kitchen kitty box. What with Mr Hunter, they did a check and kept watch. Mrs Ferris caught her red-handed. Miss Parry said this was the first time but cook says they can't be sure. Money's gone missing before.'

'She's gone home?'

'No … her family in Derby are in terrible straits.'

So, Miss Parry's frown likely stemmed from her family's troubles.

'She'll end up in the workhouse.'

'What's that?'

'They make them work terrible hard.' Maud hung Sophie's gown on a hanger. 'But it's better than starving.'

'Did she say why she took the money?'

'For postage, Miss. She was sending off bread and a whole wheel of cheese.'

'How much is a wheel?'

Maud spread her hands.

Okay, a big piece.

'Her sister's expecting her first baby and not eating enough.' Maud put the dress in the wardrobe.

'She stole the cheese as well?'

'No, Miss. It's sort of accepted, people sending off food, but even for such a heavy parcel, postage wouldn't be more than seven pence.'

'How much does Miss Parry earn?'

'Eight shillings a week.'

'And that's more than sixpence?'

'A lot more, Miss. There's twelve pence in a shilling.'

This currency was ludicrously complicated.

'She'd already sent her wages home, but said she'd repay

it.' Maud walked over to the chest of drawers, her expression pensive.

'Do you think she would have?'

'Yes, she's a good person.'

'It was Mrs Ferris that dismissed her, not Lady Lacey?'

'Yes, Miss.'

Sophie had been much younger than Miss Parry — ten or eleven — when for a dare she'd stolen a chocolate bar from a shop. If she'd been caught, she might have got off with a warning but could have received a formal caution. A police record would have stymied her Hadley scholarship.

Maud took out the nighty and dressing gown and Sophie slipped off her faithful bra.

But as Sophie pulled the nightdress over her head, her mind was humming, not ready for sleep.

Miss Parry was a child. Sophie Arundel was a *very* precarious guest and would have to tread carefully, but maybe she could give Miss Parry a second chance…

CHAPTER 34

The next morning, Sophie joined Anne for elevenses in the small drawing room.

Anne was smiling encouragingly at the red-headed maid, though the girl didn't seem afflicted with new job jitters.

After the dogs had settled and the maid had left, Sophie said, 'Can I ask about Miss Parry?'

'Very disappointing.'

'Her family are in no state to take her in.'

'Even if there are strong mitigating circumstances,' said Anne, 'this was an abuse of trust. And I can't undermine Mrs Ferris.'

'But the roads aren't safe.'

When Anne said nothing, Sophie added, 'Where's the nearest workhouse?'

Anne winced. 'Shorten. The market town.'

A town also called Shorten. Confusing.

Anne gave Sophie a resigned smile. 'I'll see what I can do.'

That afternoon, Sophie was sitting in the blue armchair reading, the dogs at her feet, when Maud bustled in, carrying a stack of freshly laundered underwear.

'Mrs Ferris says Miss Parry isn't the same as Mr Hunter, and she can come back.' Maud put the clothes on the bed. 'Never heard the like.'

Sophie looked convincingly surprised. 'So, she's back now?'

'No, Miss. My sister's gone to find her.'

'Your sister?' Sophie closed her book.

'She's taken the work van. She and her husband run Slater's bakery.'

'In the village?'

Maud picked up a clean pair of stockings. 'In the town.' She put the stockings in a drawer. 'Mrs Slater came to the kitchens after lunch with the second delivery, said Miss Parry came to the bakery asking for work and came back again because the workhouse was full.'

'Mrs Slater' must be Maud's sister. She even referred to her own sister formally.

Maud was shaking her head. 'What's the world coming to, when the workhouse turns people away?'

'So, Miss Parry's at your sister's.'

Maud shifted her weight from one foot to the other. 'They'd heard she'd been stealing, Miss, so didn't take her.'

'How far is Shorten town?'

'About five miles.' Maud ruffled Charlotte's head. 'Miss Parry will try to go to Derby, where people won't know about her thieving. But she won't get far. Mrs Slater will find her.'

Unless someone else found her first. Beard Man's face rose up in Sophie's head. She'd been lucky she'd only been robbed. Miss Parry had no money or jewellery but was slight and pretty. Defenceless.

After dinner, Maud was still agitated. 'Miss Parry's back, Miss. She's been demoted to scullery maid. Better than nothing.' Maud shook her head. 'But she's in a terrible state, won't stop crying.'

'She'll recover herself, I'm sure,' said Sophie, though she wasn't sure at all. Miss Parry might need psychological help. Keeping her face carefully blank, she added, 'She's safe and I'm glad.'

Maud set her mouth. 'Not everyone is. Mr Hunter's friends are causing trouble, saying he should come back too.'

~

In the gym the following morning, Lucy confirmed that Miss Parry's return had stoked resentment and further divided the servants. 'Last night, Hunter's mates met him in *The Crooked Gate.*' Lucy did a flurry of punches. 'He's getting them fired up, after better wages and more holidays.'

'You can put more weight behind the punches,' Sophie demonstrated in slow motion. 'Maud works long hours, only has half a day off a week. She has another half day once a fortnight, but every other Sunday has to go to church. Hardly time off.'

Lucy punched again, this time with more force. 'It's better here than most places. Miss James told me her last family made her do *everything*, cleaning, cooking, darning and minding the children, because they could only afford one servant.'

'Miss James?'

'The new maid.' Lucy steadied the bag. 'Hunter's just stirring. Of course, people could leave, but they wouldn't get another job any time soon.'

'What I don't understand,' said Sophie, placing an elegant kick, 'with so much unemployment, why hasn't Richard found a new estate manager? Hugo says good guys don't move but that can't be the whole story.'

'Men are queuing up, but he wants one with experience — and the best of them.' Lucy did another punch. 'He's offering £200 a year. Serious money.'

At teatime, when Sophie asked about Miss Parry's mental health, Anne reassured her. 'With Mrs Rawlings' kind super-vision and Maud's protective instincts, she'll recover.'

Evidently, professional counselling was a modern thing.

Before dinner, Maud provided a running commentary on the 'trouble' downstairs. Despite a decree from Mr Crawford banning Bolshevik talk, friends and acquaintances had fallen out, arguing late into the night.

'All the bolshy ones are going to *The Crooked Gate*,' Maud whispered, though they were alone apart from the dogs. 'Mr Watkins is going.'

According to Hugo, John Watkins was a very proper valet, and John was also dating Maud — Miss Conventional. So, an unlikely radical. 'Mr Watkins is bolshy?'

'No, he's *pretending,* so he can hear what's happening and report back. You mustn't breathe a word, Miss.'

'I won't.' Servants spying on other servants … hardly a recipe for a happy household. 'How many people are going?'

'At least twenty. Footmen, gardeners, all sorts.'

'No women?'

'No, Miss. They'll be drinking.'

Anne drank wine and Sophie Arundel certainly did. But then, *The Crooked Gate* was a rough pub. 'I'm glad you and Miss Parry are still friends.'

'We agree about most things. The Laceys have been good to her and she's grateful.'

Sophie nodded. The Laceys had been good to her and Hugo too — but the 'noblesse oblige' stuck in her throat.

The following morning, Sophie woke to her usual tea and toast, but Maud was uncharacteristically silent, her eyes red-rimmed.

'What's happened?'

Reluctantly, Maud faced her. 'Mr Watkins was attacked in the pub. Mr Parkes managed to pull them off before… You should see him, Miss, it's terrible.'

'You need to sit down.'

'I'm not supposed to, not with you—'

'I'm telling you to. This is more important than any … rules.'

Maud sat gingerly in the armchair. 'He's got a black eye, his lip is split, and Dr Griffiths thinks three of his ribs are broken. I've never seen anything like it.'

'He's in hospital?'

'No. Dr Griffiths says all he can do is rest.' Maud took a shaky breath. 'Lady Lacey's called the police.'

'But he'll recover?'

'Yes.' Tears rolled down her cheeks and Sophie wanted to hug her — no, she'd be more embarrassed than comforted.

Maud twisted her hands together. 'I can't face the servants' hall.'

'What do you mean?'

'There's some that thinks he got what he deserved.' She put her head in her hands and sobbed. Charlotte put her furry head on Maud's lap and Maud stroked her. 'I'll be all right in a moment, Miss.' She sniffed.

Sophie took her glass of water from the bedside table and offered it. 'You hide in here. And when you go to the servants' hall, put your chin up and pretend you're confident. After a bit, the pretence becomes real. That's what I do.'

Maud accepted the water and, after a minute or so, she helped Sophie get dressed.

Sophie left, taking Charlotte, and carefully closed the

door behind her. As she turned, she literally bumped into Hugo walking briskly along the corridor.

He was frowning. 'Is Maud okay?'

'Not really. She's crying her heart out.' A strand of hair had come loose from Sophie's bun and she brushed it from her eyes. 'At least, John's basically all right.'

Hugo beckoned her into his room and closed the door. 'Freddy's valet woke me up this morning. He overheard Dr Griffiths talking to Richard. John's *not* all right. He has internal bleeding. It's a slow bleed but if it doesn't stop, he'll die.'

'He should go to hospital.'

'They've no scans, Sophie. They wouldn't find it, any more than Dr Griffiths.'

'Does John know? Maud doesn't—'

'John doesn't want her told … any of this.' A muscle throbbed in Hugo's jaw, betraying his distress. 'But she'll have to know soon.' He drew a deep breath. 'We've become friends. Close friends. I can't take it in.'

CHAPTER 35

Sophie searched for words of comfort, again wanting to hug; but Hugo would be embarrassed, like he'd been about their 'dream' kiss.

'John's proposing this morning.' Hugo stood in front of his bed, his eyes tense. 'The vicar's marrying them after lunch.'

Sophie raised an eyebrow. 'That's … fast.'

'Special licence. As his widow, Maud will get a cottage on the estate.' He walked over to open his bedroom door. 'Mrs Rawlings has already sorted another valet. You might want to talk to her about Maud.'

Sophie followed him out and kept pace with him in the corridor. 'How can you think about servant musical chairs?'

'Actually, thinking about mundane stuff helps.' His voice was toneless, flat. He was in bits.

Sophie nodded. 'I'll speak with her.'

At breakfast, no one mentioned John, and the footmen, who usually spoke in whispers, didn't talk at all.

Half an hour later, Sophie knocked on the housekeeper's study door, though it was already open.

'Miss Arundel.' Mrs Rawlings got to her feet behind the scarred writing desk. 'You've come about a new lady's maid. I have it in hand.'

'If … the worst happens, could Miss Able have time off, as much as she needs?'

'Miss, please come in and shut the door.'

Sophie did as she was asked, keeping the dogs on a short lead, and the housekeeper gestured for her to sit on a wooden chair. Only after Sophie had taken a seat did Mrs Rawlings sit down at her desk again, her elderly face troubled.

'Miss Able now knows the reality of Mr Watkins' … situation and I've already relieved her of her duties. She has an emotional day ahead.' Mrs Rawlings turned over a page in a huge ledger. 'But returning to work may help her more than grieving in her room. *If* she has your support.'

'She does.' Like with Hugo and John, Maud was now a friend.

'Do you have any preferences for a replacement?'

'I hadn't thought that far ahead.'

'I've been considering Miss Parry, though it will put some noses out of joint. She wasn't coping well, even with Miss Able's help, and now… I thought that if she was learning new skills with you, it might buck her up.'

'Of course,' said Sophie in a rush, 'but isn't she too young?'

'Being a lady's maid at fifteen isn't usual but it's not unheard of. And she learns quickly.'

'But if other people have been passed over, won't they take it out on her?'

'If they do, they'll answer to me.' Mrs Rawlings' hazel eyes gleamed like polished steel. 'And once she's your maid, anything she says will travel straight to Lady Lacey.'

'I understand.' The promotion would be resented but would protect Miss Parry and provide recovery time.

That afternoon at three, Miss Parry came into Sophie's room, walking like she'd been summoned to a firing squad, not a new job. Her shoulders were slumped, her eyes downcast.

'How much do you know about your duties?' Sophie's tone was friendly, encouraging.

'Helping you change, Miss. Bathing. Collecting fresh linen. And hair dressing. But I've never done a lady's hair.'

'Everyone has to start somewhere,' said Sophie. 'I know things are difficult at the moment, but you need to be strong for Miss Able.'

Miss Parry looked up, surprised to be having a conversation, not receiving instructions. 'It's dreadful what's happened.'

'We're going to get to know each other and when I'm in the library or walking the dogs, you must come in here, and have some quiet time.'

'I'm sorry, Miss, I don't understand.'

'You'll have chores to do but if you're feeling over-whelmed or sad, if you sit in here, nobody will disturb you.' When Sophie's parents had died, solitary me-time had helped as much as Isha's support.

'Are you sure, Miss?'

'Quite sure. And this is between you and me.'

'Yes, Miss.'

Sophie took a tea dress from the wardrobe and laid it on the bed. 'The buttons on my day dress will take a while to unfasten but it's not a test.'

Miss Parry gave her a tentative smile.

~

Later, before dinner, Miss Parry was more self-assured, even breezy, taking on Maud's role as Gossip Central.

'I can't believe Miss Able's married.' Miss Parry took a blue dinner gown from the wardrobe. 'There's no cottage free and Mr Watkins' bed's very narrow but she's moved out of our room.' She paused for breath.

Uncomfortable discussing such intimate things, Sophie wanted to tell her off, but that could shatter her newfound confidence. 'He's very ill.'

'I know, Miss.'

'Has there been any word from the police?' A hard-pressed officer from Shorten town was investigating; John had identified two gardeners, as well as Hunter.

'Nothing, Miss.'

The next day, it was too hot to sit on the terrace, so Sophie stayed in the library, skipping lunch.

But she struggled to lose herself in a book, Maud's elegiac wedding playing on her mind. The ceremony had been performed in John's bedroom, witnessed only by Anne and Richard. There'd been no space for anyone else.

Anne hadn't met up for elevenses or tea since the assault. Richard had said Anne was ill, but Sophie knew from Maud that it had been Anne who'd okayed John's pub mission.

And Hugo was quiet, still upset.

'How are you getting on with the new valet?' she asked him, just to break the silence as they walked to dinner.

'Mr Davies is all right.'

'You've become very formal.'

'He doesn't do first names. He makes Prince Charles look casual.'

Hugo remained subdued during the meal. Everyone was. And, as usual, no one spoke about John.

But the following morning, Miss Parry came into

Sophie's room like a whirlwind. 'The bleeding's stopped. It's a miracle, Miss, that's what it is.'

Sophie sat up in bed, relief mingling with hope.

When she called for Hugo to go to breakfast, he skipped into the corridor.

'Dr Griffiths says if he takes it easy for a few weeks, he should recover.' Hugo kissed her on the forehead. 'Wonderful.'

The touch of his lips on her skin felt cold, but in a good way. She'd been as stressed as Hugo.

And that afternoon, it was Maud who helped Sophie get changed. Her normal bustling self.

'I am so glad,' said Sophie. '*So* glad.'

'It's strange. He feels better but his face is worse. Swollen very bad.' Maud started unbuttoning Sophie's day dress.

'Is Miss Parry a scullery maid again?'

'Not after being your maid, Miss. She's back to serving teas. When Miss James heard, she swore like a sailor.'

'Miss James has red hair?'

'Yes, Miss.' Maud frowned. 'It must be hard, losing her promotion so quick.'

And would add to the grudge list.

Sophie stepped out of the dress and Maud returned it to its hanger, removing a stray thread from the bodice.

With her attention to detail, Maud would enjoy sorting her first home with John. 'When will you get a cottage?'

'After Christmas.' Maud smiled, looking younger. 'I'm really glad I can stay on.'

'You've lost me.'

'Shorten's unusual, Miss. Most places, once you're married, you're not allowed to work.'

How bizarre. Anne must have changed that. 'At home, leaving work would be unusual. How would you pay for the wedding, never mind the house?'

Maud's brow creased.

'I know it's not the same here.'

Maud took something from her pocket. 'Mr Watkins bought this for me, from an elderly man in the pub, before things turned nasty. But I think it's yours.' She opened a battered rectangular box.

Her pendant. Sophie welled up. 'Oh, thank you.' Her fingers closed over the necklace, finding comfort in the familiar opal stone.

'Expensive, Miss.'

'No, only costume jewellery.'

'Costume…?'

'Not real.'

'Oh, you'd never know, Miss.' Maud avoided her eyes, uncomfortable.

Costume jewellery had yet to catch on. 'Mr Watkins bought it for *you*.' Sophie turned the pendant over in her hand. 'This has sentimental value … but Mr Watkins shouldn't be out of pocket. I'll speak with Lady Lacey. He could buy you something better.' Maud's fingers were bare. 'A nice wedding band.'

'You don't have to, Miss.' Pride and regret battled in Maud's eyes.

'I certainly do.'

Regret won and Maud smiled.

Anne joined Sophie for tea, seemingly calm and composed, and when Sophie explained about the pendant, Anne was happy to increase John's weekly pay packet the following day. But when the conversation turned to the 'servant problem,' Anne's voice acquired a hard edge. 'Preparing for the ball next week should provide everyone with a welcome distraction.'

The ball was next week? Anne's previous reassurance

echoed like a sarcastic taunt in her head. *You'll scotch the gossip—*

'Most people with family in Shorten town and Derby appreciate not going hungry but the ones from Little Shorten are more easily swayed.'

Sophie wrenched her thoughts from the upcoming ball. 'How many servants have relatives in the village?'

'Fifteen, perhaps more,' said Anne. 'It's hard. I'm second guessing people I've known for years.'

Deference here might be fraying at the edges but *trust* … that was personal. Anne didn't seem to be distrusting Sophie Arundel, but theirs was essentially the same Lacey-servant relationship: power and need, entitlement and dependence.

And Sophie's sympathies remained squarely with the servants. Only a quirk of fate thirty years ago, making Anne a guest not staff, had saved Sophie Arundel from working fourteen-hour days.

'A letter was delivered by hand last night.' Hugo gestured for Sophie to go into his room.

The familiar queasiness was back. She'd called on him the next morning to go to breakfast and just lost her appetite. 'Another note … our plan didn't work.'

'No. A different problem.'

Now relief.

Charlotte tried to put her head between Sophie's knees — a reassuring gesture — unfortunately impossible when her mistress was wearing a hobble skirt. Charlotte had already been walked, avoiding the heat of the day, and Sophie stroked her before perching on Hugo's armchair. She smoothed out her silk dress, creased by Charlotte's leaning.

'So, what's in this letter?' He wasn't holding an envelope. 'Where is it?'

'With Richard. It was addressed to him.'

'And?'

'In a nutshell, a request for shorter hours and better pay, signed by twenty-five servants. It was surreal, listening to Richard reading it out over whisky and cigars.'

Not as surreal as being excluded from manly discussions. But she only said, 'Are the requests reasonable?'

'From a twenty-first century perspective, entirely. No more than twelve-hour days and sixpence extra a week for the lowest paid. But it won't happen.'

'Will Richard sack them?'

'Most people in his position would, but he's not most people.' Hugo's favourite loud tie wasn't wonky, but he checked it in the mirror. 'He thinks Hunter's behind this.'

'I thought he was on the run?'

'Richard believes he's hiding up in Shorten town.' He turned to face her. 'Oddly, the highest pay requests in the letter are for Mr Crawford and Mrs Rawlings. They'd die in a ditch for the family, so Richard thinks it's a gambit. And I do too.' He sat on the bed.

'A gambit?'

'It's from chess. Sacrificing a pawn, to gain a greater advantage. Hunter doesn't believe the requests will be accepted. He expects everyone who's signed the letter to be sacked, and the newly unemployed to band together and attract others that are angry, about life in general and the Laceys in particular.' He gave her a cynical smile. 'The real message is what they did to John.'

Sophie felt queasy again. 'You think it was calculated?'

'Yes. But I don't think they meant to nearly kill him.' He exhaled. 'Richard's called a meeting for tomorrow, to clear the air. I'm staying well out of it and you should too.' His eyes were on her face, gauging her reaction.

'Sixpence isn't much. I should do *something*…'

'Fiddling behind the scenes, like with Miss Parry, is one thing—'

'How do you know about that?'

'Anne told Richard, and he mentioned it.' He stood up. 'Servants who resent the Laceys feel the same about us. We may be from another universe, but we *look* like the family. We'll never be seen as even-handed, so open meddling would destroy the Laceys' trust in us for no benefit. For anyone.' He opened the door.

'Were you planning a career in politics at home?'

'No.'

She got to her feet. Cynical, but she got the point.

CHAPTER 36

A few minutes before two the next day, Sophie made her way with the dogs to the older part of the main house. Going to the servants' meeting but keeping quiet wasn't *staying well out of it* but Sophie wanted to be there — not hear about it second hand. And Anne hadn't said she couldn't go...

When Sophie asked Freddy why he wasn't going, he said, 'It will blow over,' and shrugged.

His home had always been run the same way and even with John nearly losing his life, Freddy couldn't imagine that it would ever change.

Like the rest of the Manor, the large drawing room was a hotchpotch of different styles and times, altered and added over the centuries. Graceful Jacobean stone-framed windows contrasted with an ancient hearth more reminiscent of a medieval castle than a house, and the high ceiling was coffered into rectangles with the Lacey coat of arms in the centre, the royal blue 'L' outlined in gilt amidst the brown, prancing stags.

A black grand piano stood in a corner across from a

polished wooden cabinet with an enormous hearing trumpet on top — an old-fashioned gramophone. The sofas, armchairs and side tables that usually furnished the room had been replaced by rows of upright chairs.

All the servants — outdoor and indoor — were there: girls no more than twelve, older women with matronly figures, dressed in immaculate maids' outfits, and boys and men in suits or rough trousers and shirts.

As Sophie stepped over the threshold, conversation faltered. She recognised barely a handful and her insides churned. Hugo was right. This invisible army lumped them in with the family. But she wasn't like the Laceys. Never would be.

The dogs were keeping close, unnerved by the buzz of so many voices. Sunlight was pouring through the wide diamond-paned windows and the air was close and hot, laced with sweat.

Her discomfort growing, Sophie stayed at the back, beside a young gardener. She smiled at him but he blushed, making her feel worse.

Mr Crawford, Mrs Rawlings and Mrs Ferris — a stout pink-cheeked woman — were standing at the opposite side of the room, near a side door. Two chairs at the front had been set out for Anne and Richard.

Maud and Miss Parry weren't far from Sophie, seated together. There was no sign of John. Miss Parry was staring at the floor, her face obscured. Maud must have seen Sophie come in, but she didn't turn, never mind wave.

Okay, she and Maud were friendly, not friends.

Across the room, identifiable by her red hair, Miss James was speaking earnestly to a group of gardeners, her words lost in the general hubbub, and Sophie's queasy feeling increased.

She recognised it. She was Imposter Syndrome Girl,

seven years and a universe away at Hadley. Squirming, out of her depth. And now that had turned inside out. She was a posh girl by mistake—

Anne and Richard walked in and everyone stopped talking. All the servants who were seated, stood up.

Anne sat in one of the allotted chairs but Richard remained on his feet.

'We appreciate you coming.' Richard's tone was polite, without a trace of irony. 'Please sit down.'

There was no scraping of chairs. Any sound was muffled by the heavy blue carpet that covered most of the vast floor. No coughing or fidgeting either.

Absolute silence.

'You will be aware that Mr Hunter, Mr Peacock and Mr Jones are being sought by the police,' said Richard, 'following the near fatal assault in *The Crooked Gate*.'

Hunter's partners in crime were junior gamekeepers. Teenagers.

Richard was scanning the room. 'If anyone knows where they are, please inform the constabulary or one of the senior servants.'

The silence changed, deepened. A collective holding of breath.

Richard cleared his throat. 'We have received a letter requesting changes in employment conditions. No one who has signed it will be penalised. If anyone wishes to leave after this meeting, they should give notice in the normal way.'

A faint whispering ran across the room, whether of relief or surprise wasn't clear.

'If we raised wages,' said Richard, 'we would employ fewer people. That would not only affect those who found themselves without work. It would also affect their families, in the village, in Shorten town or in Derby, so I am not convinced that would be sensible.'

Sophie kept her face expressionless. She didn't buy Richard's reasoning. If he could find £200 a year for an estate manager, he could surely give everyone a sixpence pay rise?

'That said, I hadn't appreciated how difficult life has become outside the Manor.' Richard exchanged a respectful glance with Anne. 'To that end, we need to formalise the system of sending food to relatives in need and make provision for other items, like medicine.'

His audience was completely still, in shock; this was not what they'd expected.

'Everyone who has family in Shorten town or Derby should submit a note to Mrs Rawlings,' said Richard, 'listing the name, age and state of health of their relative. Food parcels can be sent like before. You know best what your relative requires. Limited to one a week per person, unless there are exceptional circumstances. Dr Griffiths will provide appropriate medicines that can be taken without medical supervision and these can be added to the parcels. Postage will be paid for by the Manor.' Richard smiled, scanning the room. 'Thank you. That will be all.'

Anne stood up, Richard took her arm and they left.

A collective intake of breath, then a whoosh of furious chatter.

'He's a good man,' said the gardener beside Sophie, to nobody in particular.

A young lad in the back row was shaking his head, of a different opinion, and as the crescendo of noise increased, Sophie slipped out the door.

Later, Maud gave her chapter and verse on the fallout — as if she hadn't completely blanked her.

'Most people are pleased.' Maud checked Sophie's tea dress was properly fastened.

'I saw you sitting with Miss Parry.' Sophie couldn't keep the hurt out of her voice and the words hung in the air.

'It's awkward at the moment. Being your maid, people assume…'

'You'll tell tales.'

'Exactly, Miss. I don't hold with all this trouble making but I keep that to myself. I needed to stay with Miss Parry. And keep my distance.'

'I understand,' said Sophie, relieved. 'John wasn't well enough to go?'

'He was, Miss, but he thought it better to stay away.' She blushed.

Sophie wasn't going to ask whether Maud was enjoying married life; she obviously was. Change the subject. 'Do you send out food parcels?'

'No, Miss. My older sisters, they must have moved. My last letters were returned by the post office.'

'Where did they live before?'

'Derby.'

'What about Mrs Slater?'

'She's got the bakery, doesn't go hungry.'

'Of course.'

That evening, when Sophie called on Hugo, he wasn't quite ready, so she sat in the armchair. Jack sat contentedly on the floor, but Charlotte took a running jump and landed with a thump on the coverlet. Sitting on the edge of the bed, Hugo predictably didn't bat an eyelid, continued fastening his shoelaces.

'I thought you'd want to know what happened at the meeting.' Sophie adjusted her pendant, so it sat flat on her neck. The blue evening gown had a lower neckline and showed it off.

He finished with his laces. 'Richard briefed me, and Mr Davies filled in the gaps.'

'Richard's been very clever, isolating the Little Shorten gang from the rest.'

'It *was* clever, but also the right thing to do.'

Sophie didn't reply. They'd never agree about this.

The following morning, Sophie was reading the paper on the terrace when Hugo joined her during a precious work break — and talked about escaped cows.

Sophie hoped they'd all get away and live idyllic lives in the countryside, but she held her tongue and nodded in a bovine way. Good practice for the ball tomorrow; these were tried and tested husband-catching tactics. Pity she couldn't go temporarily missing like the cows.

'We've been here a month.' He checked they were alone on the terrace. 'I hope our giving-up proclamation wasn't a self-fulfilling prophesy.'

She theatrically crossed her fingers and he smiled. It was just a regular smile, but the tingling was back, swirling like a restless spirit. How bizarre. Her brain had clocked at the cricket match that he wasn't interested, but her body hadn't received the memo. She cast around for a distraction. 'All those people who signed the letter ... it's strange none of them have left.'

'Not really. Letting off steam in the pub is a lot different to losing your job and the roof over your head.'

'Couldn't they camp out in *The Crooked Gate*?'

'Alan wouldn't put them up and lay on free food and beer,' said Hugo, 'any more than he would for the queen.'

'Mean to *everyone*, doesn't discriminate. Sort of good.' Sophie idly turned over the handbell. 'Maud's never thought about working anywhere else.'

'She's got too much to lose.'

'As an outsider, I can see both points of view.' She put down the handbell. 'I don't want to take sides.'

Hugo's brow knotted, his thick eyebrows nearly meeting in the middle. 'You must know, it's too late for that.'

'Unless we steal cash from the butler's pantry too and make a run for it.' She was only half joking.

'Like Bonnie and Clyde.'

'Who?'

'A couple who toured the States robbing banks in the 1930s,' said Hugo. 'It didn't end well.'

'How did it end?'

'Died in a hail of bullets.'

Freddy was walking towards them.

'Five minutes for elevenses can't hurt,' said Freddy to Hugo, as he reached the terrace.

But Hugo got to his feet. 'Already had more than five. See you in the office.' He walked off.

Freddy sat beside Sophie and rang the handbell. Then he fumbled in his pocket. 'This is for you.'

The small jewellery box had a blue velvet covering. She froze; way down the line she might marry Freddy but not *right now*. Why the hell hadn't Hugo given her a heads up? 'Let's not do anything hast—'

'It's only a watch.' He opened the box lid. 'You said you didn't have one.'

The gold strap was delicate and around the face were tiny diamonds. At the top and bottom were more glittering stones, in a matching but more elaborate platinum setting. Art deco. 'Freddy, I can't accept this. It must have cost a fortune.'

'No, a trifling amount.'

She didn't believe him but didn't want to throw it in his face. And it was a thoughtful gesture. She put it on.

'It's too loose,' said Freddy.

'No, it's perfect. I'll wear it like a bracelet.'

Miss Parry was on the terrace, carrying a coffee pot. After

she'd poured coffee and left, Sophie kissed Freddy on the cheek. 'Thank you.'

His face went a pleased pink.

When Freddy returned to the office, Sophie opened the paper where she'd left off. *Hobble skirt kills pedestrian.* She turned the page. *Derbyshire Country House Torched By Mob. Mr R. H. Bellamy and his valet, Mr Peters, died last week in the fierce blaze. Facing charges of arson and murder are eleven residents of the nearby village of Tumbury and four servants from Mr Bellamy's household.*

Hunter had riled people up downstairs and nearly killed John. What had Hugo said? *...attract others that are angry, about life in general and the Laceys in particular.* Feeling sick, Sophie closed the paper. Faced with an angry mob, what would the Manor servants do? Flee, or join in?

In the bedroom, Sophie showed Maud the watch. 'Now you don't have to tell me the time.'

Maud's face fell. 'Where did you get this, Miss?'

'Fre—Master Freddy gave it to me. It's only costume jewellery, like my necklace.'

'I'm sure you're right, Miss.' Her face carefully blank, Maud made to leave but then hesitated. 'It might be better if you left it here.'

'Why?'

'It's not for me to say.'

'Please, Maud, if I've screwed up, just tell me. I won't be offended.'

'It's just ... I got into an argument yesterday with Miss James and her friend. They were saying stupid things about you and Master Freddy.'

When she didn't explain, Sophie went with the obvious. 'Master Freddy has never held my hand, let alone done anything else.' A platonic thank you kiss didn't count.

'That's what I told them, Miss, but this watch...'

Sophie folded her arms. 'There is *nothing* between us.'

Maud still looked anxious so Sophie kept going. 'He only gave it to me because I didn't have one.'

'Has anyone else seen it?'

'Miss Parry might have.'

Maud frowned and exhaled.

She hadn't seen that combination before. She was in trouble. She took off the watch and put it on the dressing table, apprehension a dull ache in her guts. 'Thank you for helping me.'

'Having a watch is useful, Miss. This was my mother's.' Maud's watch was plain, with a leather strap.

Maud was trying to make her feel better, but Freddy's kind gesture would give the pub boast a new lease of life.

Maud left and Sophie tried in vain to read, then set off with the dogs for lunch.

Hugo was loitering in the corridor.

She told him about the torched house. 'Next time you go walkabout, check the exits.'

'Okay…' He seemed distracted. 'Where is it?'

'What?'

'The watch.'

'On my dressing table.'

'I had no idea he was doing this,' said Hugo, 'or I'd have stopped him.'

'It wasn't expensive.' But the words sounded hollow.

'Said he had nothing else to spend his allowance on. He may be a maths genius and Shorten born and bred, but he's cringingly naïve.'

'Maud made me take it off.' The Manor was a pressure cooker. And yet again she was the one being cooked.

'It's too late for that. Freddy may have played it down to you, but it came from a swanky shop in London.'

Sophie swallowed. 'How do you know that?'

'Mr Farrow recognised the packaging,' said Hugo. 'He told John and John told me.'

Freddy's valet gossiped as much as Maud. 'What can I do?' A horrible dart of panic. 'Give it back?'

'That wouldn't help. The damage is done.'

CHAPTER 37

After lunch, Anne took Sophie aside. 'You've taken it off.'

'Yes.'

'I don't know what's got into Freddy. Put it on. If you hide it, that will fuel more speculation.'

'Right…'

'I'll say over afternoon tea so Miss Parry overhears, how pleased I am you can keep the time, and that *I* ordered it.'

'I'm sorry, I didn't think, until Mau … Freddy said it wasn't expensive.'

'And you believed him?'

'No.' Sophie looked at the floor.

'I'm going to have a long talk with Freddy about your position in this house. He's not a child anymore and neither are you. Just when things were calming down.'

Sophie winced. Despite apparently fancying her, Freddy had never flirted; the watch was just a well-meant gift. He might be naïve, but it was her stupidity fuelling the gossip. 'I could miss the ball, pretend to be ill.'

'Every eligible bachelor will be there. If you didn't attend, that would only lead to more … ill-informed speculation.'

Sophie retreated to her room and confided in the dogs. 'I wish I had a time-turner.' She flopped into the armchair. 'This ball isn't a nice little party, or even a nice big party. It's a high-profile husband hunt.' She ruffled Charlotte's head. 'Right swiping sucked, but this sucks more.' At home, despite being surrounded by real boys, she'd toyed with dating sites and received texts so crude, she'd deleted them, and the apps. And she'd scoffed at marrying anyone. But here, *not* marrying — eventually — would be masochistic. She scratched Jack's head behind his ears, which he loved. 'And bailing isn't an option.'

A knock on the door, then it burst open. 'Mr Hunter's been arrested,' said Maud. 'And Mr Peacock and Mr Jones. And five gardeners.'

Sophie stood up. 'When, where?'

Maud closed the door. 'This morning, in *The Crooked Gate*. But we need to keep it confidential.'

This, from the gossip queen. 'Why?'

'To protect Mr Parkes.'

Alan had trashed her life chances here, spreading the pregnancy rumour, and didn't deserve protecting. But she was intrigued. 'I won't tell.' She sat on the bed and gestured at the armchair and after a moment's hesitation, Maud sat down.

'They arrived at the pub yesterday, made themselves at home. Mr Parkes had to order in extra beer. After they'd drunk themselves to sleep, Mr Parkes cycled here at two in the morning, woke up Mr Crawford, and Mr Crawford telephoned the police in Shorten town.'

Sophie hid a smile, picturing the butler in pyjamas, dialling out on an old-fashioned phone.

'Then Mr Parkes went back to the pub, pretended he'd never left.'

Alan was a sexist pig, but he'd done the right thing. 'Mr Parkes is a brave man.'

'They'll hang for what they did.'

~

That afternoon, Sophie met Lucy for a workout.

Lucy stretched, pushing her hands flat against the gym wall. 'The police have released my naughty five.'

'Sorry?'

'The gardeners who went along for the ride with Hunter.'

'Richard's not going to sack them?'

'No. They're all pretty shaken up. They won't step out of line again.' Lucy continued stretching. 'It's right that Hunter should be jailed for attempted murder but the idea he might be ... executed. Can't get my head round that.'

'I know.' Sophie wiggled her shoulders, trying not to think about the mechanics of being hanged. Capital punishment was a horrible reminder of how far she was from home.

'Mr Peacock and Mr Jones are too young to be executed.' Lucy stopped stretching. 'But for the people who signed the letter ... actually, for everyone, this has been a *big* reality check.'

'So, the ill feeling might fizzle out?'

'I think so.' Lucy did a flurry of punches. 'Short workout today. I've got my hands full, sorting flowers for the ball.'

Additional servants had been hired to help with flower arrangements for the ground floor, dining tables and bedrooms, and to assist with extra cleaning, adjusting menus to reflect local supplies, sourcing lobster from the coast and stocking iceboxes. Sophie steadied the bag. 'I'm learning posh dancing today.'

'I've got a better deal with the flowers.'

An hour later, Sophie set off towards the large drawing room, on the way making a mental note of doors that led out into the garden.

Trotting beside her, Jack was his normal, chirpy self but Charlotte had adopted her serious face. She knew her mistress: physically co-ordinated with kickboxing and javelin, but dancing … not so much.

'It might be fun.'

Charlotte looked dubious.

The dogs hurtled into the room, narrowly missing Freddy who was bent over the gramophone, his suit jacket unbuttoned.

The rows of chairs had gone and so had the carpet, revealing oak boards laid in polished, narrow lines.

Freddy turned a handle and adjusted something, a vinyl record began spinning, and the strains of a stately waltz echoed around the empty space.

Hugo came in, smiling broadly. 'Mr Watkins is coming back to work tomorrow. He can't lift anything heavy but otherwise, a clean bill of health.'

'Excellent.' Freddy turned to Sophie. 'I told you this would blow over.'

John had been lucky and — going by that story in the paper — so had the Manor.

'Shall we start?' said Freddy.

'What do I do?' In his over-sized brown suit, Hugo looked like a confused commuter faced with a new train timetable.

'You've never danced a waltz?' asked Freddy.

'No.'

'Me neither,' said Sophie.

'I'll show you.' Freddy turned to her. 'May I?'

She nodded.

'Hugo, you put your arm there and hold her hand. See?'

'Yes,' said Hugo. He put his arm around Sophie's waist and took her hand.

Turbocharged tingling resonated through her nerves like a guitar string. 'Sorry, give me a minute.' She took off a court shoe and pretended to remove a piece of grit. This attraction was getting positively primeval.

She took a slow breath. That was it. A subconscious survival strategy had kicked in. They saw Shorten in basically the same way, the good and bad, and her lizard brain remembered that kiss in the lane and had ramped up her lust to keep him close. It would wear off if she got home — or adapted to life here; she wouldn't need a die-in-a-ditch ally.

When Hugo embraced her again, she was prepared. The tingling settled, softer, safer, but she was still too aware of him. Focus on something else. 'Do you remember that silent disco in year nine? It was weird.'

'It *was*,' said Hugo, 'and pointless. How do you build social skills, not talking or listening to the same music?'

The event had been awkward. She'd danced with Isha; Hugo, like most of the boys, had listened to his headphones but just leaned against a wall. This was much nicer. Strange it had gone out of fashion. 'This is cool.'

'Yes,' said Hugo, stiffly, as if he were a suitor in a stuffy Victorian play.

Freddy demonstrated the steps, pretending to embrace an invisible partner. 'One, two three. One, two three.'

Cautiously, Sophie and Hugo copied him. Restricted by her hobble skirt, Sophie could only take half steps and Hugo had no choice but to do the same.

Her corset meant Sophie had to dance with her back straight so couldn't see her steps, but after a minute or so they managed to move around without stumbling.

'Sophie, you're leading,' said Freddy. 'You *have* to follow Hugo.'

'I'm having the same problem in reverse,' said Hugo. 'Not sure what that says about me.'

The dogs had calmed down and were snoozing by the piano, lulled to sleep by the music.

'Now we can start on the polka,' said Freddy, putting on a different record. 'I'll lead, Sophie, and you follow.'

Hugo stepped back and Freddy took his place. Freddy's hand on Sophie's waist felt nice but not *boom*-nice, and learning the polka proved straightforward.

When they came to a halt, Sophie felt an urge to curtsey but didn't. That really wouldn't work in a hobble skirt. 'Old-fashioned dancing rocks.'

Freddy turned to Hugo. 'Is that good or bad?'

Hugo laughed. 'Good.'

'You'll both really enjoy the ball,' said Freddy.

The following afternoon, they practised dancing again. Chairs were now arranged at the edge of the room and beside the piano for the musicians.

Smaller rooms had been designated for playing cards, cloakrooms and refreshments, and over the front drive an awning had been erected where guests would be getting out of cars or carriages; the temperature was climbing again, so thunderstorms couldn't be ruled out.

Today, the dancing felt easier, the steps more natural.

'We've got the hang of this,' said Hugo, as the polka finished.

'You have,' said Freddy, smiling. He gestured at two large chandeliers. 'This is where electric lights come into their own. With gaslight, it was very hot and stuffy.'

As Freddy walked away, returning to the office, Hugo lingered, his lips set in a determined line.

'We mustn't lose our focus on getting home,' he whispered near Sophie's ear. 'I'm sure DNA is a crucial part of this.'

Sophie frowned. 'But we're no nearer finding the other part.'

'If more than one lift — one ship — travels between universes, that would explain why the visitors saw different pictures.'

'Alan described two images, unique to him, I saw four, Lucy and Anne just saw the mansion, I'm presuming the same one. And H.G. Wells, the one here and at home, saw a sphinx.'

'So, four ships.'

'Or,' said Sophie, 'the door design changes, refreshes like a web page.'

He sighed. 'Food for thought.'

When Hugo returned to the office, Sophie went to the library and in her notebook drew a cartoon spaceship, with a destination sign over the bridge window: *HOME*. Silly, but therapeutic.

In the afternoon, she had a bath, endured the ritual of washing and styling her hair and rested, to be on top form later on. The ball didn't start until ten in the evening, dinner was served at one in the morning and, for guests not staying overnight, carriages arrived at three.

Sophie had never been a night owl, but trepidation and unyielding underwear would likely keep her awake. Anyway, retiring early was 'bad form.'

Anne's role as host involved constant checking to ensure no detail had been overlooked: carefully arranged seating plans, detailed sketches of floral table decorations, as well as last-minute changes to food and drink orders from Shorten town. It would have made the most organised person flap. Thirty families had been invited, all had accepted, and everyone expected to be personally greeted.

After a light supper of poached eggs at eight, Sophie put on a new evening gown: mega formal and fabulous. Cream silk, a slim skirt with clever drapes and folds, a simple, fitted bodice, diaphanous cap sleeves and lace around the bust line — and a two-foot long train.

Anne had given her a tiny eau de cologne bottle. Sophie didn't usually wear perfume, but she put a drop on her wrist. The orange blossom aroma sent her back to Isha's dorm, every available surface covered with scent bottles, and then to a motel room, getting dressed up for Lily's Sandhurst ball, the celebration that marked the end of Lily's army training course.

Lily would have loved this party, taken it in her stride.

Sophie's hair was piled in decorous sweeps on top of her head and Anne had insisted on lending her a diamond necklace with three overlapping tiers, resembling glittering lace. Between the diamonds were tiny oval pearls.

Since Anne would be wearing at least four rings, Sophie had borrowed one.

Maud was holding up long white gloves made of kidskin, her face resolute.

Sophie ground her teeth. 'Do I wear them over the ring? And what about my watch?'

'I should leave your watch here, Miss. Would make an unsightly bulge. You can wear the ring underneath, and over the glove you can wear that bangle.' Maud pointed to another piece of borrowed jewellery: an embossed, gold bracelet.

Like many things in this mad universe — *no* logic. Sophie took off her watch and slipped on the ring.

The gloves had to be rolled on to above the elbow, like a wetsuit in a hot changing room.

When the gloves were finally wrinkle-free, Sophie slid on the bracelet.

Maud had reluctantly made bandanas for the dogs from

the same material as Sophie's dress. Jack barked at the tall mirror, but Charlotte sat, admiring her reflection. After initial confusion as a puppy, she'd realised that what she could see was herself, not a rival.

This was Charlotte's first formal party; she hadn't been allowed to the Hadley leaving ball. Jack attended Manor social events, so Charlotte could too. Pampering dogs wasn't a modern thing — in either universe. Sophie smiled to herself, remembering a picture from a Tudor history lesson of a couple in bed and their dog asleep on the counterpane.

'I'll be here when you retire, Miss,' said Maud, checking Sophie over like a prize racehorse.

She needed to be careful not to spill anything on the dress ... when was dry cleaning invented?

'Forty guests are staying overnight,' said Maud, handing Sophie a delicate fan, decorated with idyllic rural scenes.

The fan was ivory. Don't think about it.

'At least breakfast isn't until eleven.'

'Does that make it easier?' Sophie patted her artfully arranged hair, checking it was secure.

'Not really, Miss, but with the extra help it's not too bad. And as a lady's maid, I'm not so involved in the preparation and clear up. I've done seven but Mrs Rawlings has done fifteen. Can you imagine?'

The housekeeper was as stressed as Anne.

Maud went off to one of the cloakrooms to help Miss Parry, who'd been tasked with checking ladies' dresses and hair, and Sophie took her dance card from the dressing table. Hugo had bagged the first, Freddy the second. In London, programmes or cards for balls were no longer fashionable and Anne had been toying with dropping them, but Sophie was glad to have one. If she got through this in one piece, she wanted to remember every single moment, including all her dance partners. One of them could be a future husband.

The dogs pawed at the door and Sophie checked her watch: nearly ten. Charlotte had always anticipated meal-times, down to the minute, but this wasn't part of her routine. Sophie couldn't hear anything, but Charlotte and Jack could probably hear guests arriving.

Nerves were now vying with excitement. Sophie put the dance card and mechanical pencil into a concealed pocket of her skirt and squared her shoulders.

'Showtime.'

CHAPTER 38

Hugo opened his door. 'You look … nice.'

Nice? *Nice?* She was the prettiest girl in this universe, transformed like Cinderella — not by magic but by Maud.

He was immaculate in a black, single-breasted tailcoat with silk lapels, a white shirt, detachable wing collar, thin white bow tie and a white waistcoat. His black trousers had a line of braid on each outside leg.

'You're looking pretty good yourself.'

'Not that different from Shorten black tie.' He gave her his killer half-smile.

Butterflies. Get a grip.

'I love the dogs' cream bandanas,' said Hugo, as they went to join Anne to receive guests.

'I just hope Charlotte behaves,' said Sophie. You too, whispered a voice in her head.

She lost track of names after meeting the third or fourth family and the familiar unease at meeting new people felt like a weight on her shoulders, but after a while the nerves faded. She made a special note of the Armstrong sisters.

They were both dark-haired with elfin features. Ethel was taller than her sister, with a breezy, confident manner. Alice was more serious. The sisters smelled faintly of bergamot and lemon, from perfume or soap.

'Your many universes theory is fantastic,' Ethel whispered, as they made their way towards the large drawing room, now the ballroom.

Okay, guessing 'fantastic' meant 'ridiculous.' Not 'brilliant.' Sophie felt a fresh tremor of unease. 'It's not *our* theory. It's come from scientists, based on evidence, on maths.' Well, she believed it did.

'But there is no evidence,' said Alice, reluctantly, not wanting to come across as rude.

They should have said they'd come from Australia. But changing their story now would brand them as charlatans. 'Lady Lacey came from the same place, as well as the Manor's head gardener, and the man who runs the pub in Little Shorten. And they came separately. Unlikely they'd come up with the same account, all stepping out of a lift.' Sophie fanned her face as she walked. 'But it's not really a lift. It just looks like that.'

'Father says that if it's real, it must be a carriage,' said Alice, 'like in that *Time Machine* book.'

'We think H. G. Wells invented the carriage thing,' said Sophie.

'Oh.' Alice made a disappointed face. 'That was the best part.'

They waited in the corridor, behind other guests queueing to go into the ballroom. 'Where you're supposed to come from, is it like heaven,' said Alice, 'where the dead go?'

'No,' said Sophie, feeling more uncomfortable. 'It's like here.'

'Mrs Claverley is our great aunt,' said Alice.

'Mrs Claverley?'

'She's a medium,' said Alice. 'She contacts a little girl in heaven who helps people talk to their dead loved ones.'

Sophie remembered Anne's comments about spiritualism. 'Surely, the different universes theory is as believable as talking to the dead?'

Alice raised a delicate eyebrow. 'I hadn't thought about it like that.'

'Would you go back, if you could?' asked Ethel.

'I would,' said Sophie, glad to have parked parallel universes and mediums. 'I'd only just arrived at university.'

'Gosh,' said Ethel, 'they don't admit many women. You're a blue stocking.'

'A what?'

Ethel tapped her temple. 'Very clever.'

'I'm not,' said Sophie. 'And you don't have to be. The government at home wants half the country to have a degree.'

Alice was making a fuss of the dogs, stroking them. Jack knew precisely how to behave and, hopefully, Charlotte would copy him or soon find a quiet corner to sleep.

'It cost a fortune when Edward went up to Oxford,' said Ethel. 'Father was always complaining about it.'

'I had to take out a loan,' said Sophie.

Ethel's eyes widened. 'You *borrowed* money?'

'Most people do.' Sophie moved the errant curl of hair from her face. However careful Maud was, it often escaped.

'But your family could repay it?' said Ethel.

'*I* borrowed the money,' said Sophie, 'so I'll pay it off, if I earn enough.'

'*You* have to *earn* money?' Ethel was appalled.

Not for the first time, Sophie reflected that Shorten felt unreal, but so did her old life. Mired in debt to get a degree, to get a job that paid enough to eventually pay it off… What had she been thinking? And if she couldn't get back, what would happen to her loan? Interest would pile up, wouldn't be written off for decades. Actually, if she was stranded here, it wouldn't matter.

Alice swayed and clutched at Ethel.

'My dear,' said Ethel, gently putting her arm around her. 'You should sit down. You're very pale.'

Alice briefly closed her eyes. 'It's rather hot, but I'm all right.'

'If you're sure?' asked Ethel.

Alice nodded, though her face was pasty, almost grey.

Ethel removed her arm and took hold of her sister's hand, then turned to Sophie. 'Edward enjoyed Oxford but didn't do much work.'

'At home, you have to pass the first year assessments,' said Sophie, 'or you get chucked out.'

'Mr Denning was sent down for setting fire to his room.' Ethel was amused, not shocked. 'He should be here some-where.' She glanced back along the corridor before she stepped into the ballroom and Sophie followed.

At least a hundred people, a quartet playing Mozart, footmen with shiny trays giving out champagne in shallow, bowl-shaped glasses, and too many pairs of eyes watching her. Curious, judging.

Breathe.

The air was sweet with women's flowery perfume: jasmine, rose, and other, unfamiliar musky scents. It didn't calm her nerves.

'What did you read?' Ethel asked, still holding Alice's hand.

'Sorry?'

'At college, what degree?'

'Oh, medieval English literature.'

'Sounds ... difficult.'

'You can use the modern translations,' said Sophie. 'That makes it easier.'

Across the room, Richard and Anne were standing with Herbert and the vicar. Herbert noticed Sophie and smirked — more like a snake spotting its prey than a greeting. But he looked relaxed. If he had written the notes, their plan had worked.

'Can everyone gather into family groups please, for a photograph?' Richard raised his voice above the music. 'No more than ten at a time.'

A man in an ill-fitting suit was standing behind a metal box that was shoulder high on a tripod, with a protruding camera lens. Ethel and Alice stood in a huddle with their family.

The man held up a stick. 'Don't move.'

It took about five seconds for the stick to flash and there was a longer gap between photographs while the man adjusted the camera.

Finally, the Laceys stood together. To Sophie's surprise, Freddy had his arm through Hugo's and Anne beckoned to her. Sophie went to Anne and managed to hold still, but felt overwhelmed, tearful. Publicly an honorary Lacey... Gratitude mixed with disquiet. She was standing with the family, metaphorically as well as literally.

Anne and Richard walked towards the Armstrongs and Freddy went over to the cameraman.

Freddy came back. 'He can take just us.'

Sophie linked arms with the boys and posed for the flash.

Then the musicians struck up the waltz and she floated around with Hugo, making a good bluff of knowing the steps. Like before, he was obliged to match her restricted strides. The other men on the dance floor were doing the same. She giggled. This mad fashion could hobble men too.

Hugo smiled down at her. 'You're grinning like the Cheshire Cat.'

'I can't help it. What a fab party.'

'Like the school leaving bash but grander.'

'Just a bit.' An uncomfortable memory surfaced. Near the end of the leaving ball, he'd introduced himself to Aunty Wendy. Out of the blue. And Sophie had made some lame excuse and walked away, snubbed him... She was acutely aware how close he was. Forget twerking. This was sooo sexy.

The music finished, he stopped holding her hand and she reluctantly dropped her left arm from his shoulder, readying herself for the next dance.

Freddy seemed lost for words as they whirled around to the polka, his gaze lingering on her mouth. He pulled her subtly closer; as no one could have seen, it felt wonderfully subversive. And in that moment, their easy-going friendship inexorably shifted, like the second hand of a clock.

Afterwards, Sophie was glad to sit out and fan her face, while everyone else danced the Lancers, weaving in and out of a circle of other dancers. She hadn't learned that one. Looked complicated.

Sweat was dampening her corset, on her back and front. She missed air-conditioning so badly, she would have traded a year of global warming.

A boy with a neat moustache and dark eyes was standing in front of her. 'Edward Armstrong. We met briefly when I arrived. May I have the pleasure of the next dance?'

His hair was slicked back like Freddy's had been during the visitor dates session. It wasn't a good look. 'Of course, but it has to be a waltz or a polka. I've only learned those two. Sorry.'

'I understand.' Edward turned to Hugo, who'd been standing behind her chair. 'How do you do?'

Hugo did the echo thing. 'Hugo Harrington.' They shook hands.

'We've heard all about you.' Edward lowered his voice. 'I'm sorry, but I couldn't understand it. You haven't got a time machine, like in the book?'

'No,' said Hugo.

'Our home is nearly a hundred years ahead,' said Sophie, wishing they'd given out a written summary, 'but we haven't come from *your* future.'

'I've known about Lady Lacey all my life,' said Edward. 'You've come from the same place?'

'Yes,' said Sophie.

'You should have lied,' said Edward, 'said you'd come from a colony nobody's been to.'

Hugo sighed. 'Would have been easier.'

Edward shrugged. 'Well, you're here now. Is it true you were both at the same college?'

'We were,' said Hugo.

'Shame you had your time cut short,' said Edward, addressing Hugo. 'It must have been fabulous with girls.'

'I think 'fabulous' may be pushing it,' said Hugo.

Another unfamiliar dance began, and Edward sat beside Sophie. 'Would you both like to come to our place, with Freddy? We're having a shooting party on Saturday. Great fun.'

'Um,' began Sophie. A party to murder animals … she presumed it would be animals. 'I don't shoot.'

'Ladies don't shoot,' said Edward, bemused. 'They stay inside and keep each other company.'

Lucy had mentioned this. Yet again excluded but, hey, occasionally, a good thing. She gave a resigned nod.

'We'd love to come,' said Hugo.

'And we hunt in the winter,' said Edward. 'You must come for that too.'

Sophie's lips wouldn't move.

A faint rumble of thunder. She *so* wanted it to rain.

A waltz began and Edward stood and offered Sophie his hand.

Edward was more confident than Hugo had been and led her faster around the floor, but she managed not to step on his toes.

After dancing with Edward, and again with Hugo and Freddy, Sophie began to flag so she went to the nearest refreshment room to peel off her gloves. Where practical, ladies didn't remove their gloves in public. Another stupid rule.

Back in the ballroom, she left the gloves folded neatly on her chair, accepted a glass of champagne and went with Freddy to the terrace where it was mercifully cooler.

'You are so beautiful,' he murmured in her ear.

But even as his words gave her a contented glow, a fair-haired boy with a pointed chin and arresting blue eyes stepped onto the terrace and looked curiously in her direction. She was attracting too many glances, apparently benevolent, but some guests must have heard — and believed — Alan's caustic rumour. She sipped champagne. Not cold but hit the spot. She finished it. 'These glasses are really small.'

'They're the normal size.' Half-admiring, half-shocked, Freddy accepted another full glass for her.

He was worried she'd get smashed and disgrace herself. As if.

They went inside, Sophie collected her gloves, left to put them on again, then returned and sat beside Anne.

Anne's taffeta gown was the same flattering shade of blue as her less formal dinner dress, and her tall, elaborate tiara and amethyst and gold pearl necklace somehow managed to be tasteful.

Herbert was dancing with Ethel, his face flushed and

shiny, going a little too slow and stepping on her feet. Dancers under the chandeliers glided and whirled, and the jewellery worn by the women would have out-glittered a 1970s disco ball.

'This is spectacular,' Sophie said. 'I am *so* enjoying myself.' And she was, despite the strain of behaving correctly.

'I am glad,' said Anne, elegantly waving her fan. 'Hopefully, it will rain soon and be cooler.'

Across the room, Alice was sitting alone, also waving her fan, her face pale and nervous.

'Earlier, Alice was finding the heat a bit much,' said Sophie. 'She still seems unwell.'

'Alice finds social situations stressful,' said Anne, watching the dancers.

Perhaps Alice suffered from anxiety? Isha had been on meds for stress and panic attacks since she was fourteen. So had many girls at Hadley, overwhelmed by the demands of social media and exams. Here, there was just as much pressure but a different sort: catch a husband or be pitied and poor.

Freddy was waiting near Sophie's chair, but Anne gestured at him to move on and said to Sophie, 'You shouldn't dance too much with any one chap.' Freddy winked at Sophie before sauntering off, and Anne gave Sophie a warning look.

With Freddy and Hugo off limits, Sophie was saved from wallflower status by a young man with red hair and freckles, Harry Richards, and then by a different dance partner, Albert Garnier. He was tall and slender, sported a neat brown beard and extreme 'hat hair,' as if flattened by an invisible helmet.

Dancing with Albert, Sophie looked over towards Hugo. 'Who's that with Mr Harrington?' Hugo was dancing his third or fourth waltz with the same haughty-looking girl. So much for the don't-hog-one-partner rule.

'Miss Clarissa Maine,' said Albert. 'I don't know her well. Her family live in London.'

Clarissa would suffer, not Hugo, if people gossiped. Sophie stumbled, held onto Albert's arm to regain her balance, and he gave her an understanding smile. Not handsome exactly, but an interesting face: long nose, clear eyes and a firm mouth.

As the music ended, thunder sounded directly overhead. 'Here comes the rain,' said Albert. He escorted Sophie to her seat and asked Anne to dance.

Harry Richards. Albert Garnier. Sophie wrote the names in her dance card.

Herbert appeared from nowhere holding two glasses of champagne.

'A splendid bash.' His words were slurred. Sitting beside Sophie, he put a glass by his chair and downed the other. 'I just wanted to say, if you feel like changing horses I'd be honoured.' His mouth was too near her face and his breath stank of stale vinegar.

'Sorry?'

'A bit of muslin here and there. I'm sure you understand.'

She didn't, but whatever he meant, his tone was creepy. 'I don't think so.'

He took the full glass from the floor, drank it and put it down. 'Oh, come on, we could slip away. No one will notice.'

What a sleazebag. She waved her fan in front of her face like a tiny shield. Stay cool. But Herbert grabbed her wrist, unexpectedly hard, and she dropped the fan.

'No.' She didn't bother lowering her voice.

To her alarm, Herbert stood and pulled her out of her chair. 'I like this game.'

'I'm not playing. Stop.' She scraped at his fingers but couldn't dislodge his hand. The memory of the men in the lane came back, morphed into panic. 'You're a sad fuckwit.'

People were watching, though only Herbert could have caught her words over the quartet. His grip tightened and she winced.

'What did you say?' Herbert swayed and his face turned redder.

'You heard.'

'Slut.'

'And you're a little shit.' She managed to yank her hand back. Act ladylike. 'You're drunk, sir.'

Freddy was beside her. The vicar was hurrying towards them and Hugo wasn't far behind, his dance partner's eyes curious.

Herbert smiled. 'And you're a whore.'

Her reaction was instinctive and instant. She didn't think or consider the consequences. Before she knew it, her gloved fist had connected with his jaw.

Herbert's head jerked and he crumpled.

Someone gasped.

No, *no*.

Charlotte nipped Herbert's ankle and raced off, her paws slipping on the smooth, wooden floor.

Hide.

Freddy's arm was protectively around her shoulders … nowhere to hide.

The vicar was bending over Herbert, helping him to stand. Edward was beside Anne who was standing perfectly still, her eyes round with shock.

'I'm afraid we need to leave before dinner,' the vicar said to Anne. 'My apologies, an urgent pastoral matter.' He frog-marched Herbert away, surreally in time with the music.

Alice was lying on the floor. Ethel was kneeling beside her, waving a fan by her sister's face and Harry Richards was saying, 'Help her sit up.'

Sophie gently removed Freddy's arm and went to Alice.

'Put her head between her knees.' No, that wouldn't work with Alice's rigid corset.

'Take her to our room,' said Ethel to Harry, her voice urgent.

Escape. Lie low. Sophie went with them, then helped to get Alice on a bed.

Harry turned Alice gently on her side, began undoing buttons. 'Ring for a maid, loosen her stays.'

'We've got this,' said Sophie.

Ethel said hastily, 'Harry's training to be a doctor.'

Right, not a sleazebag. Sophie opened the door and stepped into the corridor. Run.

But Anne, her face wooden, was marching in her direction.

Nowhere to run.

'What were you *thinking?*'

'He was drunk, called me a whore, was pulling me out to the terrace to … rape me. What was I supposed to do?'

'Ask for help? Freddy was right there.'

CHAPTER 39

*I*n the first assembly at Hadley, listening to the welcoming address, Sophie had been Imposter Syndrome Girl. Way too posh for her first school but, for the second, not posh enough.

You are the country's future leaders. Miss Parncutt's words had been acknowledged with a collective squaring of shoulders, but Sophie was gobsmacked. The headteacher at her primary school would never have said that. Because it wasn't true, so wouldn't have occurred to him — or his students.

Sophie didn't miss the old playground fights but lashing out was ingrained. Four weeks later, she shoved Madison hard onto the tarmac of the netball court, and in the resulting suspension interview, Miss Parncutt was blunt: 'Fighting at this establishment will get you expelled.' But she offered Sophie an unexpected alternative. 'Take up kick-boxing and use that as an outlet for your aggression.' Initially resentful, Sophie adapted, honing instinct into a respected skill.

Instinct and skill. Today, they'd ruined her. Sophie put

her face in her hands. This was the end. Numb and empty … despair.

'Look at me.'

Anne's sparkling tiara and jewellery jarred with her ashen face and hard eyes. 'Mr Clutterbuck frightened you. He was drunk and behaving dishonourably. You fell forward in a faint.'

'Everyone saw me punch him.' Sophie's voice echoed in her ears, dull, defeated.

'If we persist, repeat that you fainted and knocked him over, people will begin to doubt what they saw.'

'I can't go in there.' Women might throw punches in pubs, but ladies didn't clock drunks in grand houses… Damn crappy Clutterbuck. She hoped he'd get sacked, defrocked, or whatever happened to lecherous curates.

'If you can put a six foot drunk on the floor, you can face … awkwardness.' Anne put her arm through Sophie's. 'Chin up.'

They strolled along the passage, but it was a forced march in disguise and Sophie was hyperventilating.

When they came into the ballroom, the music seemed to fade and Anne was reintroducing her, as if she'd been ill or recently returned from Australia. 'You remember Miss Arundel? She's had a terrible shock.'

Anne retold the fainting story until Sophie could repeat it verbatim. Albert was sympathetic, as if what she was saying was entirely reasonable. So was Freddy, though he'd been right beside her when she'd 'fainted.' He was being polite. Hugo managed a disbelieving nod and his dance partner's green eyes narrowed, but she gave Sophie a token smile.

'I'm forgetting my manners,' said Hugo, ironically. 'This is Miss Clarissa Maine.'

'How do you do?' said Sophie.

Clarissa did the echo thing and smiled at Hugo, a

completely different smile to the one she'd given Sophie. A full-on flirt. Hugo flirted back.

The despair that had faded with each retelling of Anne's fake news, morphed into surprise, then hurt. Which was stupid. Of course, Hugo would be socialising, flirting. Why wouldn't he?

'It would normally be your last dance partner,' said Freddy, 'but in the circumstances … may I escort you into dinner?'

'Of course,' said Sophie, on autopilot. She peeled off her gloves. After punching Clutterbuck, removing her gloves in public was a trivial faux pas.

The dining table was laid out in its normal splendid style but made more magnificent by large silver centre-pieces featuring Shorten stags, and pink, yellow and white roses.

What had Anne said? Chin up.

Sophie sat between Freddy and Ethel. As Anne had instructed, Sophie laid her gloves neatly across her lap, under the napkin the footman had draped across her knees.

'How is Alice?' Sophie asked Ethel.

'Better, thank you.' Ethel leaned closer. 'What you did to Mr Clutterbuck was outrageous … and quite splendid.'

Beneath Ethel's earnest, conventional manner was a kindred spirit. Sophie shot her a grateful smile.

But Sophie's energy was dipping. She needed to eat. As well as familiar dishes, there was caviar, oysters, white grouse and truffles. She accepted oysters onto her plate so as not to appear odd, but only ate a truffle on toast, fruit and cheese.

After the meal, other women carried their gloves, so Sophie did the same.

Guests thanked Anne and Richard, drifted off to bedrooms, carriages or cars, and Sophie chivvied Charlotte to her room, beyond tired. She didn't want to think about tomorrow.

Charlotte slumped on the bed, Maud helped Sophie undress and Sophie made vague assenting noises to Maud's questions. An instant after crawling under the coverlet, she was asleep.

But as she floated towards consciousness the next morning, the memory of punching Herbert came sharply back. She rubbed her eyes and sat up.

Maud put the tea tray on Sophie's lap. She was acting entirely normally.

Since retiring last night, Maud must have just slept and returned. No time to hear a snippet, let alone the full version. Shouldn't repeat the fainting lie. The best barometer would be Maud's genuine reaction, untainted by special pleading.

Brazen it out.

Breakfast felt more formal with forty people. An unfamiliar footman seated her beside Clarissa, who was sitting unnaturally straight, like a cartoon princess. Was she wearing *particularly* uncomfortable underwear?

Toast and homemade marmalade lifted Sophie's spirits. She discreetly fed Charlotte, and Clarissa talked, hardly pausing for breath. 'Absolutely wonderful,' she gushed. 'During the Season, you go from event to event in one giddy whirl, meet *all* the right people.'

'Have you been to any shooting weekends?' She wouldn't be going now, but it would be useful to get info, maybe for Hugo.

'*Weekend.*' Clarissa delicately sniffed, as if catching an unpleasant aroma. She turned to face Sophie. 'Only Americans talk about the weekend ... *so* vulgar. You must say Saturday to Monday or people will think you're foreign. Or worse.'

'Worse?'

'Not the right sort.'

Clarissa ignored her for the rest of breakfast, which was no loss. Clarissa was — how had she put it? Not the right sort.

Hugo was seated a long way down the table, but Clarissa had somehow attracted his attention. Actually, his rapport with Clarissa was entirely predictable. Her demeanour was scarily similar to Madison's. They even looked alike: brown hair, almond-shaped eyes and a mouth that was slightly too big. If Clarissa hadn't been born in another universe, she could have been related. Sophie wanted to give Clarissa a good shove, but she was eighteen, not twelve. Some things could never be.

When Clarissa eventually left, Freddy took her place. 'After a late night,' he said, 'a good breakfast is just the ticket.'

'Absolutely.' She was physically restored, if not socially.

'Did you enjoy the ball?'

'Very much,' she lied politely.

'You and Hugo should learn more dances.' He gestured to a footman to pour him orange juice. 'Once you know the steps, you don't forget.' He sipped his juice. 'I could teach you.'

'I'd like that.'

Two middle-aged women were taking too close an interest. Sophie put on her innocent face and included them. 'Hugo and I need to learn all the dances from scratch. So far, we only know two.' Freddy got the hint and stopped flirting. He'd definitely been flirting.

'The shooting party should be fun,' said Freddy, in a voice loud enough to include the women.

After the last car drove off in the afternoon, Sophie sat at the dressing table in her room and looked dully at her dance card. Unlikely that any boy would be interested in her now.

She felt drained so tried to doze, but she was too wired.

Anne wouldn't lock her in a tower, but she needed to know the worst. Knowing was better than not knowing. Well, usually.

Finally, at four, she headed to the small drawing room.

Anne came in, Miss Parry served tea and left, closing the door behind her, and Sophie's nerves tensed until they should have snapped.

Sophie forced herself to speak calmly. 'What are you going to do?'

Anne ate a tiny cucumber sandwich. 'I considered asking if you could stay with Richard's great aunt. She lives near Truro.'

'Where's that?'

'Three hundred miles away. But Mrs Trelawney is elderly and old-fashioned. If you made another mistake, there would be no safety net, no rowing back.' Anne took a sip of tea. 'I can lessen the damage while you're under this roof. I can only hope I won't be called into action this evening, or tomorrow.'

A crazy rush of relief.

'My family and the Manor, this is my whole life, Sophie. *No one* is more important than that.'

Sophie cringed.

'On the bright side, many guests this morning were asking after Alice's health — and yours.'

'I still don't understand why they bought your story.'

'That punch was *so* shocking, people didn't believe their eyes.'

Like a magician's sleight of hand.

'I understand the Armstrongs have invited you to the shoot.'

'Please don't worry, I'd much rather stay here.' When Anne said nothing, Sophie added, 'Hugo accepted the invitation at the ball. He could still go?'

'A good opportunity to bolster his social credentials,' said Anne. 'Unfortunately, you need to go too.'

'But why? I could say I was *really* ill, confined to bed.'

'That would only encourage … the most unpleasant gossip.'

Sophie stared into her tea.

'Make a virtue of it, strengthen your friendship with Alice and Ethel, concentrate on embroidery and acting demure.' There was no humour in Anne's eyes. 'Jack dislikes travelling and I presume Charlotte hasn't been to a shoot before?'

'No.'

'You will need to keep her on the lead outside.'

Having Charlotte along would make it easier.

After tea, when Sophie mentioned the proposed trip to Maud, she was obviously keen.

'I've never worked anywhere else, Miss. We'll have to make up trunks.'

'I won't need loads of stuff. Just a day dress and one for dinner. It's only Saturday to Monday.'

'When Lady Lacey visits, she takes her best velvet dress for church, tweed coats and skirts. You can't wear the same dinner gown over the time, Miss. Hats, country caps, a riding habit … and think about the petticoats, hatpins and such like. And you'll need a pretty bag to carry a book and sampler.'

Off the hook with shooting, but constant pointless clothes changing and she couldn't get out of church. And delicate sewing would be tedious and difficult, with the additional problem of concealing poor results.

'What's your full name, Miss? I'll sew your initials on the bag.'

'Sophie Deborah Ellen Arundel. What are your middle names, if you don't mind me asking?'

'I don't have any, Miss. My parents used them all on my sisters.'

There must be thousands of girls' names. She'd never understand this world.

~

'Could you spare some time tomorrow to help in the office?'

Four hours later, over dinner, it took Sophie a moment to realise that Richard was addressing her. She smiled. 'Of course.' He was being polite. He must know she had sufficient time to write a novel, start her own business and write a how-to daily blog.

Anne had suggested this. To keep her occupied. And out of trouble.

The following morning, before meeting Richard, Sophie sat on the terrace and read the paper. On the front page was a black and white photograph of a fashionably dressed couple standing beside a shop window. Underneath was a short caption. *Lord and Lady Maine visit Selfridges Department Store. The popular London venue continues to prosper.*

Maine was an unusual surname. Clarissa's parents? The woman was wearing a dress with an extremely tapered skirt and a gigantic hat adorned with ostrich feathers; somehow, the outfit managed to flatter her plump figure. Her husband had an attractive, open face, but clever eyes.

Lately, every front page had featured a good news story but the headlines inside were less reassuring. *Order Restored After Bread Riot, Longer Sentences for Suffragettes Welcomed...*

Sophie checked her watch. Nearly eleven.

She walked towards the office, the dogs trotting beside her, and knocked on an open door.

Richard looked up from a shabby ledger. His oak desk was shabby too, the work surface shiny from years of use. Behind him were three more desks, arranged in a horizontal row. Rickety bookshelves lined the walls, crammed with dog-eared box files. More files were on the floor.

Hugo was seated at the middle desk, reading some sort of chart. To his right, was an unoccupied table, chaotically piled with papers. Behind the other desk was a young woman. She was moving her finger along a line of figures pencilled in a large, open book.

When Sophie stepped through the doorway, the girl noticed and smiled.

For a moment, Sophie didn't recognise her: flaxen hair neatly arranged in a chignon, her complexion clear and smooth, blue eyes bright and alert — and young, near her own age. The last time she'd seen Mrs Fletcher outside *The Crooked Gate,* she'd been defiant and exhausted and appeared years older. Sophie smiled back.

Hugo was still pointedly buried in his work.

Jack ran forward, thumped his head on a table leg and yelped.

'Heavens.' Richard rushed forward and checked him over. After a moment, Jack recovered himself and crawled under his master's desk.

Jack hadn't been in the office in a while, must have lost his bearings.

Richard gestured Sophie towards a chair by a smaller desk she hadn't noticed, tucked beside a bookcase. On the table were three thick ledgers, neatly stacked.

She sat down and Charlotte leaned against her legs. The air was stuffy and dusty, with a whiff of floor polish.

She'd expected this — basically a job interview.

Richard sat at his desk again. 'Before we begin, I would like your assurance that you will treat everything in confidence. The one thing I've been unable to change is the gossip telegraph. Nothing faster known to science.'

'I understand.'

'The office might not be neat but it's efficient. Twenty years ago, we didn't know how many cottages or estate workers we had. Until we find a new manager, I cannot let things slip. That's why I've asked you to lend me a hand.'

Sophie doubted that was why she was here but nodded.

She opened the first book: detailed records of cottages, with tenants' names, wives and children, inventories of furniture, pots and pans and cutlery, all neatly annotated with A, R, V or N.

'Keeping these records up to date will only require half a day a week,' said Richard.

'What do the letters stand for?' asked Sophie.

'Active, Retired, Vacant, Needs renovating.'

'What happens if people get sick?'

'Good question,' said Richard. 'When I took over, the Manor started paying for hospital care, and nobody loses their home if they retire or can't work. Friends thought people would pretend to be sick, exploit us. What actually happened is that working and living here is highly prized. Everyone pulls together.'

'Is there a state pension?' asked Sophie.

'There is. Five shillings a week.'

Freddy had given Hugo a shilling for their pints in *The Crooked Gate*, so a pittance—

'For men over seventy,' added Richard.

'What do women get?'

'Nothing. Life is hard for widows and spinsters, but not many men live to seventy.' Richard gestured at the piles of paperwork in the room. 'So everyone turns to the estate for support.'

Sophie leafed through the other ledgers, allocated to her because they involved families, and refrained from clearing her throat in a Clutterbuck way. 'I'll familiarise myself with these. What can I do then?'

Richard smiled. When he genuinely smiled, he looked like Freddy. 'Hugo, can you close the door?'

Hugo stood and pushed the door to, then returned to his seat.

Richard's astute, brown eyes met hers. 'Anne tries to keep herself informed but she can't be everywhere. We lost a baby last winter because the mother didn't raise the alarm in time.'

'That's awful.' She was pleased to help. Anyway, only so many baths you could have, books you could read, and the walks with the dogs were getting longer — just to fill the hours. No need to ask about salary. Less like an internship, more like Lady Bountiful.

'These projections are so detailed,' said Hugo.

'Freddy's not keen on work in general,' said Richard, 'but if there's difficult maths involved, he'll do it to perfection.'

'I'll ask him to take me through this,' said Hugo.

'Freddy will finish walking the boundary soon. He can explain the projections then. Take a break.' Richard turned to Sophie. 'You too.'

Sophie walked out with Hugo towards the garden. Charlotte sprinted back and forth, and Jack stayed close to Sophie's legs.

'Freddy's convinced himself you fainted,' said Hugo. 'In complete denial.'

'But he saw me practising in the gym.'

'Where you're concerned, he only sees what he wants to.'

Cultural conditioning could be strong, even overriding clear evidence. Freddy didn't want to believe she — or any girl — could throw a punch.

On the terrace, Sophie sat at the table under the parasol, Jack stood beside her chair and she patted him, worried by how clingy he was.

Hugo knelt on the flagstones beside Jack. 'Both his eyes are too shiny, misty.'

'Cataracts.'

'At home it would be a routine operation.'

'When did cataract surgery start?'

'I'm not sure,' said Hugo, 'but for dogs...'

Charlotte zoomed under the table and Jack carefully lay beside her, his head touching hers, and closed his eyes.

'The past sucks,' said Sophie. 'In any universe.'

CHAPTER 40

*S*till kneeling, Hugo stretched his arm out under the terrace table and stroked Jack. 'He's well cared for.' Hugo stood up and sat beside Sophie. 'And it's good you're helping in the office.'

'I guess.' Shorten Work World wasn't devastatingly depressing like going blind but still disheartening. Forget glass ceilings, this one was concrete.

'Richard means well but he puts people into convenient boxes. I know you felt excluded but you should go with the flow. And the system's more flexible than it looks. Lucy's done well.'

'She arrived here with a skill. Unlike me.'

Hugo was silent, casting around for a lie to buck her up.

Try to be positive. 'Only working half a day, I could be a suffragette.'

'I don't think even the Laceys would tolerate you chaining yourself to railings or smashing windows.'

'I wouldn't do violence.'

'You might say that—'

'I come from a long line of pacifists.'

'Do you?'

'Back to the nineteenth century.'

'That wouldn't protect you, Sophie. At home, the force-feeding of suffragettes was brutal. They were tortured.'

Torture. Sepia photos of girls from history lessons … parachuted into France in the Second World War, captured, executed. Self-knowledge hurt but she paid attention: she wasn't brave enough—

'You could be a suffrag*ist*.'

'What's that?'

'If it's the same here, they're non-violent and let men join.'

'I don't think it is the same,' said Sophie. 'Did you read the paper this morning?'

'Didn't have time.'

'There are thousands of women in jail.'

'At home it was hundreds. The justice system must be close to collapsing.'

Typical Hugo: jumping to the wider picture, analysing, his mind running in different directions. 'Forget about prisons. Women are taking up arms. This isn't a jolly campaign run by women in hats.'

'Most people know about the rousing songs and banners, but our suffragettes planted bombs, cut phone lines.'

'Like terrorists?'

'Or freedom fighters, depending on your point of view. Without the Great War, it could have turned into a full-blown insurgency.'

'I could always lobby for change in a small way. Maud told me she gets paid a lot less than John.' Equality was important, *really* important. 'Think about the Civil Rights movement, Rosa Parks on that bus—'

'How many people got thrown off buses in the States before Rosa Parks? For a gesture to become symbolic, make a difference, you have to be in the right place at the right time, and campaigning for equal pay really isn't a good idea.'

'I thought you were a feminist?'

'At home, there's still a pay gap and it was the First World War that made people even think about it. Won't happen here.' He frowned. 'You don't want to be thought weird.'

Anne's advice about behaviour repeated in her head, visions of righteous protest fading. 'I suppose you're right. I don't want to be known as a weird person. Well, more than I am already.' She rang the handbell for coffee. 'You were worried about not knowing the future, but our future's mapped out. We'll be working here till we die.'

'In sixty years, who knows what Shorten will be like?' said Hugo. 'But right now this does feel like a jail sentence. A nicely decorated prison is still a prison.'

'But we're in different jails. You're in a Swedish open prison where you can do pretty much what you want. I'm in Guantanamo Bay. And a jumpsuit would be better than a corset and hobble skirt. I had more freedom when I was nine.'

He frowned again.

'It's not fair. My crowning achievement will be getting married. How challenging is that?'

'Very challenging if you marry the wrong man. One-way ticket and all that.'

'I need to find someone who won't be any trouble.'

Hugo opened his mouth to speak but changed his mind.

'In an ideal world, I should be madly in love with him, but if it's really intense, we could fall out and then where would I be?' She rested her chin on her hand. 'Even if Prince Charming did turn up, there'd still be *issues*.'

'Like what?'

'Doing anything that doesn't involve being Lady Bountiful? When I'm wearing uncomfortable underwear and an enormous hat, I want to tear it off and … train to be an astronaut. A spacesuit would be cumbersome but have a point.'

His lips twitched. 'Definitely not an option here.'

'Glad you think it's funny. Anyway, if I can't have a normal job, I'll be pretty high maintenance.'

'I think it's a problem for both of us,' said Hugo. 'I'll have to marry someone who knows their own mind, doesn't think along conventional lines. Or I'll be bored witless.' He smiled at Miss Parry who was putting out a plate of bourbon biscuits.

After Miss Parry had poured coffee, he asked for water bowls for the dogs, in his Hugo-way. Ordering stuff from a dutiful servant was second nature, but that wasn't his fault.

She watched him under her lashes. She'd marry *him*, if push came to shove. Her skin heated in a weird surge, but she ignored it. Lizard Brain Lust was a powerful but misdirected force. Hugo spent more time with Freddy than with her. Another thought occurred. No, she'd have guessed.

And Freddy paid her compliments and flirted. She fancied him, and he was kind, and didn't take himself too seriously. Years ago, she'd discussed arranged marriages with Isha; some turned out badly, but others worked out, falling in love coming *after* the wedding. Freddy would respect her. Anne had surely seen to that. And there was no rush. 'Thirty's a good age to tie the knot. You look okay, but you're properly grown up.'

'That works at home but thirty here would be really pushing it.'

'I suppose it's different for men.' Annoyance sharpened her reply.

'A bit.' He sipped his coffee. 'But men usually married in their twenties. Oscar Wilde married at twenty-nine, for the sake of appearances.'

'So, you'll marry in a few years, *for the sake of appearances?*'

'I'm a fan of Wilde's plays and novels,' said Hugo, 'but I'm not that way inclined. Which is lucky. In the 1920s at home, gay people were jailed. Probably the same here.'

Miss Parry returned with water bowls and put them on the flagstones under the table. Charlotte drank thirstily but Jack didn't stir.

Miss Parry turned towards the garden. Freddy was walking up the lawn.

He reached the terrace. 'Coffee, yes please.'

Miss Parry disappeared inside the house.

'How was the boundary?' Hugo asked him.

'Long.'

Sophie told him about Jack.

'How horrible.' Freddy peered at Jack.

'And it will only get worse,' said Hugo.

After Miss Parry had poured his coffee and left, Freddy said quietly, 'Mr Clutterbuck has moved to his brother's estate, won't be taking the living in Derby.'

'He must blame me,' said Sophie, 'want payback.'

Freddy's brow creased. 'Payback?'

'Revenge,' said Hugo.

'He behaved dishonourably.' Freddy sipped his coffee. 'Entirely his own fault.'

'Without a living, he can't preach in church,' said Hugo. 'Yes, he could somehow make trouble, but he'll have his hands full, finding a different profession.'

'Where does his brother live?' Sophie asked Freddy. Hopefully, in the wilds of Scotland.

'Near London.'

'How easy is it,' added Sophie, 'to get from there to Shorten on the train?'

'Very easy.' Freddy reached for a biscuit. 'You still think those loony letters were from him?'

'Most likely suspect,' said Hugo. 'Actually, the only one.'

'He is an odd character,' said Freddy. 'A few years ago, he and a maid … well, she had a baby, and every day he drinks two bottles of claret, and whisky.'

'How do you know all this?' asked Sophie.

'Mr Farrow is friendly with the vicar's housekeeper.' Freddy finished his coffee. 'And Mr Clutterbuck is a younger son, so has no money.'

'He must have some,' said Sophie, 'or he couldn't fund his claret habit.'

Freddy shrugged and Hugo smiled.

As Hugo's lips moved, butterflies tapped a stupid, answering dance. Go away, lizard brain.

Freddy stood up, signalling it was time to return to the office, and Charlotte emerged from under the table, closely followed by Jack. But on the short walk, Jack kept close to Charlotte, even matching her strides.

In the office, Freddy explained about Jack's eyes.

Richard's lips compressed. 'He's only three.'

Jack was under his master's desk again and Richard bent down and patted him. 'He's been unsettled at night in the kennels, gets nervous at the slightest sound. I realise now, it's because of his eye trouble.' Richard straightened and addressed Sophie. 'Would you mind if he slept with Charlotte in your room, given their attachment?'

The bed was massive. 'No problem.' She'd talk Maud round.

That afternoon, when Sophie went to her room to change for tea, Maud jumped from the armchair like a startled frog, hiding a book in her skirts. 'Sorry, Miss.'

'No worries, you're on your break.'

'I don't have breaks, Miss, there's always chores that need doing.'

'Everyone needs breaks. I'm cool with you reading, as long as the book's not so good I drown in the bath.'

Maud's eyes widened.

'I'm kidding.' Sophie sat on the bed. 'What's the book?'

Maud reluctantly showed her. On the cover was a bug-eyed skeleton menacing a sleeping girl by a coffin. '*Varney the Vampire*,' Sophie read aloud, '*or The Feast of Blood*.' The monster was showing off his rib cage, but the girl was fully clothed. Sophie flicked through the pages. Not a 1920s *Fifty Shades*, not even steamy romance. Just over-the-top horror.

'Please don't tell Lady Lacey, Miss.'

'Of course I won't, but where's the harm?' Anne wouldn't care about Maud reading trashy books. 'I don't understand why you can't read this.'

'It's a Penny Dreadful, Miss. I'd be dismissed.'

'What's a Penny Dreadful?' Couldn't be worse than stealing.

'It costs a penny and they're ever so good.'

'Your secret's safe,' said Sophie.

Maud was visibly relieved.

'But you shouldn't be paying. The library's full of books. You're allowed to borrow them?'

'If you ask permission, Miss, but they're not as exciting.'

Sophie handed her *Vanity Fair*. She'd finished it the previous evening. 'The heroine's wicked but it's respectable. You'll love it.'

'Do I have to read it, Miss?'

'No, but there's no harm in giving it a go. If you don't like it, you can go back to *Varney The Vampire*. And you can relax. If you shut the door, the only person who'll walk in on you is me — and the dogs.'

Maud beamed.

Sophie flicked through *Varney The Vampire* again. Varney was a silly name for a vampire, but the freedom to read — anything — was important. If Maud were discovered with a forbidden book, Sophie Arundel would go into battle. Behind the scenes, like with Miss Parry.

But Anne wouldn't sack Maud. It wouldn't just be unfair; Maud was a vital part of the Supervising Sophie Team.

Sophie changed and set off towards the small drawing room but was waylaid by the fair-haired footman carrying a silver tray. On it was a small piece of paper.

Please not another threat.

She picked it up and the footman left.

Thick white paper, the size and shape of a playing card. The top corners were slightly rounded, and one was folded over. Engraved in gilt in the middle was *A. H. Garnier* and below, *Fissington Hall*. Near the bottom *P. P.* had been written by hand.

Albert. The boy she'd danced with. She turned the card over — entirely blank.

She continued on to the drawing room where Anne was standing by the window looking out at the gardens.

Sophie showed her the card. 'How did the footman know it was for me?'

'You're the only unmarried girl living here.'

'Apart from the maids.'

Anne gave her an indulgent smile. 'The turned down corner means Mr Garnier left this in person. That shows he's keen.'

A seriously interested boy who wasn't a sleazebag. Formal courting must deter time-wasters. And he couldn't be as boring as Pete.

She felt irrationally excited. This was much better than a dating app. For a start, she'd already met him. 'What does P.P. mean?'

'*Pour presenter*. It's very old-fashioned. He's asking to be presented to you.'

'I danced with him at the ball.'

'This is different,' said Anne. 'He's asking to see you by himself, to make your acquaintance. You should reply within a couple of days. That would be courteous but sincere.'

'Right.' Cool, not desperate. 'I'll suggest we meet next week. Post this tomorrow.'

'Goodness, Sophie, where to begin? Calling cards have a precise set of rules.'

Of course they did. Sophie felt an invisible etiquette blanket enveloping her, endless and suffocating.

'If we sent back his card, that would clearly signal you did *not* want him to call. And if you wrote a specific day on it, he would be very confused.'

'What should I do?'

Anne walked over to a sideboard. 'I realised you would need these, when you arrived.' She took out a stack of cards. Larger than Albert's, *Miss Sophie Arundel* was printed in a floral font and below, *Shorten Manor*.

'This is really kind of you.'

'Nonsense. Everyone has them.'

Miss Parry came in with a laden tray and, as she laid out crockery, Anne put one card aside, returned the rest to the sideboard and fished out a sleek, silver pen from a drawer.

Anne sat down across from Sophie and put the card on the coffee table.

'We need to send Mr Garnier this, with *Morning* written on it,' said Anne. 'That way, he'll call in the early afternoon, after lunch.'

'Sorry?'

'It is confusing and quite involved. I had to learn quickly how it all worked, once I was married.'

'I'm sorry,' Sophie repeated, 'you've completely lost me.'

'Everyone uses cards, to tell people they are in town or coming home.'

'Couldn't we just phone?'

'That would be easier but calling out of the blue is very bad form and not everyone has telephones.'

'I see.'

Without Anne's advice, Sophie Arundel would be a social outcast, a sad figure of fun.

'You'll soon get the hang of it.'

Miss Parry poured tea and left.

'You must establish how you feel about Mr Garnier,' said Anne, 'whether you'd accept a proposal.'

'After talking to him over tea?'

'You should at least have an inkling.'

'Okay…'

'He will stay twenty or thirty minutes. On no account should you allow him to hold your hand.'

'Got it.'

'Don't worry too much,' said Anne. 'These pitfalls only arise after at least three or four calls.'

'What about kissing?'

'No kissing, even when you're engaged, and then you'll be chaperoned.'

'Really?'

'I thought Richard's mother was using social convention to split us up. We got through it. Everybody does. I appreciate it's worse for you because of what you're used to.'

Sophie sighed. Sleeping with Pete over a weekend was hardly an exciting past. 'We got into the lift on the first day at Uni. There was no time to meet anyone.'

'But you already knew Hugo.'

'Not very well.'

There was a curious look on Anne's face. Had she guessed about the lizard brain thing? No, that was silly.

Anne handed her the pen. 'You write the reply and I'll post it tomorrow.'

'I don't get on with ink pens.' Sophie gingerly turned it over in her hand.

'You never used one at home?'

'No, just biros.'

'I've always liked the feel of a proper pen. My parents bought me one for my eighteenth birthday.'

'Would you mind writing it?'

Holding Sophie's card in place on the table, Anne wrote *Morning* in an effortless, flowing script. 'The key is to press, but not too hard.'

'Thank you for this.'

'Mr Garnier won't reply for a few days. Earlier would be unseemly.' Anne picked up Sophie's card. 'He's respectable and financially secure.'

The next morning in the gym, Sophie told Lucy about Albert's card.

'Those stupid rumours have hit the buffers, and it's not just Mr Garnier who's keen.' Lucy executed an impressive flurry of punches. 'Consensus is you'll marry a duke's son.'

'Who says?'

'Downstairs gossip mill.'

'Need to meet one first.' Shame she couldn't live with Lucy; for a moment, Sophie imagined slobbing in the cottage in her dressing gown. She steadied the punch bag. 'I think you've cracked punches. Now we can do kicks.' She did the action in slow motion.

'That's a lot of twisting.' Lucy tried to imitate the movement and fell over. She got to her feet and wiped her hands on her trousers, brushing off floor dust.

Sophie demonstrated again and Lucy copied her.

'That's it,' said Sophie.

'I'll practise the twisting action and kicks at home.' Lucy tried another shaky kick. 'The big gossip was the lecherous curate and you fainting in a ladylike way. I was impressed.'

'Don't be.' She told Lucy what had actually happened.

'*No.*' Lucy's mouth formed a perfect, shocked O.

CHAPTER 41

The fair-haired footman came into the library with a card on a tray.

Albert? So quickly? Sophie's reply had only been posted the previous day. It must have arrived at Fissington Hall first thing and — with unseemly haste — he'd delivered this himself.

And Life-Changing-Tea-Date was happening in four hours…

As they walked to lunch, she confided her trepidation to Hugo.

'The formal ritual is fascinating and, you never know, he may be too.'

'Hum.' She hadn't expected him to be mega jealous or declare eternal love, so the bleak, hopeless feeling took her by surprise. Unexpected fallout from her lizard brain.

But half an hour after Tea Date, it was Hugo that Sophie sought out — the only person in this nuts universe that would understand.

Being a Saturday, he was in his room. John answered her knock and returned her smile as he left, leaving the door ajar.

Hugo was reading in his armchair. He glanced up. 'How was Albert?'

'A complete loser.'

'Really?' He looked back at the book.

'He was keen to do tea today because he can't come to the shooting party.' Sophie sat on the edge of the bed, the dogs sprawled at her feet. 'He's bothered that Hadley had boys as well as girls and droned on for a seriously long time about hunting. I think he's quite odd.'

Hugo's head was still angled down, reading.

'Good book?'

He closed it. 'But you parted on good terms?'

'Yes.' She'd learned a lot since stepping out of the lift. The old Sophie Arundel would have told Albert to take a hike. 'Anne says I need to put him off but in a way that indicates I'm kind of interested, in case nobody else calls.' She tapped her fingers on the bed coverlet. 'After he left, I read my notes again, but I've got lift puzzle block.'

'We can't give up.'

'Never give up. Never surrender.'

Hugo grinned, recognising the quote from *Galaxy Quest*. He stood and put the book on a side table. 'The shooting party should be interesting.' His packed bags were stacked neatly in the corner of the room. 'They won't let you shoot. What can go wrong?'

They left at four for the hour-long journey to the Armstrong estate.

With Anne minding Jack, Charlotte was grumpily dozing on the back seat, already missing him.

Sophie was wearing a white veil draped to her shoulders over a hard, boxy hat. It matched her white, wrist-length gloves but jarred with her soft navy dress and matching cape. Maud had insisted she wear the hat to keep her hair protected from wind or rain. If they'd been going to a beekeeper convention, she'd have fitted right in.

Neither of the boys seemed to notice she was dressed as a beekeeper. Even Hugo, unaccustomed to travelling with someone up for fighting bees, made no comment.

As the car slowed to navigate a bend, she turned to him. 'Aren't you going to say anything?'

'About what?'

'*This.*' She gestured.

'It's a motoring hat.'

Sophie rolled her eyes behind the veil and grabbed the hat to take it off but then the rain started, strong and heavy.

In moments, the leaves of the beech trees lining the road turned shiny and battered, and all her clothes were sodden. The hat was useless as well as weird.

Freddy twisted around in the front seat, his suit and small-peaked cap also soaked through. 'Chaps shoot black grouse in all weathers, but you can stay indoors.'

Sophie smiled politely. Even if they'd been shooting clay pigeons, she wouldn't have joined in, not in the ugly 'outdoors' outfit she'd already tried on: a brown dress, bulky and coarse, short enough to show off unattractive black walking shoes, and a thigh-length, shapeless jacket.

The hat was ugly too. Nondescript brown, small and shapeless, a charity shop couldn't have given it away. She looked fifty in it. An artfully draped tartan scarf brought her age down to forty-something.

A heavy case filled the boot and in the servants' car was another one, as well as hat boxes and Sophie's huge domed trunk, which Maud called 'Noah's Ark.' It wasn't big enough for all the world's animals but had room for quite a few. Even in pairs.

The car turned right onto a main road. Dishevelled men were trudging along the verge.

'Where have they come from?' asked Hugo.

'Kilburn, Willington, Etwall … there's no work in the smaller towns.' Freddy frowned. 'They're going to Derby but the trouble there is getting worse.'

Sophie stared at her lap, *really* glad she was in the car; the memory of the attack in the lane was back, sharp as the knife point had been in her neck.

Three miles on, the line of weary humanity continued. One man was limping, leaning heavily on his companion, and Sophie felt for him, for all of them. Beard Man had been in the same state, perhaps for years. Her mother's voice sounded in her head. *Forgive those who trespass against you.* It would take time, but she would.

Reynolds turned onto a deserted side road and after twenty minutes of narrow lanes, they crossed a cattle grid and continued on a rough track through fields and eventually onto a gravel drive.

Armstrong House was smaller than Shorten Manor, more like an oversized country cottage. Still larger than Sophie could imagine affording … unless she won the lottery, or founded a start-up and sold it to someone from California.

The Armstrongs came out to greet them but everyone quickly went inside, keen to get out of the rain.

In a mahogany-panelled hall, Sophie peeled off her cape, gloves and hat and a maid took the sodden clothes away, presumably to somewhere they could dry out.

Sophie followed Ethel upstairs, keeping Charlotte on a short lead. There'd been initial confusion, as it had been assumed Charlotte would stay with other dogs in kennels behind some stables. Sophie had gently but firmly demurred, explaining that Charlotte was sensitive and unused to being separated from her mistress.

Sophie's room had a neat four-poster bed with no canopy and low mullioned windows overlooking the drive.

Heavy cloud and rain outside made the space gloomy despite lit gas lamps: slim brass pipes curved elegantly out from each wall in the shape of a swan's neck, holding smoky glass spheres. The flickering illumination was bright but soft, and corners and edges of furniture not directly underneath were shadowed and indistinct.

'I'll let you freshen up,' said Ethel.

After changing into a dry dress, Sophie sat on the bed and ran her hand over the counterpane. The worn cream brocade was inlaid with hand-stitched emerald leaves edged in gilt thread, the repeated pattern punctuated with faded red and blue tulips. Felt old.

Maud extracted a veiled funeral hat and a black plain gown made from bombazine fabric, and put them in a wardrobe with her normal care.

'That dress is hideous,' said Sophie. 'When was it made? I don't remember it.'

'It's the just-in-case dress, Miss.'

'Just in case—'

'A member of the royal family dies. Everyone has to wear black for a time. How long you have to depends on how important they were.'

A special dress to respect a famous dead person? That was bonkers. 'Have you got a just-in-case dress?'

Maud looked up from another gown she was holding, her expression bemused but patient. 'My uniform is black, Miss, so it doesn't affect me.'

So, not *everyone* had a just-in-case-dress. 'I'm so glad you're here. I feel like there are traps everywhere, waiting to catch me out.'

Maud smiled in recognition and went to the door. 'Back in a minute, Miss.'

Sophie rinsed her face, using a jug of water and a bowl on a dresser. 'Over the next three days,' she told Charlotte, 'I'm going to be the most perfectly behaved lady *ever*.'

Charlotte ignored her, distracted by new scents.

Maud returned, her face carefully neutral, which meant she was fretting about something. 'The bathroom arrangements are different here, Miss.'

'Different?'

'There's an outside bathroom for the servants and an inside one for Mr and Mrs Armstrong.' Maud got on her knees, reached under the bed and brought out a white porcelain bowl with a lid. A yellow floral motif on one side had faded with time and use. Maud left it on the floor, avoiding Sophie's gaze. 'You need to go in this, and I'll dispose of it.'

This was getting madder by the minute. 'I can't ask *you*, or anyone, to do that. It's … not nice.'

Maud folded her arms. 'I don't want to use the servants' toilet, so I'll use a commode.'

'How many servants are there?'

'I'm not sure, Miss. Outdoors as well, at least forty.'

'I could get 'sick,' so we could go back?'

Maud averted her eyes again. 'It's a matter for you, Miss, but it would be a shame. I've never heard of another house like the Manor, with so many bathrooms. If you can't stay here, you wouldn't be able to stay … anywhere.'

Sophie sighed. She'd always taken bathroom privacy for granted, well, from when she'd been toilet trained, which she couldn't remember. If she ever offended Maud, the unleashed gossip would be catastrophic, might even eclipse the phantom pregnancy. 'Do you leave while I—'

'Of course, Miss. There's paper in that cupboard. Shall I take Charlotte out on her lead, as she doesn't know the gardens?'

'Thank you.' Sophie tried to smile, but it turned into a grimace.

~

Downstairs, Mr Armstrong, Hugo, Freddy, Harry Richards — the red-haired boy who was training to be a doctor — and Edward Armstrong were gathered in the hall for the first shooting *drive*, as it was called. They were all dressed in brown tweed with deerstalker hats, reminiscent of Sherlock Holmes, except they had jackets not long coats, and knee-length socks with plus fours.

Charlotte was restless, sensing their excitement, and Sophie shortened the lead.

'Such a shame she can't join the other dogs.' Clarissa somehow managed to look elegant in an unattractive plaid dress. Behind her, a maid was carrying a dark garment, similar to Sophie's rejected outside jacket. 'Have fun.'

Shame the Armstrongs had invited Clarissa. Sophie dragged Charlotte into a quiet room dominated by a grand piano even bigger than Shorten's. Sophie imagined Charlotte bouncing and scratching the smooth, polished surface and sat well away on a cream armchair beside arched French windows. Beyond the rain-streaked glass was a smooth lawn bordered by blue hyacinths and burgundy roses, but the garden looked damp and uninviting.

Sophie took a book from her embroidered bag and opened it where she'd left the bookmark. Tawny-bright beams from gas lamps waved over the pale pages, like flames from a grate, quite different from harsh electric light. But Armstrong House smelled the same as the Manor: old stone, leavened with a hint of vinegar and lemon, and dust kept at bay by invisible servants.

Ethel and Alice came in, followed by a maid. Alice was carrying a similar bag to Sophie's, with *A. J. A.* on it.

'Can you bring me a pen?' Ethel's question was directed at the maid, but Ethel's attention was on a notebook she'd taken from a side table.

Something showed in the young maid's face. Irritation? No, more than that. Resentment. Was there trouble downstairs here too? Not an enquiry that would be welcomed from a new guest. Anyway, the sisters were oblivious to the maid's surliness.

'Would it be possible to have a water bowl for my dog, please?' asked Sophie, as respectfully as she could.

'Yes, Miss.' Now, the maid's face was carefully blank.

Charlotte put her head on Sophie's lap, realising she had zero chance of joining the shoot, and in a momentary trick of the light, the ends of her brown fur shone silver.

Alice and Ethel sat together on a pale beige sofa. 'Louise and Victoria Greenworthy will join us soon,' said Ethel. 'They came to your ball.'

Sophie couldn't remember them. 'I love your piano. Do you both play?'

The sisters exchanged glances. 'Now and then,' said Ethel.

'Is this your first shooting party?' asked Alice.

'Yes.' Sophie closed her book.

'Don't they have them in your world?' asked Ethel.

'They do, big houses get paid a lot of money to do shoots.'

Alice seemed puzzled. 'Who would *pay* to shoot?'

'Businessmen mostly, I guess it's a way of male bonding.'

Alice laughed, unexpectedly loudly. 'Male bonding, never heard that before. I suppose that's what it is.'

'We can go outside, if you like,' said Ethel, 'give them moral support.'

'I'll leave that to Clarissa,' said Sophie, before she'd thought how the words would sound.

'You don't like her?' asked Alice.

'Oh, I don't know her. I only spoke to her briefly at the ball.'

'Clarissa didn't have an easy Season last year,' said Ethel. 'She liked this Russian chap, but he was practically royalty, and he wasn't so keen when he found out her father used to be in trade.'

The maid brought in Ethel's pen and Charlotte's bowl.

After she'd left, Sophie said, 'But the family are … comfortable?'

'Heavens, yes,' said Ethel, 'but Clarissa's not from an old family.'

What did that even mean? Surely everyone's family was 'old?'

'It wasn't just the Russian chap,' said Alice, 'other girls would say horrible things.'

'Like what?'

'Let's open the doors,' said Alice.

'I don't get it.'

'What the manager says in a department store when they open, apparently,' explained Ethel. 'Her father made his fortune selling dress material and furnishings.'

Sophie frowned, remembering online gossip about snooty friends of Prince William mocking Kate Middleton's parents, who'd once worked as lowly cabin crew. 'Clarissa told me the Season had been wonderful.'

'It's important to stay positive,' said Ethel, her face serious.

Husband-hunting was a serious business. 'I appreciate you sharing that. I may have misjudged Clarissa.' Sophie returned the book to her bag. 'How long does the shoot take?'

'Today, a couple of hours,' said Alice. 'But tomorrow after church, they'll have lunch outside unless the weather's really filthy and stay out till tea, and on Monday they'll shoot all day. We always have more birds than we can eat.'

Sophie leaned forward in her chair. 'What do you do with the ones left over?'

'I've never thought about it,' said Alice. 'They don't keep that long in the iceboxes.'

'At home we have fridges,' said Sophie.

'Fridges,' said Ethel, slowly. 'Odd word.'

'There's usually a freezer compartment. Frozen food can last for months so you don't need to shop so often.'

When Ethel and Alice looked blank, Sophie said, 'You've never gone food shopping?'

'No,' Ethel admitted, 'but we walked round Fortnum and Mason last year in London.'

'It was lovely,' said Alice, 'but we didn't buy anything.'

'You're *so* lucky.' In the holidays, Sophie shopped every few days for Aunty Wendy. 'Grocery shopping's very boring.'

'Our food is delivered,' said Ethel, 'from the village.'

'We have that too,' said Sophie. 'Shopping online.'

'Online?' asked Alice.

'Sorry. We have machines. You can use them to order anything. The last thing I bought was a train ticket.' Felt like another life.

'*You* had to buy it? I don't understand,' said Ethel. 'Can't your servants understand the machines?'

'Most people don't have staff,' said Sophie. 'And most people work, so they have to shop in their spare time.'

'Goodness,' said Ethel. 'How do you get anything done?'

'We buy ready meals and go out to cafés and restaurants.'

'We went to a restaurant in London,' said Alice.

'I loved it,' said Ethel, 'but our parents didn't approve.'

'Why?'

'There can be problems,' said Ethel, knowledgeably. 'Men who've had too much to drink.'

'What kind of restaurant was it?'

'It was in a hotel,' said Alice.

'The Ritz,' said Ethel. 'I remember because the name sounded foreign.'

Very pricey. Not much chance of drunken fights there.

'It's strange, isn't it?' said Ethel, 'to think of you and us, visiting the same places but separated by, well, I don't know what…'

Sophie felt cold inside. She'd never been to the Ritz but, staying in central London with Isha, she'd probably walked the same streets. 'It's creepy. And if I can't get back, I do worry what sort of life I'll have.'

'You had that unpleasantness with Mr Clutterbuck,' said Ethel, 'but Mr Denning never stopped talking about you. I'm sure he'll ask to call.'

'Mr Denning?'

'Mr Rupert Denning.' Ethel smiled, a twinkle in her eye. 'He's very handsome.'

Sophie searched her memory. She hadn't danced with him. 'What does he look like?'

'Tall and fair,' said Ethel, 'and the most wonderful blue eyes.'

The boy with the pointed chin who'd been looking at her … curious *and* interested. 'You said he set fire to his room in Oxford?'

'He did,' said Ethel, 'but he paid for the damage.'

This Rupert obviously had issues. But he wouldn't be boring.

CHAPTER 42

'If suitors call too often, there'll be an expectation of a proposal,' said Ethel. 'If you don't like them or they're not well off, you need to be careful.'

Charlotte was asleep on Sophie's skirts and Sophie patted her absent-mindedly. She'd been careful with Albert. And she was up for round two with someone else, even a pyromaniac. 'Is Mr Denning "well-off" enough?'

'He's the eldest son, Sophie,' said Ethel, in a stage whisper. 'He'll inherit the estate *and* a title, and his family have land in the colonies.'

Consensus is you'll marry a duke's son. The guests who'd stayed over for the ball had brought their valets and maids. Rupert must have mentioned he'd liked her and his valet had gossiped…

'Most young men are not in such a fortunate position,' said Ethel. 'They try and marry someone rich from America, even go through agencies.' She took a magazine from a rack by her chair, then stood up and handed it to Sophie.

After articles on fashion, adverts for face creams and dressmakers, were companies offering introductions. *Discreet service for discerning gentlemen. Only serious applications consid-ered. References required.*

Intriguing. 'I wonder why they only target men? I quite fancy a date with a wealthy tycoon.'

'That would be scandalous,' smiled Ethel.

'You remind me of that American girl,' said Alice. 'The one we met in London.'

Ethel nodded.

What was this fascination with Americans? She was as English as afternoon tea.

'She argued politics,' said Alice, 'said we should act … decisively.'

Sophie frowned. 'About what?'

'The unrest in the cities, said we should use guns,' said Ethel.

Sophie's pacifist parents hadn't let her watch TV shows or movies involving firearms, but during weekends at Hadley Sophie had grown to love action stories, spy thrillers as well as sci-fi. *Real* guns, though, were scary—

'She was very forceful.' Alice seemed impressed but daunted.

'One of my friends is seeing an American boy,' said Sophie. 'They FaceTime every day.'

'FaceTime?' asked Alice.

'He's in America but she talks to him on the phone and can see him too, almost like she's with him, in the same room.'

'How … wonderful,' said Alice, slowly, imagining speaking on a futuristic phone.

'Was her chap over here for the Season?' asked Ethel.

'No. She met him through a dating site. She got Boston Massachusetts confused with Boston in England.'

'Dating site,' repeated Alice.

'They're a bit like these agencies,' said Sophie. 'Do you know anyone who's tried them?'

Ethel's eyebrows went up. 'Absolutely not.' Her voice was stern but her eyes were twinkling again.

'It must be wonderful to marry without worrying about money,' said Alice. Her delicate face reddened and she examined her embroidery.

Ethel cleared her throat. 'I can't think why the Greenworthys haven't come down yet.'

Alice was blinking.

Awkward. Sophie got to her feet, closing her bag to hide an untouched sampler. 'I think I'll go and get my sewing.' If Alice got stressed in social situations, it sucked that her parents had arranged this formal house party.

When Sophie came back downstairs, Alice wasn't there, and Ethel was chatting to the Greenworthy sisters about hats.

'I just wish they weren't so large.' Louise was plump with messy auburn hair. 'They're such a bother.'

'I like them. They make me feel properly grown-up.' Victoria was blonde, with a retroussé nose and large eyes — she'd look good in the craziest hat.

Sophie briefly feigned interest, then read her book.

The men returned at six, exchanging stories about misses and hits. They all had wet hair, but Harry's was completely flat, like a red swimming cap.

Wet helmet hair was better than grease helmet hair. And no murdered birds … presumably carted off to the kitchen.

After exchanging sodden Sherlock Holmes gear for suits, Freddy opted to stay indoors, playing whist with Edward and Harry, and Hugo reluctantly came out for a walk with Sophie.

Though the rain had relented, the ground was messy. Sophie had put on her walking boots, but Hugo's shoes were shiny, so they kept to the paths and Sophie kept Charlotte's lead short.

'The shoot was knackering,' said Hugo. 'I'm glad it's only a couple of days or I'd get tinnitus.'

'Tinnitus?'

'Old rock stars get it, ringing in your ears. Nobody thinks to wear ear defenders.'

'Did you enjoy it?'

'It's not difficult once you're used to the gun. Other people make a noise so the birds fly towards you.' He ruffled Charlotte's head. 'But once I realised they couldn't all be eaten before they rotted, it felt pointless. Slaughter for its own sake.'

His distaste took her by surprise. 'You'd played soldiers at school, so it's not completely strange.'

Hugo's lips pressed into a worried line, as if he wasn't sure.

She related her conversation with the Armstrong sisters about dating. 'With your British accent, you could charm a *Vanderbilt*.'

'Nobody would be interested, Sophie. The Americans have money but in exchange they want a genuine, titled aristocrat.'

His voice was giving her that nice, fuzzy feeling ... lizard brain still pointlessly plugging away. 'Rupert Denning's another option for me. He was at the ball. May leave a card.'

'That's good.' Hugo pushed his fringe from his eyes. It was way too long again. 'All that rain and standing about has given me an appetite for dinner. It's white tie. You wouldn't believe how complicated the rules are, what you wear and when, on different occasions.'

Welcome to Sophie World.

They went to the house, Hugo striding and Charlotte

bouncing, but Sophie walked carefully, feeling queasy. She couldn't face Dead Bird Dinner. Would plead a headache.

'I'm glad there'll be no grouse for dinner,' said Hugo, as if he were reading her mind. 'They have to be hung and have other things done to them. Takes a day or so.'

Enough gory detail.

In the bedroom, Maud had taken out a pale blue dinner gown, with a short train. The dress was gathered into a navy bow at the front, just above the knees to constrict the skirt. 'Does your corset need tightening, Miss?'

'Definitely not.' Any tighter and she wouldn't be able to breathe, never mind eat. 'If there's no bathrooms here, how do people have baths?'

'We send for a tin bath, Miss. The water kettles are heavy and the stairs here are terrible narrow.'

'I can do without until we get back.'

Maud smiled.

In the new gown, Sophie's waist looked tiny in a wall mirror, like she'd been photo-shopped.

She sat at a dressing table, took off her pendant and picked out an emerald ring and the embossed gold bracelet from an enamelled jewellery box, borrowed from Anne. Maud leaned over her with the heavy, three-tiered diamond necklace.

Maud's fingers fumbled behind Sophie's neck. 'Sorry, Miss.'

'Won't it fasten?'

'I've closed the clasp, but there's a tiny chain, in case the clip breaks,' said Maud. 'All done.'

The necklace glittered soft-white in the light from the gas lamps, made her look older as well as loaded, and was shouting, *Mug Me.* At home, it would have been safely stored in a bank vault, neglected but insured. She grinned at her reflection. Definitely now a trinkets person. If she ever got home, she'd buy a shedload of shouty costume jewellery.

Maud was holding the torture gloves and Sophie reluctantly stood up.

When the gloves were finally on, Charlotte pawed the door and Sophie walked towards her.

'Charlotte needs to stay here, Miss.'

'Why?'

'Dogs aren't allowed in the dining room. I'll get her nice scraps.'

Every house had different rules. One day there'd be laws against dog discrimination but not in her lifetime, perhaps in any universe. She kissed the top of Charlotte's head and Maud held onto Charlotte's collar while Sophie opened the door.

Downstairs, the drawing room was full of people enjoying pre-dinner drinks, including a young man in navy trousers and a matching jacket with gold braid on the shoulders and a decorated band collar. His dark hair was neat but not slick. The old twinge of unease, faced with new people, was back ... but she raised her chin and walked in.

Clarissa was entirely focused on Hugo, her face rapt and attentive. Victoria was beside Clarissa, her body language more formal than Clarissa's. Both women's dresses, apart from being different colours, were identical to Sophie's, down to the bow at the front. Bows must be trending.

'Lovely estate,' Freddy was saying to Alice.

'Did you have a good drive?' Sophie asked him.

'Very good, thanks,' said Freddy, still facing Alice.

Avoiding eye contact. Anne had told him to be careful. That was fine. Aligned neatly with the Demure Sophie Project.

The women began removing their gloves, so Sophie did

too. This gathering was informal compared to the summer ball so maybe the rules were more relaxed?

A footman offered Sophie a glass of sweet sherry and she sipped, listening to Freddy. Alice was listening too, seemed subdued.

Edward offered Sophie his arm, everyone else paired up, and they trooped off to the dining room like a column of soldiers.

Sophie chose the newly fashionable cold vichyssoise consommé, made with potatoes and cream, mainly to avoid mock turtle soup. She was unsure what was in it; mock-turtles couldn't be endangered, could they?

She couldn't even look at the quail dish. The complete bird minus the feet lay there prone, its eyes glassy.

Different wines accompanied each course but, like in Shorten, no one drained a glass. Sophie judiciously sipped; she didn't want to end up like crappy Clutterbuck.

Opposite her, Victoria was eating strawberries, trying not to spill any red brine. Quiet and cautious, she was endearingly unaware of her own charms.

Down the table, Clarissa was flirting with almost twenty-first century brazenness with Hugo.

'Do you know Clarissa well?' Sophie spread soft cheese on a savoury biscuit.

'Not really,' said Victoria. 'I only met her last year when I came out.'

'Sorry?' Sophie lowered her voice.

'When I was old enough for parties.'

Focus. If Victoria were that way inclined, she wouldn't casually mention it over dinner.

'Her father's a bigwig in the government,' whispered Victoria. 'The king gave him a peerage last year, though he used to be a *shopkeeper*.' Victoria said 'shopkeeper' in a fainter, slower tone, as if it were shameful.

Lord and Lady Maine... That couple in the paper were Clarissa's parents.

Hugo was still listening to Clarissa, engrossed — or hypnotised. Clarissa might be flirting like a modern girl but didn't want sex, might have no idea what it entailed. When she married, that would be a bonus, or a chore.

All these women had been training for years to catch a husband, done the equivalent of degrees. A heavy feeling settled on Sophie's shoulders, like with starting a new school or revising.

'Will you be going to town?' asked Victoria, her voice a normal volume.

'Town?'

'London.'

She needed a parallel world translator.

'We went last year,' said Edward, addressing her and Victoria. 'Stayed with the Maines and had a lovely time. The best bit was the Ritz bar and the cocktails.'

'What sort of cocktails?' asked Sophie.

'No idea, the barman selected them. American chap. Skin as black as the ace of spades.'

'Oh,' said Sophie, feeling uncomfortable. 'My friend Lily is Caribbean heritage and my best friend, Isha, she's from Mumbai.'

'Mumb what?' asked Edward.

'A city in India.'

'You should talk to Captain Charlie Fuller,' said Victoria. 'The Regiment's not long back from there.' She gestured at the boy in the navy uniform.

What was India like here? She'd hoped to visit Isha's grandparents, go backpacking. Charlie's observations would be fascinating, particularly as trekking in a corset held zero appeal.

She had no opportunity to speak to him before the ladies

retired after dinner, but the following morning at breakfast, Charlie was in the dining room, deep in conversation with Hugo and Freddy. The boys were in their Sherlock Holmes outfits again, as was Charlie.

When she neared the table, they all stood up. Even Hugo.

She took a seat, feeling awkward, and the boys sat down again.

'So, there's plenty of action,' said Charlie to Hugo, 'though it can get beastly hot.'

'Charlie's been telling us about his last posting,' said Hugo.

Sophie acknowledged a footman pouring her coffee then addressed Charlie. 'Were there elephants near your barracks?' She had a soft spot for elephants.

'No one's ever asked me that before,' said Charlie. 'Elephants are everywhere. Natives use them for carrying loads, like we use horses.'

'Are they well cared for?'

Charlie looked blank.

'The elephants.'

'I suppose so. They're just elephants.'

Seeing her downcast expression, he added, 'I've never seen any cruelty.'

A footman was standing by her chair. 'Could I have poached eggs on toast, please?'

'Charlie's been telling us about fire fights,' said Hugo.

'Sophie wouldn't be interested in that,' said Charlie, apologetically.

The footman put a napkin over her knees. 'Hugo, we should tell Charlie about Lily.' Lily was training to be an Apache helicopter pilot. Sophie had Googled it … an unpleasant weapon of war but amazing.

Hugo was avoiding her eyes. 'Lily was at school with us.' He shook his head slightly.

She got it. Explaining Lily's day job was a bad idea. Charlie wouldn't believe them.

Smiling her agreement at Hugo, she was rewarded with an answering smile, triggering the familiar tingle. There was stupid fluttering too but that might be the corset; Maud had drawn the laces very tight.

'We had a close call on the Afghan border last year,' said Charlie, his face serious.

'At home, the British army fought in Afghanistan. They were there for years,' said Sophie. 'Well, nearly a century from now.'

Charlie frowned and turned to Hugo. 'Freddy's explained where you've come from. I couldn't understand it. No time machine?'

'No,' said Hugo. 'We're from a different universe, from 2017. And that future isn't *your* future.'

Charlie was still frowning.

They were stuck with the truth now, however awkward.

'So, in *your* future, we fight the Afghans again?' Charlie took a sip of coffee and grinned. 'Shows how persistent they are, still making trouble on the border.'

'No,' said Hugo, 'more trouble than that.'

'Religious fanatics attacked America,' said Sophie.

Charlie set his cup aside. 'America? Why would they do that? How on earth did they get there?'

'It's complicated,' said Hugo, 'and Afghanistan was a hard campaign.'

'It's a hard country.' Charlie finished his bacon and eggs. 'I only joined the Regiment in '21, but both my grandfathers were in the second war, years ago.'

'Second?' asked Sophie.

'1870s,' said Charlie. 'The first Afghan war finished in … 1842.'

'Same as home.' Hugo took a sip of coffee.

Sophie's poached eggs arrived, and she tucked into them. The British had been fighting in Afghanistan forever. Who knew?

'You could do worse than join up,' Charlie was saying to Hugo. 'It's not such a bad life.'

'It does sound interesting,' said Hugo.

'I'll say,' said Freddy. 'I've never been out of England. I envy you, Charlie, all that action and excitement. What fun.'

Sophie wiped her lips with her napkin. It didn't sound like fun. And if Hugo joined up, he could be wounded, or worse. Don't think about it.

'Most of the natives appreciate what we've done,' Charlie was saying. Freddy was nodding, Hugo's face was blank, unreadable. 'But our tour's been cut short, we're back here for the foreseeable future.'

'Just your regiment?' asked Hugo.

'No, there's quite a few,' said Charlie. 'To keep order in the cities and what not.'

Hugo's face was still expressionless but Sophie knew what he was thinking because she was thinking it too. The riots in the north must be out of control.

CHAPTER 43

After breakfast, Sophie changed into a more formal green velvet dress with an elegant, if too large, matching hat. Short of faking a heart attack, she couldn't get out of church; Charlotte had — she would have howled during hymns.

The inside of the chapel was unexpectedly cold and the sermon was way too long, mainly about saints and how the congregation should behave. Sophie knelt on a cushion until her knees went numb and still the vicar droned on. Chapel at school had been a doddle compared to this.

As she pretended to pray, she thought about her parents. Clear in her head, they would never age or retire, and in this world had yet to be born or might never exist.

That first week at Hadley, her mother had sent Sophie a text. *On rites of passage: trust in God's will to choose the right path.* And Sophie had replied with kisses, like she always did. Two years later, she hadn't struggled with losing her faith. It had just gone, like her parents. If their omnipotent god materialised right now, beside the pulpit, she wouldn't worship him; he'd ignored her parents' short lifetime of prayers and watched as they died.

Human agency was just as useless. The lorry driver who'd slammed into their car as he'd scrolled on his phone had got a ten-year prison sentence, but would only serve six.

Time hadn't lessened the pain. Helplessness and fury threatened to overwhelm her, and tears streamed down her face.

'Amen,' said the vicar.

'Amen,' echoed the congregation.

She stood with stiff legs and wiped her eyes with the back of her hand.

'Sophie?' said Freddy, in an urgent undertone. 'Are you unwell?'

'I'm fine.' She fished a handkerchief from her sleeve. Should have worn that stupid motoring hat. The organ sounded with the opening notes of a familiar hymn and she gratefully focused on singing.

After church, Sophie lay on the bed, making the most of some downtime. She'd had a wobble. It would pass. And she'd mostly cracked the demure thing. Well, acting demure. What had Freddy said? *Everyone has to do their best with the cards they're dealt.* She'd use her knowledge of a possible future to help make other lives better. An invisible salute to her parents.

Maud came in and helped Sophie into a less formal dress and Sophie resigned herself to Groundhog Day.

Sitting in the drawing room with the Armstrong and Greenworthy sisters, Sophie finished the rest of *A Tale of Two Cities*, bar the last chapter. She'd read it before, presumed the ending was the same, but couldn't face checking.

Lunch was a hot smorgasbord: meat pies, boiled eggs, potato mash, over-cooked cabbage and a miniscule glass of champagne. By now in Shorten, she'd be looking forward to slobbing in a tea dress. But this wasn't her home and Maud hadn't packed any.

'I watched a shoot once, but the noise was horrid and it's always wet and cold.' Ethel poked tentatively at her cabbage. 'It's not like I'm supporting any particular chap, like Clarissa.'

'Who's Clarissa supporting?' asked Sophie.

'Hugo, of course, they're always talking.'

Go away, lizard brain.

Alice was dully rearranging food on her plate; Sophie wanted to reach out, but trying to buck Alice up might backfire.

Only one more day.

A morsel of cabbage went down the wrong way and Sophie spluttered. She held a napkin to her mouth and sipped water. What had she been thinking? Shorten wasn't home, never could be.

After lunch, she pretended to write a letter with her mechanical pencil, then peered out the window. Just drizzle. Fresh air might trump Ugly Outfit. Anything was better than embroidery.

Back in her bedroom, she took out Ugly Outfit, rang a bellpull and waited.

After five minutes, she rang again. Strange. She went to the landing and called. Silence.

She hurried down the stairs, caught her heel in her skirt and landed on the hardwood floor of the hall with an unladylike thump. A maid appeared like magic, her eyes large with alarm.

'I only fell a few steps.' These hobble skirts really were lethal.

In the drawing room, both sets of sisters were enthralled by sewing.

'Have you seen Charlotte and my maid?'

'No,' said Ethel. 'Perhaps they're outside?'

Sophie unlocked the French windows and stepped out. Maud must have taken Charlotte for a walk between drives.

Bang, bang ... *bang.*

No, they wouldn't still be out here — would they?

Her court shoes got stuck in mud so she left them and walked in stockinged feet as fast as she could. With a growing dread churning inside, she yelled, '*Charlotte.*'

A volley of shots rang out.

Barking.

Charlotte was sprinting towards her, lead attached but trailing.

Bang.

Charlotte abruptly changed direction and bolted *towards* the sound, and Sophie jigged after her, taking tiny steps like a demented marionette.

In a copse that smelled of moss and mud, Sophie's dress caught on branches and sharp twigs scratched her arms. As she emerged on the other side, the wind changed direction, driving rain into her face.

Maud was up ahead. Sophie yelled again but her shout was lost in another volley.

Charlotte was jumping about near two men. One was firing into the air, the other gazing at the sky. Charlotte grabbed a dead bird off the ground with her jaws and whirled in a circle, splattering a trail of blood.

Bang.

Sophie grabbed Charlotte's lead. Maud was yelling and another volley of shots rang out, loud and close, and Charlotte hurtled towards the house, forcing Sophie to release the lead. Sophie followed, desperately hoping Charlotte would keep going in the same direction. That wasn't a given. She was terrified *and* excited. Sophie was struggling for breath now, ribs straining against whalebone.

Clarissa was standing on the lawn, aggressively banging

the base of a walking stick on the grass beside Charlotte. Then she picked up the stick.

No way would she let Clarissa hurt Charlotte — Sophie reached Clarissa and wrestled with the stick.

'Let go,' hissed Clarissa. 'Let *go*.'

'No.'

The French windows opened, Charlotte dashed through the gap into the house and the doors closed.

Dizzy with relief, Sophie let go of the stick.

'That dog is out of control. It needs to be dealt with *now*.'

'Over my dead body.' Struggling to breathe, Sophie stumbled into the drawing room.

Charlotte was jubilantly thrashing the bird around, spraying sofas, dresses, and the piano and carpet, with its blood.

Ethel, Alice and the Greenworthy sisters were all sitting perfectly still, frozen in shock.

Sophie grabbed Charlotte's collar, hauled Charlotte towards her and shouted the strictest 'off' she'd ever given. Charlotte hesitated, confused. But didn't drop her prize. In her mouth, the unfortunate bird twitched.

Maud burst in through the French windows. 'I'm *so* sorry, Miss. I couldn't stop her. It's like she's possessed.'

'We need to get Charlotte out of here.' Sophie pulled Charlotte outside by her lead. Good. No Clarissa.

'There's a water trough, Miss.'

Ignoring a tight sensation in her chest, Sophie wrestled Charlotte into the trough and began rinsing off blood and grime. The bird had stopped twitching but was still firmly in Charlotte's jaws.

One thing at a time.

'You shouldn't be doing this, Miss.' Maud's white apron was streaked unpleasantly red. She wiped her rain-wet forehead with her hand.

'She's *my* dog.' Sophie was struggling to breathe, never mind talk. 'What the hell happened?'

'I took her out as normal, but she wanted more of a walk. I didn't mean to go near the guns. No need to.' Maud's voice cracked. 'She was on her lead but she's terrible strong. She broke away and ran off.'

Charlotte, unimpressed with being washed in cold water, was climbing out. Sophie shoved her back and the bird fell in the water with a plop.

'I ran and ran but couldn't reach her.'

Sophie tried to catch her breath. 'What were the men doing?'

'They took no notice.'

Odd. 'Then what?'

'I was terrified she'd get shot. I heard you calling, saw her running into the house.' Tears streamed down Maud's face. 'Please don't sack me, Miss.'

'I won't,' said Sophie, though keeping or sacking Maud was Anne's call. 'Charlotte can be a real rascal. It's a miracle she hasn't played up before.' Sophie took the bird from the water and laid it gently beside the trough. Its eyes were blank, dead.

Maud's crying escalated into sobbing and Sophie was relieved when a groom appeared with a blanket. They dried Charlotte before she did her messy writhing and Charlotte allowed herself to be hurried into the house and Sophie's room.

Sophie saw herself in the mirror. She looked like a survivor from *The Walking Dead*. As did Maud.

Maud dipped a handkerchief into a bowl of water on the dresser and cleaned Sophie's face.

'Help me get into another dress.'

Once changed, and with Maud guarding Charlotte, Sophie ventured downstairs. She realised she was shaking and paused in the hall. She didn't want to think how close Charlotte had come to a grisly end — like that bird.

In the drawing room, three maids were on their knees, scrubbing at bright scarlet stains on the cream carpet. All the soft furnishings were swathed in blood, streaks stretching out like ragged, ghoulish fingers.

'Miss Arundel.'

Sophie hastily turned around.

'An unfortunate turn of events.' Mrs Armstrong was in outdoor clothes and holding out a flask. 'Take a sip.' Her voice was cold but matter of fact.

Like a puzzled child, Sophie did as she was told, choking on cherry brandy. 'Where is everyone?'

'The ladies have retired.'

She didn't need to lie down. She'd grown up with monstrous fairy tales and action movies — maybe that had made her more resilient? She took a deep breath. 'Clarissa would have hurt Charlotte.' This society was only superficially like home; killing wayward dogs might be routine.

'Come with me,' said Mrs Armstrong, leading the way into a smaller room, mercifully clear of birdy blood. She tugged on a bellpull and Sophie sat opposite her across a low table. A maid appeared and was sent for tea and biscuits.

'I am *so* sorry,' said Sophie. 'She's my responsibility. I should never have brought her.'

Mrs Armstrong said nothing, waiting until tea had been poured.

A few minutes later, as Sophie pretended to sip from a delicate china cup, her brain sped up. Leave. Right now.

But go where?

CHAPTER 44

rs Armstrong cleared her throat. 'Has your dog been to a shoot before?'

'No.'

'Then you should not have brought her.'

Anne's words sounded in Sophie's head. *You'll need to keep Charlotte on a lead outside...*

'I have a duty to care for guests, however appalling their behaviour,' said Mrs Armstrong. 'You were lucky your maid wasn't shot, running around like that.'

Sophie's fingers tightened on the handle of her cup. Why had this happened *now*? After acting demure so perfectly in the face of unremitting boredom.

But Charlotte couldn't act demure — and never would.

As soon as politeness allowed, Sophie retreated upstairs. Charlotte was lying by the fireplace and her eyes rested uncertainly on Sophie. Charlotte might not understand why, but she knew she was in disgrace. Sophie kissed the top of her head. Charlotte mauled muggers but had never hurt an innocent creature. She probably didn't realise her bird prize had recently been alive. Thought it a game.

When Maud came in carrying the chamber pot, Charlotte didn't even glance at her.

Maud put the pot under the bed and after an awkward silence, Sophie said, 'You're not a vet.'

'No, Miss. A what?'

'Trained to care for animals. Charlotte's a big dog. You were doing your best. Please don't worry. I'll explain everything to Lady Lacey.' No idea what would happen to Sophie Arundel, but she could spin this for Maud.

'Thank you.' Maud managed an uncertain smile.

After Maud left, Sophie sat on the bed and put her head in her hands. What had Anne said? *If you made another mistake ... no safety net and no rowing back ... family and the Manor, this is my whole life. No one is more important than that.* Tears ran down Sophie's face, but she dried them with her sleeve, stood up, and paced like Hugo.

Anne had been so kind: defusing the Freddy debacle, brazening out pregnancy rumours, obscuring Sophie Arundel's right hook with outrageous fake news. But replacing ruined dresses and carpets and recovering sofas would cost a fortune, and Anne would have to find the money, as well as being seen to appropriately punish the culprit. She wouldn't penalise Charlotte but keeping Sophie Arundel out of sight at the Manor really wouldn't cut it. Anne wouldn't chuck her out ... maybe there was a Lacey friend or relative *really* off the beaten track, in Scotland or Ireland?

'Miss?' Maud closed the door behind her.

Sophie stopped pacing.

'The shoot's finished a day early. Today's been declared an 'idle' one because the men are satisfied with their bags.' Her face was carefully blank, loyally intent on continuing this fiction, even in private. 'The men are coming in for tea, the weather being on the turn.'

Sophie sat on the bed. 'I don't need afternoon tea.'

'Shall I say you're unwell?'

'Good idea.'

When Maud left, Sophie desperately cast around for a plan that could save the Laceys' reputation and her own. *We should install central heating. My brother in New York has it throughout the house.* America in this world was effectively further away than the space station — with slower comms. She could travel third class on the Titanic with Charlotte, staying on deck or hiding in a lifeboat in case it still sank, just a while after 1912. But would Richard foist her on his brother's family? They might be estranged—

Charlotte climbed on the bed and lay close and Sophie put her arm around her. Hugo would continue to work on the lift puzzle, might even solve it, but it could be years before she returned to England.

Maud came in and started packing.

Leaving Charlotte in the bedroom, Sophie reluctantly went downstairs.

In the hall, guests were taking turns to sign the visitors' book, the men dressed in their regular suits. As she walked in, polite chatter faltered. Hugo gave her a 'chin-up' nod and, beside him, Clarissa's lips moved in a faux smile.

'Sophie.' Freddy was by her side, taking her arm. 'The rain's stopped.' He put on the cap he'd worn for the drive from Shorten. 'I thought we could stroll.' He opened the front door and walked out purposefully onto the drive and around the house to a stretch of lawn. Then he paused and searched her face, saw she'd been crying.

Regret and unease tasted bitter in her mouth. 'I'm so sorry about Charlotte.'

'Mrs Armstrong's put out, but Charlotte's safe.'

Freddy would deliver his verdict like he did everything. Politely. 'I could go to your uncle's place in the States, just for a while? Out of sight, out of mind?'

Freddy was frowning now. His eyes were kind but there was another emotion. Understanding, or pity?

'I'd take Charlotte, but Hugo should stay. It wouldn't be fair...' She waited. If Freddy accepted her idea, that would help persuade his parents.

He took off his cap. 'Mummy wouldn't send you to America. How could you think that?'

'Well—'

'You must know, you're the daughter she couldn't have. She loves you.'

His words repeated in her head. Anne wasn't an ally or friend. She was like a mother, her Shorten mother. She was welling up.

She turned and fled to her room.

Charlotte was still lying by the grate. Maud closed a travelling trunk and looked up.

'Would you mind retrieving my court shoes from the garden?' asked Sophie. 'They're just beyond the back lawn. I'll guard Trouble here.'

As Maud shut the door behind her, Charlotte came over and leaned against Sophie's legs and Sophie drew her close. Maternal love had rescued her today, like a magic ladder dropping down to a raging sea. Anne *loved* her.

A jolt. She felt the same. And the foundation of her love was something she'd thought had gone forever: trust in the future. That Anne would not inexplicably disappear.

Sophie searched her memory for a tipping point, when she should have known what she felt, but the moments were too connected, like stitching in a patchwork quilt, each stitch stronger than the last.

Shorten had given her Hugo's precious friendship but Anne cut through everything: the stupid clothes, the need to act demure, even the need to get married. It was the little things, like the mourning dress and the boys standing up when she came towards their table at breakfast ... that moment's readjustment would always be there, but like Anne, she could learn and adapt.

Incredibly, though missing Aunty Wendy and Isha was still a physical ache, if she found the lift tomorrow and stood on the threshold, she'd hesitate.

She glanced over at the bed. Maud had laid out the cape, gloves and beekeeper hat, and Sophie put them on. The hat wasn't useless — as well as repelling bees, it cleverly concealed a blotchy face.

When she returned to the hall with Charlotte on a short lead, Freddy was signing his name in the visitors' book. 'You're supposed to write something witty, but I always write the same thing.' He'd written *Thanks for the pheasants* in a black spidery script.

Sophie wanted to write, *I'm sorry I've trashed your house,* but instead wrote, *Kind and generous hosts* before her signature.

Alice and Ethel came down the stairs, still pale and shocked. The physical damage *was* shocking, but girls here were expected to be fragile and passive — so they were. Clarissa, though, was unfazed, chatting to Hugo in her usual, incessant way.

Sophie lifted her hat veil and addressed Ethel. 'I've embarrassed myself and the Laceys and I'm really sorry for all the trouble.'

'Mama will buy new furniture.' Ethel winked. 'And I've already chosen a new dress.'

'The way you dealt with your dog and all that blood,' said Alice, 'you're like an amazon or a suffragette.'

Sophie cringed.

Clarissa was now doing a little girl laugh, relating Charlotte's antics.

Sophie turned to Mrs Armstrong. 'I'm very sorry. Thank

you for having me.'

Mrs Armstrong smiled. 'Thank you for coming.'

As ever, punctiliously polite. Stuffy manners were under-rated. Sophie shook her hand and waved to everyone else before walking onto the drive and climbing into the back of the green car with Charlotte.

Hugo got in beside Charlotte and Freddy sat in the front passenger seat. As Reynolds drove off, Freddy turned towards Sophie. 'Are you feeling better?'

'Yes, thank you.' Sophie patted Charlotte who was sitting in the seat well, exuding her regular, innocent air.

'I heard of a shooting party years ago where a chap shot a lady's dog by accident.' He frowned. 'When he saw how upset she was, he had it stuffed. He couldn't understand why she wasn't grateful.'

Sophie winced. 'Gross.'

'I only realised what had happened when we came in for tea,' said Freddy. 'Men take shooting seriously. It would take more than a misbehaving dog to distract us.'

'I didn't realise either,' said Hugo.

Good. The boys had seen nothing. She could minimise the hullabaloo and portray Maud as a fearless heroine.

'We had a guns photo taken this afternoon,' said Hugo, 'after a really good lunch.' He lowered his voice. 'I steered clear of the champagne. They're so blasé, Sophie. It's amazing more people don't get shot.'

Freddy and Reynolds in the front of the car couldn't have heard him; she'd strained to catch his words.

The wind picked up and Hugo held onto his cap. 'Char-lotte and Mau ... Mrs Watkins must have got under the radar with all the noise.'

'What's a radar?' asked Freddy.

After Hugo had gone into unnecessary detail, not only about radar, but military night vision kit, he settled back in his seat and said quietly, 'Charlie was telling me another house was torched last week, near his place.'

She leaned closer to him. 'Where does Charlie live?'

'About twenty miles from the Manor, western side of the county.'

Sophie ruffled Charlotte's head. These attacks were getting closer — and there was nowhere to hide.

'Clarissa's invited us to London,' said Hugo, sounding determinedly cheerful. 'They've had no trouble there.'

He needed to know what Clarissa was really like before he got in too deep. Any reluctant sympathy for Clarissa had vanished when she'd picked up that stick. 'Clarissa doesn't like dogs.'

'She does,' said Hugo. 'She was driving Charlotte away from the guns.'

Hadn't looked like that.

They turned onto the main road. Men, women and children were walking in a broken line, headed the same way Reynolds was. They were entirely silent, even the children. Toddlers were sitting on men's shoulders and most of the adults were carrying angular suitcases.

The car engine was loud in the quiet as they passed the first families, but no one stopped or turned around.

Reynolds slowed; people were walking in the road.

'Something else must have happened in Derby,' said Freddy. 'They're going to Shorten town.'

'How far is that from here?' asked Sophie.

'About thirty miles.' Freddy frowned. 'I know what you're thinking but we've only got space for one person, and the servants' car is filled with luggage.'

Sitting on the verge was a young girl. Her head was bowed and she was rocking back and forth, holding a doll.

'One's better than nothing,' said Sophie. 'Freddy, stop the car.'

'Very well.'

Reynolds brought the car to a stop and Sophie got out. 'Hello, would you like a lift to Shorten?'

The girl wasn't cradling a doll. It was a tiny baby, weeks old. The girl looked up, her eyes oddly blank. A child herself. Eleven or twelve.

'My sister works at the Manor,' said the girl, her voice low.

Sophie gestured at the car. 'We can take you.'

Freddy moved to the back and the girl staggered to her feet and sat in the front with the baby. Once in her seat, Sophie hauled Charlotte completely onto her lap, freeing up space in the seat well for Hugo's legs.

As the car set off, Hugo bent forward. 'What's your sister's name?'

The girl was trying not to cry. 'Miss Parry.'

CHAPTER 45

Three hours after returning to the Manor, Sophie called on Hugo to go to dinner.

She smiled at him. 'I think I crossed universes to find another mother.'

He stopped in the corridor. 'If that's what Anne means to you, this could be the end of your quest?'

'That's a cool idea.'

The dogs were racing ahead towards the dining room, Jack matching Charlotte's pace, the sound of their paws muffled by the carpet.

Sophie folded her arms. 'Anne ... I didn't see this coming.'

'The visitors' link could be a strong need, a core one.'

They started down the passage.

'If the lift appeared today,' said Sophie, 'I wouldn't go home.' The revelation about Anne hadn't affected her lizard brain. Even now, it was whirring away. But crossing universes wouldn't change how Hugo felt about her. Or didn't.

'Absolutely.' He lowered his voice. 'This gold-plates our cunning plan to fool the weird note writer.'

She stopped walking. 'No, Hugo. *Really*. I want to stay.'

He stopped too. 'You've struggled with all the restrictions this England has forced on you. That's not going to change.'

'Love trumps all that.' She checked the corridor was clear. 'But I'll never give up on the lift puzzle. I know you want to go home.' He deserved to be happy.

'Thanks.' He sounded like he was coming down with a cold. 'Lucy's wish to be a gardener or Alan's to run a pub, I'm not sure they would count as core needs.'

'And Anne could have found her Prince Charming at home. Everyone must have more than one soulmate out there or the human race would have died out.' She resumed walking.

'Yes.' He gave her an odd, tense glance as he walked beside her. 'Getting back from the shoot a day early means I'll be back in the office tomorrow.'

'You didn't cross universes to be chained to a desk.'

He shot her his resigned smile.

'But when you make manager,' said Sophie, '£200 a year is good money.'

'Estate managers are respected professionals, and they get the best cottage on the estate, but they don't get paid enough to live independently. You'd need at least £700 for that.'

'You've researched this?'

For a moment, he seemed embarrassed. Which made no sense. 'Research is good,' Sophie said, slickly like a slogan. 'Info is power.'

'I guess.' He looked towards the anteroom and his angled face in profile reminded her of the Janus faces on the church. Young, enigmatic.

No one mentioned the shooting party debacle at dinner and Sophie was grateful. Anne was behaving as she always did. Courteous, interested. A polite host. But Sophie was seeing her with different eyes.

And Sophie's thoughts kept returning to her real mother; loving and kind and killed in a pointless accident. Finding Anne was another accident, but a wonderful one.

~

The next day, Sophie met Anne for tea as usual. Understatement, or not mentioning difficult issues at all, was the Shorten way, but Sophie needed to talk.

As the dogs settled by the fireplace, she closed the door. 'I'm so sorry about Charlotte.'

'Mrs Armstrong said on the telephone last night that *you* behaved yourself. That's something.' Anne sat on the emerald sofa.

Her kindness was making Sophie tearful.

Anne gestured for Sophie to sit beside her. 'Mrs Armstrong refused to let us pay for the damage. Pride comes into these things. In time, the near disaster will turn into a funny story. You'll see.' Anne put her arms around her.

The embrace was the last straw and Sophie cried, feeling eight, not eighteen. Anne said nothing, holding her close. Finally, Sophie blew her nose on her handkerchief and sniffed.

'Mr Eddington has replied to Freddy,' said Anne, gently. 'He says the multiverse theory is sound but will only ever be theoretical.'

Sophie sniffed again. She hoped not — for Hugo's sake.

'This morning, I received a telephone call from Lady Maine.' Anne stood and rang the bellpull, then sat on the sofa opposite Sophie. 'They're happy to see you but Charlotte is too big for the town house. She should stay here. It's only for a few days.'

Shaken by Charlotte's brush with death, Sophie didn't

want to leave her, but she'd be safe with Anne. 'Are you okay to mind her, as well as Jack?'

'I'm settling in new families over the time and Richard's too busy, but we'll find someone to keep a close eye, given Jack's health.'

After tea, back in Sophie's room, Maud knew the answer. 'Miss Blackmore could do it. She knows all about animals. Shall I ask her?'

Blackmore … familiar name. Maud had talked about her during Sophie's first supervised bath. 'The girl Mr Hunter assaulted?'

'He didn't assault her, Miss. Just touched her up.'

No, 'assaulted' was the right word. But explaining that would take a while and could wait. 'Where is Miss Blackmore working?'

'In the kitchens, Miss.'

Sophie didn't want word spreading she was recruiting Miss Blackmore before Anne agreed she was suitable. 'Can you ask her to swing by tomorrow, after breakfast?' That way, she could discreetly clear it with Anne straight afterwards and give Miss Blackmore and the dogs a day to get used to each other before London.

'I'll ask this evening.' Maud put linen in a drawer. 'Mrs Arnold's in a terrible state.'

'Sorry, who?'

'Miss Parry's sister. Her husband was killed in a riot and she hadn't eaten for days.' Maud twisted the new wedding ring on her finger. 'But she'll be all right now. So will the baby.'

'I hope so,' said Sophie. 'What age can people get married?'

'Sixteen, Miss, if their family agree.'

'How can Miss Parry's sister have been married? She's not even a teenager.'

'A teen, what?'

'She's only eleven,' said Sophie, 'maybe twelve.'

'No, Miss, she's seventeen.'

This was baffling. Or did malnourished people look younger?

The following day, Miss Blackmore came by. She wasn't malnourished. Though the same age as Maud, she seemed older, had a curvy figure and the hearty air of a person who enjoyed the outdoors and the occasional pie. Maud's account of Miss Blackmore whacking a randy Mr Hunter so hard his eyes watered ... now a clear, happy vision.

Miss Blackmore got the dogs to sit, lie down and stay, her manner kind but firm. She didn't treat them as pets. More like creatures in need of training, like sheepdogs or children. Charlotte would be strictly supervised — and safe.

'Do you want to progress to cook?' asked Sophie.

'What I'd really like to do, Miss, is gamekeeping. My father used to tell me stories about Miss Fishbourne. Years ago, she was head gamekeeper on the Holkham estate in Norfolk.'

'Have you spoken to anyone else about this?'

'People in the kitchens, they joke about it.'

'I don't think it's a joke,' said Sophie. 'When I check with Lady Lacey about you minding Double Trouble here, I'll mention you'd rather do gamekeeping.'

Miss Blackmore smiled broadly and got the dogs to walk to heel.

Jack was compliant but Charlotte's co-operation wouldn't last long. 'You don't need to train them while we're away,' said Sophie. 'They're happy with walks and lying about. But Jack must be on a short lead with his bad eyes.'

'Do you want me to groom Charlotte, Miss? She's got terrible knots.'

In contrast to Jack's smooth retriever fur, Charlotte's was

well out of control. She could hardly see past her eyebrows. 'Have you groomed dogs before?'

'No, Miss, but I've done horses.'

'Bad knots you can just cut off. She can have her fur taken down to three centimetres.'

'Pardon Miss, centi?'

'Sorry, about this much.' Sophie curled her forefinger and thumb. She'd never groomed Charlotte herself, but had stayed for her first session, to ensure the girl was competent and kind. The grooming bit was easy; getting Charlotte to stand still was difficult. 'If you put her where she can see out of a window, she'll watch the birds and trees for ages, long enough for you to do it.'

'I understand, Miss.'

Shortly afterwards, Anne consulted with Mrs Ferris and then approved Miss Blackmore, and at teatime, Sophie made good on her promise. 'Could Miss Blackmore go on a game-keeping training scheme, or however you run it? She's really keen.'

'I can certainly ask,' said Anne. 'It's an all-male preserve at the moment, but that didn't stop me helping Miss Hemmings. The key is to get small concessions and when it's working, more small steps.'

'Could you put the milk in before the tea, please?' Sophie smiled at Miss Parry.

'Of course, Miss.'

Anne was regarding Sophie with wry amusement.

After Miss Parry left, Sophie said, 'I didn't like to say anything before.'

'Well, this is home now.'

The Manor would never be home. Far too grand. But home could be wherever Anne was. 'I was thinking, I could write a letter to *The Times*, explain about equality from a visitor perspective.'

'You could,' Anne said, slowly, 'but only once you're safely married. Before then, keep a low profile.'

Ironic. Anne happily conspired to help servants bag their dream jobs, yet the vision for Sophie Arundel was stubbornly narrow — marriage to a tolerant, wealthy person. But she understood. With money came security and safety; in this world, love was a bonus.

It must be wonderful to marry without worrying about money. 'At the shooting party, I had a light-hearted discussion about dating with the Armstrong sisters,' said Sophie, 'but Alice got really upset.'

Anne froze, her cup halfway to her lips. 'I thought it had been resolved.' She put down her cup. 'A very delicate matter. Can you promise you won't tell *anyone*, even Freddy or Hugo?'

'Yes.' Five weeks in Shorten had given Sophie a paranoid respect for discretion.

'It was a couple of years ago. Alice was only fifteen. The Armstrongs employed a respectable young man as a music tutor. Alice was fond of the piano and Mrs Armstrong was keen to impress potential suitors when she came out into society. After a few months' tuition, Mrs Armstrong walked in on them *kissing*.'

When Sophie remained silent, Anne added. 'She has no money of her own. It could have ruined any chance of a decent marriage. They sacked the tutor, but Alice was inconsolable. I had hoped she'd meet another more suitable chap, but she becomes so anxious at social functions, she makes herself ill.'

'She was in love with him?'

'Perhaps.' Anne sipped her tea. 'But she was prone to panic attacks and fainting fits before the tutor was employed.'

'There are no meds that could help?'

'Only laudanum. It's used for everything, from dulling dreadful pain to just being out of sorts.'

Sophie remembered. That blissful floating had been wonderful—

'It's highly addictive. Mrs Armstrong only lets Alice take it as a last resort.' Anne frowned. 'Keeping her to a routine is the key. Alice finds unexpected changes or events particularly difficult.'

'So, when I hit Clutterbuck...'

'I think that counts as unexpected.' Anne gave her a long-suffering smile. 'Alice readily accepted our doctored account and Ethel played along.'

'Ethel's very protective.'

'And Alice is pretty. She'll meet someone else, I'm sure.'

Sophie finished her tea. A world where life chances didn't depend on finding a suitable boy felt very far away.

Anne stood and went over to the mantelpiece. The hem of her skirt brushed the dogs lying by the grate but they didn't stir. 'The photograph from the summer ball arrived this morning.' She gestured to a framed, sepia picture.

Sophie jumped up to see it. 'We're clear but people in the background are fuzzy.'

'They were moving.'

'The man took a picture of me and the boys. Has that arrived yet?'

'I don't think so,' said Anne. 'These photographs are very expensive. It'll be smaller and in a plainer frame. Well, I hope so.'

'Do you have any pictures from home?'

'No. I hadn't any in my handbag and that's all I had with me. Who knows what's happened to all the photographs in my old house.'

The picture of her parents at Aunty Wendy's ... that might be taken in this universe too? If she had children, they could go to Buckinghamshire before 2011 and meet their grand-parents, or a version of them? Okay, complicated.

Sophie thought back to *The Crooked Gate*. If Alan had a reminder of home and family, he'd have mentioned it. So would Lucy. Pictures of lost worlds were incredibly precious. And none of the visitors had a single one.

That evening, as Sophie changed for dinner, there was a tone change in Maud's voice. Her chatter was so constant that Sophie often didn't listen. Maud might have been talking for a while.

'I've finished *Vanity Fair*,' said Maud, as smug as if she'd climbed Everest.

'What did you think?'

'It was good, Miss, but very long.'

True. And Maud didn't have endless days to while away.

'Is it right that London's so foggy, you can't see a foot in front?'

'Not at home,' said Sophie, 'but it could be like that here.'

'I've never been out of the county, Miss. My father went to London once. He said the noise was terrible and the build-ings so close together, only the rats get between them.'

'There are rats, but I never saw one. Your father was right about the noise though. In my London, there's always building work, police sirens and everyone rushes around. It's an exciting place.'

'Oh, I can't wait, Miss.'

Watching Hugo flirt with Clarissa in London would be torture. Think about something else. 'The photograph taken at the ball turned out well.'

'I had a photograph taken when I was little,' said Maud. 'I remember it ever so clear.'

'You haven't still got it?'

'I don't know what happened to the photograph, but it

was in the paper. There was a competition and we won a prize.' Maud's round face was thoughtful, remembering.

'We?'

'Me and my sister, Miss.'

'Where was it taken?'

'On the bench near the green.'

At their first meeting Maud had seemed familiar. That dusty sepia photo in the students' union ... *Little Shorten, 1910.* The younger child in the white pinafore dress was Maud.

In nearly a century from now, would that picture be in this world's tower block? Just a curiosity, the subjects unknown, forgotten—'

'Miss?'

'Nothing.' Sophie touched her pendant, seeking comfort in the smooth stone. Telling Maud about the photo would only creep her out.

CHAPTER 46

The next day they set off to London.

As Reynolds drove them to the local train station, Sophie could tell Hugo felt uncomfortable. The boys were wearing their suits but also swanky top hats, and Hugo kept adjusting and checking his.

But he was a rookie. Her hat resembled a huge inverted basket, matching her navy dress and cape and complementing her carefully arranged hair.

The boys took their hats off on the train. Men were always taking their hats off and on, so didn't use hatpins.

Sophie had expected a slight variation on her previous train experience: standing room only and dodgy coffee. But she should have learned by now. Her expectations were often way out — in any universe.

Maud was travelling separately with John, Mr Farrow and the baggage. Sophie and the boys were in the first-class dining car, being served lunch with all the pomp and ceremony of the poshest restaurant. But Sophie's eyes were streaming, reacting against thick swirls of smoke. She fished a handkerchief from her small handbag and wiped her face.

Apart from having no internal zipped pockets, the handbag was like a modern one: round, made from soft navy leather, with a rather stiff gold clasp at the top and a gold chain strap. Anne had advised that not carrying a bag would look odd, but the handkerchief was the only thing in it.

'After lunch, we'll go to our carriage,' said Freddy. 'It's the only non-smoking one on the train.'

Hugo was wiping his eyes with the back of his hand. 'No one else seems to be struggling.'

Freddy shrugged. 'We're used to it.'

'I've never seen anyone smoking in the Manor.' Sophie took off her short gloves. 'But then I'm banned from your after-dinner cigar sessions.'

'The servants can smoke cigarettes in their rooms,' said Freddy, 'but it's discouraged. Mummy thinks it causes a horrible disease and early death.' He adjusted the napkin on his lap. 'Is that right?'

'Absolutely,' said Sophie, 'and I hate the smell.' She wrinkled her nose.

Hugo gave her a mischievous glance. 'So missing out on cigars is no tragedy.'

She resisted a strong impulse to poke out her tongue and turned to a waiter, who was hovering to take their order. They'd been given a menu in French by mistake but it was easy to translate. Sophie chose *Soupe à la Tomate* and for mains *Coq Au Vin Blanc*, because the chicken came with peas and potatoes. The boys had steak. For pudding they all had *Quel Chantier*, a glorious mixture of strawberries, cream and digestive biscuits.

'Eton mess,' said Freddy. 'Can't beat it.'

'I don't think this was invented at home until the 1930s, and made with meringue, not biscuits.' Hugo finished the last smidgen on his plate. 'But this is mighty fine.'

Sophie's plate was clean too. 'Yummy.'

Back in their blissfully smoke-free carriage, they drank champagne and watched green fields and pretty villages speed by. And despite sitting perfectly straight and hemmed in by too-tight clothes, Sophie felt unexpectedly content.

Freddy took out a notebook from his jacket breast pocket. Pressed within the pages was the photo of her and the boys at the ball. 'A jolly memento.'

Sophie looked old-fashioned but glamorous in the picture. So did the boys. 'You'll get it framed?'

Freddy nodded. 'You'll take London by storm.'

'I hope London is able to cope,' said Hugo, from behind his newspaper. 'Perhaps we should have telegraphed ahead?'

'Take no notice, Sophie,' said Freddy, pretending to glare at Hugo.

'I try not to.'

A while later, when they arrived in London, Sophie stepped with difficulty onto a foggy platform, hampered by her narrow skirt. At least the dark fabric didn't show the coal dust from the train.

Further along the platform, the air was even greyer and thicker, and she firmly closed her mouth and started to breathe through her nose.

The boys quickened their pace and Sophie struggled to keep up. 'Freddy, what about the servants? Shouldn't we wait—'

'They'll come through later. Let's get out of this beastly fog.'

The grand roof of Saint Pancras station was the same as home, but the concourse was empty and vast: no shops, seats or cafés, and no regimented queue of taxis and people waiting in line.

But Freddy quickly flagged down a cab. It wasn't black, as Sophie had been expecting, but red, and built like half an old-fashioned closed carriage. The driver section had a short roof and a door on only one side of the cab.

Freddy was waiting for her to get in.

'You go first, I need to take my time.'

Once the boys were in, she sat backwards on the seat and slowly turned, ensuring her hat didn't push into Hugo or get dented. She managed it. Just.

'That's a serious hat,' said Hugo.

She touched the brim. 'Probably visible from space.'

'It's fetching,' said Freddy. He bent forward to the gap in the glass dividing them from the driver. '95 Eaton Square, please.'

The cabbie was smoking and the taxi interior smelled rank. Sophie put her handkerchief over her nose and mouth.

With no traffic lights or roundabouts, the cab drove at a steady speed, unimaginable in Sophie's traffic-snarled London. Horse-drawn carts clattered along next to small red buses, packed with sightseers on open top decks. Like their taxi, the driver cabs' overhead canopies offered scant protection from wind or rain.

Moving along, the air felt fresher, so Sophie took the handkerchief from her face. 'Can we go on one of those buses, Freddy? Do the tourist routes?'

'I suppose so.' He sounded unconvinced.

Sophie tugged on Hugo's sleeve. 'There's Selfridges.' Bright flags on the unmistakable, grand façade seemed to be waving to them from across Oxford Street.

Hugo just nodded, watching the pedestrians and traffic beyond the cab window.

They turned off the main thoroughfare and within moments, the roads were clear of cars or buses or pedestrians, and a deep quiet descended, only broken by birdsong.

In Eaton Square, smart townhouses overlooked a private garden enclosed by ornate metal railing. At its centre was a neat lawn interspersed with elm trees. A gravel path ran around the grass, and between the path and the railing were flowering bushes with bright yellow flowers like a fragrant daisy chain.

But when Sophie climbed out of the car, a faint bitter tang soured her tongue and throat. Smoke from coal fires.

An elderly butler opened the Maines' front door and as they trooped in, he stood ramrod straight, like a guard outside Buckingham Palace.

After the boys handed over their hats, Sophie and Hugo followed Freddy into an airy drawing room. The furniture was unfussy, the painting over the mantlepiece was brightly coloured and abstract, and an oddly-shaped sculpture by a window owed nothing to traditional taste.

Clarissa rose to greet them from a sleek sofa. Her cream brocade gown showed off her bony ankles and matching court shoes, and the shorter skirt made her seem younger and more agile, as if at any moment she could leap over a stile or perform a ballet move. 'This is going to be such fun.'

'Absolutely,' said Freddy. 'What's the plan?'

'We thought the Ritz for dinner.' Clarissa turned to Sophie. 'Would you like to go upstairs and rest?'

Had she got soot on her face? 'Thank you, but I'm fine—'

'Clarissa, it's *so* kind of you to put us up,' said Hugo. 'For us, this is the London of nearly a century ago. A historian's dream.'

Clarissa slightly raised her manicured eyebrows but only said, 'Do sit down.'

A maid came in with tea and tiny, crust-free sandwiches.

'I do enjoy being in town, but it's *much* better with friends.' Clarissa smiled at Hugo. 'You will love the Ritz.'

Just to interrupt, Sophie said, 'Do you go to clubs?'

'Nightclubs,' said Hugo.

The maid poured tea into china cups. A narrow, lime

green band circled the edge of the mostly white cups and saucers, intersected on one side by a simple pink flower.

Clarissa was repeating 'nightclubs' like a difficult medical term.

'You pay huge amounts to get in,' said Sophie, 'and the music's so loud you can't talk. It's pretty dark so you can't see much, and you have to be careful no one spikes your drink.'

Clarissa frowned. 'Spikes your drink?'

'Too much information.' Hugo gave Sophie an exasperated glance. 'People take illegal substances to make them feel better but, occasionally, it kills them.'

'Sounds ghastly,' said Clarissa.

'Why do they bother?' asked Freddy, around a mouthful of beef sandwich. 'Don't you have champagne?'

'Lots of reasons,' said Hugo, darkly. 'Teenage rebellion.'

'The bubbly of choice at home is Prosecco,' said Sophie. Before Shorten, she'd never tasted real champagne.

'Pros…?' asked Clarissa.

'It's Italian,' said Hugo. 'Very popular, particularly with young people. It's cheaper.'

There then followed a discussion about teenagers, including hormones.

Maybe she'd been hasty rejecting the offer of a rest? No. Clarissa's rapt attention as Hugo talked needed to be interrupted more than once.

'Love the new shorter dress, Clarissa,' Sophie purred, adopting her sincere face. 'Anything else I should know … about town?' Code for, why didn't you give me a heads up at the shooting party?

'It's very new. I'm sure it will spread to the country in time.' Clarissa smiled indulgently.

The boys were oblivious to the real nature of the exchange, chatting between themselves.

Sophie pretended to smile back.

CHAPTER 47

Sophie's mood improved when she found a bathroom and could get her body clean, though the same couldn't be said of her travelling clothes.

'They're ruined,' she said to Maud, back in the bedroom.

Maud examined the skirt hem, ingrained with dirt from the station platform. 'I'll scrub it with *Lifebuoy*.'

'What's that?'

'Special red soap, Miss. It does shift the dirt.'

'Is that how you sorted the ink stains on the carpet?'

'No, Miss. Vinegar and elbow grease.' Maud peered at Sophie's hat. 'A damp cloth will bring this up, good as new.'

That evening, Sophie felt self-conscious in her pale blue gown, old-fashioned compared to Clarissa's white sleeveless number glittering with tiny sequins. Clarissa's skirt was cut into different lengths in a scalloped effect to just above her ankles — and no train. Sophie took comfort in the eternal splendour of her borrowed jewellery.

In the taxi to the Ritz, Clarissa's eyelashes looked thicker. Was that mascara? And on her mouth was the faintest touch of lipstick. Sophie's mascara and lipstick were in her wheeled suitcase, literally in another world. She should buy make-up in Selfridges; Freddy would lend her the money, though how she'd repay him remained a mystery. Daring visions popped into her head but she put them aside by imagining Anne's reaction.

She stepped carefully out of the taxi in her floor-skimming dress after Lady Maine, who was grand and stylish in a heavy, trained gown. Then she followed Lady Maine, Clarissa and the boys through a gleaming lobby into a huge dining room.

Tables laid with white starched tablecloths and silver cutlery, dining chairs with oval-shaped, elegant backs … and the room's architecture was reminiscent of the swankiest sort of French restaurant: large gothic chandeliers on the ceiling and pastoral murals on the walls, flanked by classical white pillars.

Most of the customers were smoking; a few women had long cigarette holders. Sophie pictured herself holding one of the classy holder things. She could always pretend to smoke?

She sat down and beyond the smell of nicotine registered the scents of delicious cooking.

Clarissa peeled off her gloves, so Sophie did too.

Dinner at the Ritz. What a treat.

But the menu was in French, the text dense and complicated. And no prices. What was that about?

No one else seemed thrown. Clarissa and the boys were nonchalantly studying their menus and Lady Maine was perusing hers through small round glasses with only one handle.

'How good's your French?' Sophie whispered to Hugo.

'Okay.'

Sophie smiled. Hugo's 'okay' was heavy on self-deprecation. Likely he was fluent. She pointed at *Entrées*. 'Anything veggie?'

'*Oeuf Poche Florentine*. Pastry tart, sautéed spinach and a poached egg in cheesy sauce.' He read down the page. 'All the mains dishes are meat-based. You should go for the lamb. That comes with potatoes and peas.'

'I get that the Ritz is French,' said Sophie, 'but why was the menu on the train in French?'

He lowered his voice. 'Maybe to make the food seem posher? I suspect regular English food doesn't measure up.'

Freddy chose the wines. *Chateau Carbonnieux*, a French white wine, *Veuve Clicquot*, 1906, vintage champagne, and *Dow's Port*, 1896, from Portugal, would, Freddy declared, cover everyone's menu choices.

Oeuf Poche Florentine was yummy, and the potatoes that came with the main course, *Pommes Colerette*, were shaped like wine corks with grooves. Tasted like old chips.

During the pudding course, a group of seriously grand people were shown to a nearby table. One girl, around Sophie's age, was wearing a tiara and a spectacular, ankle-length gown shimmering with sequins.

Diners' chatter stopped and — with no background music — for a long moment there was awkward silence.

When the noise level rose again, Sophie said to Lady Maine, 'That girl is *so* glamorous.'

'Lady Mollison. One of the Romanov sisters, Anastasia. The family came from Russia, nearly ten years ago now. Left the Czar behind. Awful business.'

Freddy peered over his glass at Hugo. 'You look like you've seen a ghost.'

Hugo glanced meaningfully at Sophie. 'It's quite hot in here.'

She blinked, acknowledging his message. What had happened to the Russian royal family at home was too horrible for dinner conversation.

Lady Maine was reminiscing. 'They came over to London ostensibly on holiday, but never went back.'

'With the Romanovs here, have many White Russians settled?' asked Hugo, carefully keeping his voice matter of fact.

'Yes, indeed,' said Lady Maine. 'Clarissa met a charming Russian chap last year, son of a duke. Mr Nicholas something…?'

'Mr Nikolaevich,' said Clarissa. 'The son of a grand duke.'

'I studied Russian at school,' said Hugo. 'I'm not fluent but it would be wonderful to speak with him.'

'I haven't seen him recently.' Clarissa's lips compressed, put out.

'Oh,' said Hugo.

What other talents did Hugo have up his sleeve? Russian. How difficult was that? Was he good at *everything*? No. He'd struggled with learning dances and was rubbish at tennis. He was probably bluffing about speaking Russian to impress Clarissa. It was working. She was flirting with her eyes and he was flirting right back.

'How does it turn out?' asked Lady Maine, in a low voice. 'The revolution in Russia, in your world?'

'Badly,' said Hugo.

Lady Maine had addressed her question to Hugo; she wasn't to know that Sophie Arundel knew stuff too — bar conversational Russian.

'There were Russian students at our school,' said Hugo, conscious that gulags and mass starvation were also inappropriate topics. 'There was a trip to Saint Petersburg planned a few years ago, but it was cancelled at the last minute. I was really disappointed.'

'Why was it cancelled?' Clarissa asked Hugo, simpering prettily.

'Russia annexed somewhere,' said Sophie.

She finished her *Petit Pot de Crème Vanille* — not crème brûlée with a burnt crust, only thick custard — and after coffee and more *Dow's Port*, Lady Maine agreed to let everyone go to the basement bar. 'Just for a short while.'

Freddy paid the bill, which remained a mystery, though Hugo was interested enough to glance at it.

In the bar, it was mostly men drinking, sitting or standing in groups, obscured by cigarette and cigar smoke. But the chatter was relaxed.

They perched on bar stools while Lady Maine asked for a glass of water and went to sit in a regular chair across from the bar, and Freddy addressed a waiter who was mixing cocktails with aplomb. 'What would you recommend?'

'How about a *Blue Blazer*?' The young man's New Jersey accent was straight out of *The Sopranos*.

'What's in it?' asked Freddy.

'Whisky, boiling water and fire.'

After mixing the initial drink, the bartender transferred a spectacular burning liquid from one tankard to another, four times, before adding sugar and lemon peel. 'Don't drink it too quick, it's hot,' he warned unnecessarily, handing out the smoking, steaming brew in small tumblers.

After one sip, Sophie put her tumbler aside. Way too strong. Even the smell — sharp and harsh — was making her cough. 'Could I have water?'

'And for me, please,' said Clarissa.

At home, Sophie would have carried on sipping but she didn't trust herself not to lose it and snog Hugo. Did women get drunk here? She'd not seen anyone legless in the street, but she hadn't been on the street much, just a few steps in and out of taxis.

After the *Blue Blazer*, the boys had a *Gin Rickey*.

'Gin, lime and soda, absolute classic,' the bartender assured them with a swagger.

Freddy handed over a bank note, and Clarissa, with half an eye on her mother, moved her stool closer to Hugo.

A few minutes later, Freddy finished his drink, turned to Sophie and, for no obvious reason, beamed and stared into her eyes.

Freddy was handsome and kind, and Hugo clearly wasn't interested. Would be a kind of fairy tale ending, bagging the heir to Shorten—

Clarissa shot Sophie what seemed like a genuine smile.

'You should have a tramp sandwich,' said the barman. 'Soak up the alcohol.'

'Tramp sandwich?' Freddy was swaying, despite having one hand on the bar.

'Bread, butter and fries,' explained the bartender.

'A chip butty is a wonderful thing,' said Hugo, slurring his words. 'A chip butty … a tramp sandwich.' He began humming, gazing vaguely at Sophie and Freddy. '*Rebel Rebel*.'

Freddy blinked. 'Pardon?'

'*Rebel Rebel*.' Now Hugo was peering earnestly into his cocktail glass.

'What's he singing?' said Freddy, very slowly.

'About a tramp,' said Sophie.

'A destitute man? How odd.'

'Not that sort of tramp, Freddy. It means a girl who's unconventional, rebellious, um, like a suffragette.'

Freddy frowned.

'Okay, the word's a sexist insult,' said Sophie, 'suggesting a girl's promiscuous—'

'He's insulting *you*. That is not on.' Freddy jumped off his stool and advanced on Hugo, who looked entirely unbothered.

Sophie stood up to intervene. At the shooting party with Ethel and Alice, when she'd blithely dismissed drunken fights at the Ritz, she'd been tempting fate.

Clarissa had already slipped off her seat and was in front of Hugo, presenting a formidable obstacle.

But Freddy didn't notice. He clenched his right fist. 'Come on, defend yourself.'

'We should go home.' Lady Maine was walking briskly towards the bar, her shrewd eyes on the boys.

Sophie put her hand on Freddy's arm and he instantly went still, as if turned to stone. 'Hugo's not insulting me, or anyone, Freddy. It's a love song.'

'I don't understand.'

'The word 'tramp' in the song is an endearment, a pet name. And because it *can* be an insult, it makes the romantic lyrics more powerful.' She dropped her hand from his arm.

Freddy shook his head, none the wiser.

Explaining David Bowie's lyrics would be a challenge if Freddy were sober. Right now … impossible.

She held Freddy's arm again, and as Clarissa helped Hugo off his barstool she winked at Sophie. It was a 'we can sort this' wink; a mini crisis had turned her into an ally, if not a friend.

Ten minutes later, in Eaton Square, Sophie helped Freddy out of the cab, but he stumbled, and when she steadied him, his lips brushed her cheek in a clumsy kiss. He really was very sweet. At home, she might have ended up in bed with him, behaved like … a tramp.

Hugo took hold of Freddy's other arm, concentrating on putting one foot in front of the other.

Maud was waiting in the bedroom and made quiet tutting noises as she laboriously removed Sophie's gown and corset. A *Blue Blazer* fiery demon was dancing on Sophie's breath, an unfair legacy after one judicious sip.

John would disapprove of slurring Hugo, and from all she'd heard about Freddy's valet, Mr Farrow, he'd be mega unimpressed. She laid her head on the soft pillow. Hopefully, the boys wouldn't remember their near brawl. And because they were boys, Lady Maine might not consider their behaviour so outrageous that she needed to tell Anne. Freddy wouldn't care, but Hugo would…

She was in a fantastic eerie bower.

Tall black flowers and trees were towering over her as she desperately kissed Hugo and unbuttoned his shirt.

The bower dissolved into nothingness, empty and dead, and she woke with a start, disorientated.

Her eyes adjusted to the dark. In a bedroom. Safe.

Only a dream.

CHAPTER 48

'We'd have a great view from a bus.' Sophie put down her napkin. In comparison to Shorten, the Maines' dining room was modest, like a regular house. And she'd waited patiently — until the boys had eaten an enormous cooked breakfast — before trying to persuade them.

'I'm not sure,' said Freddy, sipping his fourth cup of coffee.

'I used buses all the time in our London.' Hugo was paler than usual but okay. Or using his acting skills.

'I've never been on an omnibus,' said Freddy.

'At home, you pay as you get on, with your card or phone,' said Hugo. 'It's cheap and convenient.'

Freddy made a face. 'A card?'

'A sort of money,' said Hugo. 'I'll show you my wallet in Shorten.'

'And how can you possibly pay for anything with a telephone?' Freddy put his palm against his forehead, in a vain attempt to stop the pounding in his head.

'Payment's taken directly from your account,' said Sophie,

'so you don't need cash.'

Freddy made another face.

'Here, conductors take your fare,' said Clarissa. 'I'm fairly sure.' She turned to Sophie. 'But you will have to sit with vulgar people. Really, I wouldn't go.'

Now she'd realised Sophie Arundel couldn't derail the Seducing Hugo Project, Clarissa was looking out for her … but Sophie couldn't resist a little dig. 'This London is so exciting. What harm can it do?'

Freddy exhaled. 'All right.'

Clarissa glared.

Wonderful.

Back in Sophie's room, Maud was also concerned. 'You must be careful, Miss. There'll be pickpockets and all sorts.'

'I haven't any money.'

But as they walked from Eaton Square, Sophie repeated Maud's comments to Freddy.

'I've only brought enough for the tour and lunch,' he said. 'If it happens, it happens.'

The weather was dry, so they sat on the bus's top deck at the front.

As the bus set off, Freddy removed his hat and closed his eyes, and Hugo did the same.

Sophie sympathised, remembering the aftermath of an unfortunate vodka episode with Isha. On the upside, as she'd suspected, the boys had no memory of their spat, were acting like nothing had happened.

Rebel. Hugo had called her that after their visit to *The Crooked Gate*. Hadn't been a compliment. But last night, gazing in her direction, he'd hummed a love song.

Lizard brain lust was a generic survival instinct. Maybe, in Hugo, it had just taken longer to fire up?

The late August sun on his face emphasised new shadows under his eyes and a crease between his brows. No. He'd just been drunk. A pang of fierce regret ran through her and she tried to focus on the bustling street ahead.

Men, women and children in everyday clothes, sitting upright on rickety black bikes, weaved between shabby, horse-drawn wagons and brightly coloured cars and buses, while pungent black smoke spewed from countless chimneys, mingling with petrol fumes and the sweet pong of horse manure.

A young man stood beside a bike attached to a cart emblazoned with *Walls Ice Cream* in cream letters. Not content with the sign, he was shouting in a sing song voice, 'Ice cream, cheap and lovely. Ice cream, cheap and lovely.'

His cries faded as the bus sped past him and rattled around Piccadilly Circus, where Eros, the archer statue, was taking aim at a column of spiralling smoke across the square. Painted in enormous lettering on one building was *Guinness Is Good For You*, with *Bovril, Schweppes Ginger Ale* on another.

Hugo was awake, casually holding his hat brim, pretending he'd worn top hats since kindergarten. She'd been such an idiot, lumping him in with his friends.

In that last term, when Madison was leaving for Ascot, dressed up to the nines with an expensive hat, Sophie had let rip with a sarcastic wolf-whistle and for a precious moment Madison had looked rattled. A mean gesture … and now this universe was exacting revenge. Her basket hat must have cost a fortune and she was stuck with it; even on a breezy open-air bus it didn't move, embedded like a monstrous meteorite.

The bus passengers were all wearing hats, as were the people on bikes or walking along the street. Men had bowlers, top hats or caps; women's headwear was more varied, ranging from simple and small to expensive and intricate. And most of the men had moustaches or full beards. Hipsters … before they were called that.

Freddy opened his eyes and turned towards her. 'I hope I

didn't behave inappropriately towards you last night. If I did, please accept my apologies.'

'You did nothing inappropriate,' she said, emphatically. He'd nearly punched Hugo, but only kissed her on the cheek.

'Oh, good,' said Freddy.

Hugo must have heard the exchange but didn't say anything.

Around Nelson's Column, a group of serious people from the *South London Branch* of something or other were waving banners and chanting slogans; nearby, two bored policemen were leaning against a navy, weather-beaten police box — a dead ringer for *Dr Who*'s Tardis.

The bus stopped and started again and they passed the Ritz, busy with customers and taxis, and sped on by Buckingham Palace, where the road was almost as quiet as Eaton Square. This was a smaller, more intimate London, yet to be squeezed by tourism, skyscrapers and real estate madness.

Sophie shifted slightly on the narrow bus seat. The thin cushioning wasn't designed for comfort.

The top deck was crowded now. Skinny boys in tatty trousers, jackets and caps, sat in rows, jammed in. Women of all ages, in thin worn dresses and bonnets, huddled together, their teeth yellow and uneven. One girl had no teeth at all. None of these people were tourists; they were going to or from work. And many of them were watching her and the boys, puzzled.

Sophie didn't stare back. Even if riding the bus wasn't the done thing, Clarissa was missing out.

They came into Trafalgar Square and Sophie sat closer to Hugo, secretly enjoying the tingling feeling.

The bus crossed Oxford Street and she again glimpsed Selfridges. She'd get makeup for Anne there too.

The bus thumped through a pothole and Sophie grabbed the handrail, the metal cold under her linen gloves. Westminster Abbey loomed up, solid and eternal, and they passed the Houses of Parliament, eerily identical to the building at home, resurrected after the Blitz. Would it be bombed in a future war? She wouldn't know for twenty years. The thought gave her a shiver of unease.

'This is fantastic,' said Hugo. 'I'm so glad you nagged us into—'

Angry shouting from below made the other passengers peer round, though nobody could see anything. The bus stopped.

'You must get off, I'm afraid, or I will call a constable.' The male voice rang with authority and irritation.

A dishevelled man and a tired-looking woman got off and shuffled along the pavement.

Two minutes later, the conductor came up to the top deck and addressed Freddy and Hugo. 'They couldn't pay the fare. Everything's quite all right.' Why he felt he had to explain to the boys was a mystery.

'How awful,' Sophie whispered to Hugo, once the conductor had gone downstairs. 'But he might have lost his job if he'd let them stay…'

'Dinner cost a good few pounds last night.' Hugo checked Freddy couldn't hear. 'The Great War was terrible but it brought people together. All those young men … not dead, and so many hungry and desperate. No wonder there are riots.'

'*Nothing is inevitable until it happens,*' Sophie quoted from a half-remembered history lesson.

Hugo didn't reply, his mouth twisting in a worried smile.

After the bus tour, they went to Fortnum and Mason. The famous food store was the same as home except for the Expedition Department, which was filled with the kind of supplies only a fantasist would take on a perilous quest: butter knives, sauce boats, tins of quail and foie gras, stilton cheese, lobster, boxes of wine and more mundane food, like scotch eggs — all ready to be packed into hampers to go off and conquer something.

'People didn't really take this stuff on adventures,' said Sophie, examining a beautifully illustrated packet of crystallised ginger.

'Oh, they did. I mean, they do,' said Hugo. 'The Everest expedition of 1922 carried a mind-boggling amount of champagne.'

'Do you know *everything*?' said Sophie, only half joking.

Hugo shrugged his broad shoulders. 'I just remember trivia.'

'Useful for the Christmas quiz at school.'

'Then I got glandular fever, and everything went downhill.'

'But if you hadn't got sick, you wouldn't be here with me. It was fate.' This was Hugo's chance to make a complimentary remark.

'I don't believe in fate.'

After Fortnum and Mason, they went to Selfridges and Sophie lingered on the pavement, admiring a fashion display beside a white banner proclaiming *New From Paris* in purple and green letters. Like Clarissa's dress, the skirts were shorter but still narrow, and the bodices were heavily corseted, with elaborate sleeves. Edwardian fashion with a twist. Would be a while before she could wear flapper dresses, like in the 1920s at home.

'Come on, Sophie,' said Freddy, 'let's go to the roof.'

'The roof?'

'It's wizard fun.'

Inside the store, they headed towards a splendid lift.

'Actually Freddy, I'd rather use the stairs,' said Sophie. Another lift, different location, could end up anywhere.

'Are you sure? It's nine floors.'

'We'll see you there,' said Hugo.

'I'll race you.' Freddy grinned and stepped into the lift.

Sophie took the stairs one step at a time, restricted by her skirt, but by the fourth floor had to pause to catch her breath. 'This was silly.'

Hugo paused too. 'If we ever do get home, we should get lift phobia counselling.'

'Not sure we'd get that on the NHS.'

'Might be worth paying for. Think of all the jobs we couldn't do.'

'Like what?'

'My cousin works in the cheese grater,' said Hugo, 'forty-second floor.'

'Cheese grater?'

'Skyscraper. Looks like its nickname.'

Sophie started on the next flight. She wasn't unfit; the corset was restricting her rib cage. Hugo could have raced ahead. Nice he hadn't.

'But with lift phobia,' said Hugo, 'there'd be no need for a gym subscription. We'd save a fortune.'

'If we didn't die of heart attacks.' She stopped and tried to take deep breaths.

'If we run from here,' said Hugo, 'Freddy's still going to win.'

'This corset's so tight, even walking's hard work.'

He gave her a sympathetic smile but hastily turned away.

Well, that was bizarre. He'd looked sheepish, as if he'd done something dodgy or imagined … fetish underwear. Weren't boys supposed to think about sex every seven seconds, or was it minutes? Her imagination was out of control. Concentrate on walking. If she tripped over this stupid skirt, she'd break her neck.

When they finally reached the top, she was struggling to breathe.

Hugo opened a door. 'I didn't expect this.'

They stepped out into a garden, with an artificial lake and formal fountains.

Freddy was ambling towards them, past a small statue of an embracing naked couple.

Unusual. Well, in this universe.

Freddy took her arm. 'Are you all right?'

'Just need a minute.'

'You should rest,' said Freddy.

They sat on ironwork chairs in a pergola, surrounded by fruit trees and pink geraniums in large planters.

'This is a beautiful place, Freddy,' said Sophie. 'Thank you for bringing us here.'

He smiled. 'You're welcome.'

His expression reminded her of how she felt about Charlotte: fiercely protective, with a sort of wondrous gladness. The garden started spinning. She was hyperventilating.

'Hugo, can you find some water?' Freddy's voice was far away. 'She's going to faint.'

Sophie closed her eyes and focused on breathing. Wearing a corset and the millstone hat, she couldn't put her head between her legs. In out, in out.

'Drink this.' Hugo was giving her a glass of water.

She took cautious sips. The water was wonderfully cold, with impressive ice cubes. And she felt better.

Hugo was staring as if she'd grown wings. Logical. He'd only ever seen Kickboxing Javelin Sophie, not Delicate Fainting Sophie — this was as weird for him as it was for her.

'I shouldn't have let you walk,' said Freddy.

If anyone at home had treated her like a helpless pathetic person, she'd have punched them or cursed like a sailor, but she was on a pedestal and adored and it was mighty fine. Not brushing off Freddy's supporting arm, she slowly stood up. 'Shall we stroll?'

Hugo was still staring. 'Sure.'

'Are you sure?' Freddy asked Sophie, thinking Hugo's 'sure' was a question.

'Honestly, I feel okay.'

Hugo gave her such an open, glorious smile that she felt dizzy again. She held onto Freddy's arm as inner butterflies fluttered and quivered. Get a grip. All she'd done was climb some stairs. Didn't women explore Africa in this kit? Another skill better practised from birth.

She gently extracted herself from Freddy. She could walk across the roof.

Fashionably dressed couples mingled with young women in maid's uniforms and earnest youths in suits. One boy, in a jacket and cap, had traces of soot on his face. Sophie half expected to see Mary Poppins escorting her small charges towards a film set.

They passed a café with a jaunty red awning and came to a mini golf course. Sophie had played the game on day trips with Aunty Wendy and when she played a round with the boys, she won easily.

'That wasn't fair,' said Freddy. 'You've played before.'

'I'm allowed some secrets,' said Sophie, leaning stylishly on her golf stick.

They walked on towards a wooden cabin.

'Just when you think you've seen everything,' said Hugo. 'You couldn't make it up.'

Gun Club said the sign. Attractive young women, wearing a lot more mascara and lipstick than Clarissa, were showing customers rifles and pistols. A girl of six or seven was holding a handgun, shouting, 'Bang, bang,' and, beside her, a woman in a brown dress and small matching hat was saying, 'That's quite enough.'

A shop assistant addressed Sophie. 'Would you like to join, Miss? It's ladies only.'

'Thank you, no,' she said, politely.

'The man who owns Selfridges is American,' said Freddy.

Hugo winked at her. He was saying, no need to tell Freddy we already know this. Look impressed.

She'd loved *Mr Selfridge*, really missed her boxsets. On the other hand, she was kind of living in one.

At the edge of the roof, the view was spectacular, unblemished by skyscrapers or cranes. The shop window sign had said *New From Paris* but this city — with pretty churches next to tiny homes — looked more like Paris than modern London.

They headed to a first-floor restaurant for lunch and Hugo and Sophie used the stairs again despite Freddy's protests. Freddy was a smidgen away from manhandling Sophie into the lift, but common sense prevailed.

And Sophie had learned her lesson. She took her time.

In the restaurant, a fire had been lit in an imposing marble fireplace, though it wasn't cold. They sat at a table on the other side of the room beside picture windows overlooking Oxford Street, and Sophie took off her gloves and put them in her bag.

The menu was in French again. *Petite Marmite* turned out to be a mysterious soup, nothing like real *Marmite*, and *Supreme de Volaille Khediviale* sounded exotic but was just chicken with mash. Sophie made the most of the potatoes.

Car horns and angry shouting ... she moved closer to the window.

Along the storefront, the street had become packed with people, including children, yelling and jeering, and the traffic had stopped, jammed in by the crowd. Across the road on the pavement, a policeman was attacking a young woman, smashing down his truncheon, again and again. The girl was holding a small hat to her head, trying to protect herself, but streams of blood were running down her face.

Sophie froze in horror. She'd seen stuff on *YouTube*, but nothing like this.

Another woman was lying across the same pavement, her head in the road. Her body was oddly twisted, and underneath her a red puddle was spreading out, like water from a blocked drain. Policemen were running, barging through the crowd waving truncheons. One stepped over the body in a single stride, not glancing or pausing, as if the woman was a pile of rubbish.

Sophie gulped. Why was she watching? This wasn't a movie. But she'd never seen violence like this for real and she was stunned.

Something smashed through the window and Freddy pushed her off her seat, falling on top of her.

He scrambled up. 'Hugo.'

More glass shattered and a woman screamed. What the hell was going on?

Hugo was on the floor. Everything slowed and went quiet. Sophie rolled over and tried to crawl. No, impossible in a long skirt. She stood and in a moment was beside him.

His head, shoulders and chest were entirely covered by an expanding pool of dark red blood.

CHAPTER 49

'No.' Sophie's shout turned into a keening scream. Freddy was on his knees, his face white. 'He's dead.'

Sophie wanted to die, wanted oblivion. Despair, dread … and murderous rage. She'd find who'd done this—

A desperate, guttural rasping sound. Hugo was choking. Not dead.

Sophie grabbed a napkin and wiped blood from his nose and mouth.

Hugo spluttered and breathed but blood was still streaming from his head.

First aid instructions battled in her mind with unrealistic scenes from films. 'Freddy, he needs to sit up.'

They pulled him into a sitting position against a chair, Sophie pressed the napkin over the wound and sat beside him. In what seemed an instant, the napkin was soaked and her hands were red and sticky. A jab of pain shot through her palms and she gasped.

She called over a waiter. 'We need more napkins.'

The waiter hesitated.

'A lot more.'

'Of course, madam.'

Something flew past her and hit the wall with a crack. 'Freddy, get the waiters to block off the windows with tables and barricade the doors.'

He gawped at her as if she was insane. 'Hugo.'

'I'll sort Hugo,' said Sophie. '*Go.*'

Hugo's head was lolling down. She pushed up his chin and got his head resting against the chair. The waiter returned with a pile of napkins, she made three into a pad and pushed it onto Hugo's head.

Freddy came back and knelt on the floor, his hands wrapped in bloody napkins. He was mumbling under his breath.

'What's with your hands?'

'Cuts from window glass.' He glanced at Hugo. 'He's covered in it.'

There were nurses and ambulances in the 1920s … and the store would have a telephone. 'Freddy, go check the waiters have dialled 999.'

'What do you mean?'

Right. No emergency number. 'The waiters need to phone the nearest hospital.'

'The operator will put them through.' He stood and walked slowly away, seemed mesmerised.

Keeping pressure on Hugo's wound, Sophie examined her left palm. It was covered in Hugo's blood, but also her own from too many cuts, many superficial, others deep.

Dizzy… Focus on Hugo.

The sensation receded.

Someone was touching her arm. 'They've phoned the hospital and the police.' Freddy sat beside her on the floor.

Beyond the smashed windows was a roaring wall of noise and Sophie's throat dried with fear. She must have blocked that out, coping with Hugo. And the roar was getting louder, more connected and gathering pace. She felt a gut-wrenching terror. She knew that sound, had seen enough videos, signed the petitions … a hunting pack, tearing into its prey. No ambulance would get through that.

Hugo was groaning and moving his head. Underneath bloody streaks, his face was white and clammy, but the blood flow had slowed.

'Keep still.'

He was blinking, trying to open his eyes. 'Sophie?'

'You've got a cut, a glancing blow. Everything's under control.' She'd always been a good liar.

'You're a rubbish liar,' said Hugo, his words slurred, as if he was still drunk.

Alcohol. 'Excuse me.' Sophie raised her voice in what she hoped was an unpanicky way.

'Madam?' The waiter who'd given her the napkins was picking up a brick from the floor.

'Have we any brandy?'

'Of course, madam.' He scuttled off.

Either awesomely trained or on automatic. It didn't matter.

The waiter handed her a delicate glass of brandy, and as if the furore outside wasn't happening, began clearing used glasses from a nearby table.

Sophie soaked a clean napkin with brandy and pushed the cloth firmly into Hugo's gash, wiping out glass and brick dust.

Hugo swore, the shouted f-bomb anguished and clear against the general din.

The waiter dropped his tray of glasses with a crash, an almost comic, appalled expression on his face.

Freddy looked puzzled and Sophie firmly closed her mouth, thinking the same word. She hadn't heard anyone swear in this England. Well, in the part they'd fallen into. She kept on with the napkins, giving thanks for heavy linen. One staunched the bleeding for minutes now, not seconds.

Freddy put his hands over his ears as the noise beyond the shattered windows grew even louder, and Hugo swore again and clutched at her. His eyes were open but rolling back in his head.

'You're all right,' she whispered.

He closed his eyes and went limp.

All she could do was stop him bleeding out and ensure the wound was clean. The rest was in the lap of the gods—

A scream rang out from the pavement below.

Okay, any mythical gods had their hands full.

The blood coming from Hugo's head had almost stopped. Fingers trembling, she lifted the napkin, parted the gummy tangle of his hair and suppressed a shudder: a gouge, wide and gaping. Janet's fatal wound had been a scratch...

Freddy was picking slivers of glass out of his hands. 'Is he going to die?' His voice was surprisingly calm.

'Not if I can help it.'

All but one of the windows had gone, tables were leaning drunkenly against the empty frames and the restaurant doors were barricaded with tables and chairs. Diners were crowded near the fireplace, some dazed, some crying, others in earnest conversation, their words lost in the noise.

Just discernible outside, above boos and chanting, someone was speaking through a loudhailer.

Sophie couldn't make out the words. 'What's that talking on the road?'

'They're reading the Riot Act,' said Freddy.

'How does that help?'

'Once the Act's been read, people have to leave the street or the army starts shooting.'

'A bit ... extreme?'

'How else do you clear a mob?' said Freddy, his eyes on Hugo.

Hugo's skin was white-grey and his hands were icy cold. Sophie whispered in his ear, 'You're going to be fine,' and told herself the lie sounded confident, reassuring.

Outside, noisy fireworks exploded. A pristine, regular pop, pop, pop.

Not fireworks. Gunfire.

The braying on the road faltered and morphed into chaotic screaming.

Sophie lifted up the napkin. The blood flow had definitely stopped but now she could properly see it, the yawning wound looked worse. And because the brick dust was red, she couldn't be sure the wound was clean. She asked for more brandy.

The waiter brought a bottle. She sloshed it on another napkin and quickly but thoroughly wiped the inside of the gouge again. Hugo swore and flinched and made odd breathing noises.

'I know it hurts.' She laid a fresh napkin over the cut. 'There. Finished.' She turned to Freddy. 'Keep the napkin over the wound and support him so he stays sitting up. The dress department will have needles and thread.' The ground floor might be full of looters but she'd take her chances.

'No.' Freddy touched her arm. 'Help will come soon. Listen.'

The shouting and screaming outside sounded further away.

'*Soon* won't cut it.' She stood on stiff legs and hurried towards the barricaded doors but stopped by an elderly woman lying on the floor. A wiry, white-haired man was holding the lady's hand, muttering familiar words. He was praying.

'I may be able to help,' said Sophie. She knelt, her knees crunching on glass through her skirts.

'Brick. Hit her here.' The man gestured at his own chest. 'Knocked her over.'

Red dust was scattered over the woman's white dress. There was no outward sign of injury, but her lined face was too still. Sophie felt the lady's wrist for a pulse. It was there, but erratic. Good, amateur resuscitation might kill her. Anyway, would have terrified the husband. She opened the woman's mouth and felt about. The airway was clear.

Sophie shook glass slivers from the lady's clothes, a waiter brushed the carpet and Sophie turned her gently on her side. 'In case she's sick.'

Sophie got to her feet and went towards the doors but a waiter stepped in front of her. 'Not safe, madam.'

'My name is Sophie Arundel. I need thread to stitch a wound. When I come back, if it's safe, I'll repeat my name.'

'Wait.' Another waiter was putting an ancient telephone handset into a cradle on top of a narrow metal column with a dial at its base. 'A nurse is here. Safe to open up.'

As soon as the doors were ajar, a young woman in a white apron, dress and box hat walked briskly in with a leather bag.

Sophie touched her arm to get her attention. 'Have you needle and thread, for stitches?'

'Yes, if necessary.' She scanned the room. 'How many casualties?'

People were still crying by the fireplace but Sophie searched her memory, recalling what the instructor had said on the trauma course at school. *If they're making a loud noise, they're not about to croak.* 'Two seriously hurt.'

The nurse went over to the injured woman, heard about the brick and checked her pulse. She smiled at the husband. 'More help is on its way, sir. The whalebone in her corset might have protected her.'

When the nurse moved on to Hugo and examined his wound, Sophie told her about the napkins and brandy.

'You're a nurse.'

'No.'

The girl looked puzzled but said, 'He may get away without stitches.' She delved into her bag, took out a roll of cloth and deftly bandaged Hugo's head, so the cut was kept closed. The dressing covered half his face.

A peal of gunfire outside rattled what was left of the windows, but Sophie didn't turn from the nurse. 'He needs an ambulance.'

'He's walking wounded.'

Sophie started to argue but the memory of the body on the pavement and the policemen attacking the girl made her stop. 'Understood.'

The nurse hurried off and while Freddy continued to prop up Hugo, Sophie picked out glass from her palms.

Hugo opened one eye, the one not covered by the bandage.

Relief rushed through Sophie. She felt faint with it.

'What—' Hugo put his hand on the bandage.

'A brick,' said Sophie, 'but it didn't hit you full on. You've lost a bit of blood.' Understatement was good. 'You're going to be fine.'

'People always say that,' said Hugo.

'I'm not people.' Emboldened by adrenaline, she placed a delicate kiss on his clammy forehead.

He closed his eye again. 'Now I know I'm going to die.'

'He's making jokes,' said Freddy. 'That's a good sign.'

'Yes.' She mentally crossed her fingers. Hugo wasn't sitting up by himself, still slumped against Freddy, and his face was grey.

'Is that for me?' Freddy was pointing at the bottle of brandy.

'It is, but it's not for drinking. Keep propping up Hugo.' Sophie picked up the bottle. 'Hold out your hands.' She sounded like a schoolteacher. 'Have you got all the glass out?'

'As much as I can.'

She poured brandy over Freddy's palms.

He gasped and winced. 'It stings.'

She extracted more slivers from her own palms and poured on the alcohol, hoping the remaining glass would work its way out. Most of the slashes were paper-thin cuts but they really hurt. She couldn't imagine Hugo's pain. She sat on his other side on the floor, mirroring Freddy.

Hugo opened one eye again.

'How are you feeling, old chap?' asked Freddy.

'Bloody awful.' Hugo fidgeted, his back against the chair, sitting more upright.

Freddy gave Sophie a relieved glance. 'We should stay until it's definitely safe to leave.'

Hugo grabbed Sophie's arm, trying to stand.

'Don't move,' she said firmly. 'Stay there.'

'No.'

Reluctantly, she and Freddy helped him to his feet, but Hugo slipped on the bloody carpet and nearly fell. He swore again under his breath.

'Here,' said Sophie, guiding him so he sat in the chair.

'You'll be right as rain in no time.' Freddy brought over two more chairs.

As Sophie and Freddy sat beside him, Hugo closed his eye and slumped in his chair, and Freddy held onto his arm. 'What's that word he keeps saying?' It was clear from Freddy's guileless tone that he genuinely didn't know.

The waiter had recognised the Anglo-Saxon expletive. Hearing it shouted across the restaurant had made him drop his tray of glasses. But Freddy's sheltered upbringing was a precious part of his character, his straightforward goodness, and Sophie wasn't about to trash that. Or describe the word's biological meaning, even with euphemisms. She smiled at him. 'What bad luck.'

Freddy nodded, as if he'd known all along.

Hugo's face had lost some of the disturbing greyness. Well, the bit Sophie could see. But he was gripping the sides of his chair, his knuckles white. Sophie closed her hands over his and gradually he relaxed.

The people by the fireplace had stopped crying and whispering, and outside there was complete silence.

Men arrived with a stretcher and carried away the injured woman, and waiters took the tables from the windows and — just like a regular day — began laying clean tablecloths and cutlery and plates.

Now the need for action was over, Sophie felt a surge of unexpected energy. Hugo might be okay.

'What happened again?' Hugo sounded confused.

Freddy patted him on the back. 'Just some bad luck.'

Sophie walked over to the fireplace, finding comfort in the amber flames, and examined her sore palms. Firelight danced over the pale skin and bloody cuts, turning the gridded lines shiny-red, like the aftermath of a pagan sacrifice. With luck, Hugo's life wouldn't be sacrificed today. Or ever. When he was steadier, she'd get him seated by the fire, warm and safe—

Her heart jumped and began hammering. This wasn't lizard brain lust, blindly ramping up to survive. She was in love with him, *violently, stupidly* in love. Misery ran through her, so strong and hopeless that she swayed. He didn't feel the same.

And never would.

CHAPTER 50

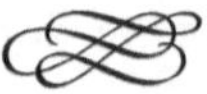

'Sophie, you were magnificent.' Freddy was beside her, holding her shoulders.

'I did trauma first aid at school—'

'I don't care. You're wonderful.' He planted a dramatic kiss on her temple. 'And Hugo's going to be all right.'

'I hope so.'

Hugo was watching them, still gripping the arms of his chair.

Was being in love a permanent thing? Was there a cure? People who fell for psychopaths and serial killers likely fell *out* of love pretty fast. But Hugo wasn't crazy or evil. The nearby fire was warm but she shivered, picturing a lonely future stretching out over decades.

'Ladies and gentlemen, the riot is over.' A sharp-suited man was addressing the room. 'But the army has advised that customers should stay within the store for at least an hour. Afternoon tea will be served shortly.'

Even after a riot, there was afternoon tea. Surely went some way to explain how Britain had acquired an empire where the sun never set. Whatever the morality of empires, the certainty of afternoon tea was a wonderful gift to the world. And Hugo's bandage was mostly white, not red.

But as Sophie relaxed, what had happened replayed in her brain. The blood … the powerlessness. She *never* wanted to feel that again. She'd have murdered the brick thrower. And if they were dragged in front of her right now, she'd kill them. In cold blood. She drew a long, slow breath. This mindless determination for revenge, even fiercer than when her parents were killed … it was shock. It would fade.

They shook glass from their clothes and Sophie went to the store's impressive ladies' loos to clean her face. In the unforgiving mirrors, her face looked pallid and her dress was sodden red. But her hat had escaped relatively unscathed. Only dented.

When she returned to the restaurant, they had tea by the fire.

'Eat a little.' Sophie pushed a plate of sandwiches across the table towards Hugo.

He ate a tiny cucumber sandwich, sipped his tea and said nothing at all.

When people began to leave, Freddy wandered over to a hole that had once been a window. The late summer day had turned prematurely dark, the sun obscured by storm clouds and driving rain.

'What are you doing?' asked Sophie.

'Checking it's safe.'

'I can't hear anything.'

'You're right. It's over.' Freddy turned on his heel, his firm mouth pressed into a tired line.

After he'd signed a credit note for the brandy and afternoon tea, Sophie said, 'How do they know you'll pay?'

'The estate office deals with that.'

How wonderful, never having to worry about your credit rating. She frowned. Why was she thinking about trivia?

She helped Hugo out of his chair. He was wobbly, so she and Freddy walked him arm in arm across the room towards the lift.

As the lift doors opened, revealing a polished mahogany interior, Hugo tensed but Sophie squeezed his arm and guided him across the threshold. He could hardly walk, never mind navigate stairs.

After the doors closed and the lift started to go down, Hugo swayed and Sophie was wholly focused on holding him up, but when the doors opened on the ground floor of Selfridges, she felt a rush of relief. Just a regular lift.

Their path to the exit was strewn with fallen mannequins and overturned displays and every store window was smashed, yet outside the street was eerily quiet.

Freddy put on his top hat and kept hold of Hugo's. 'Let's get off the main street.'

'The entrance to the tube's right there,' said Sophie, pointing to a sign.

'Never used it,' said Freddy. 'Would it be easier than taking a cab?'

Getting Hugo safely down even a few stairs... 'No.' She wasn't thinking straight.

Apart from an occasional couple or solitary person, the wet streets were deserted. If this had happened at home, there would have been police cars, ambulances and sirens.

Freddy eventually found a cab.

'Are you all right, guv?' The driver shook his head. 'What's the world's coming to?'

Sophie sat with Hugo's hand in hers, Freddy was awkwardly holding Hugo's other hand and Hugo's eyes were fixed on the back of the driver's head. Freddy's clothing was ruined but Hugo was in another league. His grey suit was now red, and his bandage looked like a clumsy stage prop.

If they ever got home, she'd never dress up for Halloween again. Fake blood overload wasn't fun when you'd seen it for real. Her corset was pressing hard into her hips. Adrenaline was ebbing away.

The butler didn't turn a hair when he opened the Maines' front door.

'Could I ask you to pay the cab fare?' said Freddy. 'We ran into a spot of bother.'

Sophie let go of Hugo, and Freddy guided him inside the house. When Hugo reached the bottom of the stairs, Sophie took his arm again and with Freddy holding his other arm, they slowly climbed the stairs.

The boys went on to Hugo's room and Sophie opened her bedroom door.

Maud turned. 'Miss…'

It wasn't often Maud was lost for words. 'We're okay. I'll tell you all about it.'

But she couldn't. Not the scene outside Selfridges, or inside. Which was odd, because the woman dying in the road, the policeman hitting the girl and Hugo drowning in blood was playing like a DVD in her head — and wouldn't stop.

Maud carefully took off Sophie's sodden hat. 'I'll pad this with paper as it dries, Miss.'

Once out of her trashed clothes, Sophie put on her dressing gown, and down the corridor Maud helped her into a bath. 'Everyone's all right, Miss. That's the main thing.'

Sophie winced as her fingers met the hot water and she willed it to wash away the replay.

'Miss?'

'It's nothing, Maud. Only my hands.'

Maud took Sophie's right hand and turned it over, then let go, putting her own hand to her mouth.

Then Sophie cried — heavy wrenching sobs.

Maud stood silently as Sophie cried herself out.

After the bath, Sophie wrapped herself in a towel, sat on a stool and tried to stop trembling. The bathwater whirling into the plug had red trails and the towel had bloody handprints.

It was illogical but Sophie felt embarrassed. 'Sorry.'

Maud left but quickly returned with a small hipflask. She unscrewed the top and put the flask gently into Sophie's hand. 'This will help, Miss.'

'I thought you didn't approve of drinking.' Sophie's voice was shaking like her body.

'This is different, Miss. Think of it as medicine.'

Sophie took a swig and fiery rum slipped down her throat. It did help.

'It must have been horrible to make you so upset. Think what you did at the shooting party … weren't put off by Charlotte or blood or anything. You're as brave as a man.'

Why did Maud think only men were brave? Sophie took another sip of rum. She likely was as brave as most men, but a bravery spreadsheet would be pretty wide — wouldn't be in the really brave column.

In the bedroom, she put the flask aside and Maud bandaged her hands, covering her palms but leaving her fingers free.

'Have a rest before dinner, Miss. You have time.' Maud plumped a pillow.

Would the replay stop, if she could sleep? Sophie curled up on the coverlet and closed her eyes.

~

On the edge of consciousness, mumbling, '*No.*' Hugo was choking.

Sophie leapt off the bed, ran to a table with a bowl and vomited, managing to keep most of the mess contained.

For a long moment, she stood there, resting her hands on the table, her head bowed. This would pass. And Selfridges The Movie needed to play itself out or it would come back worse — in years or decades, like with army veterans.

She poured water from a jug into a glass and drained it, seeing again the woman contorted on the ground. Then another memory. Admiring the window display, dawdling on the pavement … that could have been her, lying in her own blood—

Maud came in, noted the bowl and removed it without a word.

When she returned, Sophie said, 'How many hat pins did we pack?'

Maud rummaged in Noah's ark. 'Three, Miss.'

From now on, she'd insert an extra one.

'Do you think this trouble will spread to the country, Miss?'

'I don't know, but the gamekeepers have guns.' Anyone who threw bricks deserved a bullet. She pushed the thought away. Yes, still in shock.

Maud's eyes widened. 'Do you think they might have to shoot … people?'

'I'm sure it won't come to that.' Though she wasn't sure. About anything.

'Lady Maine asked if you felt able to come downstairs, Miss.'

'Of course.' The stinging on her palms had faded and the horror film had to stop soon.

Maud took out a clean corset. Hugo's blood had seeped through Sophie's dress, staining her underwear.

'Lucky you packed a spare.' Sophie's words repeated ironically in her head. Just four weeks after she'd been laced into one, going corset-less in public felt beyond slovenly, like wandering around a convenience store in pyjamas.

A short while later, Sophie was respectably dressed and Maud smiled, believing Brave Sophie happily restored.

Downstairs, Clarissa, her parents and the boys were already in the drawing room. Hugo was sitting on a sofa, wearing his brown suit. He looked dazed and his face was nearly as white as the bandage. Clarissa was sitting beside him, her body language protective and possessive. She couldn't have got any closer unless she'd climbed onto his lap — only prevented by her hobble skirt and social convention.

Sophie sat on the nearest chair.

'How are you, my dear?' asked Lady Maine.

'Fine.' Compared to Hugo, she *was* fine. 'Hugo might need stitches.'

'Tomorrow, when he's feeling stronger,' said Lady Maine.

Freddy gave Sophie a chin-up smile. His hands were bandaged like hers.

'I suppose we will read about it tomorrow,' said Lord Maine, to the room in general. 'Perhaps we should leave town? Better safe than sorry.' He paused. 'What do you think, Hugo?'

It wasn't surprising that Lord Maine would ask Hugo.

Hugo might be distressed and disorientated with a serious head injury, but he was still the fount of all wisdom. She, on the other hand, wasn't worth consulting. And that wouldn't change, even if she'd trained as a paramedic or performed open-heart surgery outside Selfridges.

'I suppose it depends whether the disorder gets worse and spreads,' said Hugo, his voice quiet and careful. 'We have riots at home, usually in the summer. But there are marches all the time. A small group got inside Fortnum and Mason a few years ago.'

'What were they protesting about?' asked Lord Maine.

'Animal rights, I think. I'm not sure.'

Silence. The entire Maine family and Freddy stared at him.

'Life went on, but in the end it's what you feel comfortable with.'

Another, slightly less baffled, silence.

Despite his pallor, Hugo appeared to be almost normal. Tension that had been making Sophie's shoulders stiff, though she'd barely noticed, eased a little.

'We should dine here tonight,' said Lady Maine.

That evening, Hugo had supper in bed and Sophie determined to carry on as normal. Or pretend to.

For dinner, she wore a new pale-cream damask gown.

Clarissa's dress was prettier, effectively silver with hundreds of hand-sewn, reflective beads. Sophie wiped her clammy forehead with her handkerchief. She didn't care. For a moment, she briefly shut her eyes against the horror film still playing in her head. No, bad idea — increased the intensity.

She coped fine with mushroom soup but when the main course arrived, she couldn't cut the cauliflower or the potatoes.

'Sophie.' Freddy was rolling his eyes up to a footman and down at his plate. His meal had been cut into small, bite-sized chunks.

If she'd been caught up in an incident at home, Isha would have made sympathetic noises, fed her chocolate cake and ice cream. That would have worked. But pretending everything was okay sort of worked too. Understatement had been refined over centuries to cope with pain and death and everything in between. Probably sustained the whole Empire.

The footman smiled at her and took her plate.

And, like most things, understatement was easier with staff. It surely deserved a memorable name? The Shorten Code. Yes, that summed it up. Almost extinct at home, but at Hadley, it had been the biggest unwritten rule: behave properly when your team lost, don't show off if you win a prize and, if you have a problem, make light of it.

The world shifted. She was back in Miss Parncutt's study. She exhaled, focusing on the present, despite the tape running in her head on a loop.

Clarissa put her cutlery together on her still full plate and turned to Sophie. 'I am so glad you were able to help Hugo.' Clarissa hesitated. 'We got off on the wrong foot, didn't we? Could you teach me some basic nursing?'

'I'm not a nurse but I can explain first aid.' Clarissa genuinely cared for Hugo. And it was clear he cared for her, didn't judge her because her father had made his money in trade.

'I have been considering the situation,' said Lord Maine, addressing the whole room. 'We should move to the country until things settle down.'

Speaking to everyone at once was evidently a Lord Maine thing.

After dinner, Sophie didn't linger in the drawing room with Lady Maine and Clarissa, grateful to retreat to a sympathetic, if talkative, Maud.

'The Maines' servants are already packing and we could leave in the morning, depending on what the doctor says.'

Sophie lay on the bed fully clothed. Make the horror film stop. Sleep.

Maud got the hint and speedily helped Sophie undress.

She'd feel better tomorrow.

The next morning, she did feel better. The horror film was still playing but easier to ignore.

On the way to breakfast, she met Freddy on the landing.

'The doctor's putting in stitches,' he said, his face grim.

Hopefully, Hugo was drugged up on laudanum.

Ten minutes later, the doctor came into the dining room. He was short and wiry, not given to chitchat. 'Give it twenty-four hours before he travels and leave the bandage on for five days. He's young and strong. Rest is what he needs. Whoever stopped the bleeding and cleaned the wound saved his life.' He walked briskly towards the front door.

Hugo really could have died. But the trauma course deserved the credit, laid on after a bombing in Manchester. How mad to think terrorism could have an upside — an alive Hugo.

Still ignoring the horror film, Sophie went into the drawing room with Clarissa and drew diagrams, trying to summarise the trauma course in an hour. She'd expected Clarissa to bail but she was calm and focused.

'You tie a tourniquet there?' Clarissa put her finger on the drawing.

'Yes, as tightly as possible, you can't worry about it hurting them more. If help doesn't arrive, you'll need to gradually loosen it but not so much they bleed out.'

'And they'll survive?'

The instructor had talked about treating casualties within the 'golden hour,' survival rates improving as medics gained more expertise during the wars in Iraq and Afghanistan.

Manage expectations. 'Most people will still die from shock and infection.'

'One can but try,' said Clarissa, her eyes still on the sketch. 'This trouble started in Spitalfields.'

'Where's that?'

'Nowhere near here. East London. But after the shooting party, I overheard my father on the telephone saying the unrest was spreading. When I asked him about it, he said we shouldn't discuss it, because it could cause panic. That's why I thought going on the omnibus was unwise.'

Bad times made for strange allies.

Freddy came in. He looked shattered.

'Elevenses.' Clarissa stood, pulled a bellpull and sat down again.

'He's still bleary.' Freddy flopped into an armchair.

'Understandable in the circumstances.' Clarissa gestured at Sophie's diagrams. 'I've been learning what to do if this happens again.'

Sophie glanced at him. 'I'll take you through the basics. It won't take long.'

Freddy paled. 'I should stay with Hugo.' He hastily stood up and disappeared out of the door.

The maid came in, poured coffee and took Freddy's cup upstairs.

'Freddy's a dear,' said Clarissa, 'and Hugo's going to be fine.'

'Yes.' The film skipped to Hugo drowning in his own blood. Think about something else. But her brain shifted to the brick thrower, making them confess...

Her mother's voice sounded in her head, silencing the rerun, turning it into a silent movie. *Forgive those who trespass against us.*

Noble, rational Sophie would triumph. Just needed time. Checking on Hugo would help.

Before lunch, she knocked on his door and, after a moment, went in. Freddy wasn't there and Hugo was in pyjamas in bed, half sitting up but dozing. On his head was a new smaller bandage that didn't cover his eye.

She turned to leave but hesitated. Maybe if he knew how she felt? Nothing to lose.

She gently took his hand in hers, but he snatched it away.

He blinked, disorientated. 'What are you doing?'

'Sorry, just wanted to see how you were.'

'I'm fine, Sophie. I'll be better soon.'

She smiled at him but inside emptiness was spreading. The tiny flicker of not knowing, of hope, had been snuffed out.

CHAPTER 51

'See you again soon,' Clarissa trilled, as they left the following morning.

Sophie turned in the taxi seat and waved, but she felt wretched, the hurt of Hugo's rebuff still raw.

When she'd helped him to the taxi, she'd worried he'd shrug her off. He hadn't. But that was small comfort. She clasped her hands in her lap.

At the station, she and Freddy walked Hugo carefully across the concourse and onto a chilly platform. At the tail end of August, Autumn had arrived with a snap.

Once seated in their carriage, Freddy said, 'We should *never* have come to London.'

Hugo was already asleep, slumped where the seat met the carriage partition by the corridor. Sophie was sitting on his other side, in case he suddenly slumped the other way. There were no arm rests or headrests, but the rich red brocade upholstery was soft and comfortable.

Sophie lowered her voice. 'Freddy, you couldn't have known.'

Her reflection in the train window was theatrically pale

— a frumpy vampire in period costume. She really needed make-up. She watched the houses and gardens speeding past. Why was she fretting about mascara and lipstick? Hugo wouldn't notice if her lashes were darker, her lips redder, or her hair was on fire. Anyway, eating was difficult enough. Applying make-up would be impossible. The cut on her index finger met around the base and wound up to the nail, like a creepy tattoo ring. Would never completely fade. The movie started. Think about something else: Anne and Charlotte and Jack. 'Everything will get back to normal.'

Freddy leaned forward from his seat opposite. 'If anything had happened to you, I don't—'

'Well, it didn't,' said Sophie, picturing a newly-groomed Charlotte, transformed into a brown labrador but with impressive, doodle eyebrows.

'Luckily.' Freddy stood and adjusted a metal dial on the wall. 'It'll get cosy-warm in a minute.' In the mellow light of the gas lamp behind him, his face was softer, more mysterious. He sat opposite her again and his lips curved in an affectionate smile.

Freddy liked her, *really* liked her. He'd only flirted at the ball and — except when he'd been drunk — never tried to kiss her. But that was consistent with strict dating rules.

When she'd first met Freddy and shaken his hand, her skin had prickled with recognition. It had made no sense at the time, but maybe she'd been given a glimpse of the future. *Their* future?

Finding Anne had felt like the end of a quest, but what if it wasn't? If she married Freddy, she could protect Hugo better and, if the country collapsed in an all-out revolution, they'd persuade Richard to move to America. Bail early, like this world's Russian royals.

The train flashed past a platform, so fast she missed the name. Only for local trains. Too many stations to count, just on this line. All those unknown passengers — happy, sad, kind, mean — en route to different destinations. *Different destinations…*

She looked out the window, her mind racing, not seeing the scenery. Instead, she was picturing the lift, gold and solid: the signs for infinity and Pi, and the sketches.

Both versions of H. G. Wells had seen a sphinx on the door in the pub, and in *The Time Machine* the statue of the sphinx was symbolic. The drawing of the big house on the lift had to represent the Manor. Apart from Alan, all the visitors lived and worked there. And if all the images were emblematic, not literal, then Alan's mansion on fire represented him burning his bridges when he'd alienated the Laceys, and the road or river that forked showed him choosing a different path, running *The Crooked Gate*.

Whether there were four ships that travelled between universes — or one, and the doors changed — each visitor *saw* their own destination.

The other sketches she'd seen made no sense but were academic now—

'Are we nearly there yet?' said Hugo, his eyes still closed.

'A couple of hours.' Freddy frowned. 'He's not well enough to go to the dining car.'

'I'm happy to stay here,' said Sophie.

Hugo opened his eyes. 'I'm up for lunch.' He stood with care and slowly walked with Freddy out of the compartment. Sophie followed, just as slowly, negotiating the narrow corridor in her basket hat.

'You should try to eat,' said Freddy, as they sat at their table. 'It will give you strength.'

Hugo covered his mouth to cough, his throat irritated by predictable cigarette smoke. 'You're right, but you guys can order. I can't face it.'

'Guys?' asked Freddy.

'Chaps,' said Sophie.

'But you're not a chap,' said Freddy.

'Um, chapesses,' said Sophie. 'It can mean girls as well as boys.'

'Chapesses,' repeated Freddy, half to himself, reading the menu.

Hugo stifled a giggle.

A good sign.

'Are you ready to order, sir?' The waiter was addressing Freddy.

'Absolutely.' Freddy turned to Sophie.

'Soup and chicken, please.' Last time, the vegetables had been soft.

The boys had steak again and Hugo cut up Freddy's meal and hers. The waiters and other diners, schooled from birth in the Shorten Code, didn't stare at their strapped hands and Hugo's bandage, let alone comment.

Back in their carriage, Hugo was soon asleep again, his breathing slow and even, and the sound was contagious. Despite the challenge of resting her hat against the wall by the window, Sophie fell asleep and Freddy had to wake them both up when the train reached their station.

With Freddy's help, Sophie safely manoeuvred Hugo off the train, and they walked in weak sunshine to where Reynolds was waiting with the car.

Hugo climbed gingerly into the front passenger seat and Sophie sat beside Freddy in the back.

'I'm a bit shaky,' Hugo said, as they set off, 'but I feel okay.' He settled in his seat and closed his eyes.

A new, pure relief enveloped Sophie and in its wake came an unexpected serenity. Hugo would never feel like she did, but he was alive and well and strong.

Reynolds drove at a leisurely twenty miles an hour, Sophie breathed in the fresh country air, and the leather scent from the seats and the purr of the engine wrapped her in an invisible comfort blanket.

'Nearly home.' Freddy put his bandaged hand tenderly over hers.

She met his soft, brown eyes and didn't move her hand. She could love Freddy.

The car turned into the sweeping drive, tyres crunching on the gravel, and Freddy shyly released her hand.

Anne and Richard were waiting on the front steps with Miss Blackmore and the dogs. Jack was sitting patiently but Charlotte, sleek and newly groomed, was straining excitedly against her lead.

The sun was glinting on the Manor's mullioned windows and the green Virginia Creeper on the gable was starting to change colour — transforming into a vibrant, welcoming red.

Hugo opened his eyes as the car came to a stop. 'The house is looking good.'

'Better than good.' Sophie smiled at Anne and Richard and tilted her hat brim to better see them.

The Manor looked like home.

EPILOGUE

His brow furrowed as he sat down to read the letter. *They arrived back yesterday. Mr Harrington was injured in a riot but will recover.*

He gazed out at the windswept green through the upstairs window and tapped his blunt fingers on the tatty, wooden desk. Three weeks since their last lift theory, confirmation they'd given up and yet…

Reaching out to a nearby shelf, he brought down a metal box and placed it on the table. His spine ached. He stretched and it faded. Couldn't complain. Given his age, he was in reasonable nick.

Fishing a key from his pocket, he unlocked the box, lifted the lid and put the letter in with the others, then relocked it.

Eddington and all those scientists couldn't find the lift. Unlikely ordinary visitors could. But if they did, he was ready.

Dealing with them wouldn't be difficult and he'd bury their bodies deep, like his secret.

He smiled to himself as he returned the box to the shelf. All would be well.

Welcome to the
🐈 **Shorten Readers Club** 🐈
🩶

**IF YOU ENJOYED STRANDED
LET PEOPLE KNOW**

Reviews are the most effective way of building awareness of a book you've enjoyed.

While I love telling people about the *Shorten Chronicles,* honest reviews bring books to the attention of other readers.

If you didn't buy *Stranded* direct from my website, I'd really appreciate it if you'd leave a review (short as you like) where you bought it.

Thank you!

Sophie's adventures continue in *Escape*, the second book of the *Shorten Chronicles*.

Buy the print book from Rosalind's independent bookshop online and directly support the author.

www.rosalindtate.com

Type the website address into your browser or point your phone camera at the QR code to go to Rosalind's shop. Click on the 3 lines to go to the main menu.

ABOUT THE AUTHOR

Rosalind Tate lives in Gloucestershire, England, and holidays on the Cornish coast. She served in the British military, then worked as a journalist and a lawyer.

Rosalind's enjoys authors' and readers' conferences, talking about publishing and encouraging new authors. When she's not behind her computer, you can find Rosalind reading her favourite books, walking her dogs, swimming, or watching sci-fi and fantasy shows.

Rosalind has three grown up children, a tolerant husband, and two utterly gorgeous dogs.

ACKNOWLEDGMENTS

To my husband, Ian. Thank you for your patience, support, and sharp, proofreading eyes.

To my late mother, who many years ago showed me how to be a writer.

To *Jericho Writers* and my editors, Debi Alper and Emma Darwin.

Thank you to our labradoodle, the wonderful Bella. You inspired the *Shorten Chronicles* after all.

And thanks also to Bella's goldendoodle kid sister, for her author guarding skills. She's called … Sophie. *What?* Okay, when we adopted her, I was obsessed with Sophie Arundel, and our energetic puppy has some things in common with her literary human counterpart. She's sassy, runs fast and is far too impulsive.

Finally, Toby deserves a mention. He was our first labradoodle and is no longer with us.

Well, in this world.

Rosalind Tate
Gloucestershire 2020

www.ingramcontent.com/pod-product-compliance
Lightning Source LLC
Chambersburg PA
CBHW051552100726
47898CB00001B/62